I0678266

Derek Takes Action

Derek has a cause but, being Derek, he also has a host of misunderstandings to sort out, mistakes to rectify and a wife to mollify

As a natural leader, he knows that beating the Railway Developers is down to him. As a natural disaster area, we know it is unlikely to go quite to plan.

In Mac Black's fifth and final Derek book the plot is stirred as poor gullible Derek tries his best and makes us laugh all the way to the end!

Please... Call me Derek
Derek's in Trouble
Derek's Revenge
Derek's Good Relations
Derek Takes Action

All Rights Reserved

No part of this publication may be reproduced or transmitted by any means, electronic, mechanical, photocopy or otherwise, without the prior permission of the publisher.

This is a work of fiction. Names, characters, places and incidents are either the product of the authors' imagination, or are used fictitiously. Any resemblance to actual persons, living or dead, business establishments, events, or locales is entirely coincidental.

First published in Great Britain 2015 by U P Publications Ltd
Head Office: Eco Innovation Centre, Peterscourt, City Road,
Peterborough PE1 2SA

Cover design Copyright © Mike Peers
Copyright © U P Publications 2015

Copyright © Allan (MacQuarrie) Black 2015

Allan (MacQuarrie) Black has asserted his moral rights

A CIP Catalogue record of this book is available from the British Library

Paperback Edition - U P Publications ISBN 978-1908135636

Kindle Edition - U P Publications ISBN 978-1908135643

FIRST PAPERBACK EDITION

9 6 8 7 5 4 2 3 1

Published by U P Publications - Printed in England
by The Lightning Source Group
www.uppublications.ltd.uk
www.macblack.info

DEREK

TAKES ACTION

by

mac black

U P Publications
2015

1

Derek Toozlethwaite stands looking out through the plate glass window at the crowd gathering across the road and on the pavement outside. It was cold and miserable. They were gathering there because of him, though deep down he had the uncomfortable feeling that this wasn't truly deserved. In fact, it all felt very unreal – almost as if he were only an actor playing a part in a film.

Stoically, he straightens his shoulders, pulls in his stomach, and polishes his steamed-up spectacles with his handkerchief, experiencing the unusual sensation of both pride and humility. In a very short time, these people would be proclaiming him their hero. That is, of course, unless the answer turns out not to be the one that they are all hoping for.

No, relax, he tells himself. *Don't behave the way the old Derek would. There is nothing to become anxious about. This time it will be clear cut. 'Cancelled': it has to be that. There is absolutely no doubt about it, but, what if they don't...? No, they couldn't. Or could they possibly decide to...? No!*

The government spokesperson is due in about twenty minutes. That person will be confirming that the plan has been changed – won't he?

It will be a relief when it eventually happens. It has been a long fight.

He is as relaxed as the circumstances can permit. Standing inside where it was warm, beside Anton, with a hot coffee in one hand and a half-consumed bacon roll in the other, it is a very much appreciated break for Derek; just what was needed to restore morale.

This place had almost become a second home to Derek. To offer his premises as a soup kitchen to those on the vigil was extremely kind of Anton because, these days, the New Astoria Eating House normally opened for food only during afternoons and evenings.

Anton arranged this out of the goodness of his old pseudo-Italian heart, God Bless Him, and both he and his son Peter had become stalwarts in sustaining the needs of the fighters' stomachs throughout the week.

Today, the crowd gathered outside the Old Astoria Bingo Hall. It made a change to be at this venue.

Although the fight had been going on for barely a month, the vigil had been along the road outside the Council Offices – serious stuff – for the last five days and nights. In fact, the tents and home-made shelters are still there, admittedly looking a little worse for wear, but all for a good cause, and now, thank goodness, able to be abandoned.

People thronged outside the Eating House because the meeting is being held at a different place. It is to be indoors, and they are waiting to enter the Bingo Hall, the palace of the common people and real home of democracy where the announcement is to be made.

Derek has been here since six o'clock this morning in the darkness, the coldness and the dampness, initially, all on his own. He would much rather have been in the warm bed beside Sally. Saying that makes it sound as if he is fighting a lone battle but that is certainly not the case. He has not been alone in 'The Fight'.

This local revolution was a team effort. He was proud of *his* people: acting on behalf of the country, some more active than others, of course. At this very moment, the ones who had been at the spearhead all along, the activists, shuffled about constantly on the move, trying to keep warm, and carrying the placards as usual. They are attempting to continue chanting in unison, but very little sound is emerging that can be heard because, already, almost all have lost their voices.

The other main protagonists, who appeared on duty here at seven-thirty, already have been across to Anton's for sustenance, so Derek doesn't have to feel too bad about standing in the comfort of the warm restaurant. This morning he has waited 'til last – as any good leader would.

Strung on the temporary barrier, erected by the local police along the edge of the pavement is the long banner, displaying the message in large letters.

GOVERNMENT SECRET PLANS FOR NEWINGSWORTH, SLATTERFOOT AND SURROUNDING DISTRICTS

–

WE SAY NO!!!!

This message is repeated in various ways on the handheld placards where each individual proudly displays a personal version of what the fight is all about.

LEAVE OUR COUNTRYSIDE ALONE!

BUST THE BANKERS!
BAN CARS
MAKE MOTORISTS CYCLE!

WHAT SECRETS?

NO FRACKING CHANCE!

WHY CAN'T YOU PICK ON
SOMEONE YOUR OWN SIZE?

YOU KNOW WHERE YOU CAN
STICK YOUR HI-SPEED TRAIN!

BRING BACK THE BIRCH!

Although unsure if the correct message is being conveyed on any of them, it is the last one, the one being held aloft by Arthur that Derek finds most questionable. Being one of the council gardeners, Arthur claims this is justified because he 'likes trees', and he is protesting about what has been done to the Amazonian forests! It would be just a matter of time before Newingsworth was denuded of timber too, he'd added. Derek is convinced he is taking the piss!

Surprisingly, little Mrs Masterton, the next-door neighbour of Alexander and Muriel, who is normally such a nosey busybody, has been a fervent supporter of the cause and very much involved. She was an early member of the team. Her placard is a little unusual too. It proclaims: HI-SPEED GAS IS A LOT OF HOT AIR. To Derek this does not seem the correct message either but, being grateful that she has been attending regularly and supporting the effort, he has turned a blind eye to it.

The television cameras crews have arrived and are out there now. Another spot on the national news channels with any luck this evening; telling the rest of the country that it is still possible for the little people to fight and protect local life. Taking a stand against government bureaucracy can still have the desired effect.

Thank goodness I discovered the Secret Documents. All has been exposed.

Twenty-seven years ago, he'd fought a different enemy – BISKO's. Back then it had been the Blytheton Road Gang versus the mighty Bisko's; they'd wanted to take away the land that the little gang played on, the scrubland that was their magical natural playground, the land they had *always* played on. This large supermarket chain decided that they wanted it, and, as was the fashion, they planned for yet another enormous unnecessary store, the sort of move that almost certainly could lead to the demise of the high street.

It had been some fight.

Back then, as only recent starters at the Primary School, they had carried the placards defiantly, the whole gang, six of them, caught on camera; they became famous overnight. The publicity had been great. It had been important to fight back, and fight they did. *If we could do it then, we can do it now,* he told himself, and...?

It had made no damn difference!

The superstore was built and still stands there to this day. Bisko's reigned supreme – they'd ridden roughshod over everybody and built on top of the natural playground! The big difference was that, back then, the opposition had been just a bunch of kids.

Not this time though decided Derek ...*When I become Prime Minister, things will change.*

"You likea my fresha bacon buttie? You wanna some morra, Derek? Orra maybe you likea now trya my apple tarta," said Anton. "My greata-grandmama's recipe – she bakeit eet afore many years ago. And thatta remind me, did I evera tella you howa she..."

"Thank you, my good friend. No more food. That was sufficient for the moment, and I'd love to hear your story, but..."

Our hero took a deep breath.

"...I must go. My people need me!"

Sad to say, what wakened him, and spoiled the culmination of a beautiful dream, was being nudged by Sally, lying half-asleep beside him; awakened, just when he was about to be recognised as...

He vaguely appreciated there was a noise coming from the other room, one that had become so familiar, especially around this time in the early hours. It was dark. He looked at the clock.

"Gerraway..." he muttered disgustedly, but deep down he knew it was his duty.

"Be a good daddy, Derek," the blonde head said sleepily from the comfort of the pillow, "ET's crying – and you know your little son always prefers *you* in the middle of the night."

2

The feeling of being a superior being was not one Derek could often claim as his – not even in his dreams. In fact, after the happenings of the weekend he had just experienced, he was delighted to be out in the daylight, to be free, and he wanted home...

It was late Sunday morning.

Andy Pandy Woodstock is a ruddy stupid pillock, he wanted to shout out to all the people milling around him in Kings Cross Station at that particular moment on that particular day... *And if I was near him at this minute I'd wring that ruddy stupid throat of his!*

He wanted to shout it out really loudly, but didn't, because it had been a very embarrassing experience this morning and anyway, no one would have listened. Everybody in London is concerned only with number one.

It will be nice to get back to Newingsworth. What a tale I have to tell Sally when I get there. She'll find it hard to believe; she might even find it funny. I wish I did. Gosh, look at the time. I'd better hurry or the train will have gone without me...

The sentiment that Derek had restrained himself from communicating to fellow travellers was very nearly a replication of that actually expressed over the police radio system, earlier in the day, by an irate Metropolitan Police Sergeant to a sheepish PC Andy Woodstock.

The call had begun quite simply as routine. The Sergeant had not expected it to lead anywhere in particular – as normal. Yes, the usual ploy, a fantastically unbelievable reason being given by a villain who'd been bundled into the police van after having been caught red-handed. Villains were always claiming to have been arrested in error by nasty policemen...

"Got a bloke here, claims he knows you," the Sergeant began. "Is he one of your snouts maybe? Says his name is Tizzle-something. Just a minute..." He referred to the sheet in front of him. "No, it is Toozle... Toozlethwaite, Derek Toozlethwaite. Know him?"

"Yes, Sarge, course I do, was with me last night, at the Annual Knees-Up; didn't see you there though. Could you not manage, or do you not like boxing. Is it too rough for a big, gentle man like you, eh Sarge?" It was said teasingly. "I won a few quid too; don't usually bet on the winner. It was a great night and didn't finish until the early hours; had to go easy on the booze though with working today. Made the start of the shift successfully on time though, hope you noticed that."

"Woodstock ...just answer the question – do you know him or not?"

"Yea, he stayed overnight at my place. Why?"

"...Because he is now in police custody."

"What? What has he done? Can't leave that pal of mine on his own, can I? Wait a minute... You are kidding me, Sarge?"

There was a long pause. This sergeant knew his team, particularly the weakest links. Not surprisingly, PC Andy Woodstock regularly fitted into that category...

"That female you live with – you are still with her aren't you – what's her name again?"

"Sophie. Sophie Clerkenwell-Brown. Why? What's she got to do with it? Is she alright? What's happened Sarge?"

"Ah..."

There was an even longer pause.

"What is it, Sarge? Has she had an accident? She's at the hospital, isn't she? Tell me!"

"The phone call, received at seven this morning from the next-door neighbour of Ms Sophie Clerkenwell-Brown, said that your girlfriend was standing beside her, hysterical, because there was a stranger in her house. She had gone into the spare bedroom and found an intruder. The guy was sitting on the spare bed, with his back to her, brazenly talking on his mobile. He didn't see her, so she rushed next door in a panic."

"Oh..." said Andy, suddenly realising something.

"The neighbour immediately phoned us and we were there in a shot and arrested the unshaven tramp for illegal entry. So, as all the other cells were full after a busy night, a Mr Derek Toozlethwaite is sitting downstairs securely locked up, with a couple of drunks. And he says he knows you."

"Oh," said Andy again.

"And he is claiming that it is *your* flat and that you knew that he was there, and that he has done nothing wrong."

"But didn't Sophie recognise him? She knows him, knows him very well."

"She hasn't seen his face. If I understand her correctly, she was more or less naked when she went into the bedroom to fetch something to wear, so, I would not expect her to have said good morning and to shake hands with a man who had obviously broken into her flat..."

"I forgot to tell her he was there, Sarge..."

"You what? Woodstock, you never fail to surprise me. How could you forget to...?"

"She wasn't supposed to be there, and when we got back it was late and she was asleep and I didn't want to tell Derek it was *her* flat or that she lived there and I crept out this morning not wanting to waken her, and anyway Sophie shouldn't have..."

"Woodstock... Stop! So, you are telling me that we have arrested a mate of yours, who had every right to be in a flat – *that belongs to your girlfriend* – because you didn't want him to think you weren't mister big-shot, right? You just didn't want him to know that you live in your girl-friend's flat, did you?"

"No..."

"*Pardon?*"

"NO, SARGE... I didn't. Sorry..."

A frustrated Metropolitan Police Sergeant ended the call, and counted to ten...

Initially, Muriel was not phased one little bit at having her married daughter appear in a foul temper at ten-fifteen on Sunday morning on her doorstep at Cloverton. Sally had walked, seriously fuming as she pushed the pram containing both baby Edwin and the poodle, Jilly, and with a large holdall full of baby-things that she'd carried all the way from the Manor.

What surprised Muriel, though, was Alexander's reaction to being instructed by his daughter to fetch the case packed with her own things. It was sitting ready to be uplifted, on the floor of the home that she'd vacated only a short time ago, he was told.

"You are such a good father," his daughter had said to him, smiling in a most insincere and patronising manner. Surprisingly, he had meekly submitted. At this moment he was putting on his jacket, about to go off to do as requested.

Alexander would not be walking back to Toozlethwaite Manor, but neither would he be driving. A recent purchase had been a trailer: a small one, for his bike. Being unable to drive and having no car could sometimes be a disadvantage and that is where the trailer helped. Bought two months ago, but not yet used, he was quite excited about having a reason at long last to use it, and that might be why he agreed so readily.

It had all been so sudden, and a surprise, Sally appearing on her parent's doorstep but, as everyone knows, a mum is the normal fall-back when life becomes too much for a daughter. It is so natural to return to the fluffy nest where it all started, to the real home. Living here all her life until she married, what else could be expected? Being here would be just like the old days again.

Muriel mused contentedly about this – to begin with.

Here was Sally, back home with her and Alexander, as it used to be, but time had brought changes: the baby, and a dog, too. Not *exactly* as it used to be!

Alexander may have been taking the path of least resistance, and he was outwardly sympathetic, but he was not pleased. Yes, he would do what she had asked of him. She would have cooled down by the time he returned, he hoped. Her being back, chomping at the bit, was just not right for a Sunday morning.

Almost like the old days.

God, they were dreadful!

This time the signs looked worrying. He'd thought that her living with Derek was being surprisingly successful, but it looked as if maybe he was wrong. Obviously, a trying experience for his daughter, living with Derek. However, having been dragged into some of their previous traumas, and having had more than twenty-five years of his daughter living at home, he could guess how difficult it could be for Derek too.

He thought that their previous upsets had been smoothed over and long forgotten – perhaps not. Sally certainly hadn't returned home in such a foul mood since well before the birth of young ET. Disturbingly, it was the categorical statement she had made, as she entered her old home with baby and dog, which made it all appear so ominous to him.

"That is it! I have had as much as I can take of that man! I am home – for good!"

Alexander was more than aware that the toleration he and his only daughter had for each other was tenuous. Duration together to be as short as possible was the norm.

"Don't forget the dog's dishes, and her food, and her basket, and her toys," she'd shouted to him as he was leaving.

Not surprisingly Alexander was wary about the future. This appeared to be serious. What the heck had Derek done? Though neither parent had yet been informed, both realised that inevitably, in the fullness of time, they would be burdened with more gory details than desired.

Yes, Sally had returned – and taken over...

Though roughly bundled into the pram, which he'd had to share with a poodle on the way over, little Edwin had been soothed by the bouncing movement during the journey; now, in the arms of his grandma, the poor fellow decided to show his displeasure. That he could be a noisy little blighter was a fact well-known by both his mother and his gran. Unfortunately, today, it would be his gran appreciating the volume achievable.

Sally was out of earshot.

Into the back room she'd gone, to sit at the piano, leaving her mother to care for a fretting baby. She'd closed the door behind her: a very sensible move in her opinion. It was not to give privacy for her piano playing, more to shut out the noise being produced by her off-spring! Mother will manage, she decided. Loosening her fingers to help ease her inner tensions and improve her playing, she sat down on the stool.

With neither her mother nor father being musically inclined, as she grew older, this room had become her domain; Sally's bolt-hole. There was nothing more pleasurable, found from previous experience when life took a wrong turn, than to sit at the piano and play.

'Dirges' were what her father termed her choices of music but, then again, anything played in a minor key at a funereal pace was a dirge to him. For Sally, playing in a minor key at a funereal pace was a way of sharing with others how she felt, and, anyway, why suffer alone she always told herself.

The phone in her pocket sounded.

Who was calling? She didn't want to know. Anyway, if it was Derek he would be ignored. She had finished with him; playing around again with Sophie Clerkenwell-Brown indeed! How humiliating it had been to see that hussy appear behind him – totally starkers!

What was it he said when he left? "An overnight stay at Andy's, in London, at *his* flat", and Sally had given him a big kiss and told him to enjoy himself. If only she'd known. It felt worse because she had trusted him. He'd departed, smiling. She'd been satisfied that Derek would never ever misbehave again because he loved only her…

What a liar!

The phone continued to ring. Resist, she told herself, but she couldn't… Just a brief look at the screen… What! Sophie Clerkenwell-Brown. That damn bitch was trying to speak to her. How could she dare! Huh!

The phone was now silent and back in her pocket.

She restarted playing but found being in Bb minor was failing to relax her. Eb minor was no better ...the tension was still there.

Having happened only this morning it was all still fresh in her mind. It kept flashing into her head, the image she'd seen on the 'face to face' with Derek on their new smartphones: a naked Sophie Clerkenwell-Brown. There she'd been, appearing in the doorway behind that conniving two-timing husband of hers – especially when it was supposed to have been a male-only weekend, with Andy Pandy Woodstock!

3

It was a certainty that Crystal Glasse would eventually become as crooked as her father. Though she didn't see much of him these days, for the little contact that did occur, he was a poor influence, although that could depend on how you looked at it. He was currently serving time in Bordam Open Prison. An open prison permitting a reasonable amount of freedom, because he had been a good boy as far as prison procedures recognised. His name was Jock Hudson; to prison staff he was 463YZ.

Crystal's mother and father never even considered getting married. Crystal had been a big mistake due to a quick how's-your-father round the back of a pub in London. Her mother had explained this to her a long time ago. Between daughter and mother, there was no love lost, though she had retained her mother's surname, liking the quirkiness of it. That was the only link to that side of the family she had kept. Nowadays there was no contact at all with mother and there hadn't been for ages.

Here she was in London again and about to catch a train to return to her home but, a little sport would be in order before leaving. Someone had been selected. She had been pretending to read while watching him. The magazine in her hands was one she'd helped herself to in the newsagent; she could have had a couple of books, and crisps, and chewing gum as well, if she'd chosen, so many people were all milling about inside the shop today, but she resisted the temptation. It would have just been because she could. The thought of actually resisting a bit of temptation for once, made her feel quite angelic and anyway, crisps were not good for the figure.

The bloke targeted had stepped from the cab at the forecourt of the busy Kings Cross Station, lifting the luggage from the vehicle himself. Obviously fit enough to do that, and good-looking too, although maybe a bit older than those she normally took a fancy to. Probably went to the gym most days, she guessed. *Wouldn't mind him chasing and catching me up a dark alley,* she thought to herself, *but not today. Today is business.*

He had headed straight to the refreshment counter, dragging the case behind and with the two holdalls slung over his shoulder. Having purchased the large coffee he had made his way a little awkwardly across the concourse, stopping to change hands on the way. Maybe he was not as fit as she had earlier given him credit for; he seemed relieved to flop onto the bench on the Station concourse.

Lacking sleep, it seemed to her …up all night with his girl-friend probably, although it could have been a boyfriend: difficult to guess these days. He looked pleased to remove the holdalls from his shoulders. These were now dumped on top of the case at the end of the bench. His attention was immediately taken up with what he found on his smartphone and he had become oblivious to those bustling around him: phone in one hand, scalding-hot coffee in the other. He had certainly not noticed that she'd joined him, sitting now, at the other end of the bench. She was attractive and normally drew attention from males, so he must be gay right enough, she decided.

It would have to be done carefully. The larger of the two holdalls would be the choice; looked as if it ought to have more valuables, though you can never be certain. The move would have to be done slickly and not be caught by the cameras, but she was getting good at choosing the right moment. *Haven't been caught yet* was the cocky thought, but there is always a first time she reminded herself, so, she'd be cautious!

She stood up. The positions of the bags could not be viewed properly from where she was. She looked around the area before doing anything else – as far as she could see there were no coppers hiding around a corner waiting to pounce, but, *easy does it*. She moved along a bit behind the bench. Yes, one bag could be removed without disturbing the other. It wouldn't do to knock the other over as she snatched the chosen one. That would be very unprofessional. Round the back of the bench she went. Ah, excellent. He was fully engrossed on the phone, using an earpiece, and watching a boy-band singing itself silly on the screen. This she could see over his shoulder as she helped herself to the holdall, and casually walked away.

The train would be leaving shortly.

In a moment she would be well out of sight, even if he were to look up now and notice his bag missing. She was going back up north, so, what could be a nicer way of saying farewell to London than by leaving with a little memento?

There was no rush to look in the bag; she could see the contents later but the name-card in the leather luggage-tag would have to be removed, just in case. She glanced at the name: CHESNEY WILFORDEN. No address, just a mobile telephone number – neither were of any interest really. She removed it and slipped it in her pocket rather than throw it in the rubbish bin. There was no sense in leaving clues around the scene of the crime, now was there!

Only another few more paces and she would be aboard the train...

4

Dozing-off with the smartphone in his hand, and not having dropped it, was thanks only to the earpiece still plugged in his right ear. Chesney Wilfordon was awake, only just. Most unlike him to do something like that, and in a public place too but, for him, it had been a very busy spell and the pressure was still on.

He looked as his watch and compared it with the station digital display – perfectly synchronised – but he'd been asleep for twelve minutes! Fortunately he'd left home in plenty of time, the train didn't leave for another quarter of an hour. Looking over the documents again would pass the time, he thought, though it probably would be unwise doing that in a public place. He should not have brought the hard copy – it was against security procedures he knew, but it wasn't as if they could get lost.

He glanced at the baggage sitting beside him, then looked again. The third bag, the one with the documents in it – *wasn't there!*

"Oh Edwin, give over," his frustrated grandmother hissed. Sally, Edwin, and the dog, had only been here for a very short time and Muriel was already worried that, for all of the life she had left ahead of her, this was to become the pattern.

What with a young child who was crying without knowing why, who would be totally unable to inform anyone anyway even if he did, a pot of milk that had bubbled over and caused a dreadful stink in the kitchen, a yappy poodle that wanted out to the garden then barked like mad until it was allowed in again, and then yapped again because ...could things get any worse?

"ET, I have a headache," Gran Donaldson told her little grandson, who didn't really seem to care, "...and I am not so sure after all, even though I love you both dearly, that I like you and your mummy to be staying here like this."

No, he definitely did not care; he just went on crying.

The phone sounded yet again: Sally's.

"Phones can be so annoying," Sally had said when she'd come through to the kitchen, laid her mobile down on the table, and returned to continue at the keyboard.

It was a clever idea for Sally not to have it beside her when she was playing the piano, but that in no way hindered calls coming through. Asking mother to keep an eye on it for her, so that she would know later who had phoned, could be of great benefit – to Sally.

Her poor mother was being driven to distraction by a baby, a dog, a horrid, burnt-milk smell, and a phone that kept ringing suddenly, and each time startling her.

Sophie what's-her-name had tried calling three times, Andy Woodstock twice, and Derek four times, and, although Muriel wanted to answer, she had been given strict instructions not to. Sally was not happy with any of them, didn't want to speak to them ...but Muriel could stand it no longer.

She could do nothing about the smell, neither had she managed to stop ET crying, nor prevented the damn dog from yapping – but she could answer the phone! It was ringing again!

"Hello!" she barked into the device.

"Sally? Is that you Sally?" It was Derek.

"No, Derek, it is not," she replied. "Sally told me not to answer this damn thing!"

"Oh, Muriel, it's you. Why are you answering it then?" he asked. "Anyway why is Sally not answering herself? Are you at the cottage? Where's Sal? Is that ET crying? Is he unwell?"

"Derek, slow down. I can't cope."

"But where's Sally?"

"She's playing the piano. The usual stuff: the 'Dead March' and suchlike," she told him with a sigh, "and you know what that means don't you?"

"But she can't have... Surely Sophie has phoned – or Andy – have they not spoken to her? They were supposed to explain. Has she listened to the message I left? It wasn't me, Muriel! Honest! It wasn't my fault!"

"What wasn't, Derek?" said Muriel, suddenly calm and interested. Maybe this was the opportunity to find out what had upset Sally. Coincidentally, Edwin had stopped crying and Jilly had stopped barking – almost as if they were listening, waiting to learn the gory details too...

"It's too embarrassing!" was the reply.

"I am not easily shocked, Derek. I know what you are like... *Tell me*."

Shortly before, back at the London station, Derek had been just in time, clambering aboard as all the doors were being closed. Moments later the train was on the move. Not having a booked seat meant searching the fairly busy carriages for one that was unoccupied, even though it might be only be a temporary resting place. The few seats lying empty had reservation tickets on them, mostly booked by passengers destined for northern destinations and who would probably be joining at a future station.

Ah, there were two without reservations, one on each side of the passage, but both were occupied by the luggage of passengers who were plainly using them as a deterrent against human company.

On the right, sitting at the window with his bag on the unclaimed outside seat, was a fat and grumpy-looking male who had spread a lot of documents all over the table. He had his head down, ignoring anything happening around him, working on a lap-top, whereas, on the left, a pretty young lady was seated. She had her holdall on the vacant seat next to the window. Her table was clear; another difference – she was smiling up at him. She nodded her head towards the seat opposite her at the table, but Derek could see it had a reserved label attached.

"That seat will be free for a long while," she said, and gave another smile. "Where are you going to?" she asked.

"Newingsworth, or rather, Slatterfoot Station," he answered.

"You'll be alright in that seat then. If you look at it, you'll see it's booked from beyond there."

He looked, and it was. "Thanks for that," he said and flopped down, grateful at this seat being his for the duration of his journey. He smiled at the young lady, she smiled back.

Thanks to Andy Woodstock's guilty conscience, when he was released from captivity by the police, Derek had at least been handed his overnight bag. The few belongings Derek brought with him had been hurriedly packed, by Andy back at the flat, and rushed over to the police station, to be handed to Derek as he was released.

The bag could now serve another purpose. It was laid strategically on the seat. He didn't want anyone to sit beside him either...

Must get hold of Sally, he thought, she'll be worried about me. He had tried phoning from the Police Station on the brief call that they permitted before he was thrown in the cell, but he had failed then to get any human response. It was Sally's mobile he had tried first, unsuccessfully, then his own home line. No answer there either, so he had finished up leaving a message on the Toozlethwaite Manor phone.

"Sorry Sally but I might not be home today. I am stuck in London, in a police cell. I have been arrested for house-breaking, but..."

"I think that should do, sir, don't you?" the nice policeman had said, as the new mobile was whipped from his hand and placed in the plastic container with his other possessions.

He wondered if she even knew yet that he was arrested. Had she listened to the message? If she has, he thought, she could be upset, unless Andy or Sophie have made contact and explained why. Sally would have been expecting him to be arriving back home by now.

He reached into his pocket and pulled out his all-singing, all-dancing, smartphone. An earlier attempt to ring her on his way to catch the train had again elicited no response from her mobile.

It did not seem the best idea to try using 'face-to-face' again, after this morning's effort. That method had been less than successful earlier and Sally appeared to have been cut-off in mid-conversation. This time it would be verbal only – but only if he could actually make contact with his elusive wife. He selected Sally's number once again and dialled, still no response.

"She could be feeding ET."

Speaking aloud was unintentional. It was heard and acknowledged by a glare from the fat gent across the passage, the one who had deliberately ignored him initially. He pointedly swivelled his head to look at the signs on the carriage windows. 'QUIET COACH' the notices stated.

"Oh, sorry," said Derek out loud again, to receive another glare that made him regret bothering with the apology.

"ET...?" The young lady opposite looked surprised. "That's the alien isn't it?"

"No, it's my son – well, his nickname. He is really called Edwin, Edwin Toozlethwaite – ET. Excuse me, but I must try again."

As Derek lifted the phone, another scowl appeared on the face across the passage, but this time Derek bravely glowered back and won the staring competition.

He tried again and let the phone ring until it disconnected automatically. He was relieved. If he had disturbed Sally doing something important she would have been most unhappy. If that had happened he knew it would have been a chilly reception. Therefore he gratefully accepted that there would be a chance to try again later.

He put the phone back into his pocket and looked out of the window at a varying landscape, now no longer just the rear views of buildings.

"Mr Toozlethwaite isn't it," said the girl. "Can you tell me what time it is? What is your first name again?"

"It's Derek," he replied automatically, "though people often call me Swea..." He stopped himself in time.

"I have come away without my watch and my mobile," she said. "It was a bit of a rush getting out of the flat."

She leaned across the table and put her hand up to shield her mouth in a confidential way. Instinctively, Derek leaned towards her across the table to hear what it was she was about to say. She was smiling, but not with her eyes...

"He is a bully..." she whispered and, with her other hand, indicated the fat bloke across the passage.

"What?" responded Derek, thinking he had misheard?

Yes, that smile was definitely false and, if he has understood correctly, this girl was in difficulty. However, he knew, oh so well, that responding wrongly to a comment because he had misheard it could land him in trouble – not uncommon when he was at home with Sally – so it seemed wise to be doubly careful. There had been enough upsets for one weekend already. He looked at the girl questioningly as she leaned forward again.

"Him ...over there; he is my wicked step-father. He is forcing me to go with him and says he'll beat me up if I don't. I must get away from him."

I am not going to become involved, Derek told himself, so, "Oh..." was all that came out as a response, and he gave what he considered to be the sort of smile that said I'm sorry to hear it, but there's nothing I can do. His phone was raised for yet another try. The girl would see where his priorities lay, and get the message.

Still no answer from Sally: why? She never goes anywhere without a mobile and, with it being the same as his: a new expensive all-singing, all-dancing model, she would surely not let it out of her reach. He certainly wouldn't let anyone have his...

"She's not answering. Must know it's me," he offered as a self-denigrating aside to the girl.

I have my own problems, he hoped he was demonstrating, but, were those vibes being picked up by the girl opposite? She should be getting the message not to expect any assistance from me – but is she?

She leaned forward again. "Will you help?" she asked quietly, but earnestly.

"Of course!" came out of his mouth before he realised he was saying it, and certainly louder than he'd meant.

He glanced across the passage. The fat ugly bloke looked up from whatever was on the laptop screen, and the challenging eye-contest took place one more.

Bugger it! That wasn't what he meant to say!

He was always doing this sort of thing – being too damn helpful for his own good. How he could possibly assist her he really had no idea. What did she hope he'd do? Talk nicely to that bloke? Is that what she would be expecting?

Did she want him to tell the man to leave her alone; warn him that if he doesn't take a telling he would be taken outside and given a really good hiding! They say that in the good old-fashioned stories, don't they? Is that what he should do?

No, of course not, so, what *should* he do?

Anyway, he had his own little problem. There was something he should be doing: his own uncompleted task, of course. He hadn't spoken to his wife yet. One more try.

"*Hello!*"

At last, thank goodness ...but she sounded different? "Sally? Is that you Sally?"

It wasn't. He had made contact with his mother-in-law.

Thinking, to begin with, that his mother-in-law was visiting Toozlethwaite Manor, then finding out that Sally was at Cloverton was a surprise. Understanding then that neither Sophie nor Andy had yet spoken to Sally came as a disappointment, and to be told by his mother-in-law that his wife was sitting in the 'music room' playing dirges on the piano was a touch disturbing. That usually only happened if he had put his foot in it but, he hadn't done anything wrong this time. Was something else annoying her maybe?

Of course, Muriel said she thought he was supposed to have been home sooner, and had to ask why he was delayed.

"...It's too embarrassing to say!" he had replied.

He knew it was better to talk to Sally directly. Though his mother-in-law sounded desperate to hear what he had to say, second-hand tales can lead to misunderstandings.

"I am not easily shocked, Derek," Muriel had pursued. "I know what you are like... *Tell me!*" but he didn't.

Muriel was not the only curious one. As Derek looked up, the girl opposite and the ugly bloke across the passage had both pricked up their ears? What was '...too embarrassing'?

"I'll speak to Sally later," he told Muriel, and ended the call.

The girl leaned over again. Reaching out, she covered his hand with hers. "You have problems too..." she murmured, gazing sadly into Derek's face.

When he noticed the eyes of the ugly bloke taking in every movement Derek quickly pulled his hand free and sat up straight. No words came from across the passage, but Derek could feel an unspoken threat. His worry was, if attacked, would anyone in the carriage come to his aid? That bloke must be at least three-stone heavier and probably three-feet taller when standing up. It was so easy to visualise!

Oh God, please don't let him stand up!

"And you have a little baby too... Awwww... I bet you are a wonderful daddy. My real daddy went away a long time ago: left Mummy and me all alone." She leaned forward once again, conspiratorially. "...And that's when *he* appeared..."

The weak smile on Derek's face exposed a less than eager person listening to what she was saying, but she was insistent. He could tell that in no way was he going to be able to deter her. He didn't want to become involved, but he couldn't stop himself. He leaned forward this time.

"How far are you going?" he asked, against his better judgement. He was being drawn in and unable to resist. She hesitated before answering.

"All the way ...if you are willing," she offered, moving her eyebrows seductively.

Derek did not know which way to look. How could she joke at a time like this? What was she up to? He gave another glance across the passage, to make sure no adverse reactions were occurring with the ugly bloke; thankfully he was engrossed with the screen.

"Aberdeen then...?" he said.

"Hmmm..." was her response. Derek thought she winked, but couldn't be certain.

To simply sit and look out at the countryside flashing by seemed the thing to do, so he did. You haven't really committed yourself, do not get involved, he repeated to himself as the girl sat back against the seat and closed her eyes and, relaxing a little, Derek did so too...

He must have dozed off because he was suddenly aware that the phone in his pocket was vibrating. He fumbled around and brought it to his ear.

"Sally ...thanks for ringing back, darling. Is everything alright now?"

"Derek, this is not 'darling', it is Andy. Sorry to disappoint you and apologies again for earlier today, but just to tell you that I can't get an answer on Sally's phone. Sophie's been trying too, unsuccessfully."

"Keep trying please, Andy. For some reason she appears reluctant to talk to me. It is almost as if she thinks I've been away for a dirty weekend!"

"Hard luck, pal, but, no doubt you are used to being in the doghouse anyway, aren't you?"

As Derek put the phone back into his pocket, the eyes of the female opened and she leaned towards him over the table.

"...And dirty weekends can be fun, can't they? Could I borrow your phone?" she whispered.

5

Sally was fairly thumping the keys now. Even with the door to the back room closed it was uncomfortably noisy. It almost drowned out the sound of the front doorbell. Muriel heard it – just.

She went to answer it carrying a noisy ET in her arms and with a white poodle yapping at her heels, and was surprised to find little old Mrs Masterton from next door standing there holding the 'Sunday Times' newspaper. *Is she here to complain about the noise*, Muriel asked herself, *because if she is...*

Why was it nowadays that her next door neighbour managed to bring out the worst in her? And it is the 'Sunday Times' too, hmmm...

Criticising this woman came to her so easily. Something to do with Mrs Masterton these days being such an annoying person! Now, if Muriel bought a newspaper, it would be the 'Slatterfoot Evening News', or the 'Weekly Gazette', because she considered it morally correct to support local community activities.

A perfectly justified criticism she decided, then felt bad. Actually buying either of the local newspapers was rare for Muriel, so, to judge Mrs Masterton as wrong in purchasing a national might be a touch hypocritical. Anyway the locals don't print on a Sunday and...

"Have you seen it?" demanded her neighbour as the newspaper was flapped around in front of Muriel's face, but flapping only for a few moments as it became necessary for the holder to whip the paper down to a lower level, as Jilly, in attack mode, squeezed passed Muriel!

"Get it off me!" came the cry as the poodle yapped at Mrs Masterton's ankles. The little old lady succeeded in doing an impromptu, but very lively involuntary dance, as she used the newspaper in an attempt to fend off the animal.

Muriel bent and grasped the dog's collar, not an easy thing to do when holding a young baby but, succeeding, she dragged the dog inside. It gave her some satisfaction to give it a kick as it passed. It had been a bad morning.

There was reluctance, on her part, to invite the visitor inside – she could be so nosy – and these days she was also choosy as to when she would deign to speak to Muriel, so it did Muriel's spirit some good to think that Jilly had startled the little busybody. Maybe, after all, the poor dog hadn't deserved the kick... Anyway, conversation inside would be impossible with the noise Sally was making!

"Look at the headlines! *The hi-speed rail line!* They are going to annihilate us!" was screeched. "It will go right through Newingsworth! How dare they even think of doing that?"

Muriel looked at her neighbour. What was she going on about? It was common knowledge that the planned route was about to be announced but it couldn't possibly be anywhere near here. These houses looked out over beautiful green pastures, and cows grazing peacefully – the perfect view. Of course the hi-speed rail line wouldn't be anywhere near here.

With an intelligent nod or two, to show that she understood the dilemma incredibly well, a sympathetic look on her face to display her depth of feeling for the subject and a baby in her arms that began to scream, Muriel chose a brief, "G' bye then..." and closed the door.

Little old Mrs Masterton removed herself from the doorstep and returned to her perpetual curtain twitching – the thing she was best at!

"Sally... *Please stop that dreadful music!*"

Now, Muriel's shout had startled poor little ET! He began a fresh, and louder, bout of crying! She felt under pressure. The stink from the burnt milk had still not cleared from the kitchen, and as for that dog! "Mother, what is wrong? Why the noise? I am trying to concentrate."

If it had been anything other than a real, live baby in her arms Muriel would have thrown it. As it was, she stormed into the music room and held the little child out to her daughter. "Oh Mother, he stinks... Couldn't you have at least changed his nappy? No wonder he's unhappy. Give Mummy a big hug, darling..." and ET stopped crying.

Muriel stomped off into the kitchen. The poodle yapping at her ankles let out a yelp as it received some of Muriel's pent–up emotion on its posterior. This time she had no regrets about her behaviour towards that little bitch...

...Then the house phone rang.

It was Thelma, Alexander's sister. Only nasty thoughts were in Muriel's head this morning it seemed. *She'll be phoning to tell me that she's found a wonderful new diet,* flashed through her brain. Thelma, being slightly overweight, was always on the lookout for good diets, *but if she dares to suggest that I should try it too, I'll...*

"Hello Thelma," she said, "and how are you this morning, darling, how nice of you to phone."

Surprisingly, it was not about a fabulous new diet that involved preparing a list of all of your favourite foods, and then making yourself sick regularly by gorging yourself on them – Thelma had been reading this morning's newspaper too.

"Incredible! This new rail route; it's to come right through a great deal of Newingsworth and looks like it will affect both Derek and Sally's place, and, our hotel! You might even be affected!"

The mood Muriel was in, she almost cuttingly asked Thelma to repeat the bit about whose hotel it was? She restrained herself and felt the better of it. Thelma and Hamish Macintosh may be running it, but the real owner, who'd had little to do with it admittedly, was Alexander.

And a diet hadn't been mentioned – yet.

Thelma chose to launch into a diatribe about the government, the rail company, and the lousy money that was likely to be offered as compensation to those who would be affected.

"Your house might be safe in Cloverton, but, if you ever want to use the train in the future, you'll have to travel an extra fifteen miles, the station at Slatterfoot is to be closed because of it. Someone is going to have to do something about this..."

Oh, oh, Alexander isn't going to like this, thought Muriel. The hotel was to be the emergency nest-egg, according to him, and although they had plenty of money stashed away, as the local bank manager he was always keen to make room for more. As for Slatterfoot Station, being keen cyclists, neither Muriel nor Alexander were inclined to use public transport too often, but there were trips made by them to farther afield places, places that called for the use of the train. No station at Slatterfoot? Indeed, that could be bad news. What will Alexander have to say about that she wondered? ...*Speak of the devil, he's back.*

"Muriel, Muriel, where are you?" he called the moment he came through the door. "You'll never believe it. Do you know what they are planning?"

The response of "Yes," from his wife came as a surprise and sort-of took the wind out of his sails. She wasn't usually up to date on matters of importance.

"Have you seen it on television?" he asked, and she shook her head. So, how did Muriel know? He was curious, but determining how she'd become aware was not the important factor. "Maybe you could switch on the television. It is bound to be the headlines. Some poor sod somewhere is bound to be losing a fortune in the process. I'll go up and change, and, when I come down, maybe I'll have some peace to read the paper."

Obviously, Thelma had picked up more detail than Alexander, Muriel realised. He didn't yet know that *he* could very likely be one of the 'poor sods'.

6

Derek was disappointed that Sally hadn't yet phoned him. Surely Andy or Sophie would have managed to speak to her by now?

He hoped it would be Sophie who made first contact with Sally. There was more chance of an explanation being understandable if it came from her. His being arrested in her flat might sound strange to Sally, but Sophie has a good way with words. Yes, he told himself, he'd rather it was her – Andy Pandy Woodstock had already made such a mess – he might just dig a deeper hole.

The girl opposite had been given a loan of his new mobile – part of her escape plan – but, once she returned the phone, that was as far as he would be getting involved. Derek was determined this time. Temporary use of the new mobile would definitely be the limit of his contribution. It was the least he could do, with her own being left behind in the rush out of her flat, as she'd explained. This brute across the passage obviously had caused a lot of trouble for his step-daughter.

As Derek did not wish to encourage confrontation with the ugly bloke, who had in no way diminished in stature during the journey, the transfer of his expensive and much-loved new phone, on temporary loan, had been done surreptitiously.

It was also done with a great deal of reluctance; after all it was new, and it was his. He didn't properly know this girl –

could he trust her not to drop it? He'd owned it for less than a week and was only beginning to understand its workings: he hadn't managed yet even to remember his own new number.

The seat opposite was currently empty; vanished along the corridor with the phone, she had: back in a moment, she'd whispered to him. The step-father had let her go without any reaction. She'd pretended it was for another purpose by announcing, as she stood up, that she was going to the toilet. It had been loud enough to be heard by most of the occupants of the carriage.

"I'll phone a pal in Slatterfoot," she'd whispered to Derek. That friend had a car and would arrange to meet the train and whisk her away – away from her wicked stepfather. Her plan had been explained in fits and starts, so as not to arouse the suspicions of the ugly bloke, and it included a part that Derek, not surprisingly, was unsure about: he was to distract the ugly bloke, by blocking the passage as she made her getaway – *she* said...

No contact yet with Sally... *Hurry up and phone please, Sal.* He still had difficulty accepting what had happened earlier today. One minute he had been sitting on the bed, in what he'd thought was Andy's flat and, the next, the bursting open of the bedroom door and being grabbed by two burly young coppers who had carried him out of the flat and bundled him into their vehicle. It was one of Andy's jokes, he'd told himself at the time; arranging for a couple of mates to get him to the station in time for his train in a very original way. If only that had been true.

The reality of it was his spending several hours in a cell with a couple of old drunks who smelt as if they could have done with a good hose down; and all because Andy was trying to pretend it was his flat.

Even worse, his friend and publisher, Sophie Clerkenwell-Brown – someone he thought he knew really well and who liked him – was the one who'd had him arrested: *didn't recognise your back apparently,* he'd been told by the sergeant, *and, anyway, she had no clothes on and she sends her apologies.* A grudging apology for mistakenly having hauled him in, was also given by the very same gentleman: "...On behalf of that pillock Woodstock!" These were the sergeant's own words and Derek could tell that, in having to say them, he was not a happy man.

There I was sitting on the bed, this morning, must have been on the phone to Sally at the time – experimenting with the face-to-face, Derek recalled. *These new phones can do so many fancy things nowadays, and...*

Oh my God!

It struck him suddenly – he was showing her what the room looked like. Could she have seen Sophie, naked, behind him? Could that be why she hung up so quickly? Surely she didn't think that... Oh dear... No wonder she's not answering her phone then. Not only would she not believe him, she won't believe a word of what Andy or Sophie are going to say either!

"We are now approaching York Station. If you are leaving the train please ensure that you have all belongings with you and, when stepping from the carriage, please take care. We are grateful for having had the pleasure of your company. Thank you for travelling with us and we hope that you will continue to use our services many times again in the future."

Derek had difficulty reconciling the male voice making the announcement with the behaviour and speech of the gent who came around earlier to check the tickets. It was definitely the same one, but he'd said absolutely nothing to anyone, treating each traveller as a likely fare-dodger. In his communication system, 'Please' and 'thank you' had figured not!

Brooding over the detail of his most recent brush with the law was impossible to avoid; he was sitting on a train with nothing else to do. A slight shudder of the carriage suddenly made him realise that he had been in a daydream, having been unaware, not only that the train had arrived at the station and been at a halt for many minutes, but that it was now time to move again.

He could see most passengers who'd left the train making their way to the exits. Being a busy station many others stood around or sat on benches awaiting the arrival of the next train. No different from the way it had been for years in this well-used junction, except that nowadays almost everyone that he could see had eyes and ears only for mobile phones, whether walking, sitting, or standing still.

Look, there's the girl who was sitting opposite him, seeming happy enough now with a big smile on her face; must have managed to contact her friend then...

"WHAT?" he suddenly yelled, drawing the attention of most of the carriage's passengers: he was wide awake now!

She didn't say she would be leaving the train here – it was to be Slatterfoot Station! Worse than that, the new phone, *his* phone, that was what she was holding in her hand – *my new phone!*

Calm down, he told himself, but that was difficult. What was she up to? She was not standing in the hot dog queue, so, she didn't go off for food. She must just have hopped off to make the call, he decided. She'd be jumping back on any second, surely. She'd have to hurry! As he watched, she continued laughing and giggling into his phone. He waved frantically but without acknowledgement.

The doors closed. There was a slight shudder as the wheels began turning. She was still standing talking and appeared to be totally unconcerned by the gradual departure. He wanted to shout to her. He waved again.

Oh no, these trains picked up speed rapidly – she had his phone – *think this through properly, but quickly Toozlethwaite,* he told himself, *her jumping off here was because... Ah-ha!* He relaxed again... *It's ok, don't panic, I understand what she's up to.*

He gave a quick glance across the passage. The ugly bloke was still engrossed in his laptop. He hadn't noticed his step-daughter standing on the platform. It showed how little he cared about the poor girl.

Clever ...it would mean that he could leave at Slatterfoot without having to employ delaying tactics with this fellow. A smart move and she'd probably ring him in a moment to say that.

Duh! He had no phone – and what about Sally? She couldn't contact him now either.

"*Oh no...!*" came out as a groan, as he leaned forward in despair. What should he do? Making rash decisions would only lead to bigger trouble. Should he run along the corridor, jump off and join that girl and they could catch the next train together; but what about the luggage – and the big bloke across the passage?

He looked out the window. Jump now and he would break his legs – there was no longer any platform! It was too late!

Derek's life was entering one of its downward spirals: a 'head in hands' moment...

"You all right, mate?" asked a male voice.

Derek looked up in surprise – at the large figure standing looking down. The ugly bloke, he was upright – and he was big. *What is he going to accuse me of? Has he realised that his step-daughter had an accomplice in her escape – and that it is me?*

"You ok? You've looked a bit peaky ever since you got on the train... You are not 'avin an 'eart attack are you? First-Aider, me... Pains... You 'avin' pains in chest? No?"

Derek was afraid to speak. He simply shook his head and gave a sickly smile, and the bloke returned to his seat to resume his scouring of the screen. His step-daughter got no mention. Maybe he was glad to be rid of her.

She's left her holdall behind. Ah, now that is it. Derek felt a spark of hope and understanding! There was no need to worry, she'd be getting her friend to drive her to Slatterfoot to meet him there, expecting him to smuggle her bag off the train without her step-father noticing, of course, and she'd return the phone when she saw him. He had been a bit hasty. Silly, he should have realised.

That very sound logic made Derek feel much better, so much so that he relaxed, positioned himself, propped in the corner and, as York Station was rapidly left far behind, dropped off to sleep...

7

"Going for a shower, Mummy, ok? Would you keep an eye on ET, and oh, the phone... Don't answer, just note who calls, please."

What a difference it can make to the peacefulness of a home: a baby having had a nappy changed, and a piano having had the lid closed.

That her husband had tried to contact her earlier was of little interest to Sally, and Muriel was chided for not obeying instructions: "Please, do not to answer calls, I said, didn't I."

Sally's becoming a right little madam, thought an already exhausted and exasperated Muriel. With little Edwin contentedly playing on the carpet with his favourite soft toy-duck, cooing every so often into its bright yellow beak, it was an opportunity for Muriel to flop down on an easy chair in the sitting room and try to relax. Sally's mobile had been placed on the coffee table, within easy reach, and easily viewed if it did ring again.

"Goo, goo, goo," said ET. He could be so loveable when he wasn't crying. Muriel looked down at the happy little figure and smiled a loving-grandmother smile, but that expression left quickly when the phone rang.

Who is it? She couldn't help herself; she'd done it again, reached out to stop the ringing and automatically pressed the green light.

"Sally?" said the female voice.

Muriel realised suddenly that she wasn't supposed to be answering Sally's phone. "I am sorry but Mrs Toozlethwaite is not available at the moment. Would you like to leave a message?" was said in a very business-like voice.

She waited.

"It's on the damn answering machine, Andy. Maybe I should leave a message... What do you think? At least I got through this time."

The voice seemed familiar; obviously one of Sally's friends, but which one?

"Sally," the voice continued. "It's about earlier this morning, to say sorry. It is rather embarrassing, but I'll speak to you later. It's just that..."

It clicked with Muriel – it was the name 'Andy', and that voice – *it's Sophie, Sophie Clerkenwell-Brown and she's my friend too, isn't she?* This was her big chance to get to know what it was all about, in case Sally was thinking of keeping this one secret – but quickly, she was going to hang up...

"Sophie, hello, this is Muriel. I didn't know it was you."

"Muriel, what are you doing answering Sally's phone? Has something happened to her?"

"No, no, no... I am the baby-and-phone-minder while she has a shower. She's not been in a very good mood. Seems upset again with Derek, I think, but she doesn't seem to want to talk to anybody. I could give her a message if you wish."

Don't push too hard for an answer, Muriel told herself, and I might get to know...

"Well, it is sort of ...delicate. Andy forgot to tell me, when he went to work, that Derek was staying in our spare room, and I had him arrested..."

"What – for not telling you? Poor Andy..."

"No, it was *Derek* I had arrested."

"Oh, my, what had he done?"

"Nothing: that's the point! I went into the bedroom, with no clothes on – as you do – to choose something to wear, and there he was..."

"Did he have clothes on?" asked Muriel sharply, suddenly thinking of her son-in-law in a new light. What had he been up to?

"I think so..."

"But you know Derek – very well too."

"I only saw his back. He didn't see me."

Muriel heaved a sigh of relief, but this was a little nougat of information that had better not be mentioned to Sally. She might jump to the wrong conclusion. She usually did!

"Unfortunately, Derek was arrested for breaking and entering my flat and put in a police cell this morning. I am so embarrassed. He's out now and should be on the train on his way home at this moment but I wanted to apologise to Sally for the trouble I've caused her."

Muriel had heard rumours of Sophie doing much worse things than that with other women's husbands, but, obviously this had been only a little mix-up – provided Sally sees it that way then all would be well, and Sally could go back home again – thank goodness!

"Right then, Sophie, I'll explain it all to her in a moment, and no doubt she will ring you herself later. I just can't understand why she was getting so upset... Oh, sorry Sophie, have to go. ET's been sick on the carpet!"

For Hammy, over-reaching for lost balls in the pond on the hotel's golf course had been a bad move today, the consequence being a wet walk back to the hotel for a change of clothing.

Well over a year ago, before the pond had even been constructed, he had joked to Thelma about salvaging the results of poor strokes, and, as he'd predicted, ever since the course was opened, the balls had splashed into the water, and been abandoned. He had been proved right. It was a fairly large surface of water and a magnetic attraction for the poorer golfer. Of course supplying a net on a fairly short pole meant most lost balls remained so, by being out of reach for the player.

The balls were normally re-useable, so, collecting them and selling them had become the routine and had generated quite an amount of cash for the local hospital. Of course, to do that Hammy had a much longer pole on his net and normally wore waders for the weekly lost-ball collection. Up to now it had been a fruitful and dry pastime – but not today.

He had been standing on the banking, wader-less, holding onto the parapet of the footbridge with one hand and reaching with the scoop, in the same way that he had done successfully so many times previously out of laziness, but this time his hand slipped. It was not all gloom and doom though. He made use of the fact that he would become no wetter if he walked about in the shallow pond. By doing exactly that, he managed to collect more little, white, round things than normal.

When he came back into the hotel, his wife almost had an accident too although hers nearly involved body fluids. She couldn't stop giggling as Hammy dripped passed her leaving a trail from the front door right through the public area. Before any guest slipped on the wet parquet floor, Kylie, who was in charge of Reception, sprang into action. She volunteered to fetch the mop and dry up the trail her boss left. Thelma was quite pleased to step in and take over temporarily at the desk. She then took great delight in recounting the tale to each visitor who appeared in the vicinity.

Thelma would have carried on giggling all day, but for the fact, that Hammy, having had a shower, sat down to read the

Sunday paper and found the article about the new rail route. She heard him from the other room. There was no smile on that man's face! The hotel and the recently finished nine-hole golf course that he was so proud of – *a rail line could be running through the middle!*

"Over ma deed body!" was his roar. Having already suffered one indignity today he was, therefore, not in the best of moods. "You urr not going tae get away wi' that, ma bonnie wee laddies, wherever ye may be. Naw, naw... dinna meddle with a Scotsman's property..." then he realised a correction was required – *he* was not the owner, "...or even a big lodgin' house that an awful-angry Scot just *manages* furr an Englishmunn!"

Alexander had returned to Cloverton, happy that his new bike trailer had served the purpose well. He had successfully pulled the load all the way from Toozlethwaite Manor – Derek gave that cottage such a pretentious name, he always thought – to Cloverton, and without stopping pedalling once. Now, that must deserve a self-congratulatory pat on the back, even though it is level ground all the way. *Not bad for a man of my age*, he told himself.

The house was nice and peaceful he noted when he returned. He'd visualised returning to a battleground – Muriel was not as even-tempered as she used to be. When they were younger she was the one who could absorb the turmoil, without seemingly being affected, by being the controlled calm in the storm of an argument going on between him and Sally.

When he returned he had gone upstairs and changed out of his cycling clothing. Wearing the Lycra gear had become a compulsion when he used the bike. It felt totally alien to even consider sitting in the saddle without wearing the proper clothes.

There was no noise in the house he noticed, so there was every chance that Sally, the baby, the dog, and Muriel had all been here together without any upsets. Super!

While upstairs he'd popped his head in to report his return to his daughter, but found that she had a migraine and was not happy at having been disturbed. Don't chance a response, he'd decided, and quickly exited that room. When he came downstairs again and went into the front room, thank goodness he moved very quietly. Baby Edwin was on the soft rug fast asleep and his wife, lying stretched out on the settee, looked to be enjoying the time-out, fast asleep too. Even the poodle was lying half-asleep, but watching him out of one eye.

He looked over at Muriel. She must be absolutely exhausted, he guessed, because she never stretched out on the settee like that. Should he close her mouth, he wondered – stop her snorting like that perhaps? No, I might waken her and that would not do at all.

It had reached the time of day for him when coffee becomes a necessity, but Muriel was asleep! He couldn't very well waken her just to have her make a coffee for him, now could he? He dithered on that... No, he'd have to make it himself.

Into the kitchen he went and put on the kettle, normally the total extent of his culinary skills. Now where was the coffee jar kept? This was a novelty for him, venturing into unknown territory. He sniffed. That smell, what was it? A pot that had obviously dried out was lying on the cooker. Looked all brown, *hmm* ...what to do? Shouldn't it be cleaned – properly? How is that done? Better just leave it for Muriel...

Ah, here's the coffee: *'Instant', I can cope with that.*

So, mug of coffee in hand, he tiptoed back through to the sitting room; both still asleep. With Sally's surprise appearance he had not had a chance to open the newspaper that morning. It would not be a Sunday without being able to sit down and relax and read the contents from beginning to end. *Better late than never I suppose*, he told himself.

All was fine until page five…

Ah yes, the High-Speed Rail Project; interesting, a map of the proposed route. The sooner the government gets approval and the project gets underway, the better, he decided, although pity the poor sods that will suffer the loss of homes and property in return for a paltry sum. Sad though it may be, it is the way of the world. Protestations will be next. As usual, individual's self-interest will wrongly fight against the greater need of the country.

The poor planning people, he reflected, have so many obstacles to overcome. It is just a pity that the public can't accept that we can't all be winners all of the time. These officials do a great job.

Of course, it is said that importance is in the detail and as he looked a little closer at the large scale map...

"WHAT!"

He couldn't help it. In his excitement he'd knocked over the cup of coffee – but what he'd read was serious stuff.

"Muriel! For heavens' sake!" he cried out. "Would you believe it? Look where they are to run the bloody thing!"

So taken aback was he by this bombshell coming his way – a major inconvenience that, suddenly, was about to affect his future – that it took a few moments to realise the chaos his loud outburst had created in the room!

On the settee, spluttering and coughing, was a wife in a state of shock at the sudden awakening, and, lying on the carpet, a baby that had been wakened with a start and was most unhappy about it, yelling its lungs out on a carpet that he had endowed with a large, brown, coffee stain, and a white poodle that resented his existence and was barking to add to the noise.

As he sat transfixed, gazing uneasily across at his wife, she rose to her feet and leaped towards him with a mad look on her face – and a crystal vase in her hand. Suddenly, the route of a silly, hi-speed railway-line seemed insignificant

He moved quickly!

The sanctity and safety of the upstairs bathroom, with a lock on the door, seemed the best place to be until the dust settled. It is obvious that rational discussion about an impending financial crisis would have to wait...

8

If the ticket inspector hadn't nudged his arm to check the validity of his ticket yet again, Derek might have slept all the way up north. As it was, he felt refreshed, but light-headed. It took a few moments to recognise the passing countryside and to realise that he was back on home territory. The train was only a few miles from Slatterfoot Station.

He smiled, it was nice to be home – and then, it all came back to him.

With his phone having been last seen at York Station in the hand of the girl who'd sat opposite, of course there had been no contact with Sally. The girl's holdall remained where it had been, on the opposite inside seat, the holdall that he was supposed to smuggle off the train for her. The seat where the girl had sat was now occupied by a stern-faced middle-aged woman. She had assumed that the holdall belonged to Derek, and her disapproving look in his direction, implied that it should be beside him rather than her, but he couldn't move it.

Derek looked across the passage – at the step-father – *he* hadn't gone, and he was *still* a big guy! He would realise something was afoot if the holdall was touched. Why wasn't he concerned though? With his eyes constantly on the laptop in front of him, he can't have appreciated just how long his step-daughter had been away – at the toilet!

The train was slowing. This was it. He had to get ready without making it too obvious …wait until the last minute, and then rush out. Take his own bag in his right hand and hers in his left, so that the man doesn't notice it, and then run.

The train came to a stop... He waited.

The doors were opened and passengers alighted... He waited.

Then he leapt up, reached over, grabbed the girl's bag, and his own – much to the surprise of the woman – and went for it!

He'd waited almost too long and nearly didn't make it.

The closing door caught his own bag, briefly – and then he was clear.

Behind, in the carriage, many disgruntled passengers had been given whacks from the two holdalls as he'd barged passed frantically. Several from the far side of the carriage, who'd been struck on the shoulder, were standing, looking out at the clumsy idiot on the platform.

The big ugly one had closed his lap-top. He was standing too, looking down at Derek and giving a sad shake of his head. "That bloke, 'e'll 'ave to look after 'imself, I tell you." His expert knowledge had to be spread to the others remaining in the carriage. "Betya 'e'll be 'avin an 'eart attack soon. A first-aider, meself, an' y'know, you get to be able t'tell symptoms. I was ready; cos, when y'are a first-aider ye'ave to be. Yup, a walkin' liability is that bloke."

These comments were directed to the whole carriage, but then, as he returned to his seat, it was the turn of the group of elderly women that were seated behind him, to hear his words of wisdom. "A married man 'e was too, but did you 'ear 'im? Tryin' to geroff wiff the bird sittin' opposite? She was 'avin' none of it – told 'im what to do wiff 'imself, she did!"

Made it! Derek heaved a sigh of relief. The doors were closed and the carriage was already pulling away from him. He was in two minds whether or not to drop the two holdalls and do a victory wave, but, with only scowling faces at the windows looking down at him, he refrained and looked away.

It was good to be back on home ground. London did not suit him; he was a small-town boy at heart. The air seemed fresher. In fact, up here on the platform of Slatterfoot Station, now that he was not being protected by the carriages, it was blowing a blooming gale. Oh, oh ...rain clouds above, but, much too windy for rain.

Wrong!

He made a rush for the Waiting Room. When he'd left from here on Friday it had been closed and redecorating had been in progress. It was obviously now finished and back in use. Unfortunately, the smell of newly-dried paint was lingering and, with the sudden downpour, everyone who'd left the train, and those waiting for the next one, had taken up residence. The windows were steamed up and the paint aroma was strong.

Not usually quite so full but, when a sudden downpour arrives it is as good a place as any to be. Is the girl in here? It was difficult to know for certain until eventually the rain subsided and people began to leave, then it became obvious – she was not.

Must be sitting waiting outside in a car in the car park with her friend. Wrong again, he was to find out a little while later, when the black cloud had at last passed over and he ventured to leave the shelter.

To an observer seeing him standing there, disconsolately, he must have seemed a pathetic figure: a holdall in each hand, in the middle of a half-empty car park that had suddenly accumulated masses of puddles, which now hid deep potholes. A pathetic figure, until he began peering in each parked vehicle – and then he became a *suspicious* one. To the stationmaster, who happened to glance at a CCTV screen in his office, he looked as if he were about to pinch a vehicle.

Derek thought the local constabulary were doing an excellent job when, five minutes after, a police car appeared. It was driven around the car park. Nice to see them check this place now and again, he thought, then he realised that he was the focus of their attention.

After his rushed exit from the train, this was unsettling. Had someone complained and given his description?

Luckily for Derek, just when the policemen were about to have a chat with a prospective car-thieving ne'er-do-well, an emergency call, relating to a car crash caused by the heavy rain, grabbed their attention and off they zoomed...

It was rather a poor home-coming. Where was she? He hadn't misread the situation had he? Maybe that girl wasn't sure how to find Slatterfoot Station or, had she to wait for her friend to arrive with the car perhaps?

She could still be en route. Yes, the train would have travelled so much faster than a car could. He'd be patient; she'd be here soon.

One hour later, Derek decided to give up. Perhaps he had got it wrong: most unlike him. There would probably be a perfectly sensible explanation for her absence. At least, if the worst came to the worst, there would be a clue in her luggage about how to make contact with her.

She might have already phoned an apology, to his home number, using his mobile of course, telling him where to meet – he had added his home number to his list of contacts while sitting on the train on the way to London – and they would arrange to do the swop: he'd give her the holdall and she'd give him the phone.

Yes, at home, there would be a phone message waiting....

When he'd arrived at the car park earlier there had been no taxis to be seen, all having been grabbed during the thunderstorm, but now there were quite a few. He went to the first in the queue and got in, then realised there was no driver in the front. He sat for several minutes, but none appeared, so he got out and went to the next one.

"A right bugger that one," was the first comment from this driver. "Goes off for a cuppa and just leaves his cab at the head of the queue to annoy the rest of us. Where to, mate?"

"Toozlethwaite Manor, please," Derek requested politely.

"Where the bleedin' 'ell is that, mate?"

I am not your mate, Derek wanted to tell him, *and would you please control your language,* he was about to say, but what came out of his mouth was: "It's along the road from the *effing* New Farmhouse Hotel, Newingsworth, mate!"

Well – it had been a long, hard day for Derek!

"Gotcha, mate..."

With Derek's detailed directions, the lane was found and the taxi driven very cautiously along the length of the dodgy surface to the front door. A multitude of puddles caused by the earlier storm still remained to hide the increasing number of potholes. Derek decided a generous tip would be required to get rid of this bloke afterwards – even he could feel the bumps. *Hope he doesn't start to suggest this has ruined his suspension. Have to talk nicely to Alexander; see if he could arrange a cheap bank loan to pay for lane repairs.*

The taxi did a tight turn. Derek watched it bounce its way back along the narrow lane. An enormous weight fell from his shoulders as he swung around to look lovingly at his own front door. He was home, but why hadn't Sally come to meet him? She must have heard the taxi.

He tried the door handle, the door wasn't usually locked, and then he remembered; she and little ET were probably still at Cloverton, with her mum and dad. She wouldn't know he'd come straight home would she? He hadn't spoken to her yet.

"Ah well," he sighed, "I can do with a cup of tea."

Automatically, he lifted the edge of the doormat for the key, but, no key. Normally one was kept under the mat. *Hold on – it's usually mine, silly me...*

He felt in his pocket, no, must be in another pocket. Oh, oh ... He tried a different pocket but no key was in it. He had managed, after a very exciting and tiring weekend, to lose his house key.

Rain ...did he feel rain? Oh noooo...

It poured down.

9

Not having a mobile was peculiar. He felt curiously detached from the real world – comparable to being in solitary confinement. Life was not meant to be like this – not being able to speak to someone whenever the urge took hold.

Only a shower, he'd hoped, but a downpour it was. There was nowhere to shelter. On some old cottages the edge of the roof overhangs the stonework and shelter is possible – but not on this one.

What a dreadful end to a dreadful day! No shelter and getting thoroughly soaked, unable to contact a wife who was probably worried sick about him but, even worse, he was unable to phone for a taxi, or to ask Hammy to nip along the road and fetch him.

Having the New Farmhouse Hotel almost on his doorstep, but not quite, was appreciated by Derek. It was the nearest place he could go for help; unfortunately though, the only way he had of getting there was to walk back along the lane to the hotel's access road. Normally, he considered the distance separating his home and the hotel to be perfect. The outside world was never too far away; just far enough not to interfere with the privacy of the cottage.

Contact with Sally could be made from the hotel, so that would be the best place to go. Possibly, Hammy might even give him a lift over to Cloverton.

Now dark, and without the luxury of street-lighting to help, it seemed that Derek found every single puddle on the way back. If he accidently slipped and went to the left he would become tangled in the spikes of the hawthorn hedge. Just as bad on the other side, losing direction and veering to the right could mean going over the edge of the banking and falling in the stream.

It was a total of one and a half miles trudged on foot, in soggy clothes, before he reached sanctuary. Of course, if it had been daylight and sunny and even after heavy rain, in the time it took him, his clothes might have steam-dried on the way, but no, it was dark, and he was cold, damp and shivering when he arrived.

Annoyingly, and it was only later that it occurred to him, he wouldn't have been any wetter if, outside the cottage, he had just taken a short-cut and walked through the stream. It would have been only a half-mile walk then.

"Straight into a hot bath for you, young fellow," Aunt Thelma declared the moment he stepped in the front entrance. She led him through to the private quarters, while Kylie, doing a little extra evening work, left the front desk and, for the second time today, fetched the mop from the back room and did her bit towards the safety of all.

"Thelma, I have to phone Sally. I must speak to her," Derek started out.

"Nonsense, that can wait another moment or two," was the response from Sally's aunt. "Let's get this bath filled with nice hot water. Off with your wet things then and we'll get them dried out."

Derek had a sudden panic; she isn't actually going to bathe me, is she? She had that Mother Hen purposeful air about her this evening, but no, thankfully, she left him to it.

He'd lain soaking for about half-an-hour, hands behind his head, pretending to be floating, and almost falling asleep while appreciating the pleasure of just lying in deep warm water thinking about almost nothing, when there was a knock at the door. It hadn't occurred to him to lock it. The door was opened, and in came Kylie.

"Towels... She forgot to leave them, oh, and some clothes of Mr Macintosh's because yours aren't dry yet. Hmm, I've seen bigger," she said looking into the bathwater as Derek rapidly repositioned his hands. "Can I help you in any other way?" she asked. That made him wonder what other extras might be supplied to *paying* guests. "Shall I pull the plug out?" She reached and did just that, and with a smirk on her face, walked out again.

The towels were warm and, as he dried himself, he felt much better. Very thoughtful of Thelma to supply dry clothes, yes ...but these were clothes that fitted Hammy!

When Hammy had been a similar weight to Derek he was a teenager, so, the temporary outfit was a 'generous' fit. Fortunately, the belt supplied held the underpants and trousers in place. With it well-tightened, the simple action of walking, although still risky, made it possible to reach the private sitting room of Thelma and Hammy without any embarrassing incidents.

"You are certainly in the bad books," Thelma told him. "Spoke to Muriel earlier. Sally's been with them since early this morning. Not in a good mood I believe. Muriel told me that she wouldn't tell her what was wrong, and, that you were reticent too when you phoned her today."

"Oh," said Derek.

"Why didn't you answer when Sally phoned you back? That made her even grumpier, you appreciate. What have you been up to?"

"Why does everybody presume that I've done something wrong?" he responded. "It wasn't my fault that I was *arrest*..." The moment he opened his mouth to reply he regretted it.

Thelma's eyes had begun to sparkle. Muriel may have failed to find out what was wrong, she said to herself, but I'll soon soften him up.

"Do you want to tell Aunty Thelma all about it?"

Luckily for Derek, the sitting room door swung open and Hammy came through.

"Sweaty! What are you doin' here at this time o' night? Oh, I like yer oufit, laddie. D'ye ken I've got troosers just like that? But why did you not buy a pair that fitted you like?"

Derek was unsure if he was having his leg pulled or not, and so ignored the comment, but appreciated the interruption because Thelma's attention had now swung onto her husband.

"You took long enough to fix the drain in Room Fourteen," she said in a dry manner. "Nice-looking girl isn't she; have a long chat did you; about plumbing, was it?"

"Aye, she's a bonnie lass, right enough," he replied innocently. "An' smart too. Her father wis a plumber she telt me. She could have fixed it herself if I'd given her a go wi' the tools. She misses her father an awfy lot, ye ken. Thought I looked dead like him: same haircut, same smile. Aye a nice wee lassie..."

There was an uncomfortable silence as Thelma processed the reply.

"Could you possibly drive me over to Cloverton, Hammy?" Derek asked.

By appearing when he did, unknowingly, Hammy had helped him out of an awkward spot with Aunt Thelma. The least I can do, thought Derek, is to help him now; *Thelma is*

in attack mode! And I am borrowing some of his clothes...
"I've lost my keys – and my mobile – and I'll have to speak to Sally. It might be wiser if I explain things face to face. She's over at her mother and father's, with ET, and she has probably been missing me. She can become a little grumpy when I am not around to look after her."

Thelma's eyebrows rose and slight smirk appeared on her face. "Oh Derek..." she sighed condescendingly. "We'll have to leave your clothes round the boiler for a while yet before they'll be wearable. You can have them back tomorrow."

"Right then, Sweaty, dear fellow," said Hammy, "let's get you back to your wee wifie."

"Have you never fancied learnin' tae drive, Sweaty – sorry – *Derek*?" said Hammy as he weaved his way through Newingsworth. "Now you are a family man, would it no' be handy tae be able tae get them out an' about a bit easier? An' I could teach ye. It's no' that hard, ye ken."

"Hammy do you know you are going the wrong way up a one-way street?"

"Och, there's nobody about at this time o' night to have tae bother with a' that nonsense. Do you need anythin' oot o' Bisko's as we are passin'?"

"No thanks, Hammy. It's amazing that they stay open for twenty-four hours nowadays. There can't be many customers at this time of night. The car park's nearly empty. To think our gang used to play on that ground before they came here. The adventures we had."

"An', after they arrived, I should have made ma fortune with sellin' the eggs tae them. Ah weel, it all went wrong didn't it, but, ye canny turn back the clock."

Bisko's was left behind. They were almost at Cloverton.

It was obvious that this was the part of the town where the money was. Large old buildings set back from the road, and for almost all of them, carefully tended gardens, well-established trees, and long driveways. At one time each of these cultivated plots of land would have been tended by a family's faithful old gardener, a man who would probably have been there for most of his life – and paid a pittance.

Nowadays, a different arrangement: during the day, the 'Fletcher and Pollock' van would be seen moving from house to house. Derek's pals had left the Parks Department and gone into business for themselves; *must be making a mint at the rates they are charging*, Derek guessed. They had a monopoly of the district, and were quite happy to keep it that way.

The house where Derek's in-laws had their home, 40 Cloverton Avenue and the other houses in this road, were only slightly more modest. They had smaller gardens at the front than the ones already passed, but still had large gardens at the rear of the houses. Arthur and Charlie looked after these too.

Number 40 also had an integral double garage but, what a waste of space. No-one in the household could drive so, no cars were required. The garage was almost empty, containing only two bikes, Muriel's and Alexander's, a bicycle trailer, and empty wine bottles, which were removed to the skip for recycling, every so often.

"Oh, oh, all the lights are oot."

"But they can't be all in bed yet. It's not even ten o'clock..." but they were.

There was still a light on next door, at Mrs Masterton's.

"I had better wait until ye get in," said Hammy. "I might be takin' ye back again if they'll not open the door for ye,

Sweaty. I suppose ye'll have lost the key for this place as weel..."

"No I haven't, and please don't call me *Swe*..." Derek stopped mid-sentence – about to lose his temper with a friend who was doing him a favour! Not wise. "No, I haven't lost it. It's sitting on the dresser back home, if you must know."

"Och aye, ye might as well have lost it then for all the good it's daein' ye," was the cheery response.

"Right. I'll give you a wave if I can get in. Thanks for bringing me over. Oh, I forgot to bring the bags."

"Nae bother. I'll cart them down in the morning, presumin' that you'll have been forgiven, an' back at the Cottage. Oh ...an' Derek, I hope that I suit these troosers better than you dae!"

Derek gave a grim smile and walked up the driveway. As he stood at the door, about to press the bell, he had the feeling of being observed, and it wasn't Hammy he was meaning. He whipped his head around quickly. Sure enough, the upstairs curtain moved, old Mrs Masterton was still up – and on look-out duties as usual.

"Right, here goes," he said aloud in his nervousness. He pressed the bell. It sounded very loud in the silence of the night. Nothing happened, other than a flicker of Mrs Masterton's curtain again.

Waking any of them from a deep sleep to answer the door would not lead to a very welcoming reception, he guessed. Should he leave them to sleep on and come back tomorrow ...but it's only ten o'clock! Why should he feel guilty?

"And anyway, I haven't done anything wrong," he said, trying to console himself a little.

Hammy was still sitting waiting.

"I'll try once more. If nothing happens this time..." He pressed the bell again. It sounded to him even louder than the first time – and then he remembered to stop pressing!

Then the barking started.

Oh, no. Jilly's here...

He waited. The barking stopped with a yelp.

Oh well ...and was about to depart, when the hall light came on. Hurrah! The thumbs-up sign to Hammy gave him the clearance to go, and off he shot like he was taking part in the Grand Prix!

The door opened. It was Sally – looking angelic – with the light behind her like that, shining through her nightdress, and she looked happy.

Derek turned and gave a cheery wave to Mrs Masterton, before stepping into the hall.

"Am I glad you are back, Daddy Toozlethwaite," Sally said with a smile. "What a lovely surprise ...for us all. To have just gone to sleep, and be wakened up by you ringing the doorbell, loudly. Welcome."

Should he step forward and take her in his arms and...? Maybe not...

His young son was making a great deal of noise at the moment; it was loud and did not sound particularly happy. In fact, he was howling his head off.

"Your son has missed you," she smiled.

And Jilly started barking again!

Welcome back, indeed...

10

The journey from Cloverton back to the cottage by taxi was short, but enjoyable. Even the holes in the lane felt less bumpy this morning and, any qualms that Derek did have about the way that Sally would be feeling towards him were proving unfounded and, Daddy noted, his baby son appreciated his return even more than Mummy did.

Sophie had eventually succeeded in talking to Sally and gave a good version of events. During the long telephone conversation Andy Woodstock had been well and truly hung out to dry and, for a change, Derek had been awarded a much-deserved sympathy vote.

He was pleased at being back with a happy wife and a contented young son. It was also a relief to return to the cottage and find that he hadn't actually lost his key at all; when he'd left for London he had not lifted it from its resting place on the dresser.

What was even more satisfying was the four of them being back home as a family again. There was little Edwin playing happily with the toys in his cot, and Sally, dear sweet Sally, actually sitting talking pleasantly with him – then there was Jilly: not quite so satisfying...

The dog had been a disruptive force and relegated to outside, having disgraced herself by peeing on the floor the moment they came back in, but Jilly was not complaining, having the freedom of the back garden. Derek's return to

Cloverton last night, had turned out better than he could have hoped. Little Edwin had been missing him – badly; as a consequence he had cried a lot, both nights. With Derek away Sally had been counting on a visit by Gran and Grandad to help out, but Grandad Smith had been ill: a touch of food poisoning: visit cancelled!

When it came to individuals that ET happily responded to, he had taken a shine to Derek's grandad. The Smiths were to have stayed over on the Saturday night during Derek's absence, because Grandad proved as big a hit as Derek with ET. A big plus was that he seemed to manage on very little sleep and wouldn't have minded the middle-of-the-night routine.

Hector on the premises overnight would have been perfect for Sally but thanks to the tummy-bug the chance of two peaceful nights' sleep, for her, vanished. Lack of sleep on top of the unexpected vision of Sophie Clerkenwell-Brown on the phone link, appearing more or less naked behind Derek, and then her discovery of the phone message, saying that he had been arrested, not surprisingly, pushed her over the edge.

Hence the result – the grumpy appearance at her parents, but that was in the past.

Derek had explained carefully the background to his wrongful arrest, and it matched Sophie's, so Sally accepted that she had jumped to the wrong conclusion. He did a good job because in the end she was so very glad that she wasn't married to Andy Woodstock!

Last night, hearing the details of what had actually happened to her presumed 'errant' husband, separately from both Sophie and Andy, and finding that their versions of the tale matched his perfectly, she began to find the whole episode to be really funny. When Derek told her of his companions in the police cell, "Imagine ...locked up with a couple of smelly old drunks. Lucky you," she'd chortled. Derek remembered it as being neither amusing, nor lucky at the time, but smiled along with her.

She was truly delighted to have him back home and all was well – other than her displeasure at his having lost the new phone! "Vanished somewhere over the weekend ...and I know not where", was how he'd explained it. Somehow Derek guessed that it wouldn't end there…

Being late, the three of them had stayed at Cloverton. Thanks to the noisy doorbell, he'd entered the house to be greeted by the howling ET and felt guilty to be the cause, so didn't mind soothing his little son to get him back to sleep. He liked it less when the wee fellow, in the middle of the night, demanded Daddy, as usual.

At breakfast, in the Cloverton kitchen, not surprisingly, of the four adults sitting there only three of them had had a good night's sleep. They were in good spirits. With ET now sleeping soundly in his pram the mood round the table was perky – for three! Alexander and Muriel were delighted to find out what all the trouble had been, and laughed about it, along with Sally but secretly, they were relieved to be losing their daughter once more, especially after her threat of permanent occupancy only twenty-four hours ago.

The fourth person, the butt of their jokes, wasn't feeling quite so jolly, having been up until nearly four o'clock and, even though it was *Daddy* who was cuddling him, his son seemed to be determined to cry all the way through the night. The cornflakes he was eating for breakfast were especially noisy in Derek's head!

"You'll now have a police record," said Alexander, "being a marked man. They'll regret having to release you and will want to get you for something else. Mark my words."

"And they'll have taken your fingerprints, won't they?" Muriel prodded. "Oh, Derek – did you wash your hands properly before breakfast? I don't want your grubby pawmarks left on this tablecloth," and the three of them laughed.

"You managed to lose your phone too," said Alexander. "Don't you have any idea where it might be?"

"No, unfortunately not," lied Derek.

"But weren't you on the train when you phoned me?" asked a rather-too-sharp-for-this-time-in-the-morning mother-in-law.

"Oh, yes, I, uhm ...do believe I was," he admitted a little reluctantly.

"So, if you chase up the rail company there could be a chance that someone found it and handed it in," Alexander added.

"Hmm ...good idea, I'll have to do that. Thanks," Derek responded. *I could do without any more of that sort of help from you, thank you, and could we please get away from this subject,* was his thought.

Anyway it was Monday and he should be back at work. A quick call apologising to his boss, Rob Sheldon at the Gazette office, took care of that.

"We will cope," his boss informed him coldly.

Derek would have preferred to walk back home as a happy family unit, it was a pleasant morning, but with all the stuff that Sally had encouraged her father to bring for her yesterday in the trailer, getting back home, sensibly, was done by taxi.

Home again, and after a turbulent weekend ...*tranquillity.* He wandered into the garden.

"Gerroff!" was shouted at the white poodle as it came rushing over in attack mode and he had fend it off with one foot. Other than that damn dog, this was the life. What a difference from the hustle and bustle of London: peace and quiet here that can't be found in the big city. Living at the edge of town, almost in the country, what could be more pleasant?

"Fore!" was yelled in the distance.

He automatically ducked and heard the golf ball strike the wire fence with some force. Thank goodness for the high fence. Yes, other than the danger from poorly-hit golf shots, and a pesky white poodle that hated him, this was the life indeed. With the bright sunshine today, looking out over the hotel's nine-hole golf course was not at all unpleasant, even if misdirected missiles took a little of the shine from the locality.

As he stood there relaxing in his own back garden, he heard the little snatch of Mozart, the ringtone of Sally's mobile. He sat down on the bench. Could do with a fresh coat of paint, couldn't it? He'd have to remember to do it, one of these days, or maybe Sally would...

Sally opened the French windows.

"That was a most unusual phone call, Derek, a young lady calling herself, Lulubelle. Said she was a friend of yours. Didn't want to talk to you personally she said, but she told me she knew my name and that she knows I am your wife, and would I please pass on a message to you. She asked me to say, 'Thank him for making me so happy, and I hope to see him again soon. You are a very lucky woman to have such a good man. He certainly did it for me. Please give him a big, big kiss to thank him for the wonderful present he gave me afterwards. It is a super phone.'"

Suddenly, life for our hero had become a little less idyllic – as another round and white missile struck the fence, this time without warning.

"And... Derek? When I checked her number, it turned out to be yours. What a surprise!" and there was a slight edge to the tone Sally was using, he noticed.

"Ah, I can explain..." he started, and hesitated – but could he? This was about to become awkward. Thankfully the front doorbell rang. "I'll get it," he hurriedly offered and shot off inside, leaving Sally standing stock still, arms folded, in the garden, with an expression on her face that even Jilly, the poodle, recognised as decidedly threatening.

Standing on the doorstep was Mr Hamish Macintosh doing the delivery of one set of newly-ironed and pressed clothes. In he came and laid them carefully on the settee.

"Kylie must have taken a real fancy tae you, Sweaty," said Hammy, with a glint in his eye. "It's not very often she'll put her hand to ironin', as far as I ken. What did you say to her to get her to do that for ye, ah wunner?"

"Yes, what was it Derek?" enquired Sally, who appeared at Derek's shoulder. "There seem to be a lot of women in Derek's life these days, Hammy."

Hammy sensed that all was not well between these two.

"Wait a wee minute, I huvnae said somethin' wrong, have ah?" he asked, genuinely.

"Of course not, Hammy," Sally replied, with a suspicious sideways glance at Derek. "Often it's what is *not* said that causes friction."

"I'll get your bags in frae the car," said Hammy, and shot back out of the room. He returned moments later with the two holdalls, and, dumping them in the middle of the room, hurriedly said goodbye and vacated the premises.

"Now," Sally started, "you have some explaining to do. Who was that on the phone to me? Lulubelle, indeed! And what have you been up to with her, and who the hell is she? And who the hell is Kylie?"

Jilly was sitting looking at Derek in a peculiar way: relishing the moment? That was the impression Derek had. *Damn dog!* That is when little Edwin chose to remind them that food was important in his life.

Sally went to the bedroom, returned with ET in her arms, stopped in front of her husband and then proceeded to explain to the hungry infant how the system worked.

"Firstly, Daddy will change our little darling's nappy, and then Daddy will do a lot of explaining to Mummy because Mummy is not happy – right?"

ET was handed over, and before Daddy could respond, Mummy stomped into the kitchen to prepare the baby's food.

Oh no, here we go... She would not believe anything he was about to say, he decided, that was very clear even before he started – but he would have to tell her. The truth must be exposed.

He followed her into the kitchen.

"I didn't lose the phone..."

"Of course, you didn't. You gave it to a floozy as a gift! So, what was it she gave you to deserve that, eh?"

"No. I gave her a loan of it, on the train. That was all. You see..." *Stay calm and do something positive*, he told himself. Regroup!

So, he left her alone, did as she'd instructed, and changed the nappy. Waiting until she came back, seated again and feeding a hungry child, he attempted once more to tell what had happened.

Unfortunately, due to a sudden attack of the jitters, his attempt at explaining the previous day's train journey was a little feeble and considerably disjointed.

"I was behaving," he explained, "like a Good Samaritan – honest. And as for that bloke that was with her..."

"Huh!" was the dismissive response.

"She got off to get better reception for the phone, at York – that was all – maybe, I think ...and was concentrating so much on making her friend understand her predicament that she failed to get back onto the train again. Simple! And the call you answered was her phoning to tell me, in coded language, that she has safely escaped from her wicked stepfather – and Kylie is the new girl up at the hotel."

"Oh, Derek, pull the other one. You'll have to do better than that..."

"Yes, look, the bags. One is mine, obviously, but whose is the other one? It belongs to her, as I told you; yes, it belongs to – what did you say her name was again? ...Lulubelle? All we have to do is open it and we'll probably find a contact address or telephone number; maybe even a note of explanation, something that will help me to find her, and stop all this nonsense. I have to get my phone back."

"Derek, we already have the means of contacting her – just ring her! She was at the other end of the line a moment ago – on your phone!"

It should have been an easy solution – but Derek was reluctant to go down that path just at the moment. There was a possibility that what he could hear would turn out not to be the answer he was hoping for. Let's stick to opening the bag, was his decision, at least that action is something I can control.

Although there was a tag holder for the addition of the owners name on the outside of the holdall, there was no card in the holder. There was no padlock holding it closed either

"I am going to look inside."

He felt slightly guilty about opening the bag initially but at least he wasn't bursting open a padlock to do it. It was the same sort of guilt he remembered experiencing when he went into Sally's underwear drawer, without her permission – the time that he, grandad, Hammy and Alexander had used her tights for their disguise. Back then, she'd made him pay. Hopefully it's not the same this time!

The contents weren't quite what he expected.

He visualised the attractive female who had been sitting opposite him for a few hours and, at the time, she didn't look like a tom-boy. The contents did not make sense.

As the items were unpacked he laid them on the settee: two formal shirts that were still in the wrapping, one of plain blue, the other, white with pink stripes; three pairs of spotted boxer shorts; striped pyjama trousers; three pairs of striped socks, a toilet bag with a shaving kit and a deodorant: all apparently for a *male* and looking as if they had been thrown into the bag in a hurry.

Is she a lesbian? Surely not, but if she is, how do you tell? Not a question he had ever asked himself. Certainly the clothes displayed on the settee were not of the feminine variety that he was expecting. Derek was confused.

Much worse: Sally was unconvinced.

The contents of the holdall were meant to give credence to his explanation; that he had done nothing for which he should be criticised – other than being a bit naive. Now, even he was having doubts about what had happened!

"But this is her bag; this was what she had on the train. She asked me to take it for her. She did! Honest!"

The bag hadn't yet been totally emptied.

At the bottom of the bag was a pair of denims, and a T-shirt, with the words on the front 'I'm a BIG boy now'. Underneath that stuff, and lying flat at the very bottom, was a folder. It contained some paperwork – and a bar-coded plastic identification card on a ribbon for hanging round the neck.

"Aha," said Derek triumphantly. "This will tell us who she is."

As the folder was lifted out, Derek and Sally experienced some apprehension. Life could be about to become a little more complicated because, stamped right across the pages, in large red letters, were the words 'HIGHLY CONFIDENTIAL'.

11

An emergency meeting had been convened and was taking place behind securely closed doors. Six people, all males, were seated around the table, each looking with curiosity around the table at the others, awaiting an explanation.

Everyone knew he was guilty, but, outwardly, he had to behave as innocently as his companions. The guilt could not be revealed.

The table was rapped to gain attention and HE spoke.

"Gentlemen, we are gathered today, because we have a potential disaster on our hands. I say potential, because the outcome has not reached catastrophic level – yet, but will be destructive if corrective action is not taken immediately. We are in danger of exposure!

"In our midst is the perpetrator. I will not name him, for the sake of 'The Team Spirit', the way some misguided training gurus would have us believe it should be done. He knows how serious his mistake is, and he knows that no stone can be permitted to be left unturned in solving his problem. He is well aware of the consequences if it were to become our problem." …Each individual shifted uncomfortably in his seat and surreptitiously squinted at the other occupants of the room, as HE continued…

"One of our sacred rules has been broken: that of possibly permitting the public to become aware of our intentions before we have decided that it is time to tell. Somewhere, someone has secret information, someone who is not in this room and who is not one of us. If the leaked information is properly understood by that outsider and our plan exposed prematurely, the consequences could be disastrous for us all. Highly Confidential means just that. I need not remind you that the consequence of such a leak could have a catastrophic effect on the careers of all of us, and all due to one simple careless action by the perpetrator."

The looks of suspicion thrown around the table continued. This group's control, of a future set to bring wealth, power and all the trappings of high living, could be jeopardised by the stupid actions of an idiot in this room, but which idiot?

"I will take this opportunity to remind us all that security is paramount. From now, there will be no removal of hard copies of anything to do with Our Project. There will be no communications electronically: no emails, no text messages. We all know how easy it is, by pressing the wrong button, to tell the world of a personal indiscretion, don't we?"

The smile was supercilious. "All contact will be personal, either face to face, or by telephone, using the allocated code names, ascertaining that you have reached the correct person with each call. Oh, and from now, 'code-speak' will be the language.

"That is all gentlemen."

No one else spoke. Bubbles had said his piece, the meeting was ended.

The only noise, as they vacated the room, was of chairs screeching on the floor, followed by soft footsteps. The underlings dispersed: Pipsqueak, Tiny Tim, Wizard, Snooty, and Dimples, pleased to leave the claustrophobic atmosphere, all but one worried in case he had inadvertently done something stupid and the guilty one relieved not to have been singled out.

12

For Alexander, cycling to work was part of his life. He was rather pleased to be fitter than most men of his age because of his cycling activities. To his own staff, at the Slatterfoot Branch of the Co-operative Bank, this was a perfectly normal activity because it had been happening for a long time. For the Head Office staff who visited and seemed to be limited to only a few visits, 'Lycra Man' was the name that had been coined by one group, and carried back, to then continue to be used when referring to him. Their name for him had become common knowledge but it didn't bother him in the slightest; he knew of considerably worse nicknames applied to his peers at other branches.

Some new youngsters from HQ were due to visit later this week.

In recent years his reputation as an amateur actor had also been established. Although a happily married man his speciality had become this ability to play eccentric female roles exceedingly well. At head office this was known and seen, perhaps a little patronisingly, as acceptable for the moment. 'It would be permitted to continue only providing it did not spoil the image of the company' was the message that fed back to him. Rather than worrying that he might step out of line and be reprimanded, he told himself that, up his sleeve, he knew a few embarrassing truths about some of the odd-balls on the board of directors.

He was an avid cyclist and actually rather proud of not owning a motor vehicle. Being a non-driver and not adding to the pollution of the environment gave him some smug satisfaction. That was as a matter of choice, not by any means for financial need because he was, as they say, well heeled. A substantial amount of his wealth had been earned by his own hard work but most of it had been thanks to a hard-working father.

Thelma, Alexander's twin – having blotted her copybook – got nothing when her father passed away. It was Alexander, who had nearly always lived in the family home and never fallen foul of his old man, who had been the recipient of a small fortune.

Two years ago, passing the age his father had been at death had been a strange feeling for Alexander. He still preferred to avoid thinking too deeply about that and, except for the period spent at University, he'd lived in the Cloverton house all his life.

Having been the manager of the Slatterfoot Co-operative Bank for a long, long time, he liked to think he was now part of the town's history: definitely 'in with the bricks'. Ask any old local worthy on a sober moment and they probably wouldn't be able to tell you who had been the previous holder of the banking post.

Modestly, he also considered himself to be the 'correct' type of bank manager: not one of those currently receiving bad press. He cared for both money and the people who were his customers.

The Company insisted that the organisation be run at a profit, of course. He accepted that and did play his part in keeping them more than solvent.

There was also considerable sympathy and understanding for the poor people who were obliged to come to him on bended knee to seek a loan. Sometimes he felt all-powerful – other times, magnanimous with it ...but in all his years as Manager he had been considered by his customers to be a fair man when it came to who should benefit from the honey pot. Slight manipulation of regulations sometimes had been necessary to satisfy what was, in his view, a particularly needy case; one that others might have rejected out of hand.

His decisions received very few criticisms from above, probably because the facts about the questionable ones had been well obscured. Long may that continue, he said to himself, thinking of the impending official visit by Head Office.

Generous thoughts were in his head today. Their father had instructed that Alexander's twin sister should receive nothing from his will and, although to his benefit, his conscience troubled him. She deserved something and he should be the one to correct matters.

The New Farmhouse Hotel was being managed, very successfully by Thelma and Hammy as a husband and wife team. The purchase of that property had been by Alexander, only a few years ago, as a wise investment towards ensuring that he would be enjoying a very comfortable retirement in the distant future, but – what the heck – he might just gift it to them. In the current financial climate, there was no guarantee that it would remain profitable, then, if it went off the rails, it wouldn't be his responsibility.

Would that be an over-generous gesture, he asked himself, or just a good business move?

More thought would be required...

Then there was the cottage.

OK, it wasn't his, having gifted it to Derek and Sally for the wedding.

The access was the problem. What a mess; potholes everywhere and always with the danger of someone slipping over the edge into the stream. That pair never had enough money for extras. They'd probably need his help but, that would have to wait. Anyway, they hadn't yet asked for any – but he knew it was bound to happen.

13

The folder was sitting on the table, dropped like a hot potato in the shock of discovering what it contained, but, he was recovering. It was lying there – tempting him – and, to be fair, ask yourself how could *anyone* resist the opportunity of peeking at 'Highly Confidential' documents?

In Derek's mind, not looking at them would have been tantamount to an admission of failure. He was an investigative journalist, for goodness sake! The word 'Confidential' alone was a magnet. Adding 'Highly' was the clincher, and, as a roving reporter for the local weekly newspaper, he was being easily won over. He would have to be nosy!

Ill-feeling temporarily forgotten and, though trying not to show it, Sally was just as eager to read whatever it was that was not considered to be fit for public display, but...

"Derek, don't!" she blurted out as he lifted the folder and began to open it. "No, it's not right! The documents belong to that girl. There might be embarrassing information about her in there."

"So, it is alright for her to have borrowed my expensive phone and not returned it, and then me not to be believed when I explain, but I mustn't look at her paperwork, in case I embarrass her? How about me? What have I suffered?"

"Derek... Is it not bad enough what you have just done – by opening her bag and handling her clothes, without then...?"

"...*Her* clothes?"

It was too late. He'd opened the folder and was looking.

"Ah-ha! Told you so: what does that say?" and he jabbed his finger at the top of the inside page. "...Government Designs! These Highly Confidential documents should never have been taken from an office, I'll bet. She's a spy! She's pinched these."

"Derek, you are being silly."

"Then why did she have these clothes? On the train, what if she had gone to the toilet and swopped outfits, she could have returned as a man and fooled everyone!"

"She didn't have to use a disguise to fool you, did she?"

Now that was cruel, and she knew it, but it did stop him in his tracks.

"Let's try to be sensible about this," he suggested. "Maybe the clothes don't belong to her, but that doesn't mean this isn't her info, now does it?"

Sally accepted that. It just didn't all make sense, but then again she often had difficulty understanding her husband.

"...And where did this file come from?" he pursued.

Together they looked at the pieces of paper in front of them, a mixture of formal typed notes and hand-written scribbles in the margins. There were also computer-generated, complicated-looking flow diagrams. Doodles appeared too, in odd spaces; had the owner of these documents been concentrating properly? Derek could see that the doodles were of a high quality and wished that he could doodle like that.

This seemed to be some sort of master plan, but, for what? Some pages were stapled together and had title headings. On the back of one sheet they discovered names in neat handwriting, not that they were of any help to Derek or Sally, and could have been the result of someone's boredom? It looked as if someone had been sitting amusing themselves – or else, these were the others in the group. Yes, these were the others, he decided. It came to him in a flash, these were *nicknames* – and for a very good reason.

"A security measure," he told her, "to use nicknames." Saying this in a condescending manner to Sally was not wise.

"You know that do you?" was the sarcastic response from his wife. "There couldn't be any doubt? A security measure..." and she read them out. "Bubbles, Pipsqueak, Tiny Tim, Wizard, Snooty, and Dimples ...Oh, Derek, how perceptive of you!"

She was not being serious enough! He ignored her. They were trying to find the full name and address of the girl who had borrowed his telephone, he reminded her, so that a swop could be arranged – but Sally had noticed something else.

"This is scrap paper!" she exclaimed.

"What?"

"It doesn't say 'Government Designs' at all. It says '*Govement* Designs'. There's been a typing error. This paper has been printed, mistake found, and then scrapped – obviously – and then used again in error."

Derek was miffed. He should have been coming out with that sort of observation.

"Well, never mind that. Let's try to identify which Government department? I wonder if they know this stuff's missing. There's a lot to read. Let's share it. I'll take this one, FRACKAREE, and you take that, TWO-SPEED-HIGH. Strange names aren't they. Could be to do with secret drugs!" He handed over three sheets stapled together. "There's plenty to read. Look at this other one – POWERY-WOWERY. Most definitely strange names..."

"Derek," said Sally, leaning over to whisper in his ear, "Drugs ...with *code names!*"

She smiled. Derek did not think his wife was treating this with the required gravity!

As they read, both began to take it more seriously – much more! They finished reading at the same time. Though details had not been absorbed, the gist was apparent.

"Are you thinking the same – a conspiracy? A secret group plotting to make a lot of money; using code names for themselves and for what they are doing, so that they cannot be identified?"

"Yes," she replied, and there was no sarcasm this time. "This says how it is to be done. Let's swop, and I'll read yours and then talk more."

Silence reigned for a short time.

"Two-Speed-High: it may sound like a new drug but it has to be code for the *high speed rail link doesn't it?*" said Derek. "And yours?"

"Frackaree? *Fracking.* It is so obvious now I have read it. No one wants to live near where that is being done, but this is a plan to ensure it will happen – everywhere and anywhere in the UK!"

A third one was absorbed together and, they concluded from what was described, that the Powery-Wowery project could only be for additional Nuclear Power Stations, again planned in detail. Locations to be wherever this secretive group chose – with no holds barred – with instructions as to how local resistance and planning restrictions are to be overcome

"Ooooh..." said Sally, as she read. "That's naughty!"

This was obviously high-level corruption involving major public projects, Derek decided after reading more of the scribbles in the margins, and appeared to be a small group who were manipulating it all and would be benefitting personally.

"It can't be actual members of the Government doing this," Derek concluded. "Six MPs couldn't reach agreement on this sort of thing. It's far too ambitious for them. It could be a clandestine group of Civil Servants; these people are out to make millions. It's like a scene from Big Brother," he added hoarsely.

"Channel four, yea ...celebrity or normal bods?"

"NO ...George Orwell's predictions, Sally; the book: Nineteen-Eighty-Four."

Sally was looking back at the details, not listening. "Could these be passwords?" she asked, pointing to mixtures of letters and numbers, "for a computer programme perhaps?"

Derek stopped. "Smart thinking, Sal, that is possible," but then, as he switched on the laptop, "No... People aren't stupid enough to write down passwords with programme names, can't possibly be that."

"Well, I have all of mine in my diary, in case I forget them."

Derek did not want to know that.

It was highly unlikely. Derek knew with this being Highly Confidential information there would be no chance of accessing a programme. It would be an intranet system, with very restricted access – but he'd give it a try anyway.

He input 'Frackeree.'

Something appeared – as it always does – a word used in a song about Fracking, he was informed. He tried entering the site but, no luck. Another option was for an Anxiety Forum, for those suffering anxiety, fear, or panic attacks. The other listed by the search engine was for a group protesting about the Fracking process; as expected, trying the reference number failed. If it was a password, there was no way of proving it.

He tried a search for 'Two-speed-high'. A long list appeared on the screen for that, but, the electronic smart-ass search engine had offered him 'High Speed 2' as an alternative.

I already had guessed that, thank you.

As for 'Powery-Wowery', a clever search engine seemed to suggest the name was used for little else other than magic spells! There certainly was a potion brewing with this lot.

Another page from the folder: Control of the 'free' press. An essential feature of the project, it said, an over-riding need – as was the control of the armed forces and police. How it was to be done was defined too. A powerful spokesperson had to be found to tackle both, one capable of using plausible language to feed the media the appropriate cover stories.

It made nasty reading. The person chosen would not only be paid substantially, he/she had to be vulnerable; perfect control of this individual would be achieved by the background threat of blackmail.

"Total control of the nation is the objective of this undercover government group," declared Derek, "and to be done without us even being aware of it happening!"

Profound words, he told himself, *and I said them!*

It was clear that power, for this group, was not the only driving force. Enormous sums of money were to be demanded of the companies being given work; in other words, bribes would be demanded from 'chosen' contractors! As far as Derek and Sally could see, millions of pounds would be changing hands – and where would the money go? Certainly not into the public purse!

And it didn't end there.

Bugging and hacking of electronic systems in the UK and foreign competitors, and severe penalties to discourage whistle-blowers were included as part of the strategy. A major upset of the currency was also planned that would permit a total restructuring of the banking system. BBC funds to be continually reduced, to create the collapse of that left-wing anti-government pest of an organisation!

"And they are only known by nicknames," said Derek wistfully. "They'll be in control – anonymously?"

"And the girl is one of them..."

"...Could be, though maybe she was trying to prevent it happening..."

There was an ominous silence. They sat staring at each other.

"She knows you have this stuff, Derek. Doesn't that put you in danger?"

Derek froze. He hadn't thought of it like that!

What they'd read was certainly threatening and a shocking scenario. It was only a quick read, but enough to tell them that this was the stuff of dictatorships. Something would have to be done! This was serious. The stuff sitting before them, it was Top Secret Government information and they had it in their home and, worse still, they had read it...

Isn't that ...*treason?*

14

The ring of the doorbell made them jump. They froze. What to do? Suddenly, they became a panic-stricken complicit couple who were caught doing something very naughty and who mustn't let anyone else know of their guilty secret!

"Hide the papers, Derek – quickly! It could be the police!"

He leapt into action and whipped the documents together, being careful not to damage any of them: Derek was very conscious of the potential value of this information. It may be treasonable information but it also was dynamite for the Media.

The folder would have to be hidden – but where? He took it into the main bedroom. Put it in the wardrobe? No. Hide it under the rug? No. ...

Ah, yes! Quickly he went next door, into Edwin's room. Don't waken him... Carefully does it... and under his cot mattress went the folder.

Now, the front door could be opened – but there was no-one standing there. The figure that was walking off back down the lane had given up, thinking that they were out. It was Millie.

"Mom," Sally shouted after her. "Sorry to keep you waiting." It had taken a while for Sally to become used to calling her mother-in-law, Mom, but now it was becoming slightly easier.

"Am I glad you are in, Honey," she said to Sally and flopped down on the living room sofa. She didn't look too happy with life this morning but, Sally concluded, having travelled to Detroit and back over the weekend would probably have been quite tiring. "I just had to talk to somebody." Millie was still resident at the New Farmhouse Hotel where she had an arrangement with Thelma and Hammy. A room was retained when she popped back and forward to Detroit. She had walked round for this visit.

Derek came back into the room, closing the door on the sleeping ET, his mother tended to talk rather loudly.

"Hi Sweaty, didn't expect to see you here today. I thought you'd be at work. I thought you said they couldn't do without you."

Derek just smiled. *Why does she have to call me Sweaty!*

"And you were down in London for the weekend, weren't ya? Have a good time, did ya? One of these 'fella's only' weekends, eh?"

"Not exactly," Sally chipped in, "and it is maybe better not to talk about it."

"Oh, one of *those* special kinda weekends, was it..." Millie said knowingly. "Too much fun, had ya? That's my boy."

Derek said nothing.

"Maybe Derek would like to make us a cup of coffee. Would you like one Mom?"

"Oh yes please, Sal."

Derek slunk off into the kitchen.

"So, Mom, you had a good visit then?"

"Not really, Honey. The flight was bumpy and uncomfortable both ways and the business has gone flat on us. In fact, it looks like I am goin' to have to sell up. Detroit ain't what it used to be, no sirree."

Since her husband died, Millie had taken control of the restaurant herself, successfully – until now. Her faithful chef, and friend, Charlie had been left with the task of continuing the good work of running the restaurant on his own since she started coming to the UK. Detroit, as a city, and its inhabitants had been going through a bad spell. 'Mickey's Joint', the restaurant, was feeling the pinch too.

"No, Sal, things aint so good over there ...at all. Folks have more important demands on their hard-earned dollars than eating at restaurants. I think I am going to have to sell up. Charlie is interested in keeping it going, but only if he can find the money to buy me out. He is talkin' about a number of his buddies poolin' resources and joining him, and he thinks he can win them over. I am not so sure... I might have to be speakin' nice to your father soon. I've gotten to think that a little loan might be needed to keep me tickin' over."

This morning, Millie needed to talk, obviously having had a troublesome weekend too, thought Sally, but Millie was not getting her full attention; Derek's weekend behaviour had not yet been properly explained – certainly not to her satisfaction. He was not off the hook by any means. Anyway what is he up to? Probably taking his time in the kitchen to avoid having to listen to his Mom's problems.

"Derek!" she shouted and freshly made coffee was brought through.

Sally's mind went elsewhere. *Derek still hasn't convinced me about his mobile!* Lent it to her, he said, because she was in trouble, he said, and he was only trying to help, he said. *Yea...*

Derek had heard most of what his mother had been saying, and, right at this moment could have done without her interruption, but like a dutiful son he made himself sit down and pretended to listen. Then he heard it: the motor scooter, phut-phut-phutting up the lane.

Now, three visitors sat drinking coffee in his living room; Gran and Grandad Smith had to apologise to Sally for the weekend.

"I d-d-didn't want to infect l-l-l-little Edwin. I was in a b-b-bad w-w-way," explained Grandad, "W-w-w-w-we w-w-w-wanted to c-c-come over but I had a b-b-bad d-d-dose of d-d-d-d-d-dia... d-d-d-dia... d-d..."

"Yea, Poppa. We can guess," interrupted Millie, "and the detail is totally unnecessary."

"...The *RUNS!*" he added, determined to finish his sentence.

Having family around should engender a comforting feeling, but for Derek it meant frustration. He wanted to look in greater detail at the papers stuffed under Edwin's cot. This was news – a world-wide scoop – important to Derek, less so for Sally; for her, the visitors were delaying her getting answers from her husband, proper answers, about this 'Lulubelle'? What really happened?

This wife could be very determined.

She'd get it out of him…

15

They'd gone – at long last, and before Sally could start to rant once more, Derek was fast-moving into Edwin's bedroom, retrieving the folder from beneath the little guy's mattress …very carefully so as not to disturb him. Sleeping a little longer would do him no harm. Edwin had slept soundly through the duration of a noisy visit, much to the disappointment of Millie, Gran and Grandad.

The folder was carried through, and the papers laid on the table once more. Derek hoped that Sally would be as keen as he was, to look at them in greater detail, but no, Sally had other ideas.

"Derek, before we do this." She was smiling, but he could tell it was false. "We need to talk," she said, "tell me again about Lulubelle, your overly friendly spy and very good friend."

"I never knew her name." He had a sudden thought…"Anyway that can't be it; nobody is called Lulubelle nowadays. Are you sure that is the name she said?"

"Yes, and Derek, does it make any difference what name she used? She has your phone."

"Ah, but you are forgetting, I have a bar-coded identification card, and all I need to do is…" …Ah yes, now there's a thing! The information in the document might give clues if read again, but where do you start with a bar code? A bar code reader obviously and Bisko's flashed into his mind:

a big supermarket with bar code readers at every till. Maybe if he nipped down on his bike and bought some bananas, and then...? ...No!

"Wouldn't it be easier just to phone her?" asked Sally.

"Ok, what's my number?"

She handed him her mobile; exactly the same as the one he was about to call. After choosing the wrong options a couple of times, (well, he hadn't had a proper chance to get to know the phone before it went walkabout) he eventually found the call made earlier and dialled back. It seemed an age before there was an answer. Should he ask her straight out if she was a spy? No, that could come later, concentrate on the name first.

"Hello again, Sally," the female voice said.

"Hello," Derek replied.

"Oh, that's not Sally, is it?"

"No, is that ...Lulubelle?"

"Nooooo – of course not!" and she laughed. "You didn't think that was my real name, did you, Derek? It is Derek isn't it? On the train, did I look like a Lulubelle to you?"

"Well, no," he said.

"So, what can I do for you then?"

"You ...I ...what?" he was totally thrown by this calm reaction. "My ...my phone..."

"Oh, you want it back, I suppose. I thought you might. It is a nice one. Sally's given you a loan of hers then?"

"Yes."

"How do you find it to use. You didn't add very many apps to this one, did you? I have found a few good ones for you."

She was totally controlling this conversation.

"Wait!" he demanded. "Your bag: it's not yours."

"What do you mean?"

"The stuff that's in it – all men's clothes."

"What? Oh, no," she responded. "You didn't steal *his* bag, did you?"

"Who's? Wait a minute. I didn't steal anyone's bag, I *saved* yours."

"My stepfather, Edgar, ohhhh..."

"What's wrong?"

"It hurts just to say his name out loud. He carried both bags onto the train. He must have put mine beside him: to stop me running off. It would have been his that was sitting beside me. Is that the one you lifted?"

"Yes," said Derek.

"That was a bit silly. What did it have in it?"

"Oh the usual stuff," and he went through the shirts, trousers, socks, pants, etc. "and *Secret Papers*." Damn, he thought, I didn't mean to say that, but, now that he had, what could 'Lulubelle' tell him. "Does he work for the government?" he asked, thinking of that 'Govement' heading.

"Oh I couldn't possibly disclose that about him, even though he has been cruel to me."

Interesting, she thought at the other end, *isn't it lucky I removed the identity card from the luggage tag? Where did I put it? What was I wearing on the train? There could be an opportunity of cash from this. A little blackmail wouldn't do any harm...*

"He hasn't caught you then?" Derek asked.

"Who?" she replied.

"Your stepfather, of course."

"No."

"Well, that's a good thing, but what about my phone?"

"Ah yes, you want it back. I am so sorry that I left the train without telling you. I am stuck here, but at least he hasn't found me. Oh dear Derek, I couldn't afford to travel to

Newingsworth to give the phone back. Unfortunately, if you still want it, you would have to come down to collect it."

"Where are you?"

"York. That would be a nice day out for you. You could maybe bring your wife and make a day of it. Visit the Rail Museum, and the Yorvik Centre, and you could walk around the walls, or go down by the river. There are lots of things to do. I'll ring you back tomorrow and fix something up. Ok?"

"Yes, fine then. Bye."

Sally was standing at his side, listening to his end of the conversation. "And what is her proper name then?"

"Bugger!" Yes, he knew there was something important he should have asked...

The grin on the face of Crystal Glasse said it all: secret papers indeed. *Thanks for that, Mr Derek Toozlethwaite.* She had no interest in anything else that might be in the bag. This little snippet was excellent for starters; she had acquired this fantastic mobile phone, and now had information that was about to be used to her financial benefit.

The label was in the pocket of her denim jacket. She remembered thinking, as she'd removed it from its holder, how clever the smart owner had been. Mr Chesney Wilfordon it said. Only his name and his mobile telephone number. *Wasn't that sweet...*

Indeed ...what a clever chap Mr Chesney Wilfordon had considered himself to be!

He knew that it was not wise to have his name and address on the label of a suitcase when he was away from home. Well, everybody knows that, but having some means of being traced seemed wise after he'd almost lost his briefcase once, when he'd laid it down in the station and wandered off without it. In case he made that mistake ever again and lost an item forever, he recorded his name and his mobile number on a name tag on each piece of luggage. Wisely, no address was divulged but a lifeline was there. London citizens are honest. He had proof of that honesty and that was why he still had his trusty briefcase. Mr Chesney Wilfordon was expecting a call at any time. It would be another example of good citizenship. Someone would return the holdall. It was rather important.

At last a call came.

Initially, he was delighted and relieved. His missing bag had been found and this was one occasion when having it returned intact really mattered. Someone on the phone was saying that she had found it near the newsagents in King's Cross Station.

Honest citizens still exist, right enough, he told himself thankfully, *I knew it.* Three cheers for the honest citizens of the world! *And this honest citizen has saved my bacon. It is simply a matter of finding a way of saying thanks when I collect my lost holdall from her.*

She continued in his mind as an honest citizen, and a lovely person, until she mentioned 'Secret Papers'.

It was an easy bluff for Crystal. She could tell she was onto a good thing by the way that he hesitated before coming out with, "...What do you mean?"

"You know..." was said in the right way, and he panicked.

She'd convinced him that she had them. *This bitch has opened the ruddy bag!* It was surprising how quickly his opinion of this honest citizen changed!

"You might want to think about what their return would be worth," she added, and heard the gulp at the other end. "Relax. There is no rush. I'll phone again tomorrow, Ches. You don't mind me calling you that, Chesney, do you? You'll want to think about how much money you will be offering me, I suppose, and I am sure you will be generous, so, take the chance to sleep on it. Oh, silly me. Maybe you won't sleep now."

He checked his phone and there was her number. Omitting to have the mobile number withheld was rather amateurish of her, Chesney Wilfordon concluded. This little lady must have thought she was really smart to come out with something like that and expect it to be successful.

"But not with me, Sweetie-Pie."

Never think the best of anyone, was something his father had been prone to believe. Maybe the old guy was right!

Before the call, Chesney had been undecided on whether the holdall had been lost or stolen. Ever since the briefcase incident, he had been particularly careful, and, he was pretty sure that he remembered where it was when he sat down. It was unfortunate that this time there was rather important information in the bag. This female had recognised that. Of course, under the circumstances getting the police involved was not an option. It must not be exposed to the public. One small crumb of consolation, she didn't sound the type to have understood what the papers were all about!

"I want you to trace the whereabouts of a caller of a mobile." This was a contact that he had not used for a while. "You still have suitable equipment, haven't you?" and the mobile number was given to his 'special friend': a man that he'd used before, who preferred anonymity and cash payments only.

This 'honest' citizen would be traced, and, no money would change hands either. Chesney was very confident about both.

"Imagine – me considering a reward… Ah well."

16

She was true to her word. She phoned the following morning, at seven am, to Sally's mobile.

"Good morning," the voice sang out cheerfully.

"Huh," was Sally's reaction, having been awakened by the blooming thing rattling on the bedside table.

"Who am I speaking to this morning?" the cheery voice continued. "It'll be Sally isn't it? So, put me onto Derek please," was the request.

Sally was tempted to hang up on this cheeky upstart. She recognised the voice from yesterday. It was Lulubelle! This female had what Sally considered to be an insolent manner.

"Derek," she growled through grated teeth at the body lying dormant beside her. "Derek!" That wakened him. "It's your friend – that girl with your damn phone!"

Her husband did not waken easily these mornings; something to do with being up in the middle of the night, at least once, for a certain demanding infant. This morning was no exception. "Leave me alone," was mumbled from beneath the duvet

"DEREK!" and that did it...

"Hello," he offered feebly.

"Good morning Mr Toozlethwaite. Aren't you up yet? And here's me up for ages and out already. Rise and shine."

"What do you want?" he mumbled, and then realised who it was. "Oh, it's you. Look I meant to ask you your correct name last night."

"Oh, did I not say. How remiss of me. Look I want rid of this phone. If you still want it back..."

"Of course, I still want it back," he spluttered grumpily, "and I'll give you the bag."

"Oh, I don't want that just now. You get the first train down, I'll meet you in the York Train Museum. Be in the shop at one pm: don't be late. All right then. See you shortly. Bye."

And she was gone.

"So, what is her name then?" asked Sally.

He just slunk disgustedly back under the duvet.

Of course, Crystal had not said her name; she wasn't totally stupid, but, it was an unusual sensation she was feeling – guilt at taking advantage of this nice bloke. He seemed so innocent ...and trusting too. Yes, she would be returning his phone, provided he arrived on time and was in the right place and she was certainly not going to be searching for him, that museum is a large place. She didn't feel that guilty!

Would he have realised that she was still making good use of his phone, she wondered? He didn't ask, but that poor innocent boy would not have wanted to know why she was out and about so early or, where she was phoning from or, what she was up to; he sounded half-asleep.

She bundled the stuff she'd so far gathered into her back-pack. Small easily-disposable items of high value were her only concern. Although there were lots of other larger valuable objects for the taking, that was not her field, but it didn't stop her admiring the quality of the paintings and clocks in the collection, displayed in the many rooms. What she was rather disappointed about was the ease by which she'd gained entry. It took some shine off the outing, her not having to use her skills properly. Had it been carelessness by the owner in setting the alarms, or was it just a poor system? Who knows, and it didn't really matter anyway.

There were several other drawers to be rifled. She laid the bag down on a chair and removed one of her gloves – her nose was itchy (and we all know that it is difficult to concentrate when the nose is itchy). The gloves were lightweight and essential and one of the reasons she had avoided detection. No fingerprints and no criminal record. Not like dear old dad – the silly old...

Getting caught was not his proudest moment, and she had been present in the house when they came for him. Most annoying: that evening, dinner was on the table, and she'd made a beautiful steak pie, his favourite. With no mother in the house, she'd become chief cook and bottle-washer. He was the cash provider up until that moment. Her old man being carted off by the police stuck in her mind, but...

Concentrate my gal, she told herself. She'd have to hurry if she was to take this stuff home and then carry out her promise to meet that mutt, Derek...

Chesney Wilfordon left London early, and was driving towards York. His 'friend' did a good job last night. Apparently that female was never off the phone all evening. It made locating the source of the calls so much easier for him. The calls had been tracked and identified as emanating from a specific semi-detached house in York – that man was good!

He was getting close. Knocking on her door would be in less than an hour with any luck, provided the satnav performs correctly.

Getting back home was rather tricky. Crystal had walked part of the way and then hitched a ride on a lorry stopped outside a roadside cafe. The lorry's destination was Berwick and would be travelling across the city. As a precaution she asked the driver to let her off on the far side of the city, well away from her own home, to ensure that her final destination would remain unknown. She then climbed aboard the circular bus and that took her as far as a mile from her place. The remaining distance was walked.

It was always a good feeling to step through the front door after doing a job, feeling confident that due care had been taken. Having a father locked up because he'd become careless, was the constant reminder to help her stay alert.

The pickings look excellent. A quick phone call to make sure Binky was there because shortly she would take the stuff to him and keep her own place free of any incriminating evidence. From then on, the sale and the money returned would be based on trust.

I'll use the Toozlethwaite phone, she decided. *He won't mind paying, he's a nice lad.* One minor problem, where was it? What had she done with it? *Oh, oh... I am sure it was in the side pocket of my anorak when I left – or was it? The lorry! Could it be in the cab?* Climbing in had been a bit awkward. It could have dropped out of her pocket then, but it might be lying on the road at the cafe. *Goodness, surely it isn't sitting on the floor of the circular bus. Which one was I on?* "You silly cow!" she yelled at her reflection in the hall mirror. "Where is the blasted thing?"

Pockets were double checked, but it was obviously not there.

The back-pack; perhaps she automatically put it in with the stolen goods? No... Keep calm. It's lost but it was not her phone. It was wiped clean of prints before she left and she was wearing the gloves all the rest of the time. It was tough, but didn't really matter now. The call could be made using her own mobile.

"Hello, Binky, the stuff; you ready for it now? Yea, good, see you shortly."

Another ten minutes, he reckoned, and he'd be there, face to face with this female who thought that she was smart enough to extract money from him – then the call came through from his 'friend'.

"Mister Wilfordon, the trace I gave you earlier. Looks like the phone is not where I said it was last night. Not surprising, someone going out and about carrying it with them, so, I did another check this morning in case you want to locate the individual. For the last two hours the phone has been pinpointed to be in a mansion house outside York, north of the city. You'll want the new location then."

17

"I am very sorry, Rob, but it is rather important, a personal emergency almost..."

Rob's response was less than sympathetic.

"Derek, we are trying to produce a weekly paper. You are remembering that, aren't you? You were off yesterday, and you are staying away today as well. There is a Thursday deadline, but you would rather sit on your backside at home doing nothing!"

"I already have some good stuff, about the wrong body being buried up at the cemetery last week," Derek offered. "Spider could access it on my PC and tidy it up in the meantime, and there are a few other usable snippets I was working on. I'll be back in tomorrow."

"You are taking advantage of my good nature," said Rob.

"And, if this works out as I hope, it could mean that we, The Newingsworth Weekly Gazette, have a scoop that the nationals will be desperate to be involved in."

"Yes, Derek – but..." Perhaps Rob did not sound as impressed as he should have been. This sort of promise had come from the young reporter so many times before. "...See you tomorrow then."

This morning, hurriedly dressed and shaved and on his way without breakfast, Derek was using Sally's phone and about to purchase a ticket for the 8.42 to London: one of the few trains stopping at Slatterfoot Station that would take him directly to York.

It seemed a long way to travel for a mobile phone, without knowing the name of the person he was supposed to meet. However, the visit would not only be to retrieve his expensive new mobile, it would be to discover the name of the owner of the hold-all, the person whose highly confidential information he almost certainly shouldn't have in his possession: info that could be of great newsworthy importance, found under the denims!

He could picture him, the fat bloke with the laptop sitting opposite on the train: the owner of the bag and the clothes, Lulubelle's stepfather, of course, but he hadn't looked like a spy either, had he?

She said she didn't want the holdall returned today, so he'd left it at home. Seemed daft when he could have brought it with him – but it was her choice. *I'll not be rushing down to her when she does want it. I'll have my phone back and she can just...*

As he sat on the train going south, a thought occurred. The denims, they were for a thirty-two inch waist and thirty-one inch leg length; if they weren't returned to the owner, he could wear them, himself. They'd be a perfect fit but...

Wasn't the girl's stepfather a big bloke?

That was a little bit odd. How would he get into them?

The satnav had fulfilled its function. Chesney Wilfordon was sitting in the car outside the highly-desirable old mansion house that his 'friend' had identified, and he was being very patient. He'd been there a while. A Bentley was sitting outside the front entrance. A red Mini-Cooper – top of the range version – was sitting there too, and some feverish activity was taking place.

When he'd arrived, the Bentley was already sitting at the front of the house. He'd stopped and parked the car at a spot where he could view the house without it being too obvious. It was at the edge of a small village and there were other vehicles near where he sat. He wouldn't be noticed. Someone was likely to be at home, but he decided to wait and observe and was glad he had.

It had been a prudent decision, because, shortly after he arrived, a Mini-Cooper roared at speed into the grand driveway. A female figure struggled to extricate herself from the bucket driving seat. She was of rather mature years, dressed in smart country quality clothing, as far as he could see, and did not look like a body to match the voice on the phone last night.

It also occurred to him, that anyone with a family like this, which obviously was well heeled, would be unlikely to be lowering themselves to attempt blackmail for a sum of money. Of course, someone could be doing it for the sport. Then again, the fact that the phone had been carried from a house in the middle of York to here this morning indicated that it could be a servant perhaps. They'd probably have to employ several outsiders to maintain a place like this.

Conflicting thoughts were disturbed when a police car came at speed along the road from York. It slowed at the entrance and swung into the long driveway and stopped outside the front entrance of this house he had come to visit.

Seems that they had been expected because they were met by an elderly red-faced man, probably the house-owner and who looked a member of the local gentry, who was immediately at the door. Much arm-waving and gesticulating by this elderly gent, who appeared used to being obeyed, added urgency to the movements of the uniformed constabulary.

Chesney restarted the engine. Now was not the time to knock the door and say, "Hello ...surprise!"

Most unusual for Crystal Glasse to have a crisis of conscience: so uncharacteristic, and driven by pity for a silly gullible male.

Poor Derek Toozlethwaite, she thought, coming down to York to have his mobile returned, and now she didn't have it to give. She honestly had meant to give it back to him. What should she do? Meet him and say 'Sorry, I lost it?' *Not on your life! He'll never see his precious phone again, but he'll get over it. We've all got our problems.*

Damn! Why didn't I tell him to bring the holdall!

The train was less crowded than when he'd travelled the other direction. This time it was easy to get a seat. An elderly gent was opposite, a railway timetable open in front of him, obviously a rail enthusiast – and eager to chat.

"Hello, young man. Good to have you aboard. Keeping good time this morning," he said, with a nod towards the timetable.

Derek gave a weak smile of acknowledgement, but offered no encouragement.

"I am Bert. Are you going to London then?"

"No, I am only going to York."

"Oh, snap! Me too; going to the rail museum then? I certainly am."

"Well ...yes," he replied, not really wanting to talk a lot this morning.

"Great museum and it'll be a great journey too. It's nice to have someone who's happy to share thoughts with. It's nice to talk," said Bert.

Derek smiled back. No ...it was more of a grimace.

"Some folk are so stand-offish and want to keep to themselves. I have travelled this route on many occasions," Bert decided to inform Derek, "and I've never been on a journey yet that wasn't exactly as it should be: timed to perfection," and his face beamed with pride as he said it.

Leave me alone...

"What did you say your name was, young man?"

"Derek," was said reluctantly He looked out of the carriage window but it did not discourage his fellow traveller. Derek guessed that he'd probably worked all his life on the railway, and never lost his enthusiasm for trains – worst luck!

"I used be a tax officer," Derek then learned; bad guess!

Without being rude, how do you tell someone who is doing no harm except being determined to talk to you, that you wanted to be left in peace? *Let it all go over the head*, Derek decided and just nodded occasionally.

Of course, it had to happen. Less than ten minutes after making the statement that it never happened, this rail expert was to experience his first stoppage on this line. For that, Derek wanted to throttle him. It stands to reason – you just don't say such things out loud.

It was a lengthy stoppage too.

They sat there listening, waiting to learn why, but no official explanation was given, so Bert took it as a gap to permit more talking. It did give the elderly gent an opportunity to explain the intricacies of the working of the British Railway System compared to that of Germany and India. Exactly the sort of thing that Derek had been desperate to learn about, of course...

With difficulty he feigned interest.

There was relief when a cheery voice announced over the communication system, "Any minute now we'll be on our way ...and we hope you haven't been inconvenienced." Still no reason given, but at least the wheels began to turn and the train quickly regained normal speed. The enthusiastic gent settled back to the serious business of monitoring the progress against the timetable – this time silently.

It was pretty clear what Bert was thinking – *will the driver succeed in regaining lost time?* His face had a concerned look. He dearly wanted to believe it to be possible.

At least he had stopped talking. That pleased Derek.

Shortly Bert's worried expression was replaced by a smile. "Yes, yes, he's doing it. We've already regained ten minutes. Isn't that incredible? I bet we'll be there on time. You just can't beat travelling by rail, can you?"

Derek smiled back, more genuinely this time, pleased that he wouldn't be late after all. He did want to arrive at his destination in good time. The museum was only a short distance from the railway station and, with any luck he would manage to have a sandwich and a coffee before he met the girl. Unfortunately for Derek, luck was going to be in short supply today.

In the middle of the open countryside the train began to slow down. It was getting slower and slower – just like climbing a hill when the engine of a car isn't powerful enough. It came to a halt. *Oh, oh! Not again.*

Silence ...then a mournful 'mooooo'.

Derek looked out and saw a herd of cows, gathered at the fence, standing and staring. He tried to stare one of them out, just like the game he used to play with Grandad when he was young. Grandad never won, though Derek suspected that he gave in deliberately to let him think he had. The cows stared back – but they didn't play the game properly. None gave in!

"Hmmm..." said Bert. "This is quite demoralising. Rather shattering my illusions. What will the tourists think? It was so much better when it was British Rail, you know."

"If it's a long stoppage, they'll put on buses," said Derek, in a superior way. "They'll want to get us there on time," then he realised that he could see a wide expanse of the countryside. There were no roads on either side of the rails.

Looking out, he could see that they were surrounded by cattle. To get to a bus, he'd have to trudge through fields of cow dung.

"We are very sorry to have to inform you that we are awaiting a replacement traction unit." At least they were being kept informed of the situation, but it sounded as if it would be a lengthy stop. "Meanwhile, may we suggest that you avail yourself of the delicious sandwiches and drinks, which are available from the mobile refreshment unit? Thank you for your patience. Have a nice day."

Food, a good idea, Derek decided. *I'll have something to eat here on the train and save time at the other end.* He was quite peckish and it was turning into a longer delay this time. Unfortunately, by the time the refreshment trolley arrived in his carriage, he found that everyone else had had the same idea. The trolley was now devoid of any food of nutritious value.

He made a purchase all the same.

"Would you like one?" he asked the train expert sitting opposite, and held out the packet of Polo mints. He was disappointed that, with little alternative, he'd had to make do with a large expensive multi-pack of centre-less mints.

As for his drink! For the very good reason that it did not taste like the luxury orange as described on the label, he regretted not offering this small carton of pink, coloured fluid to his travelling companion. Pity, he had already used the one straw supplied.

He looked at his watch. It was going to be a bit tight for time, he began to suspect.

"If we started again now, when should we reach York?" he asked the timetable expert.

"I'd say at exactly one-o-six pm," was the confident reply.

That's not too bad, she'll hang on, but, I'd better phone and say I'll be a little bit late, he decided – and dialled his own number. As he heard it ring he imagined Sally's reaction when he went home after retrieving his own phone from the girl, and, as a joke, him saying that on the way he'd lost 'her' mobile this time... "Ha, ha, joke!" he would announce, and then he visualised her face and decided – not a good idea! For certain, he'd take very good care of the one he was holding!

No answer? Why is she not answering? I'll try again in a moment.

Another mouthful of pink liquid tantalised his taste buds, and he swallowed. "Ugh!"

"Did you know that Stephenson's Rocket had the capability of travelling at no more than twenty-eight miles an hour? Wasn't that slow, in comparison to..."

"Considerably faster than we are going," Derek added, and redialled.

Why am I getting no response? The number, is it the correct one? I should have tried memorising it the moment we got the phones.

He looked at the precious calls received on this device from the girl to prove that he was dialling correctly. He was, so he tried yet again. The cows still stood staring. Derek could have sworn that one was laughing at him...

18

The train did move eventually but, by the time York Station was reached and they had disembarked, it was one-forty pm and, having failed to get through to 'Lulubelle', Derek was feeling apprehensive and he had gained a companion, whether he wanted one or not.

Bert insisted on keeping pace with Derek, talking all the way, as they hurried the short distance to the National Train Museum. It was busy, as always, with families, school groups, railway buffs, and tourists all queuing patiently at the main entrance.

Derek rushed into the shop, closely pursued by Bert. Here it was busy, and again with visitors from all walks of life, but a quick scan of the crowd revealed no 'Lulubelle', the young lady who was supposed to be waiting here to return his mobile phone!

He had hoped that it would just be a matter of grabbing it, saying a quick 'Thank you' and 'Are you all right then?' followed by a rush back to the station, to catch one of the few trains suitable for his return journey at this time of the day.

Derek looked around again, more carefully.

"Isn't it great, costing nothing to wander around the museum all day" Bert commented.

"I am not going in," Derek told him. "I am just meeting someone here, in the shop."

He was concerned with not seeing the person he remembered, and worried that a lot of girls looked very similar in his memory. Could she be here, and he was failing to recognise her? It works both ways though, he reminded himself: she would be looking out for him – that is, if she remembers what he looks like? He turned around – to find Bert still standing at his side. Derek peered passed him at the crowd.

Bert felt rejected and his face showed it. *For this visit,* he'd thought, *here is a pal to wander around with.* However, and unfortunately for Derek, Bert saw the quizzical look on Derek's face. *This young fellow needs help,* he decided, *he needs me:* and this prompted Bert to start talking again.

Derek could have seen him far enough! Bert's mouth was moving but Derek was not hearing anything being said – he was worried. The phone – give it one more try – there wasn't much else he could do.

...Still no response.

He felt bad. It was his fault that this hadn't worked out correctly. If the train had been on time it would all have been done and dusted and he would have been on his way home again, happily, with his phone in his pocket. He couldn't blame the girl, she wouldn't wait forever – why should she? She would have a busy life to lead...

Wait a minute! What was he thinking? She was the one who caused the problem in the first place! *Grrr! Now, what'll I do?*

It was close to teatime before Derek caught a train that would stop at Slatterfoot Station. He was exhausted, and hungry – and phoneless! Not true – he still had Sally's phone, thank goodness.

Bert was still his companion. He was as bright as a button. He had encouraged Derek to make use of the enforced extra time in York and had pushed Derek to explore every part of the Train Museum with him – for almost three hours! There, Bert had been, and still was, talking all the time, and showing no sign of the exhaustion that Derek was displaying.

There was very little that this man did not know about trains and train services and spare parts and the longest tunnels and the highest bridges and... The knowledge was not hidden! It was wearing for Derek, his friend's insistence on telling him about all the detail, so much so that when the train to take them home was arriving there was a strong urge on Derek's part to shove the old gent in front of it. He resisted the temptation and they boarded a very busy train.

Derek's mind was on the failure to connect with the girl but balanced, a bit, by the thought of what was hidden under ET's cot: Highly Confidential pieces of paper. Yes, something would come out of that. As they stood shoulder to shoulder in the packed corridor, with Bert still chattering away, Derek was relieved when his brain went numb!

A mobile phone was in the police car, a phone that had sounded several times, but was not heard as the car was sitting empty. No one was around. Neither was the device able to be seen due to it being down the side of the front passenger seat. It was destined to remain there until the mechanic had the chance to start next day on the planned work.

From late morning, the empty vehicle had been sitting in the car park outside York Central Police Station awaiting collection. Of course, if the car had not been due for one of the regular safety checks someone would probably have found the mobile earlier and answered the calls. The significance of yet another mobile phone, when handed in from the garage, was not appreciated right away – thought by the desk sergeant to be just one more item to sit on his shelf for ages to await a claimant.

Being called away from the scene of the theft at the Middlefield Mansion House to attend a gas explosion had caused a slight deviation from normal procedures for the uniformed policemen involved: rightly so with lives being endangered. It was the end of their shift when it came to recording the details of the crime and only then, on referring to the notebook, that the absence of the phone was appreciated. It must have been left at the scene was the presumption. *No panic*, was the reaction of Uniforms, *Plain Clothes will pick it up tomorrow.*

Next day, 'plain clothes' arrived in the form of Detective Sergeant Milne and Detective Constable Green but, disappointingly, the two detectives found no phone at the Mansion. "As usual – uniforms only ever get it *almost right*," was their comment. Could it have been dropped outside? No. Checks in the vicinity of the Police Station revealed nothing either, so, another possibility was that it had been dropped inside the car. Which vehicle was used? Where is that car? Ah yes!

So, the phone eventually was traced and now lay on the desk of D S Milne.

Here was yet another case of selective thieving from a deserted country house; small valuable items, the type of goods that could easily be sold on. Would he have any more success with this case? All along DS Milne had been sure that it was unlikely to be a gang involved. DC Green had been in agreement with him on that. With several people involved in a crime there was a good chance one would make an error. He suspected these jobs to be by an individual, and, a criminal who'd left no clues – until now!

Bizarrely, this time, this mobile phone was left behind and, thankfully, there could be a big leap forward.

It looked as if the mobile could have as much information on it that would permit him to find and convict the perpetrator without even having to leave his desk. The much-looked-forward-to and long-awaited arrest was being handed to him on a plate by the owner of the phone, the eagerly-sought thief, who'd very obligingly sent an interesting text to his own phone.

It read: *Sorry to miss you for the handover. If you will be kind enough to post the phone to me, I would appreciate it. My address is: Toozlethwaite Manor, Off Chicken Farm Lane, near Newingsworth. Thanks, Derek.*

"Oh dear me," said DS Milne, to DC Green. "Tut, tut, no post code..." but he was smiling as he said it. The crooks they dealt with were not usually so obliging. Hard to believe, leaving an address in case the Constabulary wanted to get in touch. Even better though, there were other telephone numbers from previous calls; probably be able to round up a whole gang with this...

Sitting in the flat, Chesney Wilfordon felt considerably less confident than when he had set out this morning. To confront an attempted blackmailer, had been the plan, and obtain the return of his stolen baggage and contents, but that had not happened. He was on the back foot again. Now, it was more a case of waiting for the inevitable – another telephone call.

After the police car sped away he'd watched the Mansion House for a further half-hour in the hope of seeing a female that might have matched the voice on the phone. The only happening had been the elderly woman leaving the house, struggling back into her Mini-Cooper and driving off, only to return twenty minutes later with what was obviously a bag of foodstuffs.

Was his holdall in that Mansion House, perhaps? His 'friend' seemed to think the phone was no longer in the house but the only people to have come out of the place had been the police and the elderly woman. So, where was the phone, and the 'phantom' female?

Derek shouldn't have been surprised by Sally being less than impressed by his afternoon activities in York. When he tried telling her that it had not been an enjoyable experience, failing to get the thing he'd gone for, and, at the same time meeting and having to put up with someone who was incapable of not talking, he had expected a little sympathy. However her response had been, "Are you surprised? And Derek, stop rabbiting on, please." On top of that, to have the chance to look at the hidden papers would not be possible until later. He'd been landed with nappy changing and the feeding of his young son.

It had not been a good day!

Always get rid of the goods from the house as soon as possible; Crystal had decided this long ago and today it had been achieved. Being able to relax with her shoes off and feet up watching her favourite crime programme – what could be nicer?

Having a trustworthy 'fence' meant the dirty work was being done by another. "Keep your hands clean!" That was a lesson she'd learned from her father – before he'd been arrested. *I could teach him a few things nowadays*, she told herself cockily, but, it was regrettable in the last twenty-four hours to have lost that phone. It would have been nice to have had the use of it until the cash had been extracted.

I could use a public call-box for the follow-up though, she decided, but, not tonight. I can't be bothered. Tomorrow is another day...

19

Sitting at his desk in the Newingsworth Weekly Gazette office was a frustrated Derek. The plans he'd had for last evening to do an in-depth study of the confidential information, took a knock on the head. A surprise visit from Angie and Sam and little Annabelle put paid to that, so the documents remained where they were – unread and burning a hole in ET's mattress.

Sam was to blame. He'd brought over Angie and the baby last evening to show off his recent purchase. It was an old banger of a car. Derek was disappointed, his brother-in-law had let the side down.

At least Sam was man enough to admit to feeling slightly guilty about it on two counts: firstly, he'd used some of the savings that were to go towards a house purchase and that had upset Angie and; secondly, the gas-guzzling qualities of an old banger were harmful to the environment. That, of course, was the type of thing to upset Derek.

The reason: it had been a bargain! A fellow teacher, upgrading from a vehicle that he'd inherited from his father, a snip at a price that Sam could not resist, and that he thought could afford! To Derek's question, "MOT Certificate?" there was only a blank look.

They'd stayed late and, as usual, baby Annabelle behaved impeccably even though she was up a lot later than any baby should. When compared to ET who'd been bad tempered all evening, she was the perfect child. This also upset Derek. Then, with him being up in the middle of the night – as usual walking the floor with ET, because Daddy was favourite – the son to father devotion was not totally reciprocated.

Except for Derek, work in the Gazette Office this morning was progressing reasonably, the peace being shattered every so often by the irritating buzz of the switchboard. It was only a small switchboard but all the calls into the office came through it and, sitting on Christine's desk, it gave that woman a feeling of power. There were only four occupants, including herself, but, no matter how important the call, she was the one who would decree if it would be passed over or not.

Previously, her responsibility was the large switchboard in Main Reception and there she had power over all the phones of the building's occupants, but she had become used to working in the smaller office. Somehow, the intimacy suited her. It was partly because she and one of the others had paired... Spider was her man!

Good old Spider. There was maturity in their love, Christine liked to think, but could not help suspecting that Spider's liking for good ales might have some influence in the relationship – her brother owned the Torrid Hedgehog Inn – but she didn't care.

The switchboard buzzed.

"Hello, Newingsworth Weekly Gazette. Which department can I direct you to?"

"Good morning Christine, is Derek Toozlethwaite available, please?"

"That will be the 'News and Current Affairs' Department you are after, Mr Davidson. How are you today? You are well, I hope. I'll see if I can make contact for you." The line was switched to silent.

"Derek, are you in for your father-in-law?" she shouted across the office.

Derek nodded, and smiled to himself. Christine was such a different person since Spider gave in. So, what did Alexander want?

"Putting you through now, Mr Davidson..."

"Derek, would you mind telling that dozy female on your switchboard that my name is Donaldson, not Davidson."

"Right, will do, Alexander. Is that all you phoned about?"

"No, of course not, it's about this ruddy Hi-Speed Rail route thingy. I don't like where it's supposed to be going. It's going to affect me!"

"Yes...?"

"...And from what I can see, it could be coming right through your home, and the hotel too, so I think a lot of people should be getting worried. Mrs Masterton, next door, is already up in arms about it, though I've no idea what she has to be getting excited about."

"Could it be because it affects the town, and she's just being supportive? Maybe she doesn't like the idea of the train station being closed. I don't suppose anyone does. Have you thought of asking her?" contributed Derek half-heartedly, feeling the effect of several nights on the trot attending to ET.

"I'll say one thing for her – I do believe the old biddy has come up with a name for a protest group. *SNORT!* She says it stands for Slatterfoot and Newingsworth Objectors to the Rail Trail. Not a bad idea, I'd say."

Derek mind was wandering. The Hi-Speed Link, Two-Speed-High – that was one of the documents under ET's mattress. All cut and dried if that secret information is correct. It would be a waste of time having a protest group. A battle already lost!

"Derek, are you still there?"

"Yes, sorry and you phoned me because...?"

"It's obvious surely, with you being in the newspaper business, and, being young. Get something going, my lad. Publicity! That's what's needed. Stand up to the buggers! We'll get them to change direction. Speak to you later."

A protest group...

Maybe futile in practice, but probably would be worthwhile news, particularly with a few hotheads involved, like Mrs Masterton. With a few glasses of sherry inside her she'd demolish any opposition for sure, even though she's in her eighties!

The switchboard buzzed again. It was all happening today.

"Hello, Newingsworth Weekly Gazette. Which department can I direct you to?"

"Hello, Christine love. How are ye doin' the day, eh? It's yer pal Hammy."

"Oh hello, Hammy, I never recognise your voice for some reason..."

"Ah ken, lass, I've often wished that I was mair distinctive. Could I speak tae Sweaty, please?"

"That'll be the 'Astrology and the Woman's Ailments' Department you'll want then."

"Sweaty, it's Hammy," Christine shouted across.

"Hammy, you know you are not supposed to be calling me Sweaty. You've got Christine doing it now," Derek said. Actually he didn't mind it now and again, and anyway, it's unlikely he'd ever get Hammy to stop using it completely.

"Awfully sorry," said Hammy in an attempt at English, "but I've just had a wee idea. See this Hi-Speed Railway, do ye think, that if we all got our heeds together, we could make them change the direction o' it? I'd love us tae get the better o' the folk that decides all thae stupid things."

"Have you been talking to Alexander about this?"

"Naw. Has he been on to ye to?"

"Yes, and he is suggesting a protest group."

"Oh aye, that sounds like a braw idea, an' Sweaty, are you goin' to be the organiser?"

"No, I am not. I would only report whatever you might try, though I doubt if it will get anywhere from the secret papers I've seen."

Damn! He wanted to bite off his tongue. He'd done it again!

"Whit secret papers? Ye've seen secret papers have ye?"

"Forget I said that Hammy. It was a mistake. There are none. I haven't seen any pieces of paper. I'll have to go. I'll talk to you later."

"Aye, you will that you wee rogue. You are no good at keepin' secrets are you, Sunshine? I'll see you later then, an' we'll have a wee chat aboot it..."

Of course, the walls in this office do not have ears. They are not thick enough for that. Everything that went on in Rob Burton's office could be heard outside by the other three. This is denied by them any time Rob asks if they can overhear his chats, but it is obvious that he too, takes full advantage of the benefits, from his side.

"Derek! These secrets you mentioned, would they have something to do with the scoop that you promised me? Is now a good time to come and tell me all about it?"

Damn, I forgot I told him that, thought Derek, *but I have nothing yet to go on. What can I say? Quickly – think of something! I could always mention – SNORT! Yes, that idea should pacify Rob for a short time.*

20

For several reasons Derek was fairly well known in Newingsworth, Slatterfoot and surrounding districts. Not only was he the local reporter for Newingsworth Weekly Gazette and therefore someone whose name appeared in each issue, he had written 'the book'. In his story, reviving the name of the seventies pop group, Rabid Revenge, and exposing his family connections with them had helped further his fame. Also, it had to be admitted, his surname, being rather unusual had something to do with it. Is anyone else in the world called Toozlethwaite?

However, his fame had not reached as far as York, well, certainly not as far as the Central Police Station of that city so the two detectives, who were travelling northwards to interview their suspect, knew little of him. Of course, the message kindly left by 'Derek' on the mobile, giving his address, had been helpful. From that, after a little investigation, a surname had been established.

They were on their way feeling quite relaxed about having a legitimate excuse to be on the road away from base. Although it could not be voiced aloud in the city, having the chance to get out of York was appreciated. Driving could be fun; the unpleasant part of the job was facing up to villains. As they progressed northwards it was good to see the volume of traffic diminish.

Obtaining background information about their suspect, when they reached Newingsworth, was fairly easy for DS Milne and DC Green. The first thing they found out was that Toozlethwaite did not have a reputation of being a tough nut. This they were pleased to glean from the locals, "But, you never know," DC Milne reminded his subordinate. "It's not unknown for a person's calm exterior to become maniacal rage when confronted by their crimes." It was agreed that the suspect would be approached cautiously.

They arrived in town and, first things first, a visit to a pub. From the barman, they learned where Toozlethwaite worked and were given clear guidance how to get there.

At the newspaper office, DC Green found it easy to make friends with the Receptionist at the main entrance… Not knowing what Toozlethwaite looked like, they wanted a visual pointer before approaching him, preferably without his knowing.

Green explained that he would be sitting outside in the car with his other pal, and, when 'good old Derek' passed the desk, Mary should flick the front entrance lights on and off, twice, to identify him. They were old school pals who wanted to play a practical joke on him, but it had been a long time since they'd seen each other. They wanted to be sure it was the right man.

To be honest, Mary thought that, for these two men to have gone to school with Derek, there was a rather large difference in their ages. Derek was younger. *I should have asked them about Newingsworth High School; what they remembered.* That's where she'd been and she'd known Derek back then but these two she did not recognise at all. *I hope I am doing the right thing,* she told herself – but she did what they'd asked anyway.

"There he is," said DS Milne. They watched him go round the corner to the car park, and with engine running waited to follow. They were ready!

Toozlethwaite came back out onto the main road, haversack on his back – on his new bicycle. They would not have to travel too fast to keep up.

He had only gone a few hundred yards along the road, when he stopped, and began talking to a male who was standing scratching his head in front of a stationery vehicle – with the bonnet up. They parked up and watched... *Could this be this one of the gang?*

"Be ready," said DS Milne. "If anything changes hands, goods or money, we'll have them!"

Toozlethwaite had taken off the haversack and laid it on the ground and was bending over the engine, obviously an expert. He was now shaking his head. It looked like bad news. He was standing looking in the direction of their car.

"Has he spotted us, do you think?" Green asked his boss.

"Couldn't have," replied Milne confidently. "They are being cautious off-loading the stuff. That's what I am seeing." It was true; they could only *see* what was happening.

"Sam," Derek was saying, "you've only had it for twenty-four hours and it's given up already."

It was not Sam's intention to break down at that particular spot. In fact, it was not his intention to break down at all: it just happened, but he appreciated Derek having stopped. He'd hoped to hear words of comfort from a very wise brother-in-law but he felt worse now.

"You are an American Pillock. Get your money back. He saw you coming. I'd love to be able to help but I'll have to go – sorry."

Sam was given a sympathetic pat on the back. It didn't make him feel any better.

"Did something change hands?" asked Green eagerly. "Will I go for them?"

"No, not yet," said Milne. "Give him time."

On the move again, slowly, Toozlethwaite almost caught them off guard as he swung across the road, suddenly turning to the right, into the car park of a large supermarket. The move took them by surprise but was more of a shock for the young lady driving and texting as she exited the car park. The cyclist's sudden manoeuvre almost gave her a heart attack. The wisdom of obeying the rule, about not using a mobile while driving, rapidly came home to her.

"Don't let him out of sight," Milne instructed. He was busy attempting to do a right turn but the traffic coming towards them was at its peak. Not enough to compare with York or London, but hindering any quick and easy passage.

By the time they'd entered and driven up to where bicycles were parked, Toozlethwaite had vanished and they were not the first to discover the impossibility of parking close to the entrance.

"Get out and I'll dump the car," Green was instructed, "see if you can find him in there. I don't want even to consider that we've come all this distance to lose the bugger."

The reason for the haversack on Derek's back was to carry the shopping. He had been given a list by Sally, and provided they hadn't rearranged the aisles, or the position of the stock, as they were prone to do, he could be quick and grab all the items listed and be out in no time. He was eager to be home and have a proper look at these confidential documents this evening. Each time he thought of the word 'confidential' he gave an involuntary shudder. "Got a cold coming on?" the girl on the checkout asked. "That's how it always starts with me, the shivers."

DS Milne and DC Green failed to spot him, although, while one had watched the exits and checkouts, the other had moved rapidly up and down the aisles. Fifty minutes had been wasted but, in truth, all was not lost; they had his address. Not the way they had planned to do it, but not a lot of choice now, unfortunately. It was always dicey tackling someone on their home ground. Other members of the family were likely to cause trouble. Rogues tended to band together, especially families.

With neither having checked out exactly where the address was they were totally reliant on the satnav system, and it led them into a pot-holed lane. It was really narrow, and black as pitch, a thick thorn hedge down one side and, on the other, a stream with a fair depth of water, in which it would be wiser not to become immersed. Milne was very careful. He liked the element of surprise and would have preferred to switch off the headlights, but he didn't dare. The locality made DS Milne think of stories where satnav systems could take you in error.

They'd passed a sign on the narrow road they were on. There were occasional lights along its length, no doubt, for the benefit of visitors to the New Farmhouse Hotel. It was good to have seen that because it was getting late and they had no intention of driving back to York tonight so if the worst came to the worst they could stay there overnight.

There was no wind. The area was silent except for the sound of their car engine. Toozlethwaite would have warning of their arrival. Not good! They stopped the car and got out. With the car's lights now off, they could see no light coming from the windows on this side of the cottage. The only light was shining through the little glass panel in the cottage door and it actually looked welcoming to the two policemen, but each man's thought was: *what lies beyond?*

There was a bell. When pressed it sounded piercing. It sounded loud from the outside so would not be easily ignored inside. A dog began to bark and, moments later, a child began to wail. They looked at each other. "This is not going to be pleasant," said Green to his boss, who had carefully sidled up behind him.

Milne was terrified of dogs, had been ever since a serious incident when he was six-years-old, involving him and an angry cocker spaniel: angry due to the normally peaceable animal having been poked on the nose – by the said young Milne – with a stick.

The door was opened by a woman. A lovely aroma of cooked food came wafting out. For Green, on his empty stomach, this was a comforting sensation. DS Milne didn't even notice the smell. His mind was taken up by the dog at the woman's feet. It may only have been a poodle but, to his eyes, it looked fearsome and vicious.

For the few provisions needed, Derek had been inside Bisko's for barely five minutes and had been home for ages. Enough time to have already wolfed down the delicious hot meal that Sally had spent most of the afternoon carefully preparing, which Derek had failed to appreciate – and Sally had made a mental note of the fact. "Must look at these papers," he'd said, as he rose quickly, failing to notice her frown as he shot into Edwin's darkened bedroom.

He had only just lifted out the documents carefully, from under a sleeping child, when the doorbell sounded, followed by the barking of Jilly.

"Darn!" he muttered and hurriedly shoved the folder back under the mattress. The cause of the wail that came from ET had nothing to do with either the doorbell ringing, or the dog barking, it was daddy's clumsiness! "Sorry pal," he murmured to the crying ET as Derek lifted him. Attempts to pacify failed, so he was carried into the living room.

Who had been at the door?

As he walked back into the room it was one of these rare moments when Derek took an immediate liking to someone. There were two men standing with Sally, and he had instant empathy with the elder one. For a start, he thought, in his hand he was holding a mobile phone and it was his – but even better – Jilly was circling and growling at him.

Yahoo – I am not the only one that the dog hates!

21

The pleasure anticipated by Derek on meeting these two gents was rather rapidly dissipated. The mobile phone was in a clear plastic bag and apparently they weren't just handing it back to him.

"This yours, Mister Toozlethwaite?" asked DC Green.

Jilly was circling around, growling, and it was hard for DS Milne to concentrate.

"It certainly looks like it. Did Lulubelle give it to you?" said Derek, thinking these people must be her friends.

"Lulubelle? No, not quite..." replied DC Green. "Are you going to tell him Sarge?"

"Sarge? Wait a minute. Who are you?" said Derek. "How did you find me to return it?" DS Milne's attention was definitely elsewhere. It's only a tiny dog, he was telling himself, but not believing his own words.

"Sarge?" said DC Green. He'd never seen his boss like this.

"*What?* Oh yes... We are police officers, our identification – should have been asked for this before inviting us in, you know." His eyes kept darting around as he reached into his pocket – had to keep the dog in sight...

Both brought out the warrant cards. Police officers! They've come for the...

As Derek stared at the man's face, 'HIGHLY CONFIDENTIAL' appeared, tattooed across his forehead.

Stop it! He blinked and switched his gaze rapidly to the other man. The same words were emblazoned on each of his sleeves. They were now appearing on the walls too – in multi-colours! As he looked down at the baby in his arms, not now crying and gazing up at his favourite daddy; on the little face was a frown, and the little mouth was silently saying the words, over and over: "HIGHLY CONFIDENTIAL, HIGHLY..." *but he's a baby!*

It was the sergeant who was talking. "You were in York yesterday, weren't you?"

"Yes, but how did...?"

"You left this behind. Very careless I'd say." Milne dangled the mobile in the plastic bag in front of Derek's nose.

"But I didn't..."

"Are you denying being in York, then?"

"No, but..."

"And you left the instructions for either the cash, or the goods, to be sent on to you, didn't you. I haven't yet decided which you were arranging," said Milne. "And you used your wife's phone. You are married aren't you?" He directed that at Sally.

"Of course," she replied indignantly.

"No, I asked Lulubelle to send the phone to me," Derek said.

"Who is this Lulubelle you keep referring to? No one is called a stupid name like that nowadays," Milne scoffed. "Anyway, enough of this nonsense, you've probably got stolen goods stashed away somewhere in the house. Look in the bedroom first, Green."

"Just one minute!" Sally interjected. "You are not looking at anything in this house without a warrant!" She turned to Derek. "You told me you were at the Rail Museum yesterday

– but were you really? Or, were you trying to get up to nonsense again – with this Lulubelle?"

Derek's mouth opened, but nothing came out. It was bad enough him being verbally harassed by these two policemen without his wife becoming suspicious again about everything, especially after the time he'd had with the person he had actually been with, Bert!

"I must ask you to leave this house," said Derek in his bravest manner. Looking down at Jilly still circling around the elder one and seeing the distrust on the man's face, he threw in, "...because I can't guarantee that this dog will not bite." He was bluffing, of course, but it got a reaction from DS Milne.

"Now listen here, Sonny," he said, and his hand reached out towards Derek.

With a leap forward Jilly grabbed the man's trouser leg and started shaking.

"Jilly! I was only kidding," said Derek bending down to pull the dog off. He didn't want a bill for damages to clothing, especially not one from a policeman who was obviously out to cause him trouble. What Derek forgot was his very own rule: never attempt to control this dog without wearing the gloves!

"Owowow..."

On his left arm was little ET, who started crying again and, on his right hand, a white, dangerous poodle with sharp teeth who wouldn't let go until Sally grabbed it. The baby was automatically handed to a surprised DC Green as Derek fetched a handkerchief from his pocket to wrap around his finger.

"Assaulting a police officer in the process of carrying out his duty," Milne intoned, showing no sympathy for Derek's suffering.

"Hold on," said Derek. "Can we start at the beginning again – please! I don't understand what's going on."

The finger throbbed but the pain had sharpened up his thinking. His conscience told him that they were really here because they knew he'd taken the holdall from the train, but were pretending to be here for another reason.

He could always admit to taking it, he decided, but he didn't have to say anything about the confidential papers – and see what happens.

"You know about the bag," he started," the holdall, from the train?"

Ah good, thought DS Milne, he's going to come clean and it looks like he has a lot to admit to. Give him the floor, it's his anyway...

"This one," said Derek, going behind the settee and placing it on the little table in front of them. "Maybe you'd like to sit down."

DC Green was single, and only a bit older than Derek, and actually enjoying the unusual task of baby-minding but he appreciated that it could be easier from a seated position, so he made himself comfortable. DS Milne had a slight smirk on his face as he seated himself too, happy that the pesky poodle was being controlled now, and anyway, this Toozlethwaite would be going nowhere – until he decided. He'd waited a long time for this moment. *Savour it. There is no rush.*

"This is the holdall you are looking for," said Derek. "I now believe it to belong to Lulubelle's stepfather. I suspect he could be a Government employee, or a Civil Servant."

What he was rambling on about, Milne and Green had no idea.

"I thought it was hers – but it isn't," Derek continued.

"Gerronwithit!" came from DS Milne.

"It contained a bar-coded identity tag that might be traceable."

"Oh," said Milne, feigning interest in what was being said, while thinking, 'Where's the loot?'

"It also contained two shirts, three pairs of boxer shorts, pyjama trousers, three pairs of socks, a toilet bag, a t-shirt and a pair of denims – and all for a male, and I believe all belonging to her step-father."

"Whose step-father?" asked Milne, with a quizzical look at a DC who was now absorbed in keeping a baby pacified.

"Lulubelle's; you see I lifted his bag instead of hers."

DS Milne closed his eyes and tried to remain calm but, *if he mentions that stupid name once more...*

22

Two hours later they were still there and still sitting on the settee in Toozlethwaite Manor. DS Milne and DC Green were both feeling considerably happier, each having had bacon and egg, two slices of buttered bread and cups of strong tea, rustled up and fed to them by Sally a short while ago. That was only after they had heard what Derek had to say, and only after he had given them little choice but to listen.

Derek had felt unjustifiably threatened and, being the only one who knew what had actually transpired in the last few days, he was the only one who could possibly tell the true facts. So, he talked his way in and out of his return journey from London, how he became involved with Lulubelle and her wicked step-father, and why there was a holdall in his house that did not belong to him.

How his expensive telephone had disappeared from his ownership was also explained with great clarity but he could not attempt to explain, in answer to their accusation, how his mobile had come to be in a Mansion House outside York, and eventually arrived in police custody.

The one who'd listened most carefully to every word was Sally. His wife was eager to know if he could repeat what he had claimed to her to be the true story. If it had turned out to be different with this further telling, there would have been ructions!

Of course he hadn't been involved in any stupid robbery, in any stupid Mansion House near York, because he'd been stuck on a stupid train that shouldn't have been late, but was. Then on top of that, having missed the appointment he'd had with Lulubelle to get back the phone, he'd had to reluctantly suffer meandering around the York Railway Museum with stupid Bert, who would not stop talking. The weak part of the story being that Derek had not the slightest awareness as to where his cast-iron alibi, stupid Bert, might be located.

By the end of his speech he felt mentally drained, his wife felt a little more relaxed, and the policemen were starving.

Derek had convinced them, but, there was still something odd about the phone, though not stated, that niggled the two detectives. Who could be so daft as to give a new, valuable phone to someone they didn't know? Ah yes, this fellow, Toozlethwaite, could...

Not surprisingly, the tale of woe, as explained by Derek, avoided any mention of Highly Confidential Documents. However, the bar-coded identity tag was produced with a flourish, and he suggested it might be used to trace the owner of the holdall. He admitted that he would be happy to be rid of the bag, but would be interested to learn the identity of the owner, though personal contact was not desired.

Picturing the fat bloke sitting across the corridor reminded him that he didn't want to fall foul of him, though some contact would be necessary if the documents were to be usable in the future. Without identifying the group responsible for these secret plans, his theory would not hold water, and he had promised Rob a good story.

To help the policemen, Derek gave an excellent and accurate description of the fat bloke, the girl's stepfather. He also told them that he was almost certain that the owner of the pass card worked for a government department; that information being from a source that he could not disclose. "And I'm telling you to help your search. You deserve to find him. Everyone knows that you blokes do a good job."

This was said with such sincerity that both policemen immediately thought it to be a lie! Although there was no way they could know, the truth became totally distorted when he came to describe the girl. The description he gave would lead them to someone, but certainly not 'Lulubelle': short hair (*not* long, as it actually was), with a slightly-podgy shape (whereas, in reality, she was slim and tall), with a cockney accent (though he'd no idea what her accent was). Derek was afraid that, if the policemen traced her, they might inadvertently lead the stepfather to the girl, and he would hate to feel guilty about that.

Along the way, DC Green had been relieved of baby-sitting duties. ET was now back in the cot asleep, lying on top of the secret papers – guarding them Derek liked to think.

The phone had not yet been handed over though.

"Sorry, being kept for further police checks," they told him, to be returned in a few days, possibly.

By now, Derek was feeling less pressurised, but disappointed not to get back his phone. It was a relief to think that he would probably never ever again see, or hear, of the young lady who had borrowed it, and then lost it.

"We saw a signpost for a hotel up the road. Is it any good?"

Being the only hotel in Newingsworth, the nearest alternatives being the three in Slatterfoot, Derek had no hesitation in telling them that there wasn't a better one in the town. It was late and, as a favour, Sally phoned Thelma to check that there were rooms available for the two detectives. Milne had reached the age of much preferring his own bed, but they'd decided it would be sensible to get their feet up this evening, rather than do the long drive back down to York tonight. Thelma was delighted to have another couple of paying customers using two of the empty rooms.

They left, retaining Derek's phone still in the plastic envelope. They didn't bother with the holdall or its contents, that was lost property basically and nothing to do with them Milne pointed out to Green, though they did take the bar-coded name tag. Green had contacts that could be of help. Out of curiosity he might see if the bar-code was easily traceable. Milne warned him not to get side-tracked.

For now their interview with Toozlethwaite and company was ended. They were making for the hotel. Although not far to go, they used the car. Milne drove back very cautiously along the narrow lane, having been well-warned by Derek of the ease by which a car could land in the stream.

They now were off-duty. No more driving to be done tonight so, having a few drinks before going to bed was the relaxing thing to do. It was Thelma who served them with the whiskies. When she wished them goodnight and left to go to bed, both men had four glasses of the amber fluid lined up on the table.

It was after midnight when they stopped talking shop. Eight empty tumblers remained on the table as they went quietly up the stairs to their rooms.

The text coming through on the suspect phone, still in the plastic bag, was a surprise.

"Derek – Sorry about your London visit being a bit uncomfortable, didn't expect you to be sharing a cell with a couple of smelly drunks. Glad you escaped. You'll be pleased that Sophie says she doesn't mind prison visits. Anyway, when does your case come up? Andy.'

Green was the one who had the package in his pocket. He'd heard the 'ping' of the message just before climbing into bed in his singlet and underpants. Anything coming through on this phone could be a clue related to the robbery – and this one had been sent to Toozlethwaite.

So, he'd been locked up – and escaped! Now that was interesting? Looked like Toozlethwaite wasn't as innocent as he'd made out! And this Sophie and Andy – could they be part of the gang? The boss would have to see this right away, he decided.

Going out into the corridor in his singlet and underpants was the first error; his second, was failing to keep the key-card for the room on his person; the third, was forgetting that it was a fire-safety, self-closing bedroom door; his fourth was turning right to inform DS Milne in the room next door, when he should have turned left.

The young lady, who answered the insistent knock at her door, was a little surprised to see this male visitor, but no more surprised than he was. There was a difference – she was inside her room and able to hurriedly close the door again and phone to reception to complain, whereas, he was in the hotel corridor – standing in singlet and underpants. All he could offer the elderly couple, who came out of the lift and hurried into their own room, was a smile of embarrassment.

When he realised which door he should have been knocking, he tried again. He failed to waken Milne, who'd dropped off into a beautifully deep sleep enhanced by four double whiskies. If the door was knocked any louder he would wake all the other residents, so DC Green's only alternative was to tip-toe furtively down to reception.

"Aye, lass. I'm very sorry aboot that. Leave it with me," Hammy was saying on the phone, not too happy at having been in bed, asleep, and rudely wakened by the phone ringing at the unmanned reception desk. "You're sayin' there is a sex maniac on the loose? I'll deal with it right away, aye, I'll send furr the polis, lass, don't you worry. Noo, just you try tae get away back tae sleep."

He put the phone down, and sighed. "She's just had a bad dream, the poor wee soul," he murmured to himself. "But seein' that I'm up, I might as well hae a cuppa tea."

That is when Green appeared, suddenly and silently, beside him.

"*Whit the fffffu...!*" was the friendly Scottish greeting uttered involuntarily as he pushed this maniac away, turned and grabbed the phone again. He was about to send for the police for sure now – until this policeman, in disguise, apologised and explained.

"I am locked out. Sorry!"

Hammy was never very good with systems, or computers. Not being technically minded, it taxed him severely each time to have to use this new super-duper computerised key-card arrangement. This was far more complicated than the good-old-you-can't-beat-it simple key-on-the-board system. Thelma had insisted on them having it, much to his disgust.

By the time he'd succeeded in giving DC Green access to his room once more, and he, himself, was back cosy and secure beneath the duvet, he had decided – *Thelma will be the one gettin' up if the phone rings again!*

23

Unfortunately, for Derek, having a closer look at the confidential papers was still in 'jobs pending'. Yesterday, he had been delighted to have managed to think fast enough to divert Rob's thoughts away from a particular promise. A scoop it would be, but it couldn't yet be about the Secret Papers, so Rob had been given an alternative. It was pure chance that, after the call from his father-in-law and then Hammy, it had come to him in a flash and Derek could rest at ease, Rob was now on board.

A newspaper campaign was about to begin. It was to be in support of a fledgling protest organisation called 'Slatterfoot and Newingsworth Objectors to the Rail Trail', simplified to the acronym: 'SNORT'.

Sneakily, Derek failed to mention that the name suggested for the protest group had come from Mrs Masterton. Accepting the praise from the other three in the office when it had been aired was easy enough for him; as long as she doesn't find out, he decided and, anyway, further developments were taking place as the four sat at Rob's desk tossing around ideas. Terminology had to be determined.

For starters, agreement was reached that, for all future articles, protestors would be referred to as SNORTERS. A meeting or rally would be called A SNORT and attending a protest meeting would be known as SNORTING. As his home could be affected by the publicised rail route, Derek volunteered to be 'head snorter' in the office and to search out and motivate other snorters into snorting as often as he could. He also promised to obtain as many action photographs of the snorts as possible and, in-house, these would be known as SNORTOGRAPHS. Rob was delighted.

"The Gazette will show the National Dailies how it should be done," he declared, "...providing Derek comes up with the goods!"

It was only when they thought a little deeper about the name chosen that they realised what 'snorting' meant on the street. Did they really want Newingsworth, Slatterfoot and surrounding districts to be publicised by them as 'the perfect home for druggies!' No, of course not, so, it was back to the drawing board...

Something emotive was required to raise public enthusiasm and for a spell it meant gazing into space without one inspirational thought forming for any of them, until Christine broke the silence. It was just possible that it had been found.

"How about: 'We Are Against the Rail Route'?"

That was it – eureka! The name had been decided, and there could be no mistaking the message this time. If they all chipped in, and were fast, they could knock an article together, which could just catch this week's edition, out on Saturday.

The Gazette would be taking up the cudgels – WAARR was being declared!

Although he had been expecting the phone to ring, when it did it startled him. He lifted the receiver and listened without speaking. Was it her? He said nothing and just listened. In the background there was the sound of traffic. This call was coming from a public call box, near a busy road. She was not using the mobile this time.

"Yes, it is me again, Chesney," the female voice said. "It is Chesney, isn't it? I'd hate to talk to the wrong person and divulge your guilty secrets to someone who couldn't be trusted. That would be most unfair, especially when you have money to offer me."

Was she about to give details of what she was claiming to have found, he wondered. She could be bluffing of course. He'd have to take this calmly. She'd need to prove to him that she has seen the documents.

"What do I get for my money then?" he asked. "I can manage without the clothes, you know. It would be cheaper to buy new clothing than have to pay a fortune for the contents of that bag, even though the shirts were new and expensive, you would have to agree."

"Indeed, but you know it is not only clothes that you are about to pay handsomely for."

"Oh, and you are about to tell me what it is then?"

"Now, be sensible, Chesney. Would it be wise to talk in that sort of detail over a public line like this? Anyone could be listening in. It's difficult to know who to trust, I find. Anyway, you know yourself what you have lost."

"Sorry, but I am not proceeding with this."

"Oh well, you had your chance. Obviously the media could get interested. I have a newspaper man wrapped around my little finger, by the way. One call and away we go – headlines!"

He was less confident now. Was she really bluffing or not?

"Wait! You'll have to give me some time to get money together."

"OK. I am a patient girl. You have forty-eight hours. I'll ring you."

And the call was over.

The smells in public phone boxes are absolutely disgusting, and unlikely to have been the work of cats. That was her thought as she pushed the door open and inhaled the pungent alternative – car fumes …then she had another thought; would her little friend help her? Maybe Derek would tell her what the secret is?

She re-entered the box, placed the payment card in the slot and dialled. Her mind being on the next stage must have been why she dialled Derek's number rather than his wife's. She let it ring and only when it went to the answer service did she realise what she'd done. *Wonder where I lost his phone anyway? It's probably ringing-out in a ditch somewhere,* she thought. It was still receiving calls and that was surprising, but it was an expensive one, a good battery probably.

She tried again – the intended number…

"Hello, Sally, could I speak to your dear husband please?"

"Derek!" Sally yelled towards the bathroom, as she grabbed the milk from the cooker just before it boiled over. "This is hot! Quickly, please, get this phone!" *That voice? Surely it's not... Whoops...*

"Hello," he said, drying his hands on his shirt front.

"Hello again Derek," said the voice. It was immediately recognisable to him, and definitely without any sign of the Cockney accent he'd claimed last night.

"Oh, it's you. Look, I am sorry about being late the other day," Derek said, "...and missing you. Did you wait long?"

"Me?" she responded, surprised to be receiving an apology from him. Why did he say that? And then she remembered her decision not to go to the Rail Museum. Only two days ago, but she'd forgotten all about it! *And he is apologising to me? Funny fellow...*

"Oh, that's ok," she replied. Why was he not angry? Could he know she'd chosen not to go because, having already lost it, there was no phone to give him? Of course not! Anyway, I might have just kept it.

"So, you gave it to the police then? Thanks very much. It hasn't been returned to me yet, but it might be, later today. Is that what you phoned to tell me about?"

"Hmm… Yes, yes… It's good isn't it and you'll get it back soon, hmm... yes right, Bye Derek."

But it was *not* good – the police!

Back at York Central Police Station, DS Milne and DC Green were debating current developments. The follow-up to last night's text message had confirmed that Toozlethwaite did in fact spend time in a police cell in London. The Metropolitan Police had been very helpful: wrongful arrest and released without charge. Toozlethwaite had made no mention of that, it was noted! The names 'Andy' and 'Sophie' immediately rang a bell with the contact down south. Due to the story behind the arrest spreading like wildfire through the area, a police constable named Andy 'Pandy' Woodstock was apparently still walking around with a rather red face.

Another two numbers had been traced; one was a local public call-box, the other a landline in London. Nothing much to be gained from knowing the call-box, but further checks were being done on the current location of the landline used.

Copies of the bar-code had also been distributed, this time to various government departments, including DC Green's pal from Police Training College. Obtaining an identification was considered a bit of a long shot but, who could tell? Anything that would permit a forward movement in the robbery investigations would be great.

Chesney Wilfordon was pleased that the trace he'd requested for that mobile number was continuing, especially after being told where the blackmailer's phone now was – in York Police

Station. Why it should be there he did not understand. If the phone did belong to one of the Mansion House staff, as he'd suspected it might, why was it in a police station, unless, of course, the person who owned it was there too?

If the female caller and the phone were in custody, he could forget about any further demands from the amateur blackmailer but that didn't help with the holdall. He still did not know where that was and the female was the only link he had with the bag. Goodness, maybe the police also had the holdall. He hoped not. If they had either in their control, he could be well and truly stymied!

24

That afternoon, when Derek told Alexander what the Gazette was planning to do, he was overjoyed – then disappointed.

"...But that way no one will know until Saturday morning," was his grumble. "They'll only learn about it when they buy their copy of the newspaper. We should be doing something really effective this weekend – getting things moving right away." Fly posting, or distributing leaflets through letterboxes, tomorrow and Saturday morning should be possible, "...and then we could hold a public meeting on Saturday afternoon," he proposed. "A sense of urgency, that's what's needed. Make these buggers in Whitehall sit up and take notice."

"But we'd have to print leaflets and have volunteers to hand them out and deliver them," said Derek, feeling a little bit rushed now.

"You have a printer at the Gazette, I have one at the bank, and Hammy has one at the hotel. What's stopping us? Let's get printing."

A few phone calls later and assistance had been promised from actors, back-stage crew and all the committee members of Slatterfoot Amateur Dramatics Group. Alexander had coerced them successfully into making themselves available for leaflet distribution on Friday. In the morning, Grandad and Granny Smith, and Hammy, would be in action too. They'd position themselves at strategic points in the area to distribute whatever pamphlets were produced. Sam would be working but he promised to generate some reactionary ideas in his classes that could be taken home to the parents. Exactly how he would justify that in the type of classes he took, Mathematics and Physics, was not a question Derek thought worth asking.

Although Rob, as usual, was not overly happy about the cost of a lot of the office paper being used, he agreed that it would be a good thing for the Newingsworth and Slatterfoot community. It would do no harm to the Gazette's circulation, either, if they were seen to be heavily involved, and because the information for this weekend's edition was already at the printers, and Friday was a quiet news day, he accepted that Spider and Christine could help with printing too, if they were willing.

Derek designed the leaflet using the computer graphics, achieving a slightly higher standard than the hand-painted poster he'd created back on his last protest nearly twenty-seven years ago. Was it really so long ago, he thought sadly?

The teams shot off to their respective printers and the mass production began. Hammy was on his own, using the hotel printer. Inevitably, that was bound to fail.

"Och aye, no bother," he'd said cockily.

He did try, and it was alright to begin with – until the paper jammed. Dismantling the machine should not have been necessary. Anyone with any mechanical knowledge would have known that, but he had said he could manage on his own. Thelma was unwell, and confined to bed, otherwise there would not have been a problem. It was his attempt to reassemble the parts that caused it, the pin vanishing under the... Well, wherever it went, he couldn't find it. He jumped back into the car and found it easier being a helper at the Gazette office.

It was bugging Derek but there was little he could do about it at the moment; he still had failed to make time to go through the confidential papers and work out an effective strategy for their use, but, rest assured, it was a weapon that he intended using to full advantage – when he could get round to it!

"Doesn't it feel good to lie down?" was Daisy's comment as she climbed into her side of the bed. Both she and Hector had dozed off in the chair while watching television and, at five to midnight, had awakened feeling dreadful.

It had been a busy day for them, standing on the Main Street for a considerable time distributing leaflets to passers-bye. Daisy was dubious about how many were being read properly and wasn't pleased to see the odd one blowing about in the breeze. It had been a tiring exercise, but at least they had done their bit.

"Now, about tomorrow, don't we have to get permission from Bisko's management if we are going to be outside the store giving them out?" she asked her husband.

It had been a late night for a couple of pensioners who would normally have been asleep by eleven. Reading for a half-hour usually preceded sleep for the pair of them, but not tonight, thank you. Grandad Smith was already reaching for the bedside light-switch.

"N-n-n-n-no, I d-don't think s-so. We aren't intending to be s-s-starting any f-f-f-fights, or lying d-d-down on their p-p-p-pavements are we? H-h-h-handing out l-leaflets, that's all we are d-d-doing, n-no, I d-d-don't .. I... I..."

He stopped suddenly. She turned her head. The poor old devil was exhausted, fast asleep. Granny Smith had to get back out of bed and go round to his side, switch off the light, and tuck the outstretched arm of her husband's under the cover.

Unfortunately, in the darkness of the return journey she banged her toe. She lay feeling sorry for herself for twenty minutes before eventually joining Hector in the land of nod.

Tomorrow, definitely, it would be an early night.

It had been an exhausting evening for Sally. The call from Thelma to say that she was unwell, coming immediately after having prepared an evening meal for ET and herself, meant gulping down the food and hurriedly taking her youngster in his pram, round to the hotel to offer help to her aunt. She would rather not have taken the baby but, with Derek phoning earlier to say he would be home late, there was no alternative.

Thelma was in bed, having been physically sick moments before Sally's arrival, and feeling very sorry for herself. So, straight into action went Sally, changing sheets and helping her aunt clean up. There was little choice. When that was done, though there was no disguising that she was still ill, Thelma claimed to be feeling a bit better. She decided she would stay up. Sally insisted that that was a wrong decision and packed her into bed once more.

Sally's worry was that ET could pick up the bug and, as it was a hotel, it wouldn't do for guests to start falling ill too. The visit did give her the opportunity to see this new girl, Kylie. She looked extremely flighty, in her opinion. This was the one who carefully cared for Derek's clothes, was it? However, with Hammy absent and involved with leaflets, and Thelma bedridden, Kylie had agreed to stay on duty at reception to deal with guests, at least until all were in their rooms. Very considerate of her, Sally decided, so she can't be all bad. Hammy returned about an hour later and that permitted Sally to depart with little Edwin.

As she made the way back home, unusually and in his absence, she gave Derek silent thanks and some credit for ingenuity. Being dark, the return journey to the cottage on foot pushing the pram had been made a bit safer by the addition of two torches taped to the sides of the pram. Having no street lighting along the lane, the twin beams of light, feeble though they were, made the journey a bit less hazardous.

Sally's troubles for the day were not over yet. Little Edwin was a difficult handful when they arrived indoors. Having had his evening routine upset he was rather fractious and for a long while refused to go to sleep without Daddy being there to put him down. He'd had to make do with Mummy. She was very patient and amazed herself at not becoming irritated by the continuous wailing.

It was late when eventually she got into her own bed, exhausted. Derek had still not arrived home and when he did appear, being wakened in the early hours of the morning by a husband who seemed to want to chatter was not her idea of fun.

With eyes screwed up due to his having switched on the main light, she tried to view the clock. It was two am – barely fifteen minutes since she'd dropped off to sleep! "You can't be serious!" she declared grumpily. This was not funny at all!

"Just a quick look," he said.

"No, Derek!"

It wasn't as if he was requesting a roll in the hay, was it? Although, most times these days if he did suggest anything along those lines, it was the same response.

"Look, I haven't yet had a chance to read them properly and I am desperate. Did you look at them tonight, because someone has to," he continued.

"Of course I didn't," she responded, turning over and covering her head.

"Well, I think I will," he said.

Sally sat up and glared at him.

"If you reach under his mattress and waken him, I'll... I'll..."

"I will be very careful," he said.

Moments later, the piercing yells of a distressed baby began again!

25

Crystal sat this morning in a happy frame of mind. Binky had sold the stuff. He still had the money, but there was no need to worry about not getting it. Good old reliable Binky, he was trustworthy. He did a good job. This was the bloke that dad always used, and had never let either of them down. She'd always found him honest as they come regarding dodgy deals, and that was not a claim to be made for many in the business of handling stolen goods.

A keepsake was how she thought of the little trinkets she was accumulating, one from each job she'd ever done. It was an unwise move and she knew it, but… How could she resist?

Before the stuff was delivered to Binky, she had spread all the jewellery from the Mansion on the table and sat gazing at it, and then: *make a choice*, and the ear-rings were removed. Rather special these ones, a circle of gold, with a reverse 'Y' in the centre, and filigree work as a filler. There was a brooch too, it made up the set, but she left that for Binky's disposal.

Life could be so unfair. It was beyond her why people should choose to accumulate so many expensive brooches, and bracelets, and necklaces, decorations that would probably never be worn, when so many people were struggling to pay for food and energy bills. Surely it must prey on their conscience? What she was doing would bring a little balance. At least her action had removed some of their wealth – but would they lose out? No. Insurance would balance it up again for them? They win every time.

One day when I am wealthy, she thought, *I will become a Robina Hood and give all my money to the poor – who am I kidding?*

It was two-thirty in the afternoon when it suddenly occurred to her. *I'll go north and visit Derek Toozlethwaite.* It was too late to achieve anything today and she wished that she'd thought of it earlier. She would visit him, talk about it face to face and find out what he'd actually found. *Dear Chesney obviously had something worth hiding, and Mr Toozlethwaite must know what it is.*

The chance to have had Toozlethwaite hand over the bag had been there. She had missed that and regretted it, but, it wouldn't have worked anyway. How could she have expected him to give her the holdall when she'd had no phone to give him? Anyway, if he knew about the secret papers, would he have given them to her?

Unlikely, whereas, face to face she could do a deal with him now that he knows where his phone is. He might even have it back by now. *I will twist my friend Derek around my little finger, with no difficulty I'm sure. Bet he's never been tempted to blackmail anyone; he is such an innocent. It'd be a novelty for him.* Yes, that's what she'd do and it would be worth it. It shouldn't take long to get from York to Newingsworth – wherever that was.

Finding that very few trains going north from York actually stop at Slatterfoot, was disappointing, but there was one, early in the morning.

It would mean an early rise but would help to put more pressure on Chesney Wilfordon. She knew she couldn't bluff for much longer… *I need the true facts, and yup, I don't care where Newingsworth is – I am going. When I get there, it should be easy enough to find Mister Toozlethwaite. Doesn't everybody know everyone else in a small town?*

It was all 'go' in the Newingsworth Weekly Gazette office that morning, things were buzzing, well... for everyone except Derek. Another bad night meant a less than pleasant day to come.

The phone was sounding yet again.

"Sally here, Christine. Is my dozy husband available to talk to his lovely wife, please?"

"Ah, you will be wishing to speak to our expert in the 'Ladies Fashion and High Finance' section," Christine replied. "One moment please and I'll see if he can become available."

The rather bleary-eyed expert who was performing in Christine's imaginary department of 'Ladies Fashion and High Finance' would rather not have been disturbed.

"Derek," Christine shouted. "Wakey! Wakey! It's the mother of your child!"

"Hi Sweaty," Sally said, trying to show a bit of affection, and expecting a rebuke when she called him that. Surprisingly, none came. "I am phoning to apologise for getting so angry last night, but you really shouldn't have wakened the little fellow. And I am sorry I made you sleep on the settee. I warned you what would happen, and if you'd listened..."

"Sally, I got the message, and thank you," said Derek, in the midst of an extended yawn.

"And shutting poor little Jilly out in the back garden in all that rain this morning before you left; that wasn't a very nice thing to do, was it? There was no need for the bad temper; it was only a little bite. I'm sure she didn't mean it."

"You are quite correct, Sal," he said, *you always are*, and gave another yawn. "Sally, please, I am really very busy."

"Your phone..."

Derek perked up.

"A package has been delivered from York Police that I signed for. It's your phone."

"At long last, thanks for letting me know, Sal. Would you charge it for me please, if you can find the cable, oh, and make a few calls, see that it is working?"

"Right, I'll have to go, but, Derek," she said, "you really should get more sleep," and ended the call.

Derek was already looking forward to that. There were many hours to go before it could happen – standing up, lying down, upside down, who cared, as long as it was sleep – but he knew that when he returned home, after a hard day's work, sleep would only be permitted after taking ET and darling little Jilly out for a stroll.

He'd worry about that later, a lot had to be done in the meantime. He would do it, and do it all – if only he could stop yawning.

It was late before Chesney Wilfordon arrived back at the flat.

"You have three messages," intoned the electronic voice of the answering machine. "First message: received at 2.35pm today."

Next came the human voice, the voice that is never named. He recognised it immediately. "Have an update on your trace. Tried you on your mobile but poor reception it seemed. Target reactivated. The location to be confirmed but looks like an area outside Newingsworth, will pinpoint more accurately later. It is either someone in the New Farmhouse Hotel, or at a cottage named Toozlethwaite Manor. Will confirm ASAP."

"Please press one to listen again, two to store, three to..." His brain always switched off when the electronics reached this part. "Second message: received at 4.15pm today..."

He expected it to be more detail of the trace, but it wasn't.

"This is a message from York Police for Mr Chesney Wilfordon. My name is DC Green. We have reason to believe that you have lost a leather holdall. We are not in the habit of searching for owners and returning lost property but, as you had an identity pass in the bag, we have been able to identify it as your property. It has not been handed into our system. It is being retained by the person who found it who is aware that we are attempting to find the owner and is expecting you to collect it from him at Toozlethwaite Manor, a cottage on the outskirts of Newingsworth. The gentleman is a Mr Toozlethwaite, Derek Toozlethwaite. No doubt you will consider rewarding this gent, sir. If you have any difficulties I can be contacted at York Police Station during normal hours."

Well, this was a big step forward.

"Press one if..." Get on with it! "...Third message: received at 7.15pm today," and, as anticipated, it was the unnameable voice again. "Confirmation as promised. The phone is at Toozlethwaite Manor. The satnav location is..."

Ah-ha! The holdall, had it been found or stolen at the railway station, he was still undecided, but if the messages are being sent from this Toozlethwaite's phone, and he has the holdall, then the documents are probably in his possession, but it was a female who'd phoned...? Did he have a partner?

Chesney noted the postcode for his GPS. It would be an early start tomorrow and he could look forward to a long drive.

Detective Constable Green was well-appreciated by his boss: conscientious, long-serving even though still young, dedicated – and good with babies, as proved on the visit to Newingsworth. When that lad decided to do something, he did it properly: for example – his recent success, identifying the owner of the bar-coded pass. It had been with a great deal of help of an associate from his days at the Police Training College, a contact that DS Milne didn't want to know about – involving a bit of unorthodox searching that he was unable to authorise.

Chasing criminals was the daily task. Returning lost property had to remain a 'one off', but, no matter, Milne had to give the lad his due. He'd done well.

It was also recognised by his sergeant that Green had a phenomenal memory for names and phone numbers. He envied him that skill. For Milne, unless information had been added to his notebook there was no chance of it being used. Today was an example of the way the DC's mind functioned.

As Green left the message on Chesney Wilfordon's home phone, a combination of the number and the name set his unusual memory tricks kicking into action! That number had been on Toozlethwaite's phone, the one found at the Mansion House robbery and he'd remembered that contact had been made between Toozlethwaite and Wilfordon.

Out of hours it may have been but, at this minute, Milne and Green were sitting together talking shop. Which direction to take Green's new knowledge was in the process of being discussed, a discussion taking place in the more relaxed atmosphere of the local pub because this lad deserved a pint and it was Milne's treat. Milne was hoping that, with any luck, and out of the blue, his constable would come up with another gem and move the case forward, for he was stumped.

A second pint was about to be ordered – brains need lubricating!

26

Every day at Bisko's was a busy one and a lot of people passed through the automatic doors during the working hours of this supermarket. Not so many visitors in the middle of the night though; the store never actually closed but tended to be used only in desperation in the wee small hours, but, that is an irrelevant fact. We are outside the store on Saturday morning, which, by the customer count, was about as busy as it gets.

Bisko's was situated not far from the centre of the town, though not actually on the main street. It sat adjacent to a busy thoroughfare, and was approachable from both directions. The almost constant movement of vehicles in and out of the large car park was an indicator that very few visitors came on foot, and for those who came by car it was a rare occasion to be lucky and land with a parking place close to the entrance.

For visitors using a less popular mode of transport, that is to say, a scooter, it was possible to park almost at the entrance. This gave Hector a feeling of superiority.

His shiny, bright red, Vespa 125cc GTS Super Sport Scooter was his pride and joy, obtained only a couple of years ago, an upgrade from the squeaky ancient bicycle he'd owned for aeons. It had been a gift from Daisy, compensation for the suffering he put up with when she had been a local radio personality, and the scooter was paid for from her earnings.

"Why have a c-c-c-car and have to search for a sp-sp-space and then have to w-w-w-walk a long way? With the s-s-s-scooter you can p-p-p-park outside the door, beside the b-b-b-b-big b-b-b-b-bikes – like I do?"

Being fully retired, Hector had the freedom to do whatever he wanted whenever he wanted, within reason.

For Daisy, though well past retiring age, it was a little different. Nowadays, once-a-week, on Wednesdays, she was an 'Agony Aunt' on *Little Radio fm*, but only for a short presentation, jokily responding to questions from her listeners. She'd come here as 'pillion' this morning with Hector, to do a special task. Travelling as a passenger on his scooter was tolerated by her, but not liked. At her age, now being a great-granny, holding on for grim death at the corners definitely qualified her for a place in her very own 'Agony Stakes'.

There was space to park this morning and Hector did so with confidence. Sitting alongside the large, powerful motorbikes made him feel part of the gang – the Newingsworth Hell's Angels. Though Hector didn't realise it, the other week he'd frightened the life out of one of these tough bikers in the leather gear, by asking if there was any chance of his becoming a member. As a consequence, since, they made sure they kept out of his way. No matter, it was a great parking place...

The helmets were removed and hung on the scooter. The leaflets were carried in Daisy's shopping bag, which had been zipped up and worn like a haversack. A public meeting of WAARR was planned to be held here this afternoon, Saturday, at two pm in Bisko's car park.

Daisy was feeling tense. She was disturbed about publicising the affair in this way without having first asked permission of Bisko's. It had been a novelty yesterday, wandering up and down the Main Street handing out the leaflets, but it hadn't been congested like this. Last night she'd been lying in bed worrying and had slept badly. Feeling very tired didn't help the nervousness. The thought of standing face to face with people who'd be reluctant to get involved, terrified her. These people would be there to shop, she concluded last night, and will not be happy to be harangued by a couple of old codgers. She had been on the verge of refusing to accompany Hector today, but, here she was.

It was her civic duty to help spread the word, she'd eventually decided. A stand would have to be made on behalf of the townships and, as a public spirited grandmother, she would do her duty. As long as her producer made no objection, she was determined to slip in a comment on her next radio spot.

Generally in her experience as a recipient, partly confirmed yesterday in the High Street, if leaflets were distributed to the public of Newingsworth, there was little interest shown in the content. The only purpose they tended to serve was to create more rubbish for refuse collection but, to her surprise, today was different.

Maybe it was because yesterday was a dull, miserable day. Today it was sunny and pleasant. Obviously too, these people had read last Sunday's papers and were aware that the rail link could affect them. They were concerned rather than dismissive. What they appeared to be delighted about was that someone was inclined to take action, and this morning they were happy to stop and talk about it.

"When did you say the meeting is? Here, in this car park? Right..."

"It's always the same, the damn government or the council; always one or the other, thinking and deciding that they know best again!"

"I like the name. WAARR! Yes, that's good. See you later then."

"Ridiculous. We put the buggers into office to do what we want, and this was never on the cards! Good on you mate for doing this, about time somebody did something!"

"Who's organising this, a small group, is it? Are you from the National Front? No? It'll be UKIP then. No? The Gazette! Oh, yea, that guy – you know him – Toozlethwaite, he writes stories in that paper and ...he's your grandson? ...Tell him he is doing a grand job. I bought his book you know..."

"WAARR. What does it stand for? We Are Against... Yea, I like that."

"You are doing a great job. It's a bloody shame what they're proposing. Of course I'll be back. What time? Two-o'clock? Right, see ya!"

To some people it was fresh news.

"What? They are going to close the station? So what happens to...? No, they can't just... Yes, I'll be there, don't you worry!"

Someone had expected the hand-out to be for something else. "Oh, it's not a sale of cheap carpets then. That's what the bloke was doing last week. He got chased by Security. Hope you are ok."

Daisy smiled nervously, and glanced at Hector.

"Yea," he said. "B-b-b-b-but we are n-n-n-not worried, are we, D-D-D-Daisy?"

That person left but, by now, there was a curious crowd all around them, some wondering what it was about, and others with the leaflet in their hands getting riled about it and arguing the pros and cons. Others were customers simply trying to enter or leave the store. Many were pushing the filled trolleys and finding their access blocked by a mass of bodies.

"Hector, shouldn't we move?" suggested Daisy.

"Y-yea, let's d-d-do that, b-b-b-but, c-c-c-c-can we?"

They were hemmed in, and would have to get physical if they hoped to change position. That was, until the police arrived. It was that time of the morning, the sandwich collection, the usual routine, a list of essentials to be carried by two uniformed constables each day in a police vehicle. Pre-packed sandwiches, which had to be collected and returned, post-haste, and delivered back at the station to suit the various rest breaks as they occurred. It happened every day, like clockwork, timed to the minute – but not today. Today they couldn't get easy access, they couldn't get *any* access.

A path was cleared as the Uniforms shouldered their way into the crowd. Who, or what, was causing the mayhem? That was their question ...and there was the answer – squashed in the middle was the elderly couple, holding leaflets.

"Do you have permission from the store manager for this?" the tall one looked down at Hector, who shrank a little in the police presence.

"N-n-n-n-n..." was all he managed to produce.

"Because causing mayhem, or inciting a riot, or gathering on the Bisko car park and blocking the entrance without permission, especially when police officers are collecting sandwiches, is a very serious misdemeanour, you know," tall fellow continued.

He felt a bit sorry for appearing a threat to this obviously harmless old fellow and, presumably, his wife. They'd be distributing these leaflets probably on behalf of a charity, he decided, and harmless.

"Clear the door please," the other was demanding of the mob.

"But have you seen this?" said one of the crowd, and handed the leaflet to the policeman.

It was given a quick glance, which picked out only one word – WAARR. He looked at the couple handing out the pieces of paper. They didn't look the type to cause trouble, did they? Rather old to be anarchists? As part of the generation that took delight in criticising youngsters for lacking the ability to spell, they were not setting a very good example. WAARR! Seriously wrong! Then he looked closer at the printed document.

"Hey, Geordie, do you see what this is?" he shouted to his mate. "It's that ruddy rail route. They are trying to start a campaign against it. All the houses in my father's street, including his, are going to be demolished because of this."

"Oh well, that's different," said Geordie, the tall one. "Hey, you are doing a great job here." He patted Hector's head.

"G-g-g-g-gerroff," Hectored spluttered, suddenly feeling rather embarrassed at the attention and the praise, but niggled at being patronised by someone so tall.

"Just all move back a bit then please," Geordie's pal requested, "and keep the door clear. Geordie, we'll get lynched if we don't get these sandwiches back to the station. See you all later. Two o'clock then. We'll be here."

The relief felt by Hector and Daisy at not being carted off was spoiled by the appearance of the Store Manager and his Security Man. They were coming towards them.

"Let's vanish," Daisy said to her husband, grabbing his sleeve and pulling, but they weren't quick enough.

"Ah, it's Mrs Smith, isn't it? I remember we met a while ago," said the store manager. Daisy couldn't remember his name but recognised the man. She had hoped that he would have forgotten the incident with the kettle. That had been an awkward meeting. "...And you are Mister Smith I presume." He shook Hector's hand. "Muriel phoned and said you would be here this morning. I didn't think you'd gather quite such a crowd. Well done."

Hector and Daisy had both forgotten that Muriel worked here. She had done so for a long while, although not at weekends. Being the cashier in a big place like this obviously carried some weight, because the phone call to her boss, being for a very worthy reason, had meant immediate approval of the use of the car-park, both for distributing leaflets and the meeting that was to follow. It would have eased Daisy's mind a bit if they'd known that earlier.

"You will be aware no doubt that we will be closing the store for the time that the meeting is planned." They weren't but *wow*, the town had never reacted like this before, and it seemed that word was travelling fast.

27

Alighting at Slatterfoot Station, Crystal, looking at a map of the area on the station wall, immediately realised the error in her thinking. It showed two towns, almost linked together but not quite, Slatterfoot and Newingsworth. The population at the last census was also recorded. That set her back a little.

She came out of the station exit to be faced by masses of buildings that helped justify the population figures and brought it home to her. Where was the village she'd anticipated? It wasn't at all the sleepy little place that she had imagined.

How would she be able to find Derek Toozlethwaite in over fifteen-thousand people?

Goodness, what did she know about him, other than him having something that she would like to have? Her own mobile was in her pocket. Should she try ringing his number? Of course, that would only be of use if the police had returned the phone to him. It seemed wise not to try, just in case. A wry smile appeared on her face at that thought – imagine her asking the police for help!

She was still annoyed at herself for having slipped up and been careless on that last job. Leaving the Toozlethwaite phone behind was pathetic. Whatever would Poppa think? No, he wouldn't get to know. That would be something she would definitely not be telling him on the next prison visit.

What about ringing the wife's mobile? And, that's what she did, but, before it connected, she quickly changed her mind and cut off the call. That was being silly. From her memory of the previous conversations, perhaps his soul mate would not be the best person to ask where they live. I could just ask around if anyone knows him.

He has a very unusual surname. If I simply pick on someone, but she hesitated... Come on ...in a big place like this – what chance is there? None! Only his friends would be able to help and that sort of coincidence is unlikely.

She was famished and should have bought some food on the train – too late now. Could she find a cafe, have some food, and then walk about looking for him?

It's half-past-one. Where should she start? Damn! This is Slatterfoot. How stupid! He lives in Newingsworth but not even knowing which direction that was she took a taxi.

"Newingsworth, please," she said as she jumped into the first in the rank.

"Right luvv, whereabouts?"

"Anywhere. I am actually looking for someone but I don't know where he lives."

"So, I just drive around until you spot 'im?" he said, giving her a quizzical look. "Got plenty cash, dearie?"

"Not really."

"D'you know what he looks like?" and there was a hint of sarcasm there.

"C'mon, d'you think I am stupid?" she replied indignantly

He didn't reply.

"You don't know Derek Toozlethwaite, by any chance I suppose," she said sheepishly, expecting another sarcastic comment.

"Nooo, don't know him, know *of* 'im. Know where he'll be too."

"What? You do? Honest?"

He nodded.

"I think I am falling in love with you," she beamed.

"Fine," he grinned, "...as long as m'wife don't find out."

Straight to Bisko's the taxi went and out she got. Crystal paid him generously, but, love was forgotten when she saw the crowd milling about in this large supermarket's car park. On leaving the taxi she had told herself that she was successfully whittling the search down to a more manageable proportion – she had to tell herself something to bolster her confidence, but, as she looked at the mass of faces, this was an almost impossible task.

It was the thought of missing out on a large sum of money that spurred her on. She would just have to find him – and soon. The phone call to Mister Chesney Wilfordon would have to be made tonight. Anyway, the taxi driver who'd brought her here knew that Derek Toozlethwaite was somewhere amongst this crowd of hundreds – and he was confident too.

She'd just have to look. At least, he said he knew...

Derek was pleased to have a friend at *Little Radio fm*. It was useful at times, especially when the friend was the boss. Graham 'Curly' Stockman did him proud by including the news of the proposed Saturday meeting in this morning's local activities section at eight am. The bulletin included some words from Derek explaining the purpose, and, as the morning progressed, the snippet was repeated on each half-hour.

Local radio is wonderful, Derek admitted to himself looking at the turnout – *what an amazing result!*

Everyone had their own reasons for getting involved, he was learning. Being affected or just knowing someone who was going to be affected by the sweeping proposals seemed a great motivator. Curly was no different. He wasn't sure, but he suspected that his home could be affected and, was willing to help in any way he could, without actually getting over-committed in the protest organisation.

Derek had been nominated by the group to be spokesperson. Ideas for a brief interview on radio had had to be thought up so there hadn't been much sleep for him last night but it had been worth it. A lot of people listened to *Little Radio fm* on Saturday mornings, and what he said must have done the trick.

Emphasis had been on this being a peaceful rebellion, essential to be seen and heard by those in authority as being a driving force for change, and representative of a large community. "A good turn-out is essential," Derek told them over the air waves, so that the authorities could see how all in this part of the country were reacting, and that the cause was being recognised as having ample justification. And, was his plea heard? It sure was! What a response!

Bisko's, thanks to his mother-in-law, had been very obliging. Permitting a meeting to be held in the car-park, and the manager's offer to provide microphone and loudspeaker facilities was very much appreciated. Bisko's stacker truck had even been used to place a number of old wooden pallets together to form a makeshift platform.

On top of that, the store being closed for the duration of the meeting was a great deal more than the committee could have hoped. Now, whether that had been a wise move by the store manager only time would tell. At a later date, if the day's takings were found to be dramatically down, head office would be asking some serious questions of Steven Tomkins.

Steven was banking on a great number of people attending the meeting and then drifting naturally into the store afterwards to make purchases. He sincerely hoped that they would. If not, at the almost inevitable disciplinary hearing, that being given as the reason for his decision might sound somewhat weak. It was a tough company to work for. Losing any chance of profit was severely frowned upon, but this had been done in the best interest of the community and of course, in the long run, to benefit the company: yes, that's what he would tell them.

Apprehension! That was Derek's mood as he stood beside the stack of pallets. As spokesperson, this could be either a glory moment, or an embarrassing failure. The crowd was waiting with expectations of great things. There, before him, milling around, were the good citizens of Newingsworth, Slatterfoot and surrounding districts, all of whom he hoped were in favour of WAARR. They had appeared in their masses – and it was frightening the life out of him. It was one thing having notes and sitting in a comfortable radio studio with only an interviewer and technician – quite different facing a mob!

Some comfort came from the support group being around him They, the ones who'd decided that he would be spokesperson, were laughing and chattering with happy abandonment, but they weren't about to stand up and make fools of themselves. They could afford to feel carefree.

"You'll be fine, Sweaty," said the voice at his shoulder. At least his wife was being supportive. She had brought ET with her in a recently purchased, fancy papoose baby-carrier, but, she wasn't carrying him now. "Ooh, you are making my shoulders sore, little one," she'd said, loudly enough to make

Hector feel he should be assisting. *If only he'd been standing farther away,* was his first thought but he and ET were pals, so a swop had occurred. The carrier and Baby Edwin were now hanging around Hector's neck. He was a little worried though; he wasn't at all sure how long he would be capable of supporting his great-grandson like this without falling over.

Wisely, Sam and Angie had brought their little Annabel in her pram. Alexander, Muriel, Spider and Christine were huddled together and laughing, hearing one of Spider's spicier jokes, Derek suspected.

Thelma was still unwell but out of bed and keeping an eye on hotel activities. Kylie had volunteered to be there too, working on her rest day to help Thelma. They would have to manage without Mr Hamish Macintosh.

Hammy was here at Bisko's, bustling around, as a vital part of the support group – at least he liked to think so. At the moment he was up on the pallets checking the sound equipment. Derek was glad Hammy was doing it. Not only was he ensuring the speakers would work when required, it was a good test of the strength of old pallets – if they can hold Hammy's weight...

Millie had just arrived and made her presence known by going round the group, giving all and sundry, double cheek-kisses – it was plain that for his mother it was "absolutely wonderful.." to see everyone again – although she'd seen most of them only yesterday.

Although it appeared that Hammy was the expert, when Bisko's generously offered their use this morning, it was actually Curly who came along personally to help set up the loudspeaker equipment. Anticipating that more than just half-a-dozen people would be attending was being proved correct and obviously amplification was essential or the message could be lost.

Hammy had watched over Curly's shoulder as the clever stuff was done earlier because the Scotsman lived in hope that one day he would understand how these things functioned. He was certainly not an expert but, a moment of glory was about to come for him. He was about to prove that the system worked.

"One, two... One, two... One, two," he said, and gave the microphone a few perfunctory taps – as you do – and stepped back satisfied, with a nod to the 'leader'.

"Aye, that'll be braw for ye now," he told Derek, and then in a moment of compassion added, "Well, Sunshine, are you ready? Ye're big moment, eh?"

Derek nodded, and smiled weakly. Inside, his stomach was feeling decidedly unready but, this was it!

"Hullo there!" shouted Hammy, and the speakers boomed out beautifully. "It's braw that so many of you were bothered to come oot here the day, but as my guid friend will explain, it is for a very worthy cause. So without any more bletherin' from me, I'll introduce oor leader, oor man o' WAARR, so tae speak," he was chuffed at that bit, he'd just thought of it, "*Sweaty ...Toozlethwaite – oh sorry... I meant – Derek!*" and as he clambered down the pallet steps, he avoided looking the man o' WAARR in the eye.

"Some things just come oot automatically," he mumbled as an apology.

The name Sweaty was not new to those who knew Derek: pals at school that he'd grown up with, for example, and folk he'd worked beside. They were here. Big grins on faces were dotted about in the crowd: young men with spouses, girlfriends and families that knew him of old. A lot of them had never moved away and, naturally, were here in support.

As Derek climbed the pallet steps, glad that his little group was close to him, Sally and the others began clapping their hands and chanting.

"*De-rek – De-rek – De-rek – De-rek...*"

It started quietly but grew as those around began to join in. His school pals didn't. They began their own chant, which began to spread at a much faster rate than the other and, in consequence, became much louder.

"*Swea-ty – Swea-ty – Swea-ty – Swea-ty...*"

The new chant drowned out the original until everyone in the crowd was happily singing "*Swea-ty – Swea-ty...*"

Derek's apprehension was gone, totally forgotten. This was an awesome moment. He was famous, and among his own people, and no, of course they weren't doing this to mock him. *Thank you Hammy*, he thought to himself. *This is a crowd that is united in a common cause – even if it is only a stupid old nickname.*

He would have preferred it though, if it had been... DEREK!

28

How could she have been so stupid as to think she would ever find one individual in this crowd? She was right at the back and something was happening at the front. Everyone was facing that direction, but she'd no idea what it was. She couldn't even see over the heads.

"What's all this about?" she asked the nearest person, a woman holding an empty shopping bag.

"We're here to support WAARR," was the response. "You're here for your shopping then, I suppose, dearie. Did you not know the store was to be closed for the duration of the meeting? Did you want to buy a lot?"

"What?"

"Just hang around. They'll be opening again in a short while."

"Right," said Crystal, still mystified.

That's when someone appeared at the front of the crowd, higher than everyone else that she could actually see, at a microphone, and he started talking, in a strange accent. She had difficulty making out what he announced, but, suddenly, there he was, rising into her view, the guy she was looking for. Now, how lucky was that?

"*Swea-ty – Swea-ty – Swea-ty...*" the crowd was chanting.

What's going on, she wondered? He said his name was Derek, didn't he?

She began to squeeze her way into the crowd and a bit closer to the front. He had started talking. She could see him quite clearly now. It definitely was him.

"Friends..." he said, holding his hands up as if he was about to bless the crowd.

The chanting gradually died away. He waited patiently and confidently.

"Friends, it is great to see such a magnificent turnout; each one of us here to support the WAARR effort."

There was a cheer. He smiled.

"We are not going to sit around and be bullied into giving up our homes, and our land, and our way of life, just because people who live far away have made decisions that affect us but not them, are we? Are we willing to do that? Well, are we?"

There was a reaction of "Nooo...." but not loud enough it appeared He was obviously going to work the crowd. He repeated the question, but a little louder, "*Are we?*"

The crowd response was much stronger in reply this time, "NOOOO..."

"...Of course not, and do we know who is making these decisions? No, of course we do not; faceless mandarins who hide in government offices, delighting in their manipulating of the masses. *Do we want to know who they are?*"

He paused and waited for the answer, and back it came immediately, "YESSSS..."

"...*And make them answerable to us?*" he thundered.

"YESSSSS..."

This was a very different fellow to the one she met on the train. There was power in his voice, he knew what he was doing, and he was in control of this crowd...

"The first thing we must do; and I emphasise it is 'WE' must do, is to create a petition; a petition that will be handed

175

to our member of parliament, demanding that he comes back to us with the names of whoever it is that has created this monstrosity of a plan to decimate this community we live in. We want to sit down, face to face with these people, and talk seriously about our future plans. To tell him, or them, what is acceptable to us. For many of us, it is a land that we have grown up in – and *lovvvvve*."

There was a loud cheer at that.

"We want our children growing up to enjoy the same freedoms that we have had. To have the choice and freedom to roam the countryside as we have for such a long time; a countryside that is now threatened to be taken from us. Our homes are threatened …homes where we want our kids to be able to continue to use their Wi-Fi, and their broadband, and to play their computer games, without the fear of the house being demolished while they are sitting there concentrating; all because of a rail track that no-one wants. We must do this for those who come after us. We are fighting for *their* future!"

Another cheer!

Crystal noticed that many of the people around her had tears in their eyes. Every word being said was being taken to heart, and on he went. "So, are we all going to stand together? Will you all be signing the petition? Are we all in support of WAARR?"

There was a massive cheer of "YESSSS..." and the chanting began again, this time it was "*WAARR, WAARR, we are going to WAARR, WAARR...*"

"Thank you my friends," he held up his arms, as if to give a public blessing again. "See you all here again next Saturday."

There was loud cheer once more and that was it. People were dispersing, a lot of them moving in the direction of the reopened supermarket doors and crowding inside. Crystal guessed it could be the manager she could see, standing at the side of the doorway with his arms folded and a self-satisfied look on his face. No tears in his eyes; he seemed happy enough.

Crystal struggled to move against the flow of bodies as she made her way towards the temporary platform. She could see the older man, the one who spoke first and had the funny accent, he was attempting to unplug the equipment but, as he was doing this, he must have lost balance. His arms flew up and he vanished from view.

"What the... Owww!"

The cry reached her. Those coming towards her stopped and turned round to see what had happened. The old fellow seemed to be alright, he was straightening up again. It was the body on the ground who'd let out the shout. Crystal recognised him. It was Derek.

Now, that was more like the guy she was hoping to find – the kind of guy that people sat on. Had it been accidental, the old fellow falling on him, or was Derek being the hero, trying to catch him?

"Oh! Ouch! Oh, oh..." he was saying as he struggled to get up. "What the heck were you doing Hammy? You could have killed me!"

"It wasn't meant, you dunderheed! It was these rotten damn pallets. I told ye before that they were dangerous, but would ye listen tae me? Would ye? No, you wouldnae!"

The crowd began to disperse again, but the serious looks on faces had become grins. To Crystal, they seemed to be thinking that it was good to finish off the day with a bit of slapstick. As she got closer she could see that a strap on one of the pallets had broken, but with everyone safely on their feet again, the only damage was to the pallets, oh ...and Derek!

Only a small group now stood beside the makeshift platform. All others were either on their way home, having clambered into vehicles, or still on the premises and squashed into the supermarket aisles.

Crystal was undecided. What should she do? Just go up to him and ask for the holdall, the thing she'd come all this way for, or follow him at a distance, to his home, or wherever he goes? Get him on his own, maybe? As she stood dithering, it was Derek who looked up and across at her. He blinked and then frowned, unsure today after seeing so many new faces.

I should know this person? And then he twigged: *Lulubelle!*

29

"What are you doing here? Look everyone," said Derek, a bit flustered in his surprise. "This is the young lady I met on the train; the one with the dreadful step-father – I helped her escape from him. She borrowed my phone too; her name is Lulubelle."

"No, it's not," said Crystal, giving a mock shake of the head. "Where did you get that idea from? That's a silly name. Didn't I tell you? It's C..." There was a pause. Would it be wiser perhaps to be someone else? "...It's *Katy*, of course."

"Of course it is," Sally chipped in, "and I must have misheard you." She was sounding a tiny bit sarcastic, "And I am Sally, the person who was told that silly name – by *you*." There was a cold smile on Sally's face that Derek chose to ignore and hoped Katy hadn't seen. Well, Sally could get a bit odd herself, at times; *at least, we know the girl's correct name now ...yes, it's Katy,* he told himself,.

Crystal gave a slightly strained smile to Sally in return.

"Nice to see you here supporting us," said Derek. "I didn't know you were in the district. Last I knew you were in York – when I missed you."

Hammy was helping Curly dismantle the loudspeaker system, being very careful this time where he placed his feet. He did not want to fall again on top of the man of WAARR, but even more important was that the mike and speakers were dismantled safely. If the equipment was damaged there would be no chance of having the use of the stuff again next week. Sam helped by lifting the parts to ground level, so that they could fall no farther, while at the same time watching and being ready to jump clear if Hammy were to topple again.

"I came for the holdall," said Crystal.

"Oh, right, Katy," said Derek. He tried not to show his surprise. It was strange, her just appearing out of the blue like this. She'd said she couldn't afford the train fare to return his phone and yet she'd travelled up to collect a bag for her father-in-law, someone she said she hated? What had changed? Had they made up? Was she going to return the bag to him? More to the point, how would he find out who the man was if he gave it to her?

The confidential documents – he needed to know where they came from if he wanted to use them, but hadn't had a chance to read them in proper detail... Of course, he could give her the bag but not the documents. The owner would naturally want them back when he realised they were missing and have to contact him …then he'd find out where they came from. *Yes, smart one, Derek!*

"...Do you have it with you?" she asked hopefully.

He had almost fallen asleep standing there, thinking, but with a shudder, he realised where he was and blinked. "Have what? …Oh yes, the holdall. Of course not, it's back at the cottage. We'll be going back there in minute if you want to come with us."

A very exhausted Hector staggered across with Edwin still in the papoose carrier and still hanging on his shoulders. He took great satisfaction in transferring the little fellow over to Daddy. Having done so, he straightened up, trying not to show the agony, and silently praying that Edwin would soon learn to walk …*baby-carrying was a young person's game, thank you very much.*

"Oh, how lovely," said Crystal, touching Edwin's cheek, "this will be ET I guess, and what a lovely little girl she is too."

"He's a boy!" said Sally sharply.

When asked by Derek if it would be possible for Katy to get a lift back in his vehicle with them, Hammy stopped moving a pallet, and nodded.

"Och, of course, we can always make room for a bonnie wee lassie," he said, admiring the view, and then, with the loss of concentration, managed to jam his thumb between pallets. "Ah, ah, ah... Bugger!" spluttered out of his mouth, as he struggled to release it. He prised it loose and stood sucking it as the fork-lift driver brought over his truck and took the palletised sound-equipment back inside. Dismantling the platform and removing the pallets would be next.

Hammy stood well back this time – experience told him – pallets really are dangerous!

With the area cleared they were about to climb into his vehicle when they heard a shout. It was Sam. Owning an old banger had its downside, especially when your wife and baby are sitting inside being critical, at least that's what Sam felt. Again, the blasted thing was refusing to start. Thankfully for Sam, though they had to be persuaded, Derek, Alexander and Spider were still around to help.

Hector was delighted that the scooter started into action right away. He could leave them to it. With Daisy hanging on for grim death as usual, he passed the others, now pushing unsuccessfully. He tried a cheery wave but, due to the sharp pain in his shoulders, both the wave and the smile were fleeting. It took combined muscle and positive thought-waves to move the car. It was touch and go and they'd almost reached the exit when, at last, the engine kicked-in; off went

Sam and family leaving a rather embarrassing smoke trail and the pushers, who faced a long walk back across the large car park.

Many of the others, including Alexander and Muriel had come by bike, and were gradually dispersing. Millie, who had arrived grandly in a taxi, had cadged a lift earlier from a fellow American, there out of curiosity who happened to be standing near her in the crowd.

After today's excessive mental and physical exertions, sitting back in Hammy's car was a luxury for Derek. The euphoric sensation he'd experienced on the platform was leaving him. He felt drained. There was sparse conversation inside the car, although Hammy seemed to want to chatter.

"Well, Sweaty, what are the chances of wee ET still havin' Toozlethwaite Manor to live in when he's old and grey like me, eh? It's some fight ye're takin' on. You are goin' to have to work really hard at this if you are to stop the railway line bein' here instead – we'll help ye of course!"

Derek gave a sad grin in response but said nothing.

"...But havin' a lovin' wife beside you, to back you up in everythin', must make it that much easier."

There was no response from Sally. She grimaced. Sometimes it felt a strain trying to be Derek's supportive, loving and trusting wife. Hammy turned his attention to Crystal.

"...An' what are ye called again lass? It was Katy, was it not?" asked Hammy. "But you've not really come up all the way from York the day, have ye noo?"

Crystal appreciated that the question was addressed to her, but what was this man actually saying? She looked out of the window and pretended she hadn't heard.

The vibes coming at her from another place in the backseat were not good, she sensed. *Sally has not taken kindly to me, but then again*, she decided, *I am not wild about Sally*. Derek, in the front seat, appeared to have fallen asleep. ET, in his car-seat, was trying to communicate, but no one appeared to care.

Though it wasn't a long journey from Bisko's to Toozlethwaite Manor, for Crystal it seemed like forever.

Along the lane drove Hammy, cautiously as usual, having once found his way into the stream and not liked it. He let them out at the cottage gate and went back along the lane, turning right at the end to the hotel. Was Thelma well now, he wondered? He hoped she hadn't a lot of tasks lined up for him – he had a sore thumb!

What struck Crystal firstly, standing at the front door of Toozlethwaite Manor, was the size of the place. The 'Manor', pleasant looking as it was and obviously in attractive countryside, was still only a cottage. She had expected something considerably grander and put the choice of name down to some idiot having had some crazy delusion of grandeur.

Secondly, the procedure for entry was so quaint! Lift the corner of the mat, pick up the key and turn the lock! Why bother locking it in the first place? You wouldn't do that in York – no way! Ah, a dog has begun to bark! That's why they don't have to bother. Having an Alsatian or a Dalmatian was a fine deterrent for burglars.

Derek, having opened the door, stepped back and permitted Sally, still carrying baby Edwin, to enter, followed by Crystal. The dog continued barking – it was after all a poodle! The odd thing was that it ignored Sally, the baby and Crystal, an unknown visitor but went straight for Derek's ankles, probably not happy to have been left alone at home. Crystal could see, as he fended it off, that it was plainly not for the first time because he reached over to the dresser, donned a pair of gloves, and grabbed the dog. It ended up in the back garden where it continued yelping. It hadn't even noticed her apparently...

"Would you like to join us for a meal?" Sally asked, hoping the visitor would say no.

"That would be lovely," was the answer.

"Oh" said Sally. She went into the bedroom to leave a reasonably content ET in the cot to play with his toys while she considered what sort of a meal could be conjured out of the meagre amount of food in the house. This Lulubelle, or rather, Katy appearing out of the blue had completely thrown her. Tonight was going to have been some ready-made meals bought in Bisko's after the meeting, but that had been completely forgotten.

As she came out of the bedroom Derek was fetching the holdall from behind the settee. He placed it at the door. It wouldn't be forgotten that way.

"Are you putting in the...?" asked Sally knowingly, on her way back to the kitchen.

"Oh, no, no, no," replied Derek, smiling over nonchalantly at the seated Katy.

"No sign of your phone yet – the police still got it?" said Katy.

"Oh, I've got it again, thank you. It arrived by post. It was a good idea to give it to them, saved on postage for you. I thought it was gone forever. Sorry for being too late to catch you at the museum. To be honest, I thought you might have stolen it."

"Oh Derek, how could you, after all the help you gave me. Do you really think I could stoop to that? Shame on you..."

He wished he hadn't said it now. Imagine accusing her. However, he couldn't stand chatting, jobs required his attention. Sally was dealing with food in the kitchen, so, the most enjoyable task of changing ET's nappy prior to having food, belonged to Derek. He excused himself and joined ET in the bedroom.

Crystal, left alone, surveyed the room; anything worth pinching? Not really. She thought of her last job, the Mansion House ...now that was some place. Jewellery, paintings, pieces of sculpture, furniture – it had the lot. It was a pleasant thought – to have helped herself to a little of it.

Outside, Jilly continued howling. The noise of that horrible little poodle made Crystal realise something – when she cased a joint she'd never thought to check if a dog might be inside the premises. *That was something to note: a little bit of learning*. She'd remember that for the future!

Looking around this place, it was ...comfy! That was as much as she could say about it, and, to just get the bag and get out, that would have been simplest, except, she was starving!

30

After Sally, Derek and Crystal had a hastily prepared meal together, Derek called for a taxi for his visitor. She left, thanking them profusely for all their kindness, telling them that she would have to see them again sometime soon.

Sally heaved a sigh of relief when 'Katy' went out the door. "There is something about that woman..." she said.

Derek thought that it would have been nicer if Katy had actually been here to return the phone. It was after she left that he remembered, he'd meant to tell her that the police had the bar-code pass of her stepfather's. He hope to find out the bag's owner from them but, he decided, that need not concern Katy.

With the visitor gone, ET snoozing and Sally working in the kitchen, Derek was glad of some peace and quiet; the last few days had been chaotic. It would have been near perfect tranquillity – with him slumped in his chair – if only that ruddy dog would stop barking!

The taxi was only halfway along the bumpy lane when Crystal said she was making for the station. "Going back down to York, I am," she told the driver. "Do you know the time of the next train?"

"It will be a long wait at Slatterfoot station," he told her. "Next one is sometime in the morning."

"Oh!" She hadn't realised.

"There's a good hotel along the road. It'd make sense to stay there overnight, and I've heard it's not too expensive. Never been in it myself though. Want to go there?"

So, that's what she did. It was only when she entered that she appreciated that she had already met the person at the desk.

Hammy looked up from the book he was reading – no, the book he was holding; the opening of the outside doors had wakened him. It was a young woman. She was carrying a leather holdall. He gave a sleepy smile.

"You've not been here before, then, have ye?" he enquired. "Are you for stayin'?" and then there was partial recognition. "Should I ken you?"

Crystal gave a smile, one much brighter than his had been. "You gave me a lift earlier," *You dozy old...* she almost added, but restrained herself. "How much for one night, please?" she asked him, and the terms were accepted.

One niggle Hammy had with someone appearing late like this when he was on his own, was that he would have trouble generating the disposable bar-coded key-card. So, while he had her fill particulars in the hotel register, he nipped into the private sitting room. Thelma sat sipping a sherry, watching TV, feeling considerably better than earlier. The way she'd felt earlier she would have told him to go to ...but, she didn't, and obligingly went out to the desk with him.

"Thelma," he said, indicating the young lady, "this is Miss..." and he had to glance at the open book to see the name, "Katy Glasse."

"Welcome," said Thelma, "pleased to meet you, Katy. Right let's get your room key sorted out. Hamish, please watch carefully!" He did, and did try to understand, but it was difficult for him and anyway, he reminded his wife, as he held up his hand, "I've got a sair thumb."

"You don't have one of these little free welcome packs, do you?" Crystal asked Thelma. "You know with a toothbrush, facecloth, and other useful essentials, as they say."

"But of course," said Thelma. "You left home in a rush, no doubt."

Crystal nodded her head in agreement. "My stopping was rather unexpected, I'm afraid."

Hammy lifted her holdall and led her upstairs to her room. On the way it occurred to him, that, when she was in the car earlier, from Bisko's to Derek's, she didn't have any luggage. This bag in his hand, it looked good quality and leather too. Mighty like the one of the two that Derek brought back from London, but he thought no more of it. He went back downstairs.

Relieved that the late visitor's electronic key-card worked as it should, he returned to the desk and his book. This time he tried reading the words. It was starting to become interesting when he heard the sound of a car. He checked. There were no other bookings expected. Apprehensively he watched the main door open. In walked a gentleman, carrying a small overnight bag and obviously was about to want a room.

With dismay Hammy heard the sound of their private bedroom door open, then close. It was Thelma's bedtime and he knew what she was like when she was tired – fierce!

The key-card ...he was on his own and then he had a brilliant inspiration. *What if I tell this bloke that we've nae rooms?* Then he had second thoughts. What would Thelma's reaction be if she ever found out? And that was sufficient deterrent, so he gave the gent the best welcoming smile he could summon up at this late hour, and prepared for a difficult slog.

31

"Derek, you can't just lie there in bed. Are you forgetting that Aunt Thelma wasn't well yesterday? She is probably struggling this morning and Uncle Hammy won't be much help to her. We are needed."

Debatable, he thought, but, he did as instructed and rose. Sleep was not allowed. Sally had been up for over an hour and bright as a button, but, after yesterday's busy day, with the draining effect of the speechifying, followed by the visit from Katy, and added to in the middle of the night by walking the floor with ET, he felt he deserved a bit extra shuteye.

Anyway, surely Hammy would manage – but they went.

Jilly was not pleased at being left behind – again. They were going for a walk, with the pram and the baby. Why was she not being allowed? The howling started as soon as the door closed. Sally wasn't happy going without her. Derek was more hard-hearted. He liked to think that he could get one over on that pesky dog now and then.

They arrived at the hotel to find that Kylie had appeared specially to take some pressure off Thelma: that impressed Sally. Thelma was up and about and apparently fit again and, with Kylie there too, Derek was definitely not needed and neither was Sally. He was irritated – he could have lain in bed for another hour, at least.

As breakfast was almost over, the pace back and forth between kitchen and dining area had eased off. Most guests had eaten and were relaxing, still seated at their tables.

This place runs very efficiently, Derek had to admit to himself, thanks to Thelma. She does a good job, in spite of Hammy's help!

Most of the tables were occupied and Thelma and Hammy were going in and out with pots of tea and coffee. Looking in, Derek was surprised to see Katy. What was she doing here? He really didn't expect ever to see her again, and certainly not this morning. He wandered over to the reception desk.

"Hi," he said to Kylie.

"Good morning," she replied politely as she continued scanning the screen in front of her. "Oh, it's you. Hello again, Mister Toozlethwaite. You do look better with clothes on."

Sally's ears pricked up at that.

"...At least the clothes fit you today."

Wasn't it only a week ago that Hammy implied a special favour done by this new girl for Derek? What was it, and why? It was true that Derek's activities during that particular weekend had been explained by him, to her satisfaction, but...

People were beginning to vacate the dining room. Some were coming over to the pram to admire the sleeping child, and chatting to Sally.

"Good morning, Katy," said Derek, switching his attention as Crystal came out. "Sal, look who it is."

"Surprised to see you here," Sally added.

Not as surprised as I am to see you here, thought 'Katy', feeling glad to have signed the register as that name.

"Oh, it's you. Hello again! Unfortunately there were no suitable trains last night – had to stay over." Out of the corner of her eye she noticed the good-looking bloke leave the dining room.

"Going home today then?" asked Derek and stood expecting a response, but Katy's mind was obviously elsewhere...

Just my luck to bump into them again! I would have liked to have said a bit more to the guy who sat at the next table. Quite a charmer he is. It would have been nice to have learned his name and talked properly with him. I might have a chance before I go, without an audience. Exchanging telephone numbers would be handy. Just imagine having a dirty weekend with that body. He'd only have to ask me once ...though his face seems familiar for some reason, but he may just have that sort of face. I like him. Hmmm...

The smile that came on her face was not directed at Derek. He had been blanked and knew it.

"Could I settle my bill?" Crystal had turned to Kylie.

Thelma came out, and over to her departing guest. "Hope you have enjoyed your stay, Katy, and that we see you again."

'Katy' smiled. *Why did I choose that name? I am getting to detest it; must be a more choosy next time.*

What Crystal did not know was that her interest in the good-looking bloke was reciprocated. Coming away from breakfast, in the hope of exchanging telephone numbers with the female that he'd had a few cursory polite words with, had been Chesney Wilfordon's intention. Seeing her talking with people she already knew deterred him. He would pass by just now, without being noticed. There will be a chance later, he told himself.

There were some important things for Chesney Wilfordon to be sorting out. Visiting the cottage where the phone was located would be first on the agenda, and obtaining the bag and contents with the minimum of fuss was his intention – provided it was there. However, returning and getting to know this lovely looking young woman, was now being added to his mental 'to do' list.

This morning, the manager and his wife, Thelma, had been most helpful, a lot to do with Chesney Wilfordon's technical expertise last night and Hamish Macintosh's lack of it, because it was certainly not the welcome a hotel guest should normally expect. For most, it would have been immediate departure and no one could have argued.

Imagine, on arrival having to create your own key-card for a room in a hotel, and on a computerised system you knew nothing about! Chesney Wilfordon did, without breaking too much sweat and his skill had proved a godsend to Hamish, and both ended up happy. Hamish had been grateful at not having to disturb his sleeping wife, and Chesney Wilfordon had not been required to seek another hotel in the next town late at night. Mutual benefit, plus the key-card process being explained yet again to Hamish Macintosh. He claimed to have understood – but probably didn't.

So, last night, the outcome was a bottle of whisky being shared between a grateful hotelier and his talented visitor. When the new guest and the manager parted they were slightly tipsy and bosom pals, and the hotel was silent. Thankfully Mrs Macintosh remained sound asleep as Mr Macintosh climbed in beside her.

Wilfordon had been pleased to have learned a lot about Toozlethwaite from his host and – equally important – his DIY key-card had worked!

"How's your thumb, Hammy?" said Derek.

A little tear came to Hammy's eye as he held it up. It wasn't the pain of having a black and blue digit that had engendered the moist eyes, it was the fact that someone actually cared.

"Ah'll manage," he said bravely, and then "Ouch!" as he forgot and tried to lift his mug of coffee in the usual way.

What to do next was being discussed. There was agreement that yesterday's gathering could not have been more successful, even though it had been held at short notice and in a rather haphazard way. What should be the next step?

A petition had been promised so a proper committee would have to be formed to create that, and it couldn't just be the little clique deciding it, as it had been up till now. A meeting would be required, as soon as it could be arranged. The way ahead would require careful planning.

The surprising momentum engendered would have to be maintained...

"There was no really no need to visit the hotel so early, was there? They were managing fine without us." Derek had been eager to get back home, but, insisting on making that point several times to Sally on the way back to the cottage could have delayed him – she had been sorely tempted to shut him up by pushing him into the stream!

At home in the peace and quiet he would make a phone call to Alexander; his father-in-law would know what should be done next about the petition.

Being the long-established local bank manager made him an important figure in the community. In the last few years his profile had been raised further, to a certain extent thanks to the Gazette, associated with his incredibly believable female portrayals in the Slatterfoot Amateur Players. Generally, Derek tended to look on him as a father figure who offered him wise words – though, when involved in his theatrical roles, he seemed more of a Mum!

Anyway, Derek knew that Alexander would be most annoyed if he didn't get the chance to throw in his tuppence worth! Outdoor shoes had been removed and left in the little entrance hall and, with his own super-duper mobile in his hand, he was about to dial the number – when the doorbell rang.

Having successfully lifted Edwin from his pram and transferred him to the cot, still sleeping, he should have guessed the peace was too good to last! Jilly began barking like mad, startling little Edwin into a scream of terror, or annoyance – Derek could never decide which. He lifted ET back up and attempted to comfort him as Sally opened the front door.

"Of course, come in," she had eventually said; it wasn't every day that a tall, handsome, fit-looking forty-year old, stood on the doorstep and smiled seductively at her.

"I was looking for Derek Toozlethwaite. Have I come to the right place?" he'd asked. "This is Toozlethwaite Manor, isn't it? You must be his daughter."

"No, I'm not," she'd gulped out. "I ...uhm, I am his wife."

"...Never! I was expecting someone much older. Is he in, or have I come at an awkward time. I heard a baby cry."

"No, no, please come in. Oh, but mind the dog. You are alright with dogs?"

"Oh, I love dogs. Hello, what's your name then?"

Derek came from the bedroom to see a man on his knees playing with Jilly, the fearsome poodle, and it was licking his hand. Sally was standing beside them, looking down at the scene, with a contented smile on her face. It was instant dislike by Derek for this bloke!

"Mr Toozlethwaite?" said the visitor, leaping to his feet with a disgusting display of agility. "May I call you Derek?" he continued, as Jilly sat herself down beside his feet with an expression that said "Pat me again ...please." The look on Sally's face seemed to Derek to be saying the same thing...

Derek stood with little Edwin in his arms, and scowled. Sally was about to apologise for the rude behaviour when the man spoke again.

"You are wondering who I am, of course, and why I've come into your home? Your delightful wife permitted my entry, but rest easy. I am not here to sell you anything, or to distribute religious leaflets. I am…" He hesitated. Should he use the alias? Yes, sensible as long as the police haven't told this guy who I really am. "…*Charles Devine*, and I have come to uplift my holdall."

It was a radiant, sparkling, white-toothed smile being displayed as he completed the introduction – and Derek disliked him even more. Uplift his holdall? Then this must be Katy's horrible stepfather. I definitely don't like him – but I don't recognise him either! This isn't the big, fat bloke that was on the train! This bloke is an imposter trying to steal the bag.

"What holdall?" Derek countered.

"Derek!" said a shocked Sally. Why was he behaving like this? He wasn't usually rude to people until he knew them well.

"The holdall that you have that belongs to me," said Chesney Wilfordon. The response had been in a perfectly calm and reasonable tone – and that annoyed Derek even more.

"But... Just a minute, who told you that I had your holdall?" Derek demanded.

"The police phoned me."

"Oh, right," said Derek, but offered nothing more. It's been the identification pass – the police had traced this man but had they made a mistake? Have they found the wrong person?

"I popped up from London," the man informed them both, and then switched his comments to Sally. "So, I came personally to collect it, and to thank you for finding it. It is important to me, and I came because I thought you deserved a reward."

"How unfortunate," said Sally, not wishing this nice man to take offence at the silly way Derek was behaving, "...and with you coming all that way too, especially when Derek has already given the holdall to your Katy; it was only last night too."

"My Katy?" said Chesney Wilfordon, suddenly bewildered.

"Yes, your stepdaughter. You are her stepfather aren't you?"

"...Of course," he quickly responded. "So it was given to her then?"

The visitor's expression had changed dramatically at that, he was no longer the smooth operator he'd been moments before, Sally sensed. "Yes, it was," she continued. "Has she not contacted you yet?"

Sally, for goodness sake don't mention the documents. Derek was getting a little uptight. *We don't really know who this guy is. He could be big trouble for me!*

"If you were to hurry to the New Farmhouse Hotel, just along the road, you might just catch her. She was there two hours ago. We were speaking to her then, weren't we Derek." But, Derek was back in 'mouth shut, glaring' mode and pretending to be absorbed with the child in his arms.

"Right," said Chesney, now over the surprise and giving another beaming smile to Sally. "Thank you very much for your help, and I must tell you, meeting you, Mrs Toozlethwaite, has brightened my life."

Sally smiled contently. What a charmer!

Derek had never felt more like hitting someone over the head with a large wooden club than he did now. Here in front of him was a person being adored by both an aggressive poodle and his wife! Life could be most surreal at times.

After giving Jilly another overly-affectionate pat, and ignoring Derek completely, the visitor was shown to the door by Sally. *What a gentleman,* she thought, *and such a stark contrast to the ignorant lump that I have married!*

When the door closed, Derek gave a disgusted sigh and a look of scorn in the direction of the two captivated females in the room, then, with ET still in his arms, rushed to the cot and lifted the mattress.

He had to satisfy himself that the Highly Confidential information was still where he had hidden it, and everything was under control; the folder was just as it was left. He was fearful that someone could come into the house and steal the papers back; with Katy now having the holdall it would just be a matter of time before someone came to look for the missing item.

"What do I do then?" Derek directed that question at the child in his arms. "Is this the best place to hide them? Your mummy has already said that I should take them into the Gazette Office, have Rob lock them away in the safe, but I don't want to tell him what I have done. That would implicate him and could cause a lot of trouble before I am ready. Does that seem right?"

ET contemplated for a few moments then the colour of his little face became a shade redder and, looking Daddy straight in the eye as if to tell him what he thought of the idea, he proceeded to poo in his nappy!

32

Getting back inside her own home couldn't come quickly enough for Crystal. She had to open the holdall!

The temptation to look in it had been there from the moment she left the Toozlethwaite household – but she'd resisted. The bag sat in the corner of the hotel room all night – unopened. It was carried by her onto the train and, for the journey to York it remained by her side, still unopened. Thanks to great will-power, the pleasure of exposing the contents and identifying the important item had been delayed, but, for no longer. The proper foundation for the blackmail was about to be discovered.

Though it wasn't really blackmail was it?

On the train journey she had been thinking about that, and managed to salve her conscience by telling herself that what she was doing was simply a public service. Anyway, returning misplaced property to someone deserves recompense, surely. *I am only claiming a reward!*

So, what would she be bargaining with? The bag had been opened but, disappointingly, it was sitting at her own dining table with all the items removed, and she was still none the wiser. She looked again at each item lying there. Where was it – the secret? It seemed a fairly mundane collection of items in front of her.

The two shirts seemed new, still in their cellophane cover. She tore open the packs. Clips were removed and each shirt unfolded, and given a shake. She checked that nothing had been hidden in the pockets. Six fancy socks were given the shake treatment too, with negative results.

Because of concentrating on stealing the holdall, she only vaguely remembered the appearance of the owner sitting on the bench in the station at the time, but she did recollect the erotic thoughts she'd then had about him. That guy had been…

These thoughts vanished as she held up his underwear. His choice of the spotted pattern on the boxer shorts, as they were unravelled to be displayed in all their glory, did not impress. Imagining him in these pants seemed bizarre. In fact, it seemed better not to attempt to imagine *any* male standing in front of her wearing these.

Spots on male underpants had always been a turn-off for her. It was amazing how many males she'd seen standing in 'spots'. They wouldn't have worn them if they'd realised beforehand the effect that the wrong pattern would have on her. These romances had been short.

Striped nightwear did nothing erotically for her either. As she shook open and checked the pyjama trousers, she remembered the last bloke she'd been with using this type. It was when they had been removed – the skinny legs and the knobbly knees revealed – yugh! That had been another turn-off night.

The contents of the toilet bag all seemed run-of-the-mill too; unless there was a special substance in the toothpaste, like Russian spies used to be reputed to always have in their toiletries in case of emergencies. The deodorant was pleasant enough and ordinary.

Many of these items were throwing up memories of various blokes she'd been with, and, mostly they weren't pleasant ones. All had been short-term partnerships leading nowhere close to what she thought romance ought to be.

The T-shirt – now, that she liked. In fact, it was going into her drawer. *Keep it as a trophy – might even wear it* ...and the jeans, again, with nothing in the pockets and no turn-ups where something could be hidden. No hidden pockets to store away secrets either. Could the waistband be concealing something? No.

The inside of the bag was thoroughly inspected. The stiffening on the bottom was even removed, but absolutely nothing was found that appeared to be worth the trouble.

Could it be the holdall itself? It was leather and was high quality, but secret compartments? No! Hollow handles, could it be that? No! There wasn't even writing on the bag – unless it could only be seen in a special light?

There was only one reason why she couldn't find anything: that Derek, or Sweaty as he seemed to be known, wasn't such a simpleton after all – he had removed whatever it was!

She was in a bit of a quandary. Should she give up the idea of making some money out of this, or try succeeding with yet another bluff? But, let's not panic, she told herself.

There is no rush. I'll leave it another twenty-four hours and maybe think of something. I might as well ring him tomorrow evening – from a public call box, of course.

She was relaxed about it now. Yes, calling friend Chesney from the public box was best. She could never be traced. It was the perfect way. Then she remembered – *the smell!*

Derek's intended phone call to Alexander had not happened, partly due to the distractions of a variety of little things requested by Sally, but mainly due to forgetfulness. No bother, it can be done tomorrow at work; Alexander is never busy on a Monday...

It was ET's bedtime so, while Sally gave Edwin a bath, Derek removed the folder from under the mattress and took it into the living room. He was determined that the documents would be read tonight, in detail, and with Sally's help the way ahead could be decided. Anyway, removing it from the empty cot was sensible; mustn't cause another disturbance to ET like a few nights ago. They would be read later but he couldn't leave them lying around for anyone to see; he was smarter than that.

Under the settee cushion, and there they would stay until after Edwin was bedded. That would be happening any minute now. Daddy was about to spring into action.

Thanks to little Edwin, Daddy was transformed. No longer was it necessary for Sally to gripe at him about not doing his fair share, and due to ET taking a special liking to his male parent.

Derek was brought up by his grandparents but, having seen Grandad Hector as a shining example of a husband had not made Derek the perfect housekeeper, or even an imperfect one. When she'd married him, Sally had accepted this as being normal, as the main male in her family life, her father Alexander, had been no better than Hector around the house. Alexander being well-heeled could always afford to live luxuriously, and her mother, Muriel, had insisted she needed no help from him to run her home. So, the one male that Sally knew closely, had established the rule that husbands were not meant to do housework.

That was the way married life for Sally had actually started out – in the same way as Granny Smith and her mother had continued with it – but not now, there had been changes.

Before little Edwin came along, Sally had coped with the dual role of a working secretary and a housekeeper and, although not exactly a tidy person at heart, she'd coped.

It had been surprisingly easy for her to bring about the change. At the crucial time when ET came on the scene, and, when it suited Mummy, with very little cunning or encouragement on her part she'd promoted little Edwin's love for his daddy. Mummies can be exceptionally wily when they want to be, though, it had to be admitted that ET was a quick learner. Hector, and Alexander, felt a bit sorry for the way that things had turned out for Derek.

So tonight, as usual, Derek was at the ready. There was an established routine. Bottle first, given by Daddy; burping, done by Daddy; floor walking, required for only a short while at this time in the evening, done by Daddy, and then the grand finale: ET into his cot. It was only in the middle of the night, when Derek was desperate to sleep, that a long floor-walking session occurred. The routines were wonderful and Sally was quite proud of what she'd achieved.

The compulsory after-meal-walking-the-dog was not required until later, so, at this time in the routine, with all current duties completed and offspring soundly asleep, Derek should have been able to sit down and relax – but not tonight.

The documents were spread over the table. There they all were: 'Highly Confidential' pieces of paper that, almost certainly, should never have left an office or been destroyed by someone in a secure environment!

A pot of coffee and two mugs were brought to the table and Sally sat down beside him. Where to start?

"How about 'Frackaree'?" Sally said. "...It's such a silly name and so obvious. It couldn't be anything other than 'Fracking', and nobody wants *that* on their doorstep."

"Code names, probably simple to be understandable when explaining to an MP," suggested Derek. "…Though I am not sure that this was meant to be seen by them. To me, it looks like a small group of masterminds are actually manipulating parliament, and that crowd won't realise that they are being treated like puppets."

Chesney sat in the lounge of the New Farmhouse Hotel still feeling annoyed. Who the hell did this Toozlethwaite think he was?

He obviously has no idea who I am, or what I could do to him and the fool has given away my holdall. He can't have looked inside or he would have held on to it; and him a local newspaper reporter too. He'll never know the opportunity he missed there. Now someone else has it, someone else that'll have to be traced. I'll have to get it back – but how? And, the phone calls? The female claiming that she knows the secret – could that be Toozlethwaite's wife? I could go down and confront her now. Has she been doing it behind his back and Toozlethwaite is too dumb to realise? But the voice, it sounded very different on the phone.

Oh God, I am confused. On top of that, the girl, the one I admired at breakfast and hoped to chat to when I recovered the holdall, she's gone and I don't even know her name.

That was almost as great a disappointment as the failure to retrieve the bag.

She won't live locally if she was staying here as a guest. Might stay in London if I am lucky? Maybe I could contact her when I return, wherever she stays. She was nice, and she fancied me... A look at the hotel register should reveal her name and home address. I'll do that in the morning, when the young receptionist is back on. I couldn't cope with the owner again. I'd end up producing the key cards for all the new guests probably. It is so much easier winning over females.

He was a little less confused in the morning when, after the sweet-talking routine with the receptionist, he was given a glimpse of the register and saw the name: KATY GLASSE.

She is the one who's been at Toozlethwaite's, and taken my property – and, of course, she is my step-daughter too, as I have been informed... The same young lady that I admired so much now has my holdall, so there are several very good reasons to find her.

33

He hurriedly took the key from the lock and kicked the door closed behind him. The phone was ringing, the landline. He´d heard it as he put the key in the lock. The overnight bag was dumped on the hall floor as he grabbed the receiver. *Could it be her? She said she would phone, but I mustn't sound out of breath.* He grabbed the receiver before it cut off.

"Pipsqueak?" said the voice, the male voice.

 "Oh! Oh, yes, it is, sir."

"Bubbles speaking; update required, Pipsqueak, and remember code-speak will be used. Code word is..."

Chesney Wilfordon hated the organisation's childish attempt at security, and then remembered that the telephone code-speak nonsense was a recent introduction due to his own shortcomings.

"Yes, sir, and what is it to be?"

"Don't rush me Pipsqueak. It is your goddam foolishness that made this necessary. We'll use the code-word 'Seafaring'. Got that?"

"Aye-aye, Cap'n!"

"Now don't push it, Pipsqueak..."

"No sir. Would you like a shipping forecast, or the ports visited, sir?"

He hoped his boss would understand what he was talking about – he wasn't sure himself!

"Try the weather first..." was said resignedly.

"Right ho! Today, visibility was good, initially, with long clear periods, or appeared to be, particularly looking north. Unfortunately, due to sudden squally showers, and fog that drifted in to confuse matters, visibility reduced to zero and we were unable to proceed."

"You mean you failed! The 'cargo' is still adrift?"

"Only a temporary period of unsettled conditions, I'd rather say, sir. Tomorrow, it looks so much brighter, particularly northeast. Our vessel will be untying and sailing in that direction."

"Have you ascertained that the cargo has not been recognised for what it really is? Pipsqueak – have we been compromised?"

This is ridiculous, two grown men, of superior intelligence, talking in a manner that even a stupid schoolboy would find demeaning...

"...Pipsqueak, are you still there?"

"Of course, we haven't ascertained the exact location yet, sir, but of course you realise that action will be taken to ensure secrecy. A shot across the bows to begin with, but then, it could be necessary for the pirate concerned to end up in Davy Jones' Locker, to guarantee that secrecy remains watertight."

"...In whose locker? What are you talking about now, Pipsqueak?"

"Leave it to me sir. My cutlass is sharp. Our Treasure Island map will be safely returned."

Oh how he hated this sort of nonsense. *Yes, I did take the documents from the office, but I didn't deliberately lose the damn things!*

"Pipsqueak, have you really been out of the harbour?"

"Indeed sir, but I have had to return to my safe haven, so to speak."

"You are at home then, just sitting on your backside! Why didn't you say that?"

And that was spat out by his boss in a disparaging way, as if after all the chasing around he hadn't been trying. ...*But that wasn't Seafaring-speak! Why only me doing it?*

"Negative, Skipper. Even though it could be a choppy sea tomorrow, with a straight course, we are hopeful that the cargo will be recovered by ...eight bells, later in the week. A few details will be sorted out in the meantime."

"...Eight *balls*? What are you on about ...and later in the...? It had better not be too late!"

There was a silence. Should he have responded? What could he say?

"Pipsqueak, have you been drinking?"

"No Cap'n, but a tot of rum is about to be issued to the crew very shortly. The crew thinks that I deserve one too."

After this stupid conversation it could be the whole bottle!

34

There was a celebratory mood in the Gazette office this morning. Normally Monday was never a good day to begin a week with but, today was different. The weekend's activities had proved fruitful in many ways and everyone was feeling perky for a change.

Sales of the newspaper had exceeded normal Saturdays, and there had been a great turnout at the meeting. Ideas galore for future editions of the paper were tumbling out and being added to the whiteboard. Even Christine wanted to have a go at an article – a first for her. They had all been there and all four would be contributing their personal angle about the occasion for the next issue.

In addition, Rob, having gone along with the office camera, was particularly proud to have caught action photos of Hammy's topple off the pallets, and a follow-up of the flattened Derek. He had also taken good crowd shots of the reactions to a fired-up Derek spouting forth. The headline to be added to the whiteboard was already in Rob's head: 'SWEATY leads us into WAARR', but, knowing Derek, there could be objections to using that. He'd never liked his nickname.

Firstly though, Derek was eager to point out, there was the simple matter of the promised petition. What the heck do you print on something like that? They were at least in agreement for how it should start: 'We, the undersigned, do hereby declare...' but, as far as words that the four could agree on, that was as far as they managed!

Eventually, after a prompt from Derek, they did agree – to subcontract the task to Alexander. Well, he was the Bank Manager, a pillar of the community, so he must know what should be said. Christine was allocated the duty of obtaining his agreement.

"Mr Davidson," she started as she was put through to his office, "Oh sorry, got it wrong again, didn't I? Mr Donaldson, this is the Newingsworth Weekly Gazette, Christine speaking. And how is our dear friend today?"

"Hmm..." was the suspicious response from the other end. "Not particularly good, if you must know Christine, but what can I do for you?"

"Well ...we were wondering, no, Derek suggested ...that because you don't usually do much on a Monday that you would appreciate a little challenge, and that you would happily take on the task of devising the WAARR petition. You are sure to know the correct wording to be used, he said."

The others in the Gazette Office sat listening, willing the man at the other end to say yes.

"And we would all be ever so grateful to you. You would be absolutely wonderful I'm sure."

Good girl, keep it going, they all silently prompted.

"It would be so easy for you, Mister Donaldson, I'm sure." She was quite proud of herself, correctly remembering his name this time, but...

"Afraid things are a little bit abnormal," he said.

Oh, oh!

"No, sorry, can't help."

"But, Mr Donaldson..." And with that the call ended.

"Derek, the man says NO," Christine reported back.

Glum faces looked at her then at each other.

"Better just do it yourself then, Derek," said Rob. "At least we've given you a start. *We, the undersigned, do hereby declare...*"

Derek was gazing into space looking for inspiration when Christine threw in, "Derek, do you know you will have to do it on-line too? Everybody does."

"When will you have your big story ready, Derek?" shouted Rob from inside his office.

After the euphoria of the weekend, his speech-making achievement, and the adoration of the crowd, his bubble was well and truly burst. It was back to basics.

The pressure was on; this was what life was really like but does a newspaper man ever let something beat him? It was simply words, and words were his speciality, but all Derek could think of was *...Help!*

It was early evening before it came, the phone call; the one that should have come yesterday. Chesney wondered why she was late. *Losing confidence in her ability to bluff maybe? Although, if she now has my holdall...*

He let it ring out for a while before lifting the receiver. He said nothing. Nothing was said at the other end either, though, similar to the last time, he could hear the sound of traffic passing. Was she using the same phone box? There was a spluttering noise and the phone disconnected.

He wasn't to know that, by pondering for several minutes on what she was about to say, and then taking a few deep breaths to steady her nerves, Crystal Glasse had almost passed out from the effect of her current environment. It was a question of survival!

She was at this moment standing outside the phone box, trying to get over that dreadful feeling of impending asphyxiation. This time she took deep breaths while on the outside, and, when she entered the box, jammed the door partially open with a half brick, making the smell slightly more tolerable.

When his phone sounded again he was in no rush to answer. Let her wait. This could be a battle of nerves.

"Hello Chesney," the female said, sounding surprisingly confident for someone he considered to be bluffing.

"Yes. Who is calling please?" He could bluff as well as anyone. "Is it Sally, the delightful Sally Toozlethwaite?"

There was slight pause at the other end, as she wondered why he'd used that name. "Of course it isn't." *Relax,* she told herself, *I'm in control.* "Surely you can't have forgotten me already. I am the one that you could make very happy; add a little to my pension fund, make me rich. All you need to do is behave like your normal self, generously, and you'll get back what you have lost. I shouldn't have to explain it all to you again, Chesney dear."

"I don't think you have anything of mine."

"Oh, but I have. Do you want to know your shirt size for instance, or would you rather your waist measurement? The bottle of aftershave, want to know the make? That's a turn-on but – I don't care for your choice of underwear, I have to tell you. Spots, hmm..."

She is still bluffing – but he felt slightly less certain. "Well, tell me more," he said sarcastically. Push her a bit.

"Metric, or British sizes?"

"Just tell me!" This was becoming annoying.

"Neck, size fourteen and a half, it says on the shirts, waist, thirty-two inches, and leg length thirty one; boxer shorts – blue dots, red dots, and ...oh dear Chesney, pink dots. How could you?"

This was unsettling, sounding less like a bluff.

"What else do you want to know?" she asked teasingly.

"The papers – what about them?"

"You don't mind me opening them up in a public place, and reading an extract then?"

"No, don't do that!" He was beginning to get annoyed. She was making a fool of him.

"Chesney, admit it. You want to talk about money, don't you? How much did you say they were worth?"

He was breathing deeply. It was clear to him now.

"Ok little lady. You think you are very smart, but we'll see how smart you are when I send someone round to collect! If I were you I wouldn't open the door to any strangers for the next few days, Miss Katy Glasse!"

It was her. He had eventually recognised the voice. He disconnected the call without giving her time to respond, and sat back with a grim smile on his face. She was being very awkward and it looked as if, for the moment, she had the upper hand. Also, it looked like the Toozlethwaites could be blameless – but only if she really has them!

It was time for action. Humouring her was over. Provided he'd read the situation correctly, he knew who she was. The girl he fancied; the one who'd been talking to Toozlethwaite in the hotel; the 'Katy' that Toozlethwaite's stupid wife mentioned; the one whose address he'd wheedled easily from the girl in reception, all one and the same.

Wasn't it convenient that she lived in London, and, almost within walking distance? A visit right now will probably catch her on her way back from a local call-box...

He rushed out of the flat. The lift couldn't come quickly enough for him. He wanted it over and done with as soon as possible. What a shame she'd turned out to be the one he fancied, the first time he'd felt like this in a long time. What a waste, but better to know what she's like before any entanglement. It would be strange to have to confront her in these circumstances, hiding his true feelings…

He didn't have to though, he'd had no chance. No-one of that name stayed at that address – because the address didn't exist!

Escape from the phone box in York couldn't come quickly enough for Crystal. A quick check that the paper with the clothing sizes was in her pocket, wouldn't want to leave clues around – like when she'd forgotten that stupid mobile.

The smug smile on her face said that she'd succeeded. She'd bluffed him yet again – very successfully too. He was a worried man. Only a little more work would be needed and then some cash would be coming her way.

The macho bravado he was trying to display impressed her. *'I'll send somehow round to your house' – yea, and yah-boo! There is no way that you will find out where I live, matey!* But had she imagined it? Had he really called her ...Katy Glasse?

35

Alexander wasn't the most exciting person to face across the table at breakfast on a Tuesday morning. Muriel would be the first to tell you that, having lived with him for thirty plus years with almost exactly the same routine every working day. If she had been interested she could have read the pages of whatever broadsheet he was holding up in front of him, though she never did. Normally, it would be the Guardian. It was there as usual but, this morning, the Times, the Telegraph, the Daily Mail and the Sun sat beside him too. All lay folded on the table. This morning, he was simply glum.

"Not going into work today," he told her.

Earlier, he'd phoned along to the newsagents and asked for all these newspapers to be delivered. Was he unwell, she asked herself? She wouldn't dream of asking him that sort of question to his face; even if he was, he would deny it; he considered that, by cycling the way he did, illness was being prevented. Something was wrong, and in a big way. No doubt she would learn shortly.

She made toast, placed it in the rack, took it over to the table and laid it in front of him. He was gazing into space. The kettle boiled, the teapot was filled, infused, and a cupful poured out for him. Still the vacant stare. She sat down and reached for the marmalade. His hand shot out and grasped hers from across the table.

"Muriel," he said, now looking straight into her face, "I have bad news."

She wriggled uncomfortably. How bad? She feared the worst, and what would 'the worst' be? She said nothing. *Let him come out with it in his own time. Don't rush him* ...but he pulled his hand away again, and without saying anything, opened the Guardian and began scanning the pages.

The crunching noise as she ate her toast seemed deafening to her. The only other noise to break the silence was the rustle of the newspaper pages being turned.

Page after page was scanned by him. No detail was being read. Obviously he was searching for something in particular. His cup of tea lay untouched, pushed aside to permit the newspapers to be spread out.

Muriel rose and cleared the dishes from the table. Still he looked at the newspapers. She wanted to hear him tell her what was wrong but she had her work, didn't want to be late today. There would probably be a phone call from Derek to arrange the next WAARR meeting. He would be presenting the petition to the committee, and then she would have to negotiate with her boss to have it available for signing by the public in Bisko's.

"Hope Steven Tomkins agrees," she said, voicing her thoughts.

"What was that? Who is to agree?" asked Alexander, as he turned over the last page of the Sun knowing that it contained only football, and he was not in the least interested in that.

"What? Oh sorry," said Muriel. "I didn't mean to speak aloud. I have disturbed you."

"It's all right. There's nothing in there yet. Bad news yesterday, from Head Office, looks like Slatterfoot Branch could be closing."

"But it's your bank, Alexander. They shouldn't be doing that," said Muriel with genuine concern. "What'll happen to you?"

"I'll become part of the great unwashed, lazing around all day with nothing to do. I'll have to rely on a working wife bringing in some pennies to keep us going."

He smiled sadly.

"It's me they are after, I guess; dug my heels in once too often. They are using the excuse that the effect of the high speed rail link will reduce the local need, but that doesn't make any sense to me. Of course, there's always on-line banking and, if that had been given as the reason..."

"Oh dear, Alexander, the Bank is your life. Isn't there anything you can do?"

"Oh yes indeed. Give all the support I can to Derek and his petition. Get the rail route changed so that it doesn't affect this area; take away one excuse at least. I wonder if Derek still needs help with that petition. We have to win this WAARR!"

"Television coverage, that's what we need," said Rob. "Derek, are you still busy?"

Derek looked up with a glazed expression on his face, overload written all over it.

"Ah, yes," said Rob – thought for a moment, and switched his target: "Spider!"

So, instead, Spider was landed with the task of thinking of a ploy to ensure campaign coverage would appear on TV screens.

No one could doubt Spider's enthusiasm. Contacts had to be a start. Derek's pal, Curly, at *Little Radio fm*, he would know of someone; and he did. All that was needed now would be a reason to entice the cameras. Spider sat and thought, and thought, and ...and eventually inspiration came. Maybe, he could ask Derek nicely for an idea? ...but Derek was asleep at his desk.

DC Green now knew the owner of the holdall, or at least an identity for the person whose bar-coded badge had been in the bag that Toozlethwaite 'acquired'. It was a leap of faith him phoning and leaving the message on the answer-phone, and what if it wasn't that person's hold-all? Should he care? No. Anyway, it would be up to the individual to make contact with Toozlethwaite if he wanted it back.

Lost property should not have been taking his attention, DS Milne had reminded his underling – his concentration should be on stolen property! So, he'd taken it on himself, as a personal challenge, and getting the result from his Police Training College buddy had been gratifying. Good having buddies. The Force was with him. No information came back from the government contacts.

How the identity was acquired and who had issued the badge was not offered by his college pal but that was not of Green's concern. The name, current address, and a telephone number were gratefully received without prying questions. Green had done a little of this sort of thing himself and knew the consequences of being caught 'at it', achieving a trace, and breaking many rules in the process. It was better not to know; he had a result and that was what mattered. That way, a long-standing, telephone-only, friendship could continue – and perhaps come in useful on another occasion.

He sat, alone, in the office in York Police Station looking at the telephone number written on the piece of paper, thinking hard. That telephone number – why was it familiar? He was convinced that he had come across it before, and, in connection with some criminal activity. Concentrate!

Got it!

This was one of the numbers that appeared on the phone found at the scene of the Mansion House robbery, a home number that had not yet been followed up. That phone belonged to Toozlethwaite. Toozlethwaite had visited York and the bar-coded badge came from the hold-all that had been in Toozlethwaite's possession; Toozlethwaite said he didn't know the owner of the hold-all – yet he'd had phone contact!

Last week, Toozlethwaite was accepted as innocent. His personal presence at the crime scene had been accepted as impossible. He'd been eliminated as a suspect in the actual theft. However, had that been the correct decision?

Chesney Wilfordon was the name. London was this man's home base. If the hold-all was his would he want it back? There must have been a connection between Toozlethwaite and Wilfordon. Could they have been working together? Was Wilfordon the one at the Mansion House, and Toozlethwaite, the mastermind? No, Toozlethwaite wasn't smart enough surely! Did Toozlethwaite think the bar-code identity would not be found, or had that been a deliberate ploy? Could the holdall have contained the stolen goods? Had this all been pretence by Toozlethwaite to put them off the scent?

Maybe I'll have a word with the boss. There are too many questions...

After Rob showed his excellent photos of Hammy's kamikaze fall, it was Christine's moment of glory. What she had to offer was Hammy in freefall – live action captured on her mobile. She had been keeping it a secret, wanting to sit and giggle at it on her own.

Hammy could be the star if they used the film, suggested Spider. Facebook or YouTube might be where it could be displayed, well, as a first step at least. He acted quickly and the action movie was on-line almost immediately, with an important message, and within a very short time it was remarkably successful as an attraction to advertise the next gathering: *Another even more spectacular kamikaze leap to be done by Mr Hamish Macintosh on Saturday at 2.00 pm in the Bisko's Car Park during the petition-signing ceremony.* It was an open invitation to come along and support him.

"I know of a company that organises bungee jumping," Christine had offered.

"Yessss!" proclaimed the other three.

"It's done from a tall crane," she explained.

"Yessss!" they once more cried in unison, getting even more excited.

"Hammy will love it."

"Yessss!"

This was terrific, an attraction with pulling power. Spider could now use the name that Curly supplied and made contact with the BBC. Yes, sounds good, was the response, we'll be there with TV cameras, was the promise.

Spider could sit back with his feet up on the desk. He'd done his bit. His objective had been achieved, the only trouble looming was – when would Hammy be told, and who would tell him?

36

Working at home today was the plan but, when the buzzer sounded, Chesney was already having difficulty concentrating. Someone requesting access was not a surprise. He had been expecting a visitor. The 'Katy' girl would be delivering the holdall to his doorstep and then demanding money, of that he was fairly certain. She would have found his address. Annoyingly, for all his previous cockiness and his smart attempt at detection, he did not know hers.

The small screen showed two males standing outside in the rain.

"Yes," he said into the speaker, "can I help you?"

"We'd like to speak to Mr Chesney Wilfordon."

"And who are you?"

"Detective Sergeant Milne and Detective Constable Green," was stated gruffly by the older-looking one, "...from York Constabulary."

He released the door catch, and they entered. Chesney stood looking at a screen showing the rain splashing on the now empty pavement. A short delay then a knock at the door. It felt ominous. What did they know? It wasn't a social call so, should he offer to take their wet coats? Should they be welcomed inside or kept on the doorstep?

He opened the door and stood looking at them until the older one broke the silence.

"It might be better if you invited us in sir. It could be confidential matters we are about to discuss and I am sure you would prefer your neighbours not to hear."

They held up warrant cards for his inspection.

"Of course, please..." and he stepped aside and waved them into the flat.

"Would you mind if we remove our wet coats, wouldn't want to mess up your carpets, had to park a good distance away unfortunately."

"Yes, yes," in a bit of a daze as he reached out for them. "Sit down, please."

One sat in the main settee, the other at the far corner of the room.

"We have reason to believe that you were in the vicinity of Middlefield Mansion House on the outskirts of York on the morning of..." and the notebook was referred to, "one week ago, on the Tuesday," the notebook again, "on the ...fifteenth, yes the fifteenth." It was the younger one, who was taking control and, as agreed beforehand, taking a chance on their theory. The notebook was being referred to, unnecessarily, by Green because his boss thought it would be more convincing that way. "Is that correct, sir?"

"Well..." He hesitated. How did they know that? "I might have been."

"Ah-ha," said the younger one, with a glance over at his boss. It looked as if the bluff might work.

"And is it true that you are aware of a Mister Toozlethwaite, a Mister Derek Toozlethwaite?"

"Well, I..." That's when he recognised DC Green's voice. This was the person who left the phone message telling him who had the holdall and gave him Toozlethwaite's name. "You obviously know I know that name... You informed me."

"Ah-ha," and gave another glance to his boss for approval. He received a nod to continue.

And I think you are a very clever boy too, was the sarcastic thought passing through Chesney Wilfordon's head.

"...And, that between you and Toozlethwaite, a robbery was carried out at the said Mansion House, the goods then being transferred in a leather holdall that has been identified as belonging to you."

"*No!*" Chesney Wilfordon replied.

"Ah-ha," came out automatically from the younger one, but this time there was no glance of approval. "Oh..." This was not per the script at all. "Did you say 'no'?"

"Yes. What gave you this crazy idea?"

"But you admitted you were there, at Middlefield Mansion House on the day. Is that not correct?"

"Yes, but I was outside, watching your guys rushing about. I didn't know there had been a robbery."

"You were outside?" and now it was the older man, having stood up and come over, who was looking down at him. "Why?"

"I was trying to get back my holdall."

There was a silence. The two detectives looked at each other, then, back at him.

"What made you think that you'd find your holdall at Middlefield Mansion House?" asked DS Milne.

"The phone," he told them.

"Ah ...*the phone*..." repeated DC Green.

"Terrible echo in this flat, anyone else notice it?" said Chesney.

"Very funny, sir," said the Detective Sergeant, but he was not smiling. "You had the phone with you, then, and lost it."

"I was never on the premises, it was not my phone, and I was trying to identify who had tried to ring me from it." He avoided using the term blackmail related to that first call. He would prefer to deal with Katy on his own. This was personal – and then it suddenly occurred to him that maybe he did know that female's address – it could be where the phone had been located the previous night!

Milne looked at Green.

"You're mobile number is?" Chesney was asked by Milne. Milne looked at Green, but there was no reaction as they were told it.

"And your home phone number is again?" asked Milne, and, as the suspect stated his number, Milne watched Green's face. Would this be one he remembered?

"Ah-ha, yes," said Green. "That number was on Toozlethwaite's, an outgoing call on the evening preceding the robbery, I think that was."

Chesney Wilfordon looked quizzical. There was no reference to any notebook.

"I think maybe it would be better if you accompanied us to the local nick, sir," said DS Milne. "I'm sure the Met boys will give us the use of some space and let us get on with it more quickly. I'm sure you'd agree – it's a long way back to York."

A little later, when the phone started to ring, Chesney Wilfordon was unavailable and the flat was empty.

37

Chesney was driving and on his way north with a clear destination in mind. Why hadn't he thought of it before? That early trace he was given of the location of the mobile, it had been for a semi-detached villa in York. The phone had been sitting there for almost eight hours before it appeared at Middlefield Mansion House. In fact that villa had been his target before he diverted to the Mansion House. If it was where she lived, as he suspected, he would soon find out.

At least this time I know what she looks like, and I have her name. The whip hand is mine this time. It would be perfect if she is the one who opens the door. She won't know it's me she's been phoning until I choose to tell her. She'll see me only as the guy she met at the hotel last weekend. She fancied me as much as I did her: I could tell.

The time spent at the police station yesterday had proved nothing, and in the end he was thanked for his co-operation and for having attended willingly. He also received an apology for the misunderstanding and any embarrassment it may have caused him. Learning a bit more of his side of the story had convinced the policemen. They were surprised that he didn't have the hold-all. They had expected him to have collected it from Toozlethwaite and were confused at someone else having claimed it.

He realised how unpleasant it could have been if they had removed the holdall in the first place. For them to have discovered the documents and understood what it was all about could have been disastrous. At the very least, it would have become public knowledge – and it could have happened!

Almost there – a Satnav is a wonderful device.

What should I tell her when I arrive? That I am madly in love with her? She seemed too level headed to fall for that. That I need her help? That certainly is true. That she's getting no money and please, would you give me back my pieces of paper... Hmm, that would go down like a lead balloon...

But, what if she doesn't have them?

Why should I have doubts? She sounded confident on the phone, but was she being truthful? She's blackmailing me, probably a born liar – and an expert at extortion! She has a special talent. I liked that girl from the moment I saw her and irritating though it is, I like her even more now. Probably not the first time she's done this. Yes, I am the amateur here.

He pulled up in the road, short of the address he'd been given, and sat surveying the scene. It was a pleasant-looking area, houses well-maintained, and most of the gardens reasonably well-tended, not spectacular, but neat and tidy. He looked at the number on the nearest door and worked out which he would be aiming for. Ah, the only one that looks particularly untidy!

Sitting in the car was the easy part. He waited a little longer, observing. He could see no-one about at all, kids were still at school. When he was sure the road was deserted he got out and tried knocking the door, but, no answer. Had the journey been a waste of time? Couldn't just leave, he decided, he had a lot to lose. He must have patience...

Meanwhile, back in Newingsworth...

"Whit? Say that again? You are wantin' me to do what? A Bungee Jump! I thought I didn't hear ye right. Ye must be kiddin'! Away ye go..."

"But Hammy," said Derek, "we thought it would be a brilliant idea, and it'd be even better if you wear your kilt. Anyway, it's not as if you are being asked to dive into a bucket of water or anything silly like that, but it has to look spectacular. The crane has already been arranged. Remember it is to encourage the TV coverage, and it could be your contribution to the WAARR effort."

"Away an' fa'. If you were askin' me to do the Highland Fling or maybe even the Full Monty, I might have considered it, but, a Bungee Jump? Naw, naw, naw!"

"Look you are obviously undecided about it, so I'll leave it with you to think about. Thelma, your dear wife, thought it would be a good idea."

"It's the insurance money she's after. We've no' been married all that long, but, I ken her very well – an' I'm not goanie change my mind!"

Chesney had waited for nearly an hour. Some children with mothers had returned from school and came along the road a while ago. These kids were now playing near the car. A ball hit the side of the vehicle every so often and he was tempted to get out and give them a mouthful, but he resisted. Two women came back from shopping and stood chatting but as far as the person he was hoping would appear – nothing.

I will stay another half-an-hour maximum and then give up if she doesn't show.

The only activity around the houses had been a young fellow putting leaflets through letterboxes – until now! There she was, looking as gorgeous as she did when he saw her at the weekend: *sad that I can't trust her; it is almost certain that she will be trouble. Why am I doing this*? The secret information, it had to be found.

She'd gone inside. Could he safely leave the car with these kids galloping around? Would it still have wheels when he returned?

Did the bell work? He wasn't sure. He pressed again and waited. No, it definitely didn't. He knocked. No one came. He knocked again. Movement upstairs, the curtains twitched. He pretended not to notice and looked the other way. Still no answer so he tried once more. Ah, that was more like it.

This time there was a sound behind the door. It opened, only a fraction and on a security chain. She was hidden behind the door.

"I don't want any of what you are selling," said the voice he recognised.

"I am not selling. I came to visit a pretty young lady who left me behind at the weekend and didn't say cheerio."

"Who is this?" said the voice still from behind the door, sounding a fraction more interested.

"You might recognise me if you peeked," he suggested. "The hotel?"

The face looked out of the gap.

"Wow! It's you. How did you...?"

"Are we going to carry on this conversation through a part-open door?" he asked. "You do remember me, don't you – Charles Devine? We didn't get the chance for proper introductions, Katy."

Oh God, why did I choose Katy but it sounded so different when he said it. She opened the door and invited him inside, *probably foolish to do this*, she thought, *but, when you like someone...*

"The place is a mess. I've been out all day and just got back."

227

"I was passing," he lied, "and wondered if I could see you again."

"Passing? But how did you…"

"Well… I thought if I am in the area it would be nice to meet again and talk to you properly this time, maybe over a meal?"

And there it was, he saw it, his holdall, sitting in the corner of the room. At least, he was almost certain. He would have to check at a suitable moment.

"I could rustle up something," she said, "and we could have it here, if you are not in a hurry."

"That's the cheapskate's way if I give in to that," he said, "but, if you are happy, then so be it. I happen to have a couple of bottles of wine in the car."

That was easy, he thought, as he returned with the wine and poured two glasses. It was to be a quickie meal from her emergency stock, she told him.

"So it's thank goodness for microwaves then, Katy." He smiled, and she liked that smile. "Where would we be if…?"

When she went into the kitchen, he took a chance and glanced inside the holdall, better to be sure. Yes, it was his. He recognised the shirts, though they were no longer wrapped in the cellophane packaging and looked a bit crushed. He decided to do nothing yet and see how the evening developed.

It was later, after they'd eaten and consumed a few glasses of wine that Crystal's thinking became freer and her tongue a bit looser. Three glasses, and progressing to a fourth was her tally. Less than one had been consumed by 'Charles' but he had successfully made it look as if he was keeping pace with her. Avoiding red wine would have been wiser, she would tell herself later, because afterwards she usually regretted the things she'd said. Someone always could recount to her how she had embarrassed herself, and it was usually words she could not remember.

"Can I ask you something?" she said, looking into his eyes. "Has a handsome guy like you ever been caught shoplifting?"

"No, I was much too good at it to be caught," he lied. He would have been terrified to have done that sort of thing.

"Me too, but how about picking a lock? My dad taught me how."

"No, can't say I have ever managed that. Can you do that?"

"Yes, easy-peasy. How about house-breaking? I bet you have done that, surely..."

"Noooo... Can't claim to have done that either, but you have, I presume you are about to tell me."

"Have you ever tried blackmail? No. You have led a very sheltered life, Charles. May I call you Charlie? That can be fun, you know. You can just pretend – if you are good at it. I am. There's this guy Chester, who thinks I have something important of his, but..."

Her mobile interrupted. *'Hey, Mister Tambourine Man, play a song for me...'* was singing out piercingly.

"...I haven't. Just a minute," she said reaching for the phone, then, standing with a little difficulty, finished the remains of her wine in a gulp, and made her way towards the kitchen door.

"I'd better answer this..."

38

Derek had intended phoning earlier in the week but what with the campaign, and the Gazette, and ET in the middle of the night... OK, he had to admit to himself, he forgot! It was Sally's phone he was using this evening. Katy's number was already on it from one of her earlier calls.

"Hello," said the voice that immediately began giggling.

"Hello, Katy, it's Derek. Am I interrupting you?"

"Katy? Oh yes, that's me," and the giggling began again. "Who is speaking please?"

"It's Derek, Derek Toozlethwaite. Have you forgotten? Are you all right?"

"...All right? Me, all right?" and again giggling. "Why would I not be...? (*hic*), pardon! Who is it again?"

"Derek! You saw us – my wife and I – at the weekend. Are you at home?"

"Yes, I am. So nice of you to ask, and, to tell the truth, I am enjoying a little drinkiepoo... Wait ...it is Sweaty – that's your real name, isn't it? Of course I know you. It was a wonderful speech!"

"Listen Katy, just to warn you. I meant to phone before this but, after you left on Sunday we had another visitor."

"Oh that's nice..."

"...and he was pretending to be your step-father..."

"But I don't have a... Oh, yes, maybe I do!"

"...but, he looked nothing like him, I could see that; this bloke said his name was Devine, I think."

"I know that name – no I don't – yes, I..."

"Sally thinks that she may have said your name to him and told him that you were up at the hotel. He didn't look big and fat like your stepfather, he was more my build, but a cocky charmer. Don't know what he was up to – he was after your bag. We were worried, in case he..."

"Is he (hic) handsome?" she asked hesitantly.

"Sort of... Yugh! A charmer..."

"Oh my God!" said Crystal. "Devine! Charlie! It's him then. I shouldn't have... He's in the other room!" The call ended rather abruptly. She wished she hadn't drunk the wine so quickly.

Claims he fancied me does he but it's not me he is after at all – it's the holdall! Should never have let him in – got to get him out of the house!

It took a lot of courage for her to open the door and go through to join her visitor again.

"Oh dear," she said, trying to think quickly though not very clearly, "that was my Pa – in a vile mood now! He's on his way home and he could tell that I have had a drink. He gets very annoyed because he knows it affects my health. I shouldn't do it but..."

"When he arrives I'll tell him it was my fault," Chesney offered chivalrously.

Make something up, anything, she told herself! Get him out of here before he attempts anything. Mustn't let on that I know what he is up to; he thinks he can hoodwink me! Trying to get that bag indeed! Anyway what would he want it for? It's Chesney's!

"Oh no, Charles, he's already been in prison for serious assault on my last boyfriend – he's still in hospital. He'll only shout at me, but you... I am afraid that he'll... It could get serious! You had better go – and fast."

This was not what 'Charles' wanted. He still didn't know if she had the documents, but she had the bag and he needed that back to be sure. It was still sitting there. Should he ask her for it, or grab it and run? He was given the chance to do neither.

"He'll be here in a moment!" she said, desperately grabbing his arm and pulling him to his feet.

"I will have to see you again," he told her, feeling pressurised and unable to do anything about it.

"I'll ring (*hic*)," she replied and rushed him out of the front door. She waved and went back inside quickly as he climbed into the car

Where did it all go wrong, he wondered? Surely she wasn't bluffing again?

It would be a long drive ahead so he was glad that he had only taken one glass of wine. It would be just the thing if he were to be picked up for drunk-driving in York and then have to face two detectives on their home territory. They would relish having a good reason to lock him up, he imagined.

Oh, oh! She wasn't bluffing – there he is!

The figure staggering along the pavement was getting closer and looked menacing. The car was started, and Chesney Wilfordon was quickly on his way.

As Joseph Topper approached his gate, he hardly even noticed the big car that roared away. As usual, he fumbled with the stupid gate latch, eventually stumbling up the path, fearful of the reception he would be receiving from his wife for returning home late, worse for drink. On one occasion, when he'd been like this, he'd got it wrong and gone to the next door neighbour's door, but young Crystal had been quite pleasant about it, he recalled, not like his blooming wife was about to be (*hic*)...

In Newingsworth, Derek couldn't understand Katy's reaction this evening. Forewarned is forearmed, as they say, and at least he'd tried to help, but she sounded slightly tiddly. He hoped she'd taken in what he'd said. Wouldn't it be terrible if that bloke were to cause trouble for the girl because of us, he thought?

Derek had been busy, very genuinely. He'd been organising, motivating, and gaining much needed publicity. It was his belief that all the adults of Newingsworth and Slatterfoot and surrounding districts should be encouraged to be involved. Nobody should be permitted to sit back and be only a passenger.

Tonight, he was once again reading the confidential paper that described what was about to be the government's approach to 'Two-Speed-High'. The process of controlling the population had already begun; that would be the information fed to the media, which appeared the other weekend.

How could the documents he was holding be most effectively used and would he suffer if he proceeded, he wondered fearfully? It was explosive material. It could turn out like the whistleblowing of Snowden, he'd exposed Government secrets and paid for it.

The banner headlines and an exposé of corrupt practices were being visualised by Derek. Realistically, it could lead to the closure of the newspaper through political pressure. Yes, it could happen.

Would he get backing from the others if they were told and would the team be brave enough to take the risk? Rob knew nothing of these secret papers – yet. No-one did, other than Sally. Would the Gazette be 'done for' if they dared to print?

Perhaps an alternative, without involving the team, might be to use the information surreptitiously, maybe put pressure on someone in authority?

Success by going to a single MP would be unlikely. One wouldn't be able to influence a rebellion. Forces much more powerful than the elected members were at work here. It would have to be at the highest level, in the department that created the plan.

Get to the man in charge. Whisper in the ear of Mister Big; let him know that we know too! On top of all that, there is the other matter – the Bungee Jump and Hammy...

Chesney Wilfordon had grudgingly developed a sneaking admiration for Toozlethwaite, even though he was causing him some headaches. He was turning out to be quite a character, grabbing and holding the interest of the media; obvious from the photos and articles after that initial event. What he had achieved at the weekend had been remarkable, whipping up the crowd at the Saturday rally and creating good publicity for his cause at the same time. It was the main topic of gossip at the hotel when Chesney was there, and the one generating most of the gossip had been Macintosh.

Oh dear, Macintosh! Was it any wonder that he couldn't operate his own computerised systems; he never concentrated. He made sure everyone was aware of his involvement: of his friendship with Toozlethwaite; of being a WAARR committee member. He was too concerned in chatting with everyone, even though not many guests understood what he said!

The gossip after breakfast in the hotel that Sunday had been about the next meeting being planned for this coming weekend. It had even been given a mention earlier this week in the Guardian: '*Strong reaction from a local community to the planned route of the hi-speed rail link; actively pushing ahead in opposition. There is to be the signing of a petition this coming Saturday in the town's supermarket, and to be followed by a spectacular event, details of which are being kept as a closely guarded secret.'*

That was not what he had been scanning the newspapers to find. All week, all the papers he could get his hands on were being scoured and on-line gossip checked. He was dreading finding any mention of his lost paperwork but, so far, nothing. His mind today dwelt on more pleasant thoughts: Katy, though she appeared to be a bundle of trouble.

He really liked her – even though she could turn out to be an experienced crook.

He was home. When he left her place last evening, he noticed in the rear view mirror that her father had gone in the wrong gate. *He wouldn't have given me any trouble while he was in that drunken state,* he told himself confidently. *I could have pushed him over with one finger. I'll bear that in mind in the future, if there is a future with that young lady.*

One thing was clear, although she had the holdall, by her own slightly tipsy admission, it looked like she was bluffing about the documents. Thank goodness she didn't realise who he was, he thought. There would be little chance of any romance in the future if that were to be exposed.

If she didn't have the papers, where were they? Did Katy pinch the holdall originally, or was it someone else; and how was Toozlethwaite involved? Could he have them? He seemed to have had the bag for some time, and his being a newspaper reporter too! It would be a catastrophe if he had already found them and was about to make use of them.

It had been a bizarre evening for him at Katy's, a bit like 'truth and dare' with the questions she posed. 'Have you ever broken into someone's house?' she'd asked. 'No,' had been the answer, but, having now thought about it, maybe that would be what was required. He would have to do something!

There would be little chance of getting an honest answer, no matter who he asked about the documents, Chesney realised, so he would just have to check for himself.

He wondered if they were in Toozlethwaite's home. Could soon find out, there was to be a WAARR rally on Saturday; his house would almost certainly be empty then. His wife would be there in support, like last time. She'd even taken their little one along to cheer. So, Newingsworth again – he'd be making a special uninvited visit to Toozlethwaite Manor on Saturday and didn't mind that they wouldn't be there to welcome him... *I'll stay at the same hotel and if I book in advance, perhaps I won't have to print my own key-card!*

39

The Gazette office was deserted when Derek hurried in – perfect. The idea had suddenly occurred to him, the chance to make an important phone call to a Government Department, privately; it might speed up the whole process.

The office should be empty for a while.

Spider was over at Bisko's organising the electronics for the weekend. Mr Tomkins, the manager, had been extremely co-operative and supportive and was providing more advanced equipment for Derek's speechifying. This weekend he would be having the use of a mobile radio-signal mike that would permit him to wander rather than have to remain in front of a fixed-stand microphone. Rob was along at *Little Radio fm*, meeting with Curly to attempt to persuade him to arrange a live broadcast at a future rally, and Christine was doing the most important daily activity at this time of the late morning, the food. She would be uplifting the hot sausage rolls from the home bakers in the High Street for the lunches of Spider, Rob, and Derek. She preferred water biscuits and cheese herself. She was also going to pop into the bank next door and talk over an article that Alexander was writing for next week's copy of the newspaper.

A special telephone number had been acquired by Spider, from goodness knows where, that would, apparently, obtain direct access to the Government Department that deals with the Rail Route. That number was dialled by Derek.

"Hi Doris," said the male voice. "Did you manage to get twenty-two down? I think it is 'catastrophe'. It matches sixteen across, 'turmoil'. I think I win then – my sort of day. ...*Doris?*"

"This is not Doris," said Derek, wondering what number Spider had come up with.

"Oh," was said in a slightly camp way.

"I'd like to speak to the official in charge of the Hi-Speed Rail Route,"

"Oh, you would, would you?"

Derek had an inspired thought. "Yes indeed, but for security reasons I'll refer to him as 'Bubbles', you know who I am talking about, don't you? You, being part of the team, should know that when the code name is used, immediate action must be taken. It is rather important and I don't have all day to chat to an underling who has nothing to do but compare crossword clues with a colleague. I don't want to have to report that, so, please, put me through, right away."

Derek was surprising himself these days, brazenly doing things that he'd meekly shied away from in the past, but only when the mood spurred him on. Today he was being spurred. It was exhausting though because he was living on his nerves during his working day now, and felt brittle, but it was doing the job.

"Oh, right," and the voice sounded a little hurt. "Who shall I say is calling, sir?"

"Just tell him it's..." and he had another inspiration, "...tell him it's Pipsqueak."

"Hold the line, please."

The line remained silent for an uncomfortable length of time. Derek thought that he had failed this time. He'd gone too far, expected too much, he told himself as he held on. Had he been disconnected?

"Can I help you?" said a voice that was used to being respected, a voice that would normally be in control.

Derek felt slightly less confident now, but pushed himself.

"You'll have heard of us, I'm sure. WAARR: 'We Are Against the Rail Route'. I am speaking on behalf of the people of Newingsworth, Slatterfoot and surrounding districts who are reacting to the oppressive manner of the Government imposition of the Rail Route."

"Hmm..." said the voice.

"This is to warn you that our petition will be reaching your department very shortly, and it seemed only fair to tell you in advance what you are about to be faced with."

"Hmm..."

"...And give you the opportunity to react by considering the surrounding unused ground in the area as a more suitable route. If you do not take heed, then be prepared for further action. I know of 'Two-speed-high', and the rest, and if you do not take immediate action I will expose your dastardly plan to the press."

"Hmm ...and you used the name 'Pipsqueak'. Is it Mister Pipsqueak? Where did you learn that? Do you have a real name?"

"Ah-ha..." said Derek and hung up. That wasn't too bad for a first attempt, he told himself.

"What was all that about?" asked Rob, having come back into the office at the end of the conversation, almost frightening the life out of Derek.

"A little something that I have up my sleeve," was Derek's sly reply.

It made Rob wonder though if, maybe, Derek was getting too big for his boots?

Tomaskins was called into the large palatial office.

"My tea is getting cold, a fresh cup, please, and quickly, and Tomaskins, that call, why did you put it through to me?"

"I thought he was one of your *very* close friends, sir. He called you Bubbles."

Tomaskins left to make fresh tea, leaving a slightly bemused senior person gazing after him, and wondering if Tomaskins was, after all, 'getting past it'.

This would be a day for cleaning the house – and thinking.

Having flexible working hours had always been appreciated by Crystal, and, with her type of work, they don't come much more flexible than the freedom to choose whether 'to do a job', or not. A life of crime inherited from a father who was a habitual criminal was not the sort of inheritance that was normally shouted from the rooftops but, for Crystal it was in the family, a craft, and one she was continuing with pride. He had taught her well.

The training had begun enthusiastically, on her part, the moment she left school.

Of course, her tutors were unaware that her father's occupation was not the High Court Judge named on the school records many years ago. That piece of paper was filled in by Crystal herself in her best handwriting; the form she was supposed to have passed to her parents for completion. No-one questioned it when it was returned. She was encouraged to apply for university, with the objective of progressing into law. It was to give her the opportunity, her tutor had said, 'to follow in daddy's footsteps'.

No amount of persuasion by her career advisor could convince her that rejecting the acceptance of her University application was the wrong thing to do. Unfortunately 'Papa', due to his courtroom commitments, was never available to visit school to discuss his daughter's apparent rebellion.

The career advisor had to suffer the humiliation of failure. That this poor girl was obviously kicking aside the traces to do her own thing, was his conclusion: wanted to be different. What a shame. What must her father feel...?

'Papa' was delighted. His one and only daughter choosing to follow him in his chosen career – housebreaking and robbery – was a particular delight. Anyway, he couldn't have visited the school on the day they wanted because he had been in court, right enough – but in the dock, again.

As well as receiving verbal instruction and practical tutorials at home, by far the best coaching for Crystal had been 'on the job'. Breaking and entering, using the good old plastic card, as well as the bent wire, became a particular skill of hers. Choosing the premises to be tackled was always done with care. No use going for something beyond her capabilities her old man had always insisted, skilled though she was becoming, and gloves always had to be worn on a job. He also abhorred violence.

Her skill was honed over many of her maturing years. The working rules were headed by a simple maxim of her dad's, 'Don't get caught!' and she had heeded that conscientiously. Unfortunately for her father, it was more of a case of 'do as I say, not, as I do', because, for Dad, it was a regular result of his chosen occupation. He often found gloves a nuisance and would sometimes take a chance; sensitive fingers were more effective for his skill to succeed. As a result of the failure of his most recent venture, he was once more languishing at Her Majesty's Pleasure in Bordam Open Prison.

The bag pinching had come as a delightful surprise to Dad on the first day that she'd tried and succeeded. Very little value came from the contents on that first attempt, but her initiative had impressed him. This had been a prowess developed by Crystal herself.

It was surprising how proud that man was of his daughter.

Today, she was missing him. There was normally no problem with her being on her own in the house. She was quite happy in her own company and her many past boyfriends had been deliberately short-lived affairs. Mostly, meetings with them had been restricted to public places or back at their pads – never in her house. She was particularly wary of those who became curious about the work she did, especially those who wanted to know where her money was coming from.

Now and again it would have been comforting to have someone to talk things over with – someone she could talk to honestly – but her confidence had been shaken by the surprise visit of Charles Devine – and Chesney's holdall; why Charles wanted it still made no sense.

He was a bit naughty too, plying me with wine but I like him, he is lovely. Hmm... Who knows what could have happened – if that Derek hadn't interfered... Drinking wine had been unwise, it always had loosened her tongue. Had she said anything she shouldn't have? That she couldn't remember was disturbing, and she was unsure what to do next.

Dad would have known.

40

The second public meeting was nearing too rapidly. Derek was beginning to have regrets. After being up for a large part of the night rewriting the speech for today – a speech that he was still unhappy with – while pacifying a fretful ET, at this precise moment he would rather have been returning to his bed than going into town.

Sally had been insistent that he couldn't start the day on an empty stomach, especially a day that required him to be on top form and inspirational for the people who would be at the rally. He gave in and did what she'd said. A large bowl of grapefruit had been consumed, followed by bacon and eggs and black pudding, and two slices of toast, but now he wished he hadn't.

"I don't feel well, Sal. Could it be flu, do you think?" he asked her. "I feel dreadful."

"Nonsense," she told him, recognising cold feet about the rally. "A hot toddy – that's what your Gran would recommend I'm sure," Sally replied chirpily. "Do you want me to make one for you?"

"But, shouldn't I go to bed and sweat out the fever if I drink that?"

"I'm sure it would work without doing that."

The potion was mixed; half a glass of whisky, a drop of boiling water, oh, and four spoonful's of sugar, that's what Granny Smith recommended, wasn't it?

"Phew, that's powerful stuff," Derek admitted after downing it in a single go. "It's a good job I am not driving."

Cleaning his glasses to read the blurred print of his typed pages didn't seem to make much difference. He sat down. Warm, isn't it? His tummy felt funny-peculiar.

"Derek, Thelma phoned, I'm going up to collect the baby food. Hammy was supposed to drop it in on the way past but forgot. I'll use your bike. Keep an eye on Edwin. He'll be waking any time soon."

Sally left. The house became peaceful, ET asleep in the bedroom, Jilly asleep in her basket, and Derek, on the settee sitting blinking and trying to remember when he'd last had an eye test. He fell fast asleep...

Hammy had left earlier and driven down town to Bisko's to organise the platform again. This time, he would be making sure that no pallets were used that would not comfortably support his weight. He was still suffering the effects of his fall on top of Derek – Derek hadn't softened the blow enough, and, as for his thumb...

Hammy was not on chauffeuring duties for Mr Toozlethwaite and his missus this time. Alternative transportation for Derek's contingent had been volunteered, last evening, by someone else and it had arrived. It was to be Sam's old banger today, and Sam was at the door, but it took the combined sounds of the doorbell ringing, ET yelling, and Jilly barking her head off, to rouse Derek and remind him of today's excursion.

Sam had Angie and little Annabel with him. They were sitting in the car. It was a dishevelled-looking Derek who answered the door and asked them to come in. Derek felt rough and it was getting late and Jilly wasn't helping matters by jumping about, getting excited with the entrance of the visitors and yapping continuously. Sally hadn't yet returned from the hotel with the essential baby food. Before leaving, ET would have to be fed and have a nappy change immediately afterwards. Derek felt under pressure.

"Derek, I've been meaning to ask you," said Angie.

His eyes cleared sufficiently to appreciate that he was receiving a mean look from his sister. It immediately made him feel guilty.

"Did you encourage Sam to buy this ...this ...what's the term over here for a clapped-out hard-to-get-insurance-for old car – a jalopy? Was it you, Derek?"

What a question to be asked when he was barely awake, with an odd feeling in his stomach and unable to think straight... As usual, thought Derek, he was being blamed for the world's catastrophes.

Thankfully, Sam interrupted. "Angie, sweetheart," he said. "Do you have to go on about it? No, it wasn't Derek. I did it all of my own accord. I've said I am sorry. What more do you want?" Before Angie had time to answer with the list of demands that had been festering, the front door opened and Sally was back.

"Hello everyone, sorry, I am running late. Thelma was desperate to chat. Derek, you have fed ET, haven't you?" and no, it hadn't occurred to Daddy that there was sufficient food for several more meals without panicking.

"Sally ...don't feel well ...really."

"You'll be alright once we get going," she assured him and rushed to feed a starving child. "Have you fed the dog?" Derek's sheepish look of failure received a silent glower in return. He felt that she was being a smidgen less than sympathetic, then Sam, like a real gentleman, offered to deal with Jilly's needs.

"No, thank you Sam," said Sally graciously. "Derek will get it."

He struggled to his feet. The smell from the half-used tin of dog food, even though held at arm's length, was not the most pleasant sensation for him in his condition but, he dutifully fulfilled the task. At least Sally was looking after the nappy-changing.

Eventually, they were ready to go. Jilly was in the huff as usual because she wasn't allowed to go with them. Derek told her to go into her basket and bent down to give her an affectionate pat, but pulled back quickly when he saw the sharp teeth.

Important things to be done were remembered by Derek as the others made their way into Sam's jalopy. He checked a) that the confidential documents were still safely hidden under the cot mattress, b) that the speech was in his hand, and c) that the front door was safely locked.

As he climbed into the front seat beside Sam, he realised that he was wasting energy. It was inevitable, wasn't it? He would have to climb out again in a moment; the car would not start and he would have to get back out, and be the one who had to push the darn thing …but he was wrong. The engine started first time. Feeling delighted to be wrong was most unusual for Derek. Sam had a little smirk on his face. He could obviously read Derek's mind.

Driving with fingers crossed was not the best way to do it, but it was becoming a habit with Sam, and luck could play a large part in the short journey along the lane. As he moved off in first gear he had to avoid the many potholes – for the sake of the car's old springs – while ensuring that he did not drive too close to the edge, or they would all finish up in muddy water. This lane had a bad reputation.

"Oh Derek, ET's dummy," Sally suddenly exclaimed from the back. "I've forgotten to bring it, sorr-ee!" The two males looked at each other.

As the car came to a screechy halt, Derek cautiously opened his door, careful to avoid scratching the paintwork on the thorn hedging that ran along the length of the lane. Sam wondered why Derek bothered, the surface already had a multitude of scratch patterns from previous owners.

Wisely the engine was kept running: no use tempting fate. Derek was back quickly, dummy in hand and out of breath but feeling slightly better by being in the fresh air and having a little exercise, and off they went again. It had been a dry spell so at least the potholes were all visible.

The railway sleepers that made up the bridge and the main access road from the hotel were reached with the springs apparently continuing to function.

Sam relaxed. Derek relaxed. It was now plain sailing.

They were still on a minor road, but now on a surface that was like smooth glass by comparison to the lane. The main road was reached without mishap, and Sam turned towards Newingsworth. Unfortunately as he uncrossed his fingers, the engine stalled.

Sam smiled at Derek to reassure him. "It started first kick minutes ago," he said. Derek was not reassured. Sam tried the starter and the car did not start. Sam tried again. Several more attempts failed to achieve the desired result.

"Derek? Would you mind?"

Having been asked so nicely by Sam, how could Derek refuse? He got out. As he bent to push, the two-tone blast from the horn of the lorry startled him; obviously a driver not expecting an obstruction like this on a main road into town – and Derek was queasy again, visualising what could have happened. He wiped perspiration from his face. He felt seriously unwell. Little obstacles that are placed in the path of life, are there to be overcome, he told himself philosophically, took a deep breath and looked in the direction they were about to go. A slight gradient, thankfully downhill, and he started to push. It was still hard work but this time the engine kicked-in quickly. Sam's fingers were crossed once more and Derek climbed back in.

Valiantly he tried to hide it but, already, he was mentally and physically exhausted.

41

From behind the hedge Chester Wilfordon watched them climb into a ramshackle version of a car... he was grateful that the countryside surrounding the cottage gave him choices for hiding. The e-map had been studied and the various alternatives for a secret visit to Toozlethwaite Manor had been worked out. However, being a total amateur at housebreaking – in fact, this was to be the first time – attempting this in broad daylight meant his being extra cautious.

For him, checking the planned programme for today's events was easy, at least as far as Toozlethwaite's movements were concerned. The WAARR committee had been doing a very good job, spreading the word about the next event and actively encouraging community involvement.

The population of Newingsworth, Slatterfoot, and surrounding districts, had been queuing each day in Bisko's to sign the petition. *Little Radio fm* had been keeping everyone up to date with the increasing signature total. The daily newspaper, Slatterfoot Evening News, carried the same sort of information. It also had daily interviews with selected individuals who had signed. These articles concentrated on the losses interviewees would suffer due to the inevitable compulsory purchases and the financial and emotional suffering. This was being given the full works.

The other local newspaper, Newingsworth Weekly Gazette, had chosen to feature local heroes, alive or dead, and the daring battles they'd fought on behalf of the community. Thanks to Derek Toozlethwaite's own imagination though, there had been a lot of artistic licence used in these tales and he relied on readers not wishing to verify details for themselves.

By far the best communications to the masses, however, had been the YouTube clip of the old plump guy, Macintosh, toppling off the platform onto the leader, Toozlethwaite. That had gone viral very quickly, as these things do, and had transmitted the message beautifully to many parts of the globe that normally would not care.

'THE WAARR SPECTACULAR: GET TO BISKO'S AT 2.00PM SATURDAY TO LEARN THE NEXT STAGE IN THE CAMPAIGN. NOT JUST SPEECHES – SEE THE 'FAT GUY' DROP FROM A GREAT HEIGHT THIS TIME. AFTERWARDS, YOU CAN DO THE SAME BUNGEE JUMP AND BE FAMOUS TOO!'

Chesney Wilfordon never failed to take advantage. It was useful having made friends, before, with Kylie, the hotel receptionist. Women seemed to like him though he was unsure why. Was she smart enough to realise that he was obtaining information from her? He'd feigned interest in the WAARR Campaign.

Being a Newingsworth girl herself, she was extremely proud of what was being done to save the local community, particularly because her boss, Mr Macintosh, had become a star on YouTube! Her knowledge of the man who was now a local hero, Derek Toozlethwaite, was also a subject she was pleased to talk about. Chesney had to be careful not to appear too pushy in these chats. Let it spill out naturally from her, he decided, and spill out it certainly did.

"Did you know that Derek Toozlethwaite's wife was up here a short while ago? This morning, you've just missed her. Her aunt is my boss, you know. Hurrying back to get ready for this afternoon: she told me that; leaving at one o'clock they are, to go down to Bisko's. Today, Mrs Macintosh is going to hear Derek Toozlethwaite's speech too. She missed it the last time."

"Is that so? It must be very exciting living so close to a famous person," said Chester Wilfordon.

"Oh yes, Chester. Can I tell you this?" and she giggled. "You won't tell anyone else will you, but, before he became famous, I saw him without any clothes on!"

"Who?"

"Derek Toozlethwaite!"

"No...!"

"Oh, I shouldn't be saying things like that, should I?" and she giggled again, obviously enjoying the telling. "Oh, are you expecting rain? You are wearing wellingtons. You know it hasn't rained here for ages, Chester?"

"Don't want to get my good shoes messed up," he explained, "because I might take a wander over the fields."

"Not going to the rally then? That is disappointing. I'd hoped that you would have come back, Chester, to tell me all about it. I like hearing your voice."

Oh, oh! She was flirting with him. That's not what he wanted – just information.

As he stood hidden in the bushes, he heard the car splutter down the lane at a depressingly slow speed. It was fortunate that he had waited because Toozlethwaite suddenly appeared in a rush, went back into the cottage, and out again and then hared back down the lane, and the engine revved again. It was quiet enough this morning for him to be able to hear it go for a distance, maybe something to do with the direction of the light breeze, and then it stopped suddenly. A horn, blaring angrily, came to his ears. Why had they stopped, he wondered, and hoped they were not returning. A few moments later he heard the engine restart and gradually fade away completely.

It was more uncomfortable than he thought it would be, squeezing through a thorn hedge. Rather prickly! It had to be done if he were to avoid crossing the bridge at the end of the lane. He would have been seen too easily that way.

Slithering down the banking of the stream was not difficult but his gloves picked up mud. Into the stream he stepped. It was only a couple of metres wide and should have been easy enough to cross but catching a foot on some debris on the muddy bottom threw him off balance, and the next thing he knew he had two wellingtons full of muddy water.

"Damn!" Only a couple more steps and he would have been over and dry. Now it was awkward clambering back up the steep banking carrying unexpected ballast. He would have much preferred dry feet, or at least, not to have heavy water-filled wellingtons at the end of legs that were not used to this sort of exercise.

At the top of the banking the removal of each boot to pour out the water, and having to do it in a seated position, meant his trousers became soaked and mud-stained. He had not bargained for this. He'd brought only one pair of trousers this weekend and look at the state of them!

It was at that moment that he chose to ask himself, *what am I hoping to gain from all this?* He was able to supply an answer of course: a rather important document, containing the top-secret information, the loss of which was his fault. *Will I be successful? Of course I will, provided Toozlethwaite actually has it in his house.*

He stood up. What a mess! How could he sneak back into the hotel looking like this? That girl noticed the wellingtons, how could she possibly miss the messed-up trousers? And he had nothing to change into. *Can I have them cleaned? Focus! Get it over and done with.*

He tried the door; locked, of course. What else could be expected? He should have brought a jemmy. Idiot, why hadn't he? He'd break the glass panel and reach in ... but what to use?

There was a noise from inside, a snuffling sound. Was someone actually in the house after all? Had the wife stayed at home? Was he going to have to bluff it out? He rang the bell – and immediately the barking began! He'd forgotten about the dog. No one came to the door. It must have been the dog he'd heard.

What was its name again, Julie? No, it was Jilly.

There was a letterbox low down on the door, the bane of a postman's life. He looked through the opening – at the face of a white poodle.

"Hello girl," he said gently. "Who's a good Jilly?" Then he did something that Derek would never have believed: he poked his hand in the letterbox. Jilly licked his fingers. "Good girl." He removed his hand gently from the letterbox and heard the dog give a disappointed whine.

Kneeling on the doormat gave the moment of inspiration: he'd remembered his father comparing country folk and townspeople. There is a greater trust of the human race when you live in the country, he'd told him.

Was it possible?

Could the door key actually have been placed trustingly under the doormat?

Chesney lifted it. Look at that! Hard to believe but his old dad had been correct. Even in this day and age, here was

someone gullible enough to trust the rest of humanity...
Muggins!

The door was opened, cautiously. She'd licked his hand but he wasn't sure how the dog would react to him actually entering.

He needn't have worried, she was delighted, bouncing around and so pleased to see him again.

The nice man had returned.

42

All was not well on the Bisko's car park. A crowd was already gathering but thankfully, they were not aware that today's plan was proving shambolic. Derek was feeling slightly better but struggling to remain calm. He tried telling himself that there was plenty of time, desperately trying not to make a big issue of it. *Hammy will be won over.* However, the man they were attempting to convince was being supremely obstinate! He took exception to being told by Derek that it was a bit thick of him pulling out at the last minute, to which Hammy retorted that he'd never agreed to do it in the first place – a fact that Derek had chosen to ignore.

"Onywey, who'd want to drop doon from a muckle big platform in the sky? No' me, or do I look daft?" he asked grumpily, and before anyone had the chance to answer his question, "I told ye before, ah'm not doin' it!"

"Now, don't go off in a huff," Thelma added, just the words to make Hammy want to do exactly that.

Derek looked at Sam. "Would you?" he asked, and gave his most engaging smile, but the reply of "No! Oh Jeez, no!" was immediate.

"And don't bother with me either," said Alexander very quickly.

"Spider?" Derek asked plaintively.

"I'd need a doctor's line," Spider offered lamely.

"We have to have something to give this mob. We promised them that you would do a bigger jump than last time, Hammy."

"Ah've told ye – *naw!*"

They all stood looking up glumly at the mobile bungee-jumping platform suspended on the long steel structure, almost in the clouds it seemed, but sitting unused and about to become a massive anti-climax. What do you tell a crowd that has appeared in anticipation of watching a plump gentleman step bravely off the edge, who was now saying, NO?

"Could I make a suggestion, Derek?" said Sam. "What about – you go up on the platform?"

"What?" came from Derek – in the form of a squeak!

"…And, do the speech from up there? That would be unusual."

"But..." Derek thought frantically, suddenly feeling unwell again.

"Sam, that is a brilliant idea, if I might say so," added Alexander, "and wearing the mobile microphone Derek, it won't matter where you are standing."

Steven Tomkins, the store manager, was now actively involved with the group. This week he had had been very helpful and acquired a mobile microphone system for Derek's use.

"We'll have to make sure the range is good enough," he said. "You'll be very far away from the equipment, you know. Oh, and Derek, you will remember to say that Bisko's supplied the speaker system won't you?"

Derek looked up at the platform. Yes, it was very, very far away and it was little wonder that Hammy refused. He, himself, was not convinced, reluctant to buy into a scheme that might put him at risk, but... "If I did that, it would only be for the speech. I would not be jumping." He was hoping for a response of, 'Oh well, it wouldn't be worth it then,' but that didn't come.

"I can visualise you standing up there, Derek. It would be very dramatic, my boy," said his father-in-law. "For you, this could even go down as a major moment in history."

"Guaranteed to be on the national news tonight, I'll bet," said Spider, "and the front pages of the nationals. You will be talking to the world if you stand up there," ...*but it would be even better if you fall off*, he was thinking.

"You'll have tae be awful careful o' the wind when ye're standin' up there, sunshine," said Hammy, glad to no longer be targeted. "Just one wee blow and, *whooooosh*, ye'll be flyin'. Aye, ye'll love it, laddie."

Derek looked once more at the machine that was waiting for him – a cantilevered affair, the long strap and harness sitting ready. It looked much worse than it really was, because he was standing directly below it, he decided as he tried to convince himself.

It would be folded down to allow him to step onto the platform and all he'd have to do then was stand and hang on to a bar as it rose again into the clouds. He'd make the speech, to a wondrous audience who would be admiring his bravery as well as the clever words that he'd be saying, and that's it. Massive cheers, and then down he'd come, off he'd step, and everyone would be happy. *A piece of cake!* He imagined the spectacular reaction.

"Right, let's check that the mike will work at that height," he said, trying to avoid looking up at the platform again in case his new-found confidence wavered.

"One, two; one, two; testing; one, two." The voice of Steven Tomkins was coming through loud and clear from the far end of the car park.

"So, we'll not be needin' a platform after all?" suggested Hammy, looking at the stacked pallets with suspicion.

"Yes, we will," said Derek. "Why don't you lot go on to it, together, as a committee, and sit there while I am up on the..." His voice broke as his eyes drifted heavenwards – pigeons were circling up there! *This is not a good idea!* He thought how stupid he might be about to become but forced himself to continue. "...And then Our Cause will be seen to be not just a one-man band. Our strength is in our teamwork!"

"Aye, that'll be righ'," said Hammy, under his breath.

"Someone will have to help me," said old Mrs Masterton, the latest one to join the committee. "I don't want any silly nonsense like he had last week," she added with a nod in Hammy's direction, "Not at my age!"

That she'd been at the sherry, as usual, and would have been safer standing where she was, was obvious to those in the vicinity, but she was determined to be seen as one of the team. Alexander said he'd help her.

It was getting near the planned time for the start of the rally and the car park was filling rapidly with more people still coming in the entrance. Customers in the store were being urged to leave so that the doors could be closed during the gathering. As far as the crowd could tell, it was all going like clockwork.

"Derek, nearly time to start," Alexander called to his son-in-law. The platform had been lowered and sat there, ready for boarding.

"I don't need any straps on me," Derek was protesting to the Bungee Jump owner. "I'll hold on to the rail. That's all I need. I'll be ok."

"Sorry, but you will have to wear the normal harness," he was told. "No one goes up without that. I'll strap you to the rail as well and you keep that on until the red light goes off.

Don't jump until the green light shows, and I give you the thumbs up from down here."

"I am not jumping," Derek repeated. "I will make a speech and then you can let me down again. Others can jump later if they are daft enough."

"Chickening out already are you? Most people wait until they are up there."

"It's only for the speech!" Derek was getting excited and short tempered. He had never done this sort of thing before, in fact, probably no one had ever been daft enough to do this, but ...*as publicity, it should be perfect!* A smug thought boosted his resolve once more: *I'll say it was my idea!*

He stepped onto the platform and was clipped to the rail. The long rope lay coiled at his feet. That would certainly remain coiled, he told himself and tried to think pleasant thoughts as the platform began to rise quite quickly.

"All the best, Sweaty," said Hammy, shaking his head sadly. "Ye'll need it!"

Don't look down... No, don't.

As he rose the chanting began. Sally tried to lead with "Der-ek, Der-ek," but was drowned out by the much more emotive one of "Swea-ty, Swea-ty." In no time at all, the cantilever arm was at its maximum and the platform had stopped rising. Derek stood there wondering why it was still vibrating, and then realised it was not the platform – it was him!

Get a grip – and don't look down!

The chant had changed. It was now: "Jump Sweaty, jump Sweaty, jump..."

Don't look down!

He held up his arms. There was an enormous cheer – and then an expectant hush. He clasped his hands together in front of him, in supplication, and there was another cheer, then the hush, and he began to speak.

"Ladies and gentlemen of Newingsworth, Slatterfoot and surrounding districts; brothers; comrades; dear friends – today is the opportunity for us to move forward in a giant step in our campaign to usurp authority; an authority that is attempting to dictate a policy totally contrary to the wishes of the people, us, the ones who elected them. They want to destroy the life we lead, a life that has been going on in the same way for centuries, the life handed down by our forebears; a life that we love."

Has that made it appear that we are living in a third world country? Maybe I could have expressed it in a better way?

But on he went.

"Let them be clear about what we are saying. This is WAARR! We Are Against the Rail Route!"

As his voice echoed majestically off the supermarket walls, he paused for effect, and to give time for a supportive cheer from below.

"As good citizens you have been dutifully signing the petition all this week. To date there are thirty-three thousand names included."

Another pause, and another cheer. He just hoped that the person receiving the document did not look too closely at the names because, even he could see that although different names were stated, often the writing was the same for several entries, and he wondered how it could be explained if the end result showed thousands more than lived in the area...

"But, we all know that that will not change any of their plans for demolition. A piece of paper will mean little to the authorities. We need action." Pause for a cheer. "We must face them down. Let them know who runs the country. Let them know that, we, the people, are the masters of this grand part of the universe. Pause. We must fight them in the corridors of power; we must fight them on the highways, in the high schools, in the post offices, in the supermarkets. We must fight them in the cowsheds..."

He was warming up and no longer grasping the safety bar. His free arm was needed for the dramatic gesticulations, and anyway he had a safety strap attached to the bar. The pigeons were even listening to him, circulating around, wondering who this was with the effrontery to invade their air space...

"As I stand here looking down on you all, I see dedication, I see enthusiasm, I see determination, I see a power for the betterment of our society, the ability of the good people of Newingsworth, Slatterfoot and surrounding districts to force a change to poorly thought-out plans. And I must share my secret with you: I know of the scheming that has gone on behind closed doors, scheming that will make fortunes for those individuals who consider they can control us! We must be courageous!"

In reality, Derek could tell nothing from the faces of his audience; to do that he would have had to pluck up the courage to actually look down; the courage he spoke of was certainly not his!

"What we must now do – together – is to show our strength. We will go onto the streets. Civil disobedience is called for – peaceful obstruction of normal life. We must involve the rest of the country in our fight."

An inspirational moment occurred as he looked beyond the surrounding rooftops towards the railway station and the lines going north and south.

"Normal society will have to be given a severe shake. It is time for the peaceable silent majority to create a ruckus. The whole country must become involved. We could stop all trains running north and south. Yes, we'll disrupt timetables by our physical presence. We will make them listen to us. Slatterfoot Station, the station that they are intending to remove, will be ours: that will be our next objective. If one of us has to be a sacrifice to show how serious we are, then so be it. The storm clouds are gathering. Those against us must beware. Are you all with me?"

There was a massive cry of "YESSSSSS..." from down below.

"Are we ready to march?"

"YESSSSSS..."

Alexander, Spider, and Hammy, looked at each other. This was happening too quickly. *What have we let ourselves in for? What is he thinking about? Why is he dragging us with him, and – did he really say: sacrifice?*

The cry from high thundered from the loudspeakers.

"Yes! This is WAARR!"

43

Earlier, Spider had subconsciously hoped that Derek would change his mind and actually do the bungee jump, so he sat with the camera ready to record it in video form for immediate use. It would be great publicity. Unfortunately, there was little hope of that actually happening, he'd told himself.

But, as it turned out, Spider was wrong and, as can happen in these situations, the cause would not be due to only one reason. Obviously, Derek, by releasing the short safety strap from the side rail, had been stupid. It was there to serve a meaningful purpose. However, being restricted to a position that prevented him from being seen at the best angle by the cameras below, niggled him. He'd decided to correct it – but that aspect was only a contribution.

It wasn't that he stepped too far forward either. It had been just enough to permit him to improve his position and take up a picturesque pose. There was no breeze and, except for the flapping of the wings of nearby pigeons, the air was still. His hand left the rail for only a few moments as he positioned himself and took up a pose that Nelson on his column, or Napoleon on the plinth, could have taken pride in. (Maybe, whoever had been first should have trademarked it!)

There he stood with one hand behind his back, holding his notes out of sight, and the other tucked in his shirt. He imagined it to be perfect for the camera shots.

From down below I must look magnificent, he told himself with a conceited smile.

Doing the speech standing up at this high platform was for spectacular effect, so, he had made the most of it. With his head held high and chin proudly jutting out, he felt the part – a natural leader, and then he chanced a glance downwards...

The moment he did that he knew he had made a mistake. Suddenly he felt queasy. The feeling from earlier had returned, but, he forced himself to remain upright and to retain his composure. *Grin and bear it*, he told himself, but that didn't help – and then came the clincher!

A pigeon was won over by the pose and what is more natural for a pigeon to do when exposed to a statue of Nelson, or Napoleon, than to alight on the statue's head! Though Derek was feeling poorly he had forced himself to stand stock still to be photographed from below. He looked like a statue – until the bird landed!

It was the mad swinging of his arms that probably caused it in the end – the sudden and uncomfortable feel of the bird's claws on the skull causing the extensive panicky arm movements. The bird's reaction was a sudden fluttering to escape, accompanied by the natural result of any bird being startled, relief of the bowels.

As the pigeon left hurriedly, unfortunately, so did Derek – over the front edge!

"Whaaaa...! Nooooooo...! Ahhhhh…!" was the plaintive cry that came from the loudspeakers as down he dropped.

"Wow..." was the admiring noise from the crowd, followed by the now familiar "Swea-ty, Swea-ty, Swea-ty..."

He dangled, bouncing up and down, unable to do anything to stop the seemingly perpetual motion, feeling more and more unwell with each bounce.

The committee, all of whom dutifully had done as requested and displayed the team spirit by sitting on the platform underneath a now dangling Derek were the ones who suffered the indignity of having to watch the contents of their hero's stomach splatter around their feet, and where it splattered was much too close!

The crowd thought this to be wonderful – the little extra they'd hoped for.

What a man!

Sweaty Toozlethwaite had just demonstrated to everyone that he was game for anything! Obviously, this was someone who knew no fear and would fight long and hard for his people and the just cause!

A man that can be trusted to go all the way – a man to follow!

The crowd cheered like mad!

Derek could only dangle, helplessly...

44

Chesney was inside the cottage. Finding the tin of Sally's favourite biscuits and feeding several to Jilly had sealed the friendship. The normally snappy white poodle was happily following the visitor around the house. Chesney convinced himself that if she could have talked she would have been pleased to disclose the whereabouts of the documents to him. As it was, she couldn't, and he hadn't – found them, that is.

He'd looked in all the places he could imagine anyone would hide them: the wardrobes, the cupboards, under loose rugs and cushions, under the chairs and settees. All drawers had been checked to no avail. He'd even tried under the mattresses of the double beds in the main bedroom and the guest room without success. Could they be taped to the underside of a table or chair perhaps? Nope! *Is there a loft?* Yes, there was, but it looked from the paint that the cover had never been opened since modernisation of the cottage.

Chesney felt at home in this cottage. It seemed a comfortable place to live, peaceful and remote, not too fancy, but with one glaring flaw: no security. He was padding around comfortably in stocking soles – dry socks too. Though he hadn't found what he was looking for, there had been one benefit of being in the drawers; he'd purloined a pair of Derek's socks. He was convinced that they would never be missed because there were lots, mostly loose single socks, with only a few sorted as pairs. It had been a difficult task finding two to match but he had, and that was what he was wearing.

He'd also noticed Derek's wellingtons sitting in the little entrance hall as being identical to the ones he was wearing. So, these would be the ones he would be putting on, when he left.

However, it looked as if Chesney could be leaving empty-handed as far as the documents were concerned. He was even beginning to doubt that they had ever been inside the cottage at all! Had he been mistaken about Katy? Did she really have them? Was she playing a double bluff perhaps? Of course, Toozlethwaite could be carrying them about with him. It was most frustrating – it could be any damn scenario. They had to be found: if they fell into the wrong hands...!

His trousers were still soggy. He would never be able to sneak back into the hotel without being noticed, and someone was bound to ask questions, that receptionist for certain. He was closing the wardrobe door when it occurred to him: the solution that he'd found for the socks; would it work for the trousers? Toozlethwaite was about the same build. If a pair of trousers went missing, would he notice? Was there a similar pair of denims in the wardrobe? Ah yes, so, if the wet ones were hung at the back they would dry, eventually. He double checked the trouser pockets. It wouldn't do to leave any obvious evidence behind.

Yes, that's better. A perfect fit, much more comfortable.

"Another biscuit, dog?" he asked the white poodle, and a handful of biscuits came from the tin again. Jilly scoffed them off promptly.

The printer! The computer printer had a closed flap. That hadn't been checked. He stepped over, but was disappointed once more. There was a document underneath that began 'Ladies and gentlemen of Newingsworth, Slatterfoot and...'

What a load of drivel, he concluded, and gave up reading. It wasn't what he was looking for.

This had not been a successful venture. He looked around the room. He had been careful to keep everything he touched in the same place, no mess, and no fingerprints either. The gloves had been worn from the moment he stepped in the front door. *Ah, but what about the letterbox?* He'd put his hand through, hadn't he. That would have to be wiped just in case. His handkerchief took care of that. The front door was lying open.

To have free passage through the front door was not normal for Jilly. The lead was always applied going out that way. For the dog, the fence around the back garden was the maximum freedom permitted, unless accompanied on a walk. Jilly's new friend didn't seem to know that rule, nor did he even notice her trotting out. He was concentrating on cleaning the fingerprints from the brass surface.

Chesney stepped back inside again, had another look in each area as a final check, and went back to the entrance porch. His own wellingtons were put in the exact same position as the ones he was putting on, the door was closed, locked with the key, and the key replaced under the mat in the precise position where he'd found it.

He had failed. If it were true what she said about housebreaking, would Katy have had more success? But, of course, Katy could be the one who had the file...

He pondered on those thoughts as he crossed, more carefully this time, back over the stream.

It was a much subdued Derek that climbed out of Hammy's vehicle. He, Sally and little Edwin, were offered the return journey from the rally by Sam but, thankfully for Derek, Hammy suggested that, because he was going directly back to the hotel, they might as well be with him and Thelma. Just as well because, as usual, Sam's vehicle failed to start.

Even though he considered himself to be suffering from shock after his unintended fall from the heavens, Derek still felt slightly guilty at leaving Spider, Rob and Alexander to take turns at pushing Sam's old banger.

Derek had been the only one to have any mess on his clothes. It was noticeable to Hammy and Thelma after Derek and family left the vehicle that the sickly odour remained. The man was no longer with them, but his aroma lingered on.

Sally stood outside for a moment and waved as Hammy drove back along the lane. "Let's go and see how smelly Daddy is doing then," she murmured as she carried the little one inside. Normally being the blame of bad smells in the house, ET just smiled up at Mummy.

The first thing she noticed was the mark on the carpet. Derek had failed to remove his footwear and, ill or not, rules were rules. He should know how easily footprints made a mess on this covering. He'd been told so many times before, how could he have forgotten?

"Derek. I hope you are going to clean the carpet," she shouted as she placed ET in his cot.

"Sally, I am already in bed, I am not feeling good at all. What's wrong now?"

"You have made marks on the carpet. Why didn't you remove your shoes?"

"I did," was the plaintive – *I should be getting sympathy* – reply from the bedroom.

"You didn't, you know. The evidence is right here in front of me."

The bed made a creaking sound as he rose reluctantly to appear at the bedroom door – in his stocking soles.

"Did you take them off in the bedroom then?" was the next criticism.

"They are in the hall. Look, there! Do you think I'd be stupid enough to walk into this house with outdoor shoes on?"

She had to give him that one – like a good boy, he had remembered – and his shoes were where he said.

"Oh, well," she had to concede a point this time, but persevered, "So, when did you make the mess then?"

In the meantime, Derek had slipped back onto the bed.

No reply. She would give up on that – for the moment!

The sound of Grandad's scooter broke the silence. The phut-phut-phutting, that was so easily recognised, gradually got louder as he approached the cottage, going slowly and carefully navigating the potholes like everyone else. Sally opened the front door as he cut the engine. He and Granny Smith dismounted, removed their helmets and in they came. Shoes were removed automatically. Sally's rules were rarely argued about by anyone other than Derek...

"We won't stay long," said Daisy. "We only came round to congratulate Derek for this afternoon. That brilliant speech and then the fun of the bungee jump. That was a real surprise, even though he'd said he felt unwell. I didn't think he would do it."

"Is he all r-r-r-r-right?" asked Hector. "I have some c-c-c-cans of b-b-b-beer with m-m-me for him. Wh-wh-wh-where is he?"

"In the bedroom, Grandad: cup of tea, Daisy?"

"Oh yes, dear, and do you think I could have one of those biscuits? The ones you like, they're my favourites too. Hector won't want any. Can I lift little Edwin?"

"Derek Toozlethwaite!"

Sally's yell came from the kitchen. Hector stopped in his tracks at the side of the bed, as Derek sprang to a seated position, suddenly sensing trouble.

"Have you been at my biscuits?"

The pained look on Derek's face caused Hector to step back out of the firing line. The footsteps were coming from the kitchen in the direction of the bedroom and, thankfully, any complaints would be directed at the figure on the bed, rather than at him. Sally appeared at the door with a face that said trouble, then she stopped suddenly and looked around.

"Daisy, is Jilly in there with you?"

"No dear," came back from ET's room. "She's not in here."

"Derek, where is Jilly? You were last to leave the house earlier. Did you let her out into the back garden before we left?"

"No," came from the bed.

"What did you do with her then?"

At that point Derek decided that by rising from the bed he might be less vulnerable. Any feelings of grandeur that he might have experienced at the rally had rapidly dispersed. This was real life in Toozlethwaite Manor and as usual everything was considered to be his fault. Derek was on his feet now; so much for recuperation. *Might as well be up*, he decided as the approaching noise of a car gave advance warning of more surprise visitors, and indicated the urgent necessity for Sam to replace the exhaust.

"Hi everybody," said Angie as she opened the door and entered. "Sam," she shouted back through the door to her husband, "bring Annabel's baby food with you, please, "...and Sally's favourite biscuits. They are in the Bisko's bag."

Sam kicked off his shoes, left them beside Angie's, and came in carrying Annabel in her carry-cot in one hand, and the biscuits in the other. Sally lifted ET from the cot and carried him through to join the party.

"Thank g-g-goodness for the b-b-b-biscuits, Sam. S-S-S-Sally's eaten all of h-h-hers and b-b-b-blaming poor old D-D-D-Derek." Hector received a glaring look from Sally for that remark, and regretted it immediately. "...W-w-w-ant a b-b-b-beer, Sam?"

There was a knock at the back door.

Oh God, who is it this time? Derek thought. *I am not in party mood.*

Sam was closest and opened the door to Hammy, Thelma and two dogs. He stepped aside quickly as Cornelius leaped in and made straight for his favourite person in the bedroom doorway.

"Oh no..." Derek could see what was coming ...the big, lollopy, sandy-coloured Labrador hit him in the chest and sent him tumbling backwards. Luckily, he had failed to progress much beyond the bed again and toppled gratefully onto a soft landing. He struggled there to fight off the affectionate Labrador, avoiding its slobbery tongue.

Sally's interest switched as the little dog Hammy released from the leash took her attention. "Jilly!" she exclaimed, and the little white poodle dashed straight for her. "Where have you been my precious little darling? I was worried sick about you," and Jilly became the centre of attention.

"This wee blighter was annoying one of oor guests in the hotel, would ye believe. She was just standin' outside the door of one of them, howlin'."

"That's a bit of an exaggeration, Hammy," Thelma interrupted. "Sally, she was only whining outside a door in the corridor. She isn't normally allowed out on her own is she?"

"What have you been up to my little one?" The question was asked with the dog's face held close to hers, but Jilly refused to answer, especially with the others staring. "It was your master, wasn't it? He doesn't like you and he tried to lose you, didn't he?" Again, Jilly refused to answer.

Derek didn't consider it worthwhile defending himself. Absorbing the blame seemed simpler and, anyway, he couldn't be sure that the dog hadn't nipped out when his back was turned, but why was she in the hotel? That thought was banished by the need to rise rapidly from his horizontal position on the bed.

Cornelius had decided to become even friendlier.

45

Chesney Wilfordon was reluctant to admit that he had yet to discover the whereabouts of the Secret Documents, but the phone call to the boss would have to be made. He should be informed of the lack of progress – but not yet. Hopefully, leaving the call for another few hours would do no harm. Courage would be needed...

Who's got them? Toozlethwaite, or that pretty little Katy?

Sitting in the office, door locked, surrounded by his electronics, he ought to have felt safe – but he did not. What they were doing had never troubled him before but, previously, exposure of the scheme had been considered to be impossible.

The panic was all due to him!

The documents should never have been in his bag.

It had been an egotistical 'I am brilliant, look what I can do' moment. He was intending to read them during the weekend break, but copying them and taking them with him had been plain stupid – and then to lose the pesky things! He'd missed out on a short holiday too! It would cost a fortune if they weren't found; not just costly for him. If details of the documents were leaked at the wrong time, even though identities could be difficult to trace, the whole project would fail. The backing they was getting from the top would be exposed too. A private organisation surreptitiously being aided by a very senior Civil Servant: an individual using

Government equipment: an individual who had detailed inside knowledge of Government procedures: all could carry a hefty penalty.

Chesney Wilfordon knew that secrecy had been, and still was paramount, but what more could he do?

The phone call would have to be made; get it over with...

It was ringing.

No response... Oh well, at least he'd tried...

Then, when he was about to give up, it was answered.

Damn!

"Hello," the voice barked.

"Ah, this is Chesney Wilfordon speaking, is that...?"

"Code-speak please! As if the situation is not bad enough, man? And you are directly through to Bubbles." Bubbles tut-tutting was ominous...

"Listen carefully, for this call we will use..." There was a moment of hesitation. "Huh! ...Weather-speak." The Boss did not sound in a good frame of mind. "And now, perhaps you would condescend to supply me with a forecast," he continued, "and a good one I hope because my barometer is registering very high pressure currently – thanks to some idiot! So ...the black clouds are lifting, we sincerely hope."

It wasn't the words that were threatening – it was the growl in the voice!

Chesney gulped. He did not have good news... "Negative," he said. "A red sky in the morning, the sailor's warning..."

"Oh no, that must not be, Pipsqueak! It is not good enough and you must sort it out immediately! The sharper the blast the sooner it is past, as they say... And you should be remembering that the pot of gold at the end of the rainbow is at stake!"

"How could I possibly forget that sir, but, if you want to see the sunshine," offered Chesney, "…you have to weather the storm…"

There was a silence… Had they been disconnected?

"I have to warn you, Pipsqueak," said Bubbles eventually, "that when your joints hurt, it heralds a storm, so, look out! Unless you, personally, make hay while the sun shines, I will make sure the storm is fierce and that your joints really hurt – together with various other parts!"

Chesney flinched. "Is that a threat, sir?"

"How very perceptive of you," Bubbles responded. "I hope for your sake that the bad weather looks worse through your window!"

"Oh, yes, I understand. Hmm… The rain in Spain falls mainly on the plain."

"Pipsqueak, what the blazes are you talking about?"

"Sorry, just threw that in, to maybe lighten the mood. You can rely on me sir. We will not give up even though it becomes a hurricane. "

"Nothing less is expected of our Senior Weatherman. Full-time dedication, above and beyond the call of duty, coupled with a positive forecast, will be the only things to prevent this apocalypse! Continue to search for your safe haven in the storm, so that your barometer of happiness may rise effectively… *What the hell am I talking about now?*"

That mumbled question did not seem to call for an answer… How much more? Two grown-ups behaving like silly schoolboys, but…

"WILFORDON!" was loud and clear. "GET YOUR RUDDY FINGER OUT!"

"Affirmative. Understood. Digit extracted, sir!"

Chesney Wilfordon replaced the phone on the cradle with a deep sigh.

46

It was Sunday morning. Alexander and Muriel had arrived on their bicycles with a selection of newspapers to find Derek and Sally still in pyjamas.

While the bed was still warm, Derek had been hoping to slip back under the covers for a few extra hours. What with the crowd leaving late last night, his tummy feeling less than healthy and, as usual, ET wakening him in the middle of the night, he reckoned he deserved some extra time – but no chance.

He brightened up when he saw the printed reports. Yesterday's rally had become big news. They'd made the front page of many of the nationals – at least, Derek had.

'IT COULD BE A SWEATY WAARR!' said the Observer's headlines.

'A DROP OF SWEATY' was in the Times.

'SWEATY – MAN OF THE PEOPLE' was the choice of the Sunday Mirror.

In oversized print, the Sunday Sun had gone for 'SWEATY EXPOSES A BIG BOOB'; though they did go on to explain in the text that the boob was committed by the government department by choosing that route for the intended rail line. The sub-heading posed the question 'Who made this silly decision?' So, at least they were all being supportive.

There were pictures too. Every newspaper had successfully obtained a shot of Derek, dangling helplessly from the bungee rope. It looked like a public hanging!

In every one, a lot of column inches were consumed by a warning to the rail-using public that the Eastern rail lines had been targeted by the WAARR group. There was every chance that bodies would be chained on the line in the area of Slatterfoot Station. It would wiser for travellers, this Saturday coming, to alter plans and stay home, or better still to make their way to Slatterfoot Station and support a worthy cause.

This was not a plan decided at the meeting at all, and not even one that Derek, in his inspired moments, had spouted on about. It appeared to be deliberate scaremongering by the press, the media moguls getting even more brassed-off with current government policies than the general public, and taking every opportunity to stir it!

Last night, short items on news programmes of various television channels had given publicity related to the previous day's rally. Beneficially for the cause, these had been repeated several times. Derek and Sally found this out from Alexander and Muriel who were at home watching TV when all the others were at the cottage.

"And what an expression on your face, Derek," said his mother-in-law, "I thought you were about to burst. It was really funny!"

Derek could have managed without that comment.

"And when did the idea of tying yourself to the railway track occur to you?" Muriel continued. "You never mentioned it at any of the meetings but it's in several of the stories. Won't that be dangerous?"

"I didn't say that – and anyway that is being stupid. For me the next stage is to be a protest march. We'd start off at

Bisko's – our home base now – and go all the way through Newingsworth and Slatterfoot to the station."

"Oh, that's a disappointment..." said his mother-in-law. "I was looking forward to seeing you tied on the line."

Derek hoped that she was pulling his leg, but...

"Well, are there any better suggestions than a march?"

"I think that is very practical, Derek," said Alexander.

"Yes, and get tied to the rails the *following* week!" added Muriel.

"Look I lived dangerously yesterday. If danger is what you want, it is someone else's turn. I've done my bit."

"You can't suggest that others should do it if you are too chicken to do it yourself," said Alexander, in order to stir things up.

"But I didn't suggest it!"

"I agree with you, Derek," said Sally passionately, turning to her father. "My Derek has taken enough risks this weekend, and he is right. It should be the turn of somebody else, surely – so how about yourself, Daddy?"

Alexander almost choked on the mouthful of coffee.

"A good idea Sally," said Muriel. "He's always getting others to do the silly things."

"It's not silly," Alexander spluttered back. "It's too damn dangerous!"

"Nonsense, you can do it," said Derek, determined to get his own back. "You could be tied to the line, and..." a dramatic pause, "you could be dressed like an old-fashioned heroine from the silent movies, with a blonde wig and full make-up, it would make a perfect scenario for the cameras."

Derek sat back and waited for the protestations, but none came.

Alexander looked at him in wonderment. Where did these ideas come from? This was par excellence; another chance for him to show how good he could look in female clobber.

Detective Sergeant Milne was at home in York, relaxing after a trying few days of senior management criticism. Breakfast was over. Sitting with a mug of coffee beside him, to be consumed when cool, he was reading a Sunday newspaper, the Independent, his usual and only Sunday newspaper.

This man was not caring about WAARR with the same enthusiasm shown by Derek and his associates, but, it seemed WAARR news was hard to avoid. He was interested today in Toozlethwaite's antics because yesterday morning there had been a further development related to the unsolved crime – the one that occurred recently on his patch when Toozlethwaite's phone was found, and for which he was receiving a great deal of criticism.

It was Green who'd come into his office with the news. A girl, who worked for many years at Middlefield Mansion House, where the robbery took place, had been passing a local pawnshop in York. Something in the window caught her eye.

What she'd seen was a brooch of an unusual shape. She recognised it as the one that the lady of the Mansion had owned, one that was stolen recently. It was a gold circle surrounding an upside-down 'Y' – looked a bit like a CND badge – with filigree. It hung on a gold chain and was inlaid with small, valuable stones. It was certainly unusual, probably unique and quite valuable. Cynically, DC Green suspected that the girl had recognised it, probably because she'd had her eye on it herself – to pinch at a suitable time. He had seized the item as evidence and it was safely locked up in his boss's desk drawer in York Police Station.

The pawnshop manager, Harold Bissell, was interviewed by Green and questioned about where he acquired the brooch. Someone pawned it, had been the response. Would he be willing to identify who brought it in? Of course! He'd then given the impression of wanting to be helpful and immediately offered to describe the man.

Green had his own suspicion as to who it was most likely to be, but, the description given to him was nothing like the appearance of Binky Ross.

Binky had been working this area for a long time and was well known to both crooks and police. Every so often he was pulled into the station because no-one else could be found. Of course, the man usually succeeded in convincing the arresting officer that he had been on another planet at the time.

When Milne was told that a description had been eagerly supplied and although he would have loved it to be true, he was unconvinced. From his experience of this particular pawnshop manager it would be information conjured up to please a policeman.

However, as he sat drinking his coffee and perusing his Sunday newspaper, that description, repeated to him yesterday by Green, was still fresh in his head.

He looked closer at the photo of the dangling figure, then the full-face correct-way-up version of that same individual included with many other shots of yesterday's WAARR demonstration.

Interesting...

Though it was obvious that Bissell must have used his imagination and would be protecting the real person, on the page being held open by Milne – from the angle the photo had been taken, and the description given by the pawnshop manager – it was a perfect match for Toozlethwaite!

47

What a crowd-puller Sweaty Toozlethwaite had come up with this time!

BANK MANAGER'S RAILWAY LINE SACRIFICE WILL BE NEXT WEEK'S BIG ATTRACTION.

Monday morning's newspapers had made a meal of it. This was the detail they chose to add to their version of the Sunday papers' stories about the 'the sacrifice of a volunteer – a body on the railway line'. Speculation was rife, as to why this particular person should have put himself forward for the selfless act. Of course, the spark for the obituary-in-waiting could have been due to the slant put on the Press Release by Spider – perhaps it was unwise to have mentioned Alexander Donaldson by name. It had become greatly personalised.

It disturbed Alexander somewhat when he read it. Derek's idea was good and he had been all for it when they'd been at the cottage on Sunday, highly enthusiastic in fact, but seeing it in print, he was less sure. It made it all sound so final – for him.

Only a stunt, he kept saying to himself, but at work, it had become preferable to remain inside his office as much as possible. When he'd appeared in the general area of the bank it was embarrassingly uncomfortable. It was the way customers looked at him pityingly.

"Couldn't cope with the job," was the gossip.

"Poor soul ...but he's had a good innings."

"I hear his wife's about to leave him. Relies totally on her, he does. He can't even boil an egg. Better going quickly than starving to death slowly, I'd say."

Finding bunches of flowers being left anonymously outside the bank entrance when he arrived for work on the Tuesday, made him feel rather guilty. How could he tell them that it wasn't really to be the end for him, without them feeling foolish and him becoming disliked and ridiculed? It would be easier to suffer it for the week, and then give them a nice surprise when he arrived back safe and well.

Oh, but then, they might be disappointed!

The mood of his staff was dismal. No longer was there the jolly banter to keep the day from feeling long. It was now Wednesday and only ten o'clock but it seemed, for everyone working with him, the day would never come to an end. The eyes of the girls, Jane and Cheryl, were bloodshot from breaking into tears every so often. It only took one little old lady, who'd been a customer since a schoolgirl, to enquire gently, "How is he today?" and the tears started again.

The male employee, David, was just as bad. He couldn't look his manager in the eye any more. If he tried, he finished up vanishing to the toilet to avoid breaking down in public.

"Mr Donaldson, Head Office on the phone, sir," Janice sobbed. "They want to speak to (*boo-hoo-hoo...*)"

"I'll take it in the office, Janice, thank you."

"Alexander, this is Jack, Jack Evans. How are you old man?"

"Oh hello, Jack, haven't spoken to you in a long time. I am not doing too badly, thank you, how are you."

"You don't have to put on a brave face for me, old chap. We've known each other a long time. Look I am well aware of what has caused this. I was totally against it."

"Oh, were you Jack. That's nice to know." Trouble was that Alexander was not clear why Jack was calling.

"I didn't realise just how badly it would affect you, and..." There was a pause as Jack Evans regained his composure. "...And, Alexander, I promise you ...that I will do all that is in my power to have the decision rescinded. Closing your branch, one that has been highly successful – destroying the life of one of the best managers in the company – is totally wrong. Just hold out, old boy and please, don't do it!"

"Thank you Jack, for your very kind words."

"Good man, Alexander, hold on, life can continue."

Alexander sat back in his chair and smiled. He had begun to feel a little more comfortable: incredible, the power of newsprint. He almost felt at ease with his demise...

Meanwhile, in York Police Station, DS Milne and DC Green were in serious conversation.

"But what if you are right, Guv, that Toozlethwaite is involved in some way?" said Green. He looked at the newspaper photo again. "Could it be that this time that pawnshop tosser, Bissell, is actually telling the truth?"

"Yes ...and that Toozlethwaite was doing the fencing for whoever carried out the theft," mused Milne, "...although it is a long way from his home. Would he have come down to York from Newingsworth to shift the stuff, do you think?"

"Well, they do say it is not wise to plop on your own doorstep, don't they?"

"But Toozlethwaite has never appeared on our horizon before. You did check the records didn't you?"

"I did. The only involvement with us I could discover was that one in London, and he wasn't charged. Wrongful arrest, in fact, that was."

There was a moment of thoughtful silence. Milne was beginning to dislike this Toozlethwaite intensely. He looked away from the photograph, folded his hands behind his head, and leaned back in the chair. The blank ceiling was more appealing.

"Could I make a suggestion, Guv? This was to be my weekend off and I fancied going away but, if I went to Newingsworth, to that hotel we were in, I could have a couple of games of golf on their course. At the same time I could ferret about a bit re Toozlethwaite, see if there is any gossip. For starters, the young girl on reception seemed to know what was going on, but..."

"...But to do that, you would have to have expenses because you would be on police business? Is that what you were about to add?" Milne sighed.

"How perceptive is that for a boss, eh? Thank you, Guv," DC Green smiled.

48

She hadn't phoned back yet, but the call was bound to come – at least Chesney hoped she would try one more time. He would be very disappointed if she didn't. As a con artist he considered she deserved high marks but, as a blackmailer, the jury was out; at some point she would have to prove that she had the goods. However, failing to find what he'd been searching for at Toozlethwaite's place had thrown the likelihood back at the secret documents actually being in her possession. He should have grabbed the holdall when he'd had the chance.

Crystal was in her own home, dithering. Her approach last time appeared to have worked reasonably well, but there was little left to bluff with. It was decision time.

...Phone... Don't phone... Phone... Don't phone... Phone... Don't phone....

Last one... *Phone...* She had counted out the matches from the box to decide the choice.

She would phone!

"...Chesney?"

"Yes," the recognisable voice answered, but oh dear, her confidence had gone. She couldn't do it. Should she just hang up?

"Am I glad you called!" was his surprising comment, and caused her to hesitate. "I was hoping you would," he continued. "How are you and how is your father doing?"

My father, why has he asked about my father?

"Fine, yes he's fine," she managed to get out. Did he know him from prison?

Oh no! He was going to tell her he shared a cell with... *But, wait a minute, the voice?*

He sounded like...

"He certainly seemed the worse for wear the other night," he informed her.

He'd seen him recently then. Was he a prison visitor – but how did he know the connection with her? Her father wouldn't say that she...

Who am I blackmailing?

"You saw him?"

And that's when it struck her: the voice – it was her visitor from the other evening, the heartthrob – he'd been to see her at home!

It's Charles Devine – and he knows who I am, how humiliating; but he doesn't seem bothered? But, I thought I dialled Ches...

"Sure did. Look, wanted to thank you. You gave me some good ideas that I used," he continued.

"I did?" *Yes, it really is him!* "Are you...?"

"Of course I am," and he chuckled.

"But you are Charles, Charles Devine; that's what you told me, but that's not your proper name is it – Chesney...?"

"Oh, what does it matter what I call myself. I thought you would have recognised my voice right away, and, as I was saying: housebreaking... Yea, I tried it. And it worked, or maybe answered a question for me. So, I am willing to give you ten thousand pounds for the documents, and no questions asked. So, don't bother with the blackmail attempt, Katy pet. I am willing to pay. These pieces of paper are very important."

At the other end, Crystal had flopped in a chair in astonishment. She was going to try for two thousand!

"Are you still there?" he asked with concern. "Look, I am willing to accept that maybe you do not have them. If that is the case, I think we could come to an arrangement and you could help me. Whatever – I would like us to go out for dinner."

"...Your treat?"

"Yep, and, if you bring the stuff, I give you the money and we have dinner, or, if you don't bring it, we still have dinner, but we talk, about the future – and what we do next."

"...The future ...what we do next?"

"Yes ...a deal?"

Had he convinced her?

"You are damn right, it's a deal!"

He had…

Two days later and, there they were, sitting facing each other, awaiting the arrival of the food, about to enjoy a candlelit dinner in an award winning restaurant, the Black Swan.

He'd driven up from London and picked her up from her home in York.

"Is your father in tonight?" he'd asked when he phoned ahead to say he was almost there. He would be staying in the car and sounding the horn, ready to roar off quickly if her male parent were to appear, storming down the path. That had been decided beforehand, so, he was delighted when she said he wasn't there this evening. He resisted asking the supplementary question of 'Where is he then?' and settled for not having to be concerned by a threatening presence.

However, as they left Crystal's place, seeing Joseph Topper leave by his own front door and walk down the path, next to Katy's, confused him. Why did she say earlier that her old fellow had already left, and, why did he always use the next door neighbour's pathway? It made more sense when he was informed that old Joseph was not her father. He still resisted the temptation to ask where her father was. The information was not offered by Crystal.

On the way in the car, the chat by both had been restricted to small talk. Sitting in such close proximity was certainly intimate, but, being unable to observe each other's facial expression, to recognise if a truth or a lie were being dispensed would have been too taxing. The name he'd called himself when he visited her last time had been Charles Devine. Chesney made no mention of 'Charles' during the journey, but neither was Crystal's real name disclosed. When it came to untruths, deep down, each acknowledged the other to be a very capable performer.

It was a top-class restaurant that he'd chosen but, with each being on guard and cautious with the words used, the starter was eaten and the plates removed with little memory remaining of the quality food they'd consumed moments before.

"Katy... What a lovely name," he said at one point. "My mother's name was Katy."

Crystal felt really awkward when he came out with that. Should she tell him that it wasn't actually her name and, that each time he said it, it made her detest it even more. Worse still, how could she possibly say anything unkind about his mother's name?

She was concerned – but unnecessarily. His mother's name had been Maureen Sybil Matilda Wilfordon, nee Trimble, and her nickname at school, he'd been told, was Mo. His 'Katy' was manufactured for this occasion.

At what juncture the subject of money, secret documents, and blackmail, should be broached was a rather difficult one for him. She had brought his holdall with her, and it was sitting in the car. She'd placed it on the rear seat without making any comment whatsoever. He was desperate to open it and see for himself that the document file was inside – but that would not be gentlemanly behaviour. He was determined to portray a good image, so, the holdall was still sitting in the car, closed.

It was Crystal who broke first.

"Chesney, I must be honest with you," and he anticipated this to be the revelation that she did not have the documents. "My name is not Katy..."

Chesney almost choked on the mouthful of red wine, and grabbed for the napkin to reduce the damage.

"What do you mean? It is not...?"

"No, it is Crystal. Crystal Glasse. Sorry about that."

"Sorry? Why be sorry," he smiled. "What a cracker of a name!"

"I didn't want to say anything about Katy, but I don't like it, and with your mother having..."

"Oh, yes, dear mother..." but he couldn't force himself to tell the truth about that. "Crystal, yes I like that, but tell me please, were you joking when you talked about shoplifting and housebreaking that last time?"

"Did I say that?" she responded. "Chesney, or is it Charles, surely you didn't think I would tell you that if I actually did that sort of thing."

His face fell. He had been hoping she would have said it was true.

"Mine *is* Chesney," he admitted.

"Then again, *Chesney*," she added, "I might not *now* be telling the truth."

His face brightened once more: it was the moment to ask about the papers.

"Do I give you the money?" was blurted out. "Do you have them with you?"

"Oops!" and she looked slightly embarrassed. "Well, no, not actually with me."

"Be honest with me this time – please..." he said seriously.

She saw he meant it, so perhaps a little honesty on her own part would not go amiss.

"No, I don't have them, and never had, and I'm sorry that..."

"No, I don't mind. It means that you are a useless blackmailer – but a brilliant bluffer." He had a broad smile on his face now. "I think we could make a great team! If you don't have them, it must be that idiot Toozlethwaite who took them out before he gave you the bag."

"So?"

"Would you like to help me get them back from him?"

"A great team?" she asked tentatively. "Would it just be for this job?"

"I hope not," he said. "I like the long term idea, but, who cares about that just now. I've drunk too much. I can't drive you home. Either we get a taxi and I come back for the car tomorrow – or we get a room..."

Her smile said, forget the taxi!

49

It was late afternoon on Friday. Kylie was still on duty when DC Green came into the hotel. He looked as if he were here to enjoy himself, as he struggled through the front swing-door with the weekend bag in one hand and the golf clubs over his other shoulder. He almost came a cropper, but he made it and when he saw her he smiled. She recognised him and smiled back.

This time, he could relax without having to look after his DS, and he was being paid expenses! He had tried chatting to Kylie at Reception on the morning of the previous visit and would have liked to have spent more time with her. His boss, chuntering-on about it being late and getting on their way back south, had kept that contact much too brief. Maybe this time he'd have some success.

"Hi Kylie, doing anything tonight?" were his first words.

"Hmm, you are a cheeky one, aren't you? Not content with behaving like a sex maniac the last time you were here, you are just in the door and starting again. You are a definite danger to any clean-living girl, you are. I remember how you..."

"Ah, now that was a mistake," he said, hurriedly. "I was..."

"Only joking," she grinned. "Now, if you had knocked on my door in the middle of the night..."

"What would have happened?"

"Wouldn't you like to know; but I am not doing anything special tonight, in answer to your first question."

It was his turn to smile broadly. This might prevent the next couple of days being all work and no play. She was a sexy little chatterbox. He could find out about Toozlethwaite while having a good time. Yes, this was going to be a very enjoyable weekend.

Kylie was late arriving for work next morning, and Stuart Green was late down for breakfast. Hammy was covering Reception until Kylie arrived.

It was DC Green's misfortune that, when he appeared to go into the Dining Room, Hammy just had to say hello again, then had to update him on a considerable number of happenings since the last visit and, as a consequence the young policeman almost missed his last chance for a cooked breakfast. He didn't though. That would not have been good customer relations and Thelma knew that. He got off with a smiling "tut, tut..."

By being in the dining room at that particular time, he did miss something, and that was the arrival of a couple who'd booked a double room for Saturday night only.

Since DC Green sat down to eat, Kylie had arrived and was again on duty. She was the one to book the new guests in. Neither she, nor Hammy standing beside her, had recognised the name that the room was booked against – Mr C Devine – but the faces of the two individuals who came in the front entrance were certainly familiar.

"Good morning, I have a room booked," the man said, and gave no sign of recognition to either of the two behind the desk.

There was no attempt at flirting with her this time, Kylie noted.

I wonder, is this his wife, or his bit-on-the-side? But, I recognise her as well.

Either way, he was pretending never to have seen Kylie before.

"If you'd like to sign the register, sir," Kylie said, opening the book, and handing him a pen, while giving the female another look. It was Katy Something-or-other, wasn't it? She was also pretending never to have seen Kylie before.

Can't be his missus, they were both here at the same time a few weeks ago, in separate rooms. Hmm...

"It'll be a key-card ye'll be wantin' then," said Hammy. "An' it was jist the one room, wasn't it, that ye'd ...eh, booked. Aye?"

Kylie noticed the furtive glance that went between the two males.

"Yes, of course," answered Mr Devine.

"Oh dearie me," sighed Hammy, "a key-card..."

He scratched his head and looked at the male visitor, who looked as if he could sense what was about to be asked of him, then, like a magician, Hammy produced the one that Thelma had prepared last night. The look of relief on the man's face was obvious.

"Not a do-it-yersel job this time, eh?" said Hammy, with a chuckle as he handed the card to the gent, who didn't smile. *The lassie has no idea whit am talkin' aboot!*

Hammy took them upstairs, made sure they had access to the room and left them to it. He had to get ready. He had to leave in a little while; preparation for a long walk meant good socks and stout shoes.

"There's nothin' worse than sair feet," he confided in Kylie.

In the dining room, DC Stuart Green wiped the remains of the egg yolk from his plate and sat back, contented. For him the previous evening had been everything he could have hoped for, both for the policeman in him and the cool dude that wanted out. An Indian curry followed by a visit to a badly-lit corner of the only nightclub in the area, across at Slatterfoot. Kylie made his Friday night something special.

That's how he became aware of the WAARR plans for today. To be honest though, Kylie wasn't the only person that could have told him of all the details that were being circulated but, she was the nicest...

It was when he was leaving the dining-room after his delayed breakfast that he saw them: the two latest guests to arrive at the hotel.

He was standing chatting to Kylie when they came down the stairs together and made for the exit. He immediately recognised the male, even to remembering his telephone number. The constable stepped back. A bit of a coincidence that fellow being here. The girl was familiar but he couldn't quite pin down why he should feel he recognised her.

He asked Kylie who she was but the name didn't click. In his line of work he met a large variety of people every day and got to know quite a few very well, the disturbing thought was – most of them were criminals.

Nothing had come of the suspicions the two policemen had had of Chesney Wilfordon. *Strange though him calling himself Devine – a dirty weekend?*

Although Wilfordon had been interviewed by Stuart Green and his boss not so long ago, and they'd sat face to face in the interview room, he didn't recognise the detective standing beside the desk. Always useful, thought Stuart, to have the advantage.

A dual role was being performed this weekend, he reminded himself. Not just a detective – he was here for golf too, but it wasn't worth going onto the course until the afternoon. A walk along the access road would probably be just as good: help his breakfast go down – essential if he had to eat lunch.

"Not going to the rally then?" Kylie enquired.

"No thanks – golf has a stronger pull."

Stuart was never properly off duty and, for DC Green, suddenly it clicked. The girl – her father, he knew her father. That's what it was. Last year, at her home. He smiled to himself as he remembered. Under the circumstances, saying to this girl that he knew her father would not be a good idea: he had been part of the team arresting him. Jock Hudson, currently Bordam Prison, but her name wasn't Katy, as it said in the register. *Think...*

Crystal! Crystal Glasse, that's it, yes!

"I'll see you later!" he shouted across to Kylie and blew her a kiss. Hammy, who was walking along the corridor, and about to leave at that precise moment, waved back, but gave Stuart Green a suspicious look. Male guests didn't usually blow him kisses.

It was a fine day outside and pleasant enough to sit in the sun and do nothing, and that is what Stuart Green did. He watched Hamish Macintosh come out with his large Labrador, obviously about to leave for the demonstration.

The friendly dog ignored its master's instruction to 'Heel, Cornelius!' and wandered over to Stuart. Only after being patted by him did Cornelius deign then to jump, as instructed, into the rear of his master's large vehicle. Hamish Macintosh climbed into the driving seat and off they went.

Crystal Glasse and her male friend had been sitting in the sunshine too, farther along the terrace. As soon as the vehicle moved off, Stuart noticed that they were on their feet and had begun walking hurriedly in the same direction. It appeared to the detective that they had been waiting for Macintosh to leave, and his curiosity was roused.

I promised myself some exercise?

He followed.

They were well ahead and walking faster than he normally would. They vanished from sight, round a bend in the road. As he reached there, they were no longer walking on the road. They were in the bushes heading towards the stream. He stopped, just out of their sight in case they turned around. What were they doing?

They'd forced their way through the hedge and could no longer be seen. If they had come for a dirty weekend, vanishing into the jagged bushes for some rumpy-pumpy seemed daft. Wouldn't the soft bed back at the hotel be more comfortable?

As it was, the soft bed in the bedroom had already been well disturbed; they hadn't come all this way just to do a bit of burgling. Chesney had already explained in the room about the lane being screened by hedging on both sides running along the side of the stream. They would wade over but without Crystal getting her feet wet. He would be carrying her on his back.

He failed to mention his previous mishap, the wet trousers and socks. Remembering that, as they squeezed passed the gap in the hedge, caused his confidence to waver slightly.

That someone could have noticed where they'd gone, hadn't occurred to either Chesney or Crystal. They were on a mission and hadn't looked back, using the same route that Chesney had on his last visit to Toozlethwaite Manor.

It would have been less hazardous if they'd walked along and over the rail-sleeper bridge at the start of the lane, but that would have been too obvious to any onlooker. It would also have meant a considerably longer distance.

At one time there must have been a footbridge at this spot, a long time ago though. Some rotted timbers sticking out of the undergrowth remained, giving support and helping Chester to slide down the slope, cautiously. He helped Crystal to do the same and she clambered on his back.

As he stepped into the flowing stream this time, it was less the fear of slipping and falling into the water and more that his breathing would be stopped before he reached the other side. Crystal was terrified, grasping around his neck with a grip that tightened with each step and was bound to leave a mark. He was relieved to reach the other bank and suck in gulps of air. It was more pleasant with his hands on her bottom, assisting, as she climbed the banking.

Knocking on the cottage door was precautionary only. They'd seen Macintosh, the hotel owner, leaving a short while ago to drive down to collect Toozlethwaite and his family. By now they should be at their rallying place; Chester had heard Macintosh make the arrangements on the phone and was pleased not to have asked, or appeared too inquisitive and drawn attention to what he and Crystal were doing.

No sound came from inside today. "No one in," he smiled at Crystal, and bent to lift the edge of the doormat. There it was – the key. "Isn't it that sort of careless security that encourages criminals?" he said.

Stuart Green could see all this. In the bushes on the other side of the stream he was hidden and watching curiously. He'd been afraid he might be accused of being a voyeur and was relieved that their intention was not open-air shenanigans, but what were they up to?

They were at the door of the man he was here to investigate. He remembered the suspicion of the connection between the two men so, were they here as friends or visitors? They had obviously intended this, but used an unusual route, through the stream. Now, was that just laziness or familiarity? They were knocking. No one in, it seemed. They were smiling to each other. He had lifted the doormat, they'd unlocked the door, and now, they were inside the cottage, Toozlethwaite's cottage.

I wonder, thought DC Green, if Toozlethwaite knows?

50

Hamish was transporting Thelma, Sally, himself, and little Edwin to the rally, and the two dogs were with them in the vehicle.

The dogs were making Derek feel uptight and he wished the journey to be over as soon as possible. He would have liked a better seat, but he would have felt a heel complaining, so he decided to suffer it out.

In Derek's opinion, having Cornelius in the back without a proper mesh guard between the dog and the passengers, was stupid! To be honest though, nobody was affected by that, other than Derek.

"Gerroff!" he kept saying to the lolloping big Labrador that would not settle and delighted in licking his ears and the back of his neck at every opportunity, totally ignoring Sally sitting in the other rear seat on the opposite side.

Derek was his friend.

It was way beyond his comprehension, that he could be disliked, so intensely, by a white poodle called Jilly, yet at the same time adored by a stupid mutt called Cornelius.

Jilly was with Sally. She should be left at home, Derek had suggested to Sally before they left, but because Hammy was taking Cornelius Sally decided Jilly should be there too and would sit on her knee. Having the car seat, with little Edwin, between him and his wife, suited Derek, as long as she held the dog tightly. There was always an evil glint in that dog's eyes but, then again, Derek probably looked the same to the poor defenceless creature.

What a relief for Derek to arrive and climb out at the Bisko's car park.

They were all about to embark on a five-mile protest march to Slatterfoot Station and Derek was pleased to see that a large crowd was already congregating even though it was early. Hordes of people were trekking through Bisko's large doors. Steven Tomkins, the store manager, was certainly not grumbling about that. If they entered, there was every chance that they would make a purchase. He was relying on that to use as his defence when Head Office decided to call him to account. The figures, so far, were supporting his argument that business had not suffered due to closing the store during the demonstrations. Although sales of non-food stock were slightly down for the week, he was anticipating that that would be balanced by the money being spent on food and drink that afternoon.

Even with extra staff it was a struggle keeping shelves stocked with life's essentials – these being currently crisps, chocolate bars, giant packs of toffees, lemonade and other soft drinks, and cans of beer. The sandwich bar was almost empty too, as were the shelves of cakes. It was hard to believe that all the rubbish that was about to be crammed into mouths, was to sustain them for a march of only five or six miles. What was about to be consumed over the next few hours appeared to be more than enough to last a fortnight for a native in the Amazonian jungle. So, Mr Steven Tomkins was far from grumbling – he was overjoyed!

The iced buns, crisps, toffees, chocolate bars and beer were generally stuffed into rucksacks that were on backs, or over shoulders, although some simply had plastic carrier-bags, paid for as an extra. Almost all the family groups looked slightly overweight. Starving for the following five days would not prevent their trousers still being tight!

There were some who were holier-than-thou but these were few and far between. They were into healthy dieting, had carrots, and apples, and bananas, and the bottle of sparkling water with them. To emphasise this ultra-healthy living, this lot carried their food in clear plastic containers in one hand for the world to see, and, in the other hand, the essential bottle of water. Also, they liked to think of themselves as being environmentally conscious citizens and had brought their own clear plastic carrier, but purchased the fresh products in the store to fill it in the same way as all the others.

All were getting prepared for a happy day of protesting. The weather was pleasant, perfect for planned picnics on the march or at the destination.

Granny and Grandad Smith had arrived before Derek and company. Baby Edwin was transferred to the pushchair and Grandad given the responsibility of the pushing the pram. No objection came from him. It was so much easier than supporting the papoose sling – he could hang on to the pushchair for support.

Some members of the band were standing, in their uniform, waiting for their buddies. The Salvation Army Hall being planned for demolition on the predetermined Rail Route had fired the organisation's fervour and their Captain had volunteered the services of the band. However, to Derek, the individual band members looked a little less than enthusiastic, but at least they had turned up. They probably would have preferred to remain static, playing at a street corner, rather than on a five mile march. Derek thought, uncharitably, that the exercise would do their waistlines the world of good. The gent with the big drum, especially, looked portly. He was already perspiring profusely while just waiting for the others. In his hand was a half-eaten beef burger that he continued to consume.

Looking around, Derek could see that generally it was a good turn-out of family groups and that the more enthusiastic amongst them had brought placards. Each showed WAARR clearly. Being made individually they looked less like the 'factory mass-production' placards often seen on this sort of occasion. The wide variety of colours looked bright and cheerful and would be good for publicity photographs.

Thinking of something to catch the eye and the public's attention – a novelty expected by both the participants and the media – had been difficult this week. It was Alexander who came up with the inspiration this time – people on stilts. It was a member of the Slatterfoot Amateur Dramatic Group who had mentioned that he had a nephew who, with a couple of pals, did that sort of thing. Derek's invitation for their attendance had been accepted and they were making their way from Darlington. They hadn't arrived yet.

The car park was filling. Passengers were spilling out and still rushing into the store for food before it closed. It was beginning to look like another big turn-out. Promises had been made that people would be joining the march as it progressed through the town, so if this was how it looked to start, the end result should be terrific.

A van pulled into Bisko's. On it, painted in garish colours, were the words 'Zipoo and Pals'. Three young lads leapt out and started to remove their props, obviously the stilt walkers who would be leading the procession so Derek went over and introduced himself. He thanked them for coming such a distance.

"Can you cope with five miles?" he asked them.

"What?" was the response, "Uncle Tim said we would be fooling around in the car park for an hour or so, but five miles? Hmm..."

Derek's face fell. "Oh, so, does that mean...?" he started.

"Only kidding," laughed Zipoo. "We take big steps. It won't seem like that to us."

Derek's face brightened again. "Great. You'll be leading – in front of the band."

Shortly, before they started to march, he would have to make his speech. He checked that the piece of paper was still in his pocket. "Hammy, is the microphone ready?" he asked. "Do the loudspeakers work alright? Have they been checked?"

"Och aye of course they have. Has the team ever let ye down? Ye're gettin' yourself all worked up about nothin' as usual. Relax man. Enjoy yourself, an' here, have some highland toffee!" Yes, all was under control.

Derek gazed around.

Zipoo and his pals look good, Derek thought, as they strode around the car park. *How they balance is amazing, but what happens if the kids get overexcited. It must be very easy to be knocked over.*

The remaining members of the Salvation Army band had arrived. It was to be a grand line-up; three trumpets, two trombones, a euphonium, a side drummer and a bass drummer. They should make plenty of noise.

"You're on in a wee minute, Sunshine, it's time for you to be startin' to rouse the rabble," Hammy prompted.

"Right, here we go then..." Deep breath. Once he got started it was easier, he'd found, but for the first moments...

"Ladies and gentlemen, boys and girls, welcome to another WAARR rally. It is very pleasing to see so many here starting with us this afternoon. Are we feeling good today?"

At least he was off, he'd managed once again, but it was a desultory response to his question and demanded a repeat... "I said – are we feeling good today?" ...he shouted loudly into the loudhailer this time. The loudhailer was not as effective as the previous week's system, but the increased volume of his voice had an effect.

"YESSSSS..." bounced back this time.

"We'll be off in a moment, but a big thank you to a couple of groups helping us out today. Firstly, 'The Newingsworth, Slatterfoot and surrounding districts Salvation Army Band'. They're are with us all afternoon."

"Hurray..." came from those nearest to Derek, the rest of the crowd were not caring too much.

"That must be one of the longest names for a band that there is! And, all the way from Darlington – you've already met them – we have Zipoo and his pals."

This time, there was a great cheer from the children and the parents in the crowd, so, it was obvious who the favourites were. The two dogs joined in by barking enthusiastically. In acknowledgement, Zipoo and his Pals smiled and waved to the crowd, and received another cheer; the band members glowered at each other.

"Zipoo and his pals will lead the parade today. Now, something else before we begin, about how we conduct ourselves. You have all been on your best behaviour at the previous two gatherings, for which I thank you."

"You were the worst behaved," yelled someone from the crowd, and that got a laugh. Derek smiled tolerantly.

"Yes... The media is here to watch us. They will tell the world what we are like, and it is important that we show everyone who sees us that we mean business, that we will not be dissuaded, and that we are approaching this as good people who are doing our best for the futures of our families and the surrounding countryside that we love."

He got a rousing cheer for that. They were listening now and they were on his side.

"Therefore, we must do everything in a peaceful, non-aggressive manner. And so, if we are all ready, let's march – for WAARR!"

The loud cheer that came out spontaneously merged into the chant of "Swea-ty, Swea-ty, Swea-ty..." as everyone began to form into a column, but the noise gradually diminished as they entered the main thoroughfare.

The special musical arrangement that the band master had knocked together for this occasion had been drowned out by the shouting, but then gradually began to be heard. It was a brass band version of selections from 'The Sound of Music' and was very tuneful and cheerful, pleasant to hear – to begin with... It would be repeated many, many, many times during the five mile walk.

51

They were in, with maximum ease. Not a splinter of wood, not even a chip of the paintwork, yes, certainly the easiest way to open a door had to be by using a key. So simple!

There was something different about the place today, and it wasn't just the dishevelled state of a house abandoned because the occupants were short of time and had to leave quickly. It was Chesney who was first to twig.

"The dog: no dog today. Hope it hasn't escaped again. That's what happened the last time I was here. Followed me back to the hotel and howled outside my door."

"You didn't tell me that," said Crystal.

"Hmm, yea. I was afraid that someone might have become suspicious. I stayed inside the room until the hotel owner took it away."

"I don't think it even noticed me when I was here," said Crystal, "but, if it is not here, I am glad." She looked out the window to the back, and no sign of it there. "They could have taken it with them."

"Well, I am sorry not to see it again. I could have played with it while you search. Now I'll have to sit and twiddle my thumbs."

"Yes," Crystal agreed. "With only one of us disturbing things our visit is less likely to be appreciated. Although, the state of the rooms, stuff strewn about, I don't think anyone would actually notice."

The house, today, was worse than usual.

Sally had tried hard to change since getting married and, on the whole, had vastly improved in avoiding clutter, but sometimes it felt as if it was just not worth it: it could all become untidy again so easily, what with a young baby, a dog, and Derek! Today, before leaving for the rally, had been one of those days!

As Crystal began her search for Secret Papers, Chester lay back on the settee and put his feet up and started to read today's copy of the local Gazette. Last week's antics were prominent.

An article on the habits of feral pigeons explained why Derek's head had been such an intriguing attraction, and then went on to tell the world how a Mrs Gregg, of Carleton Lane, Slatterfoot, had a cat that specialised on bringing 'not quite expired' pigeons back into her house regularly. She had posed a question that the reporter was opening up to public discussion. 'Could, and should, these pigeons be eaten? Is this type of pigeon nutritious and does anyone have a recipe for pigeon pie that she could use?'

The Gazette failed to hold his attention.

"I looked there!" was the call that came every so often from the sofa, as Crystal went about her search. She knew that it was vital for the papers to be located; his future depended on it, but his interfering was irritating. Having the feeling that someone was looking over her shoulder was disconcerting. She had become used to working solo.

"Fancy a cup of coffee?" he asked. Rather than just sitting around reading rubbish he would do something useful.

"I hope the papers are here, and that your suspicions are correct," she said. "What will you do if I don't find them?"

She looked over at him.

The grim look indicated to her – he didn't know!

"No coffee for me," she said. "Make sure you clean the cup carefully and return it to where it was – no clues remember."

Chester made himself an instant coffee, helped himself to the last of the biscuits from one of the tins, and sat down again. He was trying hard to appear unconcerned, but he was getting worried, nothing found yet.

The living room had been thoroughly checked, as had the kitchen, and the bathroom, and she was now completing the main bedroom, disturbingly for him it was with no success. The only place remaining was the other bedroom, the one with the spare bed and the child's cot.

Chesney stood gazing out of the rear window. The golf course was being used by a few guests. It was a pleasant view. His mind started wandering. It could be great living in an area like this, away from the bustle of the city, settled down with a wife, and a dog, and maybe even a few kids. If everything got back on plan, he would be able to leave London behind, he could even come back up here and settle, maybe buy that hotel and transform it into his personal mansion. Offer enough money and Macintosh would hightail it back to Scotland, no doubt, but, the future depended on finding those papers!

"Anything yet?" he turned and shouted to her.

"No..."

He turned back to the view. *Ah well, dream on...*

"Did you check the cot," she shouted, "...under the mattress?"

He turned and looked at her.

"No," he said, feeling foolish because, there they were, in her hand – the papers! This beautiful, luscious, young, lady house-breaker was holding his documents. Toozlethwaite had taken them.

Crystal was pleased to have succeeded and she could see that he was impressed. She felt a warm comfortable glow. This relationship could only blossom after this, and she was not thinking criminally.

Her previous call at this house had not impressed her, she recalled, and she'd had no wish to return. Having done so, this time was no different, but, as it was a job, and as had become her practice, she was taking a small souvenir to remind her of this visit. When doing the living room search she'd noticed Toozlethwaite's phone sitting on an arm of the settee. He'd obviously forgotten it.

Chesney needn't know that it is now in her pocket.

He was quite happy to get his lost property back, and anyway, Toozlethwaite had had the cheek to steal the papers that should have been hers. From her view, that made him just as naughty as she was, and, for what she knew of 'dear' Derek, he would never know where he'd left his telephone anyway.

"We can go now," said Chesney with a large grin. And out they went, carefully replacing the key under the mat, and leaving the mat at exactly the same angle they found it.

Being a detective constable can be really boring at times: the hanging around, in case something might happen, a bit like today had been – until now, but sometimes it turns out to be worth it. He moved back so they wouldn't see him when they crossed over the stream again.

Stuart Green watched them slip carefully down the bank. The girl climbed on Wilfordon's back again, and he, now carrying a document file, stepped cautiously a little farther into the running water. There was a moment of uncertainty. The bloke stopped and regained his balance, and adjusted the hold of the female, before they successfully crossed over and clambered up the bank again.

With luck, as they passed, they'd be talking about what they'd been up to, and he would hear, he told himself. Frustratingly for DC Green, the couple smiled smugly to each other, but said nothing.

He had no intention of informing them of his presence at the moment. He was content to watch for clues. Had they broken into Toozlethwaite's home? No. They'd used the key; it could have been prearranged with Toozlethwaite. Had they delivered anything? Not as far as he could see, unless it had been something small: could have been a payment they were making – in cash? Had they removed anything? Possibly: the bloke was holding a folder when they came out, but if they'd stolen something it would have to have been small or it would have been visible to him.

Do nothing for the moment, was Stuart Green's conclusion. According to Kylie, they were staying overnight, plenty time to reach a decision, but, wasn't this to be his relaxing weekend as well? *I came here also for golf,* the off-duty detective reminded himself. *So, for a while, I will concentrate on beating the living daylights out of a little white ball!*

52

Hammy said he would take the two dogs on the lead and stay at the outside edge of the group, to avoid tangling with the band in front of them. Derek was quite happy with that arrangement. It would keep a 'loving' Cornelius away from him and would also give Jilly less chance to nip his ankles!

It gave Derek freedom to keep an eye on what was happening around them. He could chat to bystanders and encourage them to join, if they hadn't already decided to do so.

Other than 'The Sound of Music' driving everyone insane, though no-one would admit it, the march itself was proving to be a success. It was now a massive crowd protesting on foot today, and, with many having turned out in fancy costumes, there was plenty for the media's cameras.

Spider was being cameraman for the Gazette today. He was in the company of several guys from the national newspapers. Derek was particularly pleased that the television cameras were here too, from both BBC and ITV. He hoped footage would make its way onto Sky as well. Even if it didn't, overall, it was excellent publicity for the cause.

They were getting close to Slatterfoot Station, in fact, it was now in view. It had all been going so well – but he should have known it couldn't continue.

It was the dogs! Well, it wasn't totally their fault. They'd been walking for five miles but no one had thought to bring a bowl to give them water or even had been thoughtful enough to give them a tit-bit when eating their on-the-move snacks, so they made their own arrangements...

Derek had noticed something that was very obvious as they walked along. One was that almost everyone at the side of the road was holding a mobile phone, and very few were not referring to it – and that is when he appreciated that he did not have his with him.

Where did I leave it, he wondered?

Could it have fallen out of his pocket in Hammy's car?

I daren't have lost it – after all the fuss with Katy!

What would Sally say if he had?

Unfortunately, there was little he could do about it just now, so it was pushed to the back of his mind, but the other thing he'd noticed – almost everyone was stuffing food into their mouths, happily feeding plump bodies.

That's when the problem occurred. One large gent, who'd had his fill of eating, happened to throw down the remains of his sandwich carelessly, just as the band was passing. Dogs have a keen sense of smell, they also have keen eyesight, and the two that Hammy was holding also felt that, with empty stomachs, they would benefit from that food.

Both made a lunge for the remains, which threw Hammy off balance. He was jerked forward, and as he started to fall, reached out and almost grasped the shoulder of the bass drum player. Being caught off-guard caused the player of the big drum to fall forward too – into the trombone player, which was very unfortunate for the cornet player who took a blow on the back of his head from the trombone. He fell forward too, smacking his lips on his own cornet mouthpiece – and wasn't happy.

It was a bit of a shamble – no ...it was chaos!

The crowd was brought unexpectedly to a halt, trying to avoid treading on the fingers of the bass drummer, who was under his drum and struggling to rise...

Eventually the situation was rectified – but only after Hammy was given a clout by the bass drummer who, in turn, was thumped by the cornet player with the swollen lip. Incidentally, the dogs shared the sandwich bits between them and ignored all the fuss.

Not surprisingly, when they reached the station and stopped, the round-up speech by Derek, this time, was an anti-climax. If someone had organised the loudhailer to be at Slatterfoot Station to permit him to be heard, it would have helped. He tried to thank everyone for attending and to tell them that the following weekend the gathering would be outside the station itself, but very few heard him.

The final indignity was when almost everyone realised that, having walked for five miles without making special arrangements for the return journey, that they were now at least five miles away from their homes and transportation!

53

DC Green would not, after all, be contending only with a little white ball. When he said what he was about to do, two worthy opponents were suggested by Kylie. Two visitors, Ms Glasse and Mr Devine, the two that he had been spying on, were about to come back downstairs in a moment to pick up two sets of clubs and go out for a game. They'd asked Kylie if she knew of anyone who might care to join them.

"I told them you would probably like some company," said Kylie.

"Oh..." said Stuart.

After being a Peeping Tom, and having suspicions about their antics, it felt a little strange for DC Green initially, but he guessed it would probably not be noticed by the other two. Meeting other players in this way and playing together for the first time was usually awkward to begin with.

"Charles Devine," said the man, "but feel free to call me Charlie. Everybody does, and this is my very good friend, my very, very good friend, Katy."

There was no sign that either of them recognised him. Stuart returned with a nod the beaming smile that came from 'Katy'. He was then rapidly forgotten as she directed a soppy-loving-look in the direction of 'Charlie'. They seemed very pleased with themselves. This might prove to be an interesting round of golf, thought DC Green, and a great chance to find out a little more about them.

"I believe the course was designed by Mrs Macintosh, herself," said Chesney. "The young lady on reception told me that when she was young, and still at school, she was a champion golfer. I don't play enough, get really rusty, how about you?"

"Fair to middling, I'd say," said Stuart modestly, deciding not to mention the handicap of four, he currently held.

"Match play, a tenner a hole – are you up for it?"

"I sure am," said Stuart, feeling confident. He would go easy on Charlie, and not take unfair advantage.

"I am not very good," Crystal said. "I couldn't compete with you two, but I'll try and hang on."

Crystal played off the same tees and proved to be considerably better than 'not very good', in fact she was disturbingly good. Chesney was no slouch when it came to it either. It seemed that DC Stuart Green was not the only one hiding a light under a bushel.

Taking his first drive was not normally any problem for Stuart.

Today it was, and he could not afford to hold back. It even looked as if he might struggle to keep pace! A deep breath and...

"Attaboy..." It was a great relief to have hit it so well.

They had the course to themselves and, with no others to hold up play, they made good progress. Thanks to Thelma's clever design, each found a fair share of the hazards but also displayed expertise by escaping and all returning to safety.

By the sixth hole, they were level – all three of them!

"What do you do for a living?" asked DC Green to Charles. "Or do you not have to work, a secret millionaire?"

Chesney Wilfordon smiled self-assuredly at Crystal Glasse.

"Not yet. Ask me that question in a couple of weeks and I will be saying – yes, indeed, a millionaire! Everything is about to work out fine, thanks to my friend Crys... *Katy!*"

"Your old man about to pop his clogs then?" asked DC Green.

"Hell no, but it's strictly confidential, man; I am in IT. We have a very successful games company and it is all about to happen."

"What is?" said Stuart.

"Can't tell you that, Stuart, old boy, sorry, but I can say that for us it has been a very productive day. As a matter of interest, what is it that you do for a living? You are obviously not a millionaire."

"Me? I'm a policeman..."

Now that shook them up. Chesney Wilfordon eyebrows furrowed, but he made no comment. He'd been so full of himself, he was only now remembering – they'd met before – in different circumstances.

DC Green was delighted with the effect his answer had – knocked them both for six on the next hole, concentration gone, and poor approach shots. Obviously, a guilt complex was involved, well, that's how he read the situation and it delighted him immensely. He now wished they'd been on 'stroke' play rather than 'match'. He would have been much farther ahead. It didn't last though.

By the next hole the concentration had returned and he had to witness some magical getting-out-of-trouble shots that gradually pulled them back level, but he didn't give in.

Being a nine-hole course, and going round the second time, experience of playing each hole a short time before, provided the opportunity to avoid the hazards that previously had been hidden. All three were determined not to lose.

The second time they passed at the rear of the Toozlethwaite cottage it was obvious that someone had returned home. The white poodle was barking in the back garden, and shouting could be heard, disturbing the peace and quiet of the sparsely populated golf course.

DC Green saw the special attention given by the other two to those premises. The regular smug self-satisfied smiles that they shared would have gone unnoticed if he hadn't been aware of what had happened before. Some earlier comments were making sense.

As for the golf, the situation was now critical. Each male had had a chance to lead, then lost it. The score seesawed back and forth until the final hole, neither was ahead. It was all to play for.

On the green, Chesney putted – missed. Stuart, in turn, missed.

It was going to be a tie – almost certainly.

Chesney putted – his final one, he hoped – and it hit the back of the hole.

Come out again, wished Stuart – but his wish was not granted – in it went.

Final putt for Stuart...

Align this shot carefully. Settle down. Comfortable stance: gently pull back the head of the putter. Keep a good line …and …

A mobile phone went off in Crystal's pocket and kept sounding!

The ball went so close – but gently rolled past the hole. He had miss-hit it!

"Hard luck, Stuart," said Chesney with a smile.

Stuart turned and looked at Crystal.

She didn't even notice him. The mobile was in her hand but she wasn't answering the call. She stood with the device in her hand, looking at it with a large grin on her face, before pressing the little red button, and the sound stopped.

DC Stuart Green grudgingly handed over the tenner.

54

Derek was exhausted when he arrived back at the cottage in late afternoon. He reckoned when he returned that the phone should have been where he'd left it. Trouble was, he wasn't sure where that was. He'd looked all over the living room – the most likely place, and then he'd tried the other rooms, but with no success at all. The pockets of his clothes had been scoured. It was not showing itself.

"Sal, could I borrow your phone for a moment please?" he asked.

"Why?"

"I've mislaid mine somewhere in the room," he bluffed, "and if I dial my own number I'll hear it," and he tried. "Oh, oh… If it is ringing it is out-with earshot, or I've gone deaf," he joked. Somewhere, someone was hearing it, he hoped.

It wasn't in Hammy's car, he'd checked on the way back, and he'd just proved that it wasn't here in the cottage either.

"Derek, you can be so careless at times. How can you keep losing it?"

"I don't know," he said, and the levels of the voices were rising as tempers began to fray a bit. "Do you think I'd be trying to find it if I knew where it was?"

He stopped suddenly, and his voice went quieter.

"The door was locked wasn't it? You came in first, didn't you?"

"Yes – and you saw that the key was in its usual place. Why?"

"I don't know," he replied. "It's just a feeling," and he hurried through to Edwin's room and lifted the mattress. "They've gone! Damn! Someone has been in the house and taken the confidential documents, Sally."

"Phone the police, they've probably taken your phone too," she said.

"Can't do that, what would we tell them? That someone stole the documents that we stole in the first place?"

"Derek, why are you saying, *we?*"

It was a while later that the knock came at the door.

"Hello again," the voice said. "You might remember me, Mrs Toozlethwaite – DC Green from York Constabulary. Is Mr Toozlethwaite in?"

Derek had fallen asleep in the chair. It had been a hard and a not totally satisfying day for him, taking into account lost phones, vanished secret documents, and injured band members. In his half-asleep condition he recognised the voice at the door. *Oh dear*, he guessed that this caller could be making his day even worse!

"Hello again, sir," said DC Green. "Nice to be back. Mind if I go over a few things once again with you? Had a good day then?"

He's taking the mickey, decided Derek. News travels fast when there are hordes of cameras about!

"Some points we didn't get clear on the last visit, if you don't mind."

Derek was tempted to respond with ...*And, if I do?*

"We didn't ask you about your car."

"What car?" Derek said. "I don't drive, I can't drive, and I have never wanted to drive! I only have a bicycle!"

That set the detective back a bit. No private transport! A fence moving stolen goods between here and York, on a bicycle or public transport? It seemed extremely unlikely.

"I was hoping you had found my phone for me again."

"No, I haven't, and I didn't know you'd lost it again," said DC Green.

"He never stops losing it, it seems," threw in Sally.

"Mislaid it, have you?"

"No, I haven't, at least I don't think so, and before you ask, I've tried ringing the number, several times."

"Ah yes, your number," and the young detective astounded them by recalling, and stating out loud what the number actually was, without reference to anything other than his memory.

"And I think someone may have pinched it!" said Derek.

"Oh, that's rather serious," said DC Green. "What makes you suggest that?"

Might as well get it off his chest, Derek decided, "Because, they have also taken..."

"...The last of my favourite biscuits!" shouted Sally from the kitchen.

DC Green went back to the hotel satisfied that Toozlethwaite was not involved in either the jewellery theft, or the 'fencing' of the goods from it. He was the wrong type; sadly, he appeared to be too innocent. When he returned to the hotel there was no sign of his golfing partners. Kylie said that they were on the premises.

"In their room, coming down for a meal this evening, they told me," she said.

"How would you like to join me for a meal here, tonight?" he asked her.

"Like a busman's holiday, but if you insist."

"That's a good girl," he said, and was glad he didn't have to insist – he would have. He'd had an idea...

For Kylie it was strange sitting in the dining room with Stuart. It was the first time that she'd been in here as a guest of one of the guests, and certainly the first time to be served a meal by her bosses.

Thelma looked surprised when she came to take the order, but nothing untoward was said. Tomorrow she would be subjected to a lecture regarding employee behaviour towards guests, Kylie presumed, so she determined to make the most of tonight!

She noticed that Stuart's attention was not directed fully towards her. He seemed to be observing the couple he'd played golf with today, who were sitting a few tables away. Other than a cursory nod in his direction on entering, they were ignoring him.

"Stuart, what are you up to?" she asked quietly.

"I am going to try something, forgive me for a moment." He put his mobile on the table, flat in front of him, and input a series of digits, then covered the phone with his hand. Another phone sounded in the dining room, causing everyone to look in the direction of Crystal Glasse's table. Kylie watched as the mobile was brought out, the telephone number checked and the choice made to answer the call. She held it to her ear and, from the look on her face, something was amiss. She looked again at the screen and held it to her ear once more, and then gave up and ended the call. The phone was left on the table.

"That was your call wasn't it," whispered Kylie.

"Yes," he nodded, "just confirming something. I'll explain later. I will try once more to make sure it wasn't a coincidence." He did, and Crystal went through the same routine. Stuart didn't speak, but this time disconnected at his end first.

DC Stuart Green smiled. It was working out as he'd begun to suspect and, he could see clearly that she was wearing the unique ear-rings again, which matched a brooch in his boss's desk. The phone call to his boss could wait till after dinner. Next week should turn out fruitful for the team but the rest of his weekend would be much more relaxed.

He then concentrated totally on Kylie, and they had a lovely evening.

55

"What can we do next?"

That was the current question being asked because, as far as the protest group was concerned, success was breeding success. It was a maxim that seemed to fit the current scenario, and Derek could feel proud that he had been instrumental in being the cause of at least some of it. The rallies were gaining followers all the time, although he was worried that, at some point, more physically active political groups would latch on and cause trouble.

The march yesterday had not been as successful as the previous meetings, but having had a headline grabbing incident again, it had certainly not been a failure. Every newspaper this Monday morning was displaying exactly the same headline – BLAME THE DOGS OF WAARR!

The articles were describing the Saturday march in varied terms. None portrayed it as an outright success but the media had, once again, given support and kept readers' interest. The very large group of people attending had ensured its being seen as a display of massive resistance, as was clearly stated in each report.

...Except for the Sun, of course.

BARKING MAD – THEY FELL FOR IT! Sub-heading: DOGS banned by band.

'It was a Sweaty boob, as far as this reporter is concerned, to allow mad dogs in on this march, and in no way should

Toozlethwaite have permitted Hamish Macintosh, one of the maddest of the organisers, to have taken the poor animals along. "I almost hit the woof," Sweaty Toozlethwaite confided afterwards, showing his displeasure, "and, as for the Salvation Army – fighting amongst each other..." It was a good day out for the masses but not up to the death-defying antics of last week by any means. This reporter expects more from you, next time, Sweaty! Still waiting for the Bank Manager's hara-kiri! I am definitely going to be there to cheer that.'

The quote was certainly not from the mouth of Derek, but it did tend to match his unspoken thoughts at the time.

The police had been involved, but only a little. Thankfully, the force had maintained a low profile at each rally, possibly because it was mostly family groups involved, and that they had been behaving impeccably; there had been no need to intervene or become officious. Could it be that the policemen were also sympathetic to the cause? At least they'd helped everyone back to their feet so that the march could continue and, except for one cornet player, the Salvation Army boys were still able to play – even though it was yet again their selection from the 'Sound of Music'.

Derek believed that there was a great deal of sympathy all over the country for what they were doing. The majority of the population was being calmly supportive of the cause, and unhappy about the government's attitude. The government was working to suit its own agenda rather than working for the will of the people.

Ask the man in the street these days and the comment is always: 'Those in power no longer care for the little person. Being ridden over rough-shod by a government has always had to be tolerated – but only for so long!'

It had to remain being a non-physical protest. Provided that there was no bad behaviour and the gatherings remain peaceful there should be no need for police intervention. Anyway, until now, it had seemed that anything physical had been limited to one person, Derek!

Oh, and Hammy…

…And the Salvation Army Band!

"What should we do now, ET?" Derek asked the child in his arms. The middle of the night, the early hours of Tuesday morning, possibly not the best time to be discussing strategy, but something would have to be done to maintain the momentum of the rallies. It would have to be new and original. His brain wouldn't switch off so readily these nights. However it was unlikely that a great deal would be offered by his very young son.

Proper undisturbed rest was called for, and all pressure removed. That was badly needed by Derek. He had already decided that once this Rail Route was sorted out, and WAARR achieved the demands, life for him could become somewhat ordinary again. How he'd be when it did end he could not imagine. The adrenalin flow had kept him going, and while it lasted he would bear up.

The now silent child he held was still open-eyed.

"I should have listened to your mother. Your mother is a great woman. She always knows the right thing to do. She said to take them into the Gazette office and put them in the safe and I said, not yet, and look what's happened. They've gone – been pinched – stolen – purloined, and how was it done?"

Baby Edwin gazed up into his daddy's face, pondering the question.

"At least I had the chance to read them properly last week. If I sat down just now I might even be able to record most of what was written, no, I mean it!"

The reassurance was necessary because ET's disbelieving look implied, *Yea, and pull the other one!*

"The trouble is that without the hard physical evidence of the documentation who would believe what I'd be exposing? If it is MI5 or some other secret Government Agency who took them, will they have passed them back to Bubbles already? He must have been informed that they'd been recovered. But what if he doesn't know yet? Maybe I should chance it."

ET made no comment. Derek took that as a good sign. It was certainly out of his control; the vital pieces of paper that he had been relying on for leverage had vanished.

"Under your mattress seemed the perfect hiding place. I suppose it was safe only as long as you were looking after them for me; on guard, so to speak."

Edwin's eyes blinked up at him. *Oh dear, is that a tear?*

"No, no, little fellow, I wasn't blaming you. How could anyone suggest that you did not care? I know you do, and you want me to succeed, don't you? And I want you to grow up being proud of your father, even though he is called Sweaty..."

"Put him back in the cot, Derek love," said Sally gently, but it still made him jump.

He looked down at the little one in his arms, now in a deep sleep. He kissed his forehead and laid him down.

"Come back to bed. You need some rest."

"You are right, Sal, but I'll not sleep."

He said it confidently, because he had decided, he would take a chance...

Rob never complained. All the happenings since Derek became the main focus of the local rebellion had generated considerable mileage for the Gazette. The weekly exploits from the rallies had created ready-made stories and photographs. The papers were now selling incredibly well at a time when most other newspaper sales were falling.

No need for anyone to chase around wondering what could fill the pages these days, but because of Derek's regular absences from the office far more work than normal was being handled by Christine, Spider, and Rob. It was more usual for Derek to be doing the lion's share, but leave well alone, Rob concluded. Normality would return soon. They would cope. A knock on the door brought Rob out of navel-gazing mode. Derek was in the office – an attendance day for him.

"Rob, got a minute?"

"Of course I have, Derek, if it is to do with Gazette work, for a change."

This had to be a private conversation, and safer if Spider and Christine were not involved and worked on. Derek closed Rob's door. Last night he had decided, he would bluff it out. He would pretend that he still had the documents.

"Rob, I mentioned before that I had some secret information, highly confidential stuff that could affect the Gazette if it were made public. How would you feel about publishing Government Secret Documents?"

"No problem, Derek. Just put them in my in-tray and we'll have them on the front page on Saturday and then we'll all run away to Moscow, or Hong Kong, or the Isle of Man – somewhere safe – like you do!"

Rob turned his head away and continued skimming over the information currently on his screen. He is being a tad sarcastic, thought Derek. "I am being serious. I have come across some papers that are really hot; the sort of stuff that the Nationals would love to sink their teeth into. I haven't brought copies with me, and they are in a safe place, but I can assure you they are real."

Rob's attention returned to Derek. "Hmm... What sort of stuff are we talking about?"

"Top Civil Servants, it looks like, and a conspiracy affecting major projects likely to make them a fortune – at our expense, well, I mean, the public's expense."

"Oh ...sounds interesting." Derek had his full attention now.

"But, if it was published in the Gazette, the odds would be stacked against us avoiding jail, I think. It is a big can of worms."

"We wouldn't be selfish then. I do have contacts, at the Nationals, who would be delighted to have that sort of information and be brave enough to use it. We could take some credit and, if actions on this document expose that laws are being broken we should be safe, if the big boys are on our side. We'd use the real Power of the Press."

Derek smiled. Rob was being very positive about it.

"I am glad you have not embroiled Spider and Christine in this," said Rob, "because nothing can be guaranteed for our safety if we go ahead. These guys will have powerful friends."

"I agree. Now could I make a phone call from this office, a special call, on behalf of WAARR – apply some background pressure? You can listen in."

"Help yourself."

So Derek dialled, using the same telephone number that Spider found last time that had been successful.

"Hello, can I help you?" It was the same camp-voiced answer as before. "Is that an outside line? How did you get this number?"

Being a bit stroppy today.

"Still doing the crossword," said Derek, "...instead of what we should be doing, are we?"

"How do you know...? Who are you wanting then?"

"I wish to speak to the head of your department," and he said it his most commanding voice.

"He doesn't take calls from the public, sorry."

"I want to speak to Bubbles so put me through immediately. Tell him it is Pipsqueak."

"Oh, his special friend..."

There was silence. Nothing was happening this time. Had he been cut off?

"Yes?"

He was through, it had worked.

"You might remember me, or rather the organisation WAARR. I spoke to you a short time ago and made a suggestion."

"Oh..." was said in a most disinterested tone.

"That the route of the high-speed rail line should use waste ground rather than the destruction of our town."

"Oh, yes," and the voice had the cheek to yawn!

"We will be disrupting rail services this weekend and I am sure we will be causing a few more headaches for you as the weeks progress, unless you approach this in a reasonable manner."

"And you are the ringleader, no doubt. Am I right?"

Derek gulped. It sounded menacing the way he said it.

"Toozlethwaite, yes, your name has been brought to my attention," said the voice. "I don't normally waste my precious time talking to small fry. I am afraid something will have to be done to stop this annoyance in the future."

"What do you mean?" This man knew his name!

"You will see, my good fellow, you will see..." And the conversation was ended but not by Derek.

He stood up, shaken. That hadn't gone as he'd hoped at all. That man must already have the secret papers. He had known where they'd been, who'd had them – me – the only person in the country called Toozlethwaite!

Rob looked at him, expecting him to say something, but Derek was stunned. He stood and opened the door, went out and sat at his desk. He hadn't taken account of someone like that talking back with a threat – and knowing his name. He looked at his hands, they were shaking, and suddenly he didn't feel so cocky. What next?

Something else he had not considered when he went into Rob's office – the office walls, they were paper thin: Spider and Christine heard everything he'd said.

"Good on you, lad," said Spider, and Christine nodded in agreement.

Derek felt anything but good.

56

There was a deathly hush in the corridor, disturbed only by the click, click, click, of the built-up leather heels of his bespoke shoes. As he minced along, each footstep from the wooden floor echoed in the empty passageway. It was an unusual occasion, his being on this floor of the building – the Upper Sanctum.

He knocked on the door. His ambition was, one day, to have his door unlocked and opened by a Private Secretary like this, although, thinking realistically, it was unlikely ever to be fulfilled. It was a recognised fact that reaching this level in the organisation was accomplished only by having contacts of the highest order, and that also required the inclusion of several top-ranking relatives festooning the family tree, with one, preferably, being governor of a national bank – of any country – except Central Africa!

"Wait," he was told.

He stood, immobile, as the inner door was knocked gently, and opened by the underling to announce his presence. A muffled grunt was heard and the underling reappeared. Permission to enter was granted before further movement was attempted. He went inside.

"Sit," was the next instruction given, this time from the room's occupant.

He did as instructed, his upbringing having encouraged immediate compliance of a superior's request. Hesitation was failure.

Now, perched on the edge of the solid oak chair with the red leather cushioned seat, in front of the large oak desk, he looked in awe at the six telephones, each of a different colour, arranged neatly and evenly across the surface. Other than the assortment of phones, a blank notepad and a fountain pen were all that sat on the highly-polished surface.

No computer or electronic devices were to be seen, unnecessary when underlings existed to deal with the mundane.

Being expert at reverse-reading of upside-down documents on other people's desks, he noticed that the notepad was not totally blank. In small printing that taxed his eyesight, at the top corner of the pad almost like a doodle, were three words: Bubbles, Pipsqueak and Toozlethwaite ...no, not familiar names.

He dared to raise his head and look beyond.

Behind the desk the eyes scrutinised him.

He looked down again: dangerous to attempt a staring competition with a superior as senior as this. The silence continued. Being of a high level himself, at interviews, he had subjected his own staff to this type of treatment, so he should be used to it, but this was being inflicted on him with such admirable skill.

"Watkins is it?" was suddenly grunted in his direction.

Watkins gave a start, and nodded. "Yes Sir."

"Don't recognise you."

"No Sir," was deemed sufficient, he thought ...then added, "Two floors below, Sir."

"Harrumph. ...Tomaskins!"

The underling immediately appeared silently behind Watkins' chair.

"The tea, man – where's the tea?"

Tomaskins left the room. Watkins sat in silence expecting the next move to come now from the man opposite. None came, only the constant stare. It was a relief when Tomaskins re-entered, this time carrying a tray with a pot of tea, and one teacup – that he proceeded to fill and give to his superior, who grunted, "Right, to business," when Tomaskins left. "You are the head of the department responsible for this fiasco of a new rail route, are you not?"

"Yes Sir," Watkins replied, thinking, that's not a very nice way to talk of my largest project, thank you very much!

"What? Speak up man! Can't hear what you are saying."

"Yes Sir, I am responsible for the fiasco of a new rail route."

"That's better. I am talking to the correct person then."

"Yes Sir."

"No need to shout, man. Control yourself. Now, you see the telephones. Look at them closely. One of these is a direct line to and from the Prime Minister. Do you understand?"

"Yes Sir."

Oh, oh, Watkins was suddenly afraid. He was about to be asked to guess which one and, if he got it wrong, it could mean the end for him. A lifetime's career ended on a whim. He'd used that sort of technique himself to remove staff that crossed him.

"It is the red one," he was informed, before he had the chance to answer. "And do you know what I dislike intensely about it?"

Oh, thought Watkins, a different game... "...The colour, Sir?"

"No, of course not, man… Watkins, I hope you are not treating this matter lightly!"

"Oh no, Sir," he said rising from the seat in a panic.

"Sit!"

Watkins obeyed, and waited. The cup was seized and the tea consumed, while the eyes continued to stare at Watkins. "I'll tell you what I do not like, Watkins."

"Yes Sir."

"I do not like it when that phone rings. And do you know why?"

"No Sir."

"…Because, when that phone rings, the Prime Minister wants to speak to me, and why would he want to do that? Close your mouth and just listen, you silly man. He wants to complain, and I do not like that, because, it means that somewhere, in my many departments, someone has failed to do their duty correctly."

"Oh!"

"Ah, the guilt is obvious, Watkins. Do you wish to confess to your sins or do I have to draw it out of you?"

"I, eh… I don't know what you are talking about, Sir. We do our best always. There are constraints of course, sometimes regarding finance…"

"What nonsense, man! That should never be a restriction – not in my Departments."

"No, Sir. So, what …what …what is it that…?"

"I'll tell you what, Watkins. The Prime Minister's cousin is unhappy; something about you ruining his ruddy pig-sty with the line of your ruddy rail route! A pig-sty that has been in that position for hundreds of ruddy years! Of course, what does Lord Whatshisname do? He reacts! He complains to his cousin, and when the Prime Minister is unhappy, who is the one who is blamed for getting it wrong Watkins?"

Thump!

"Me!"

As the final word had been emphasised by the large clenched fist hitting the top of the desk, Watkins blinked and wriggled uncomfortably.

"And who is the one who is about to shoulder the blame because I am unhappy, Watkins?"

"...Me, Sir?"

"...Of course, Watkins. And you are the one who is about to correct it, aren't you – and very quickly too?"

"Yes Sir. Of course, Sir."

"But, Watkins, pray tell me; how did you, and your little department, decide where this new rail line should go?"

Watkins took a deep breath...

"Well Sir... To be honest, we have to thank our computers for that. Ehm... The programme was code named 'Crow's Flight', and, ehm ...we input the pertinent information. The rail line had to be the shortest distance linking our designated northern-most conurbation with London, and, with the shortest distance being the straight line, we accepted that it would inevitably be at a price. However, with the effect being felt by towns and buildings outside London, that was considered inconsequential."

Watkins was feeling slightly more confident now, talking about his favourite subject.

"To simplify construction, the terrain selected was based on the minimum of tunnelling, and bridge building, etc. The environment could not be ignored so, material from the demolishing of areas of townships decreed as dispensable, obviously, is being absorbed by route levelling.

"To achieve the admiration of the public, and avoid any negative reaction, travel times will be impressive and, with stops being limited, many rail stations have been deemed superfluous. Some have been designated as heliports in areas where key civil service personnel reside. Of course the costs, for the daily private helicopter transportation of selected personnel, have been carefully obscured.

"UK seismic recordings for the previous fifty years were incorporated, as were the locations of mines, caves, and planned fracking developments. Predicted sea levels related to global warming are also accounted for and, to discourage determined road users, not only has the computer devised the optimum route for the rail line, it has identified which motorways and highways to close – or rather, those to be allowed to run into disrepair.

"Full utilisation of the new rail system will be required to assure its success. And that, Sir, is a simplified explanation of a very complex project but, I am pleased to say, one that is now finalised."

The eyebrows opposite rose, initially in surprise, and then the face relaxed into a superior almost-smile.

"Finalised, Watkins? Oh no, not yet. You have surely forgotten something."

"I would certainly hope not, Sir."

"Pray, remind me why you are here, Watkins."

"Oh!"

"Oh, indeed. A certain pig-sty belonging to the Prime Minister's cousin, Watkins?"

"Dear me! Sorry, Sir. Of course, Sir."

"...So you will be correcting some of the silly things that your silly little computer is suggesting then..."

"Of course, Sir. A regrettable oversight. How could it have been missed? Thank you for bringing it to our attention, Sir."

"I think you'll find, that is why I am here, Watkins, and you are two floors down."

"I understand, Sir. We will action it right away."

"Just do it quickly!" the senior voice hissed and the face became threatening once more. "I do not want another phone call like that again." Watkins sprang to his feet. The interview was over. "Tomaskins! Show this man out!"

"Thank you for your time, Sir."

Watkins stood and bowed and went backwards towards the door.

"Oh, and Watkins..."

"Yes Sir?"

"It would be wise to ensure that we do not meet again. I do not like you."

"Yes Sir, of course, Sir..."

57

A very important announcement was being made at Westminster that would be destined to be the new theme for this weekend's edition of the paper – if everyone worked really quickly. The news broke immediately from the press conference and reached the Gazette office very shortly after: excellent timing for a weekend rag. It was Thursday and there was time to change Saturday's edition.

'The Rail Route has been changed! It is no longer to be directed towards Newingsworth, Slatterfoot and surrounding districts. It is to be about twenty miles east of the original route.'

There were smiles, and cheers and from Rob, a promise of extra pints, as soon as the paper could be updated. They'd done it, or at least Derek had and he was about to be the star of Saturday's modified Gazette. The headline for the front page had been decided without question.

'IT WAS SWEATY WOT DID IT!'

He was being given full credit in the office, but, like the true professional he was, he knuckled down with the rest of them – there was a deadline to be achieved. Then the phone started ringing, and ringing, and ringing...

"Could Sweaty Toozlethwaite be available for an interview?"

Who was calling?

"BBC, we want him for 'Newsnight' tonight."

Then, "We would like to interview you on our breakfast programme tomorrow, and on the lunchtime programme too." That was SKY.

"Could we come round to the gazette offices? We are eager to do a personal documentary about Sweaty Toozlethwaite," said ITV.

Derek had rapidly become a hero.

It was absolutely wonderful that the campaign had been successful. The world was giving credit to the WARR group's effective campaign, with recognition of Derek Toozlethwaite having been the driving force; as the press proclaimed: All thanks to SWEATY DYNAMITE!

Derek himself put it down to the power of good old-fashioned blackmail. He was convinced that he had frightened that shadowy group of code-names: the fear of being exposed having been the real driving force.

He did wonder though, why success still came – even after the visit by MI5, because they had to be the ones who had raided the cottage last weekend. Who else could it possibly have been? They did the Government's dirty work didn't they?

It had been a good job the place was empty when they called, he thought… No one was hurt. *It could have been rough if I'd been there and put up a fight, and if Jilly had been around, she would have had fun with them! No, she would probably have gone for me!*

Surprising though, after stealing back the Highly Confidential Documents, to have given in and changed the route? Surely, they must have realised that there was nothing left to be threatened by.

They could have just forgotten about me...

But, what if I haven't been forgotten? Could I still be arrested for theft? I wish I'd never seen the ruddy papers! Gosh! Could I be tried for treason?

As the weeks passed, the threat of retribution faded a little from Derek's thoughts and it no longer was the fear it had been. So many other good things had happened, and not just for him, although having a super, duper roadway – that led all the way from a new bridge over the stream almost to the front doorstep of the cottage – made such a difference. Seeing the old railway sleepers stacked in the field beside the new bridge was a reminder of what had been before and it had cost Derek nothing.

Alexander had appeared out of the blue. "I am really proud of you, Derek," he'd said, as he patted him on the back. He had then put both arms around him and given him a manly hug. Such a display of affection from his father-in-law was most uncharacteristic and Derek, for the first time in many years, blushed brightly.

"As a special thank you for the many things you have achieved for the two towns and the district, I am willing to pay for the path to be repaired – without you having to ask or having to repay a loan: my little gift to you."

Alexander later disclosed that, after the episode of his threatened hara-kiri appearing in the press and the rail route being changed, the great business acumen he'd demonstrated over the years had been recognised by the directors. The Slatterfoot Branch of the bank would be remaining open and he would continue in charge until he retired, or chose to depart.

The largesse shown to Derek, by Alexander, was also extended to his own sister, Thelma, and her husband, Hamish Macintosh. Arrangements were underway for the hotel to be transferred permanently to the ownership of Mr and Mrs

Macintosh. This removed some of Alexander's feelings of guilt at having being the wealthy member of the family, at the expense of his twin sister, for all those years.

Derek was being urged to other things too. He'd been encouraged to stand for the council. People kept telling him he would have a landslide in the voting, but he was reluctant to get involved in that sort of thing. Over the weeks, being aware of the Government Secret papers, he'd recognised the effect of excessive power. It could lead to corruption and he'd rather not go in that direction – yet!

Since no longer being involved in organising or participating in the WARR group, Sally and Derek had seen a lot more of Angie and Sam. Being a schoolteacher, and into computer games himself, Sam has been trying to encourage his brother-in-law to relax and play along with the latest crazy game.

It was all about politics, but with a darkly-manipulative theme where you were the master controller of the government and the people, anonymously. It could let you do whatever you wanted. It was really three games in one and seemed to be popular with all ages. It was called 'LIBTORLAB?' and selling so fast that it was nearly always out of stock. Anyway, Derek was not wild on computer games but maybe, one day, he'd give it a try...

Oh, there was one other thing, a personal phone call to Derek from the other side of the country, a plea that he might have difficulty ignoring.

"Please, Mister Sweaty Toozlethwaite, we need you here. We'll pay you anything you want. You could help us. We beg you on bended knee, just come over. They are going to build a railway line – right through our town!"

Sally was totally supportive when he told her of the request, and, at the office, Rob was all for it too. Alexander,

Sam, and Hammy said they would give him any help he needed, and they would help drum up other assistance for him the minute he gave the nod.

Other odd things were happening. His arch enemy, Jilly, had developed an inexplicable friendliness towards him – no nips for twenty-five days – and although it probably wouldn't last forever, little Edwin was sleeping right through the night – and so was Derek.

Life was no longer a strain; he wasn't panicking when something went wrong; in fact, he felt like a new person. And even stranger – though maybe to do with at last being acknowledged for his heroic qualities – in Derek's mind something that had bugged him for so long, no longer did!

Yea, man... It had taken on a lovely satisfying sound in his head. It was the name ...*Sweaty.*

58

Simon Gove was delighted. As the founder and owner of the small software company 'Govement Designs' he was proud of what had been achieved, especially at how his small team of five males carried out the preparation work in a pressured atmosphere of the highest security. The value of 'Govement Designs' had rocketed to an astronomical level; he had hit the jackpot; the timing and strategy had been perfect. The computer games market had been poised, waiting, desperate for something new, and adults and youngsters went wild for it, just as he had anticipated. It could not have worked out any better.

It may be a sad sociological fact, but, today you are nobody, and incapable of claiming super-geek status, if 'LIBTORLAB?' is not in use on your smartphone, laptop, PC, or your personalised head-mounted smart-glasses, at least once every twenty-four hours.

The subversive political three-game package of 'FRACKEREE', 'TWO-SPEED-HIGH', and 'POWERY-WOWERY', turned out to be exactly what the public craved. The CD pack has been selling like ...well, selling at a level that any cleverly well-thought-out secretive campaign should be achieving – by the bucket load! Excessive demand, when purchasing on-line, had already caused system failure several times.

The public was sick of real-life political manoeuvrings. This has become the way to kick politics into the fun park; a game to play that is even dirtier than real life; the chance to become the Master Controller, and take advantage of all human gullibility's.

It could be played in private, or against nasty on-line challengers on the way to work, or while waiting for the kids at the school, or – with a few beers to help the thinking process in the pub. A lot of loving relationships were in the balance due to the growing habit of 'LIBTORLAB?' being taken to bed!

The fuss about the confidential stolen documents, though not forgotten, was well in the past, more than a month since that was put to bed: and nothing did actually leak. It could have turned out to be a catastrophe. If a rival company, or the press, had got wind of what was about to explode onto such a sensitive market, the whole strategy would have failed. The game was designed to make a fortune for its creator. It was doing it good-style with the fortune building by the minute as each newcomer became addicted.

"Haven't you been too generous with the triple package?" he was asked. "Shouldn't you have sold each game individually, and made even more money?"

"No," he replied, "that would have been greedy."

He knew that it might not have been like this; Chesney Wilfordon almost ruined it. Perhaps that young man will be a little more cautious when he gets out of the prison, him and his thieving girl-friend – housebreaking – oh dear!

Yes, Simon Gove had had great plans for that young gent, but not now.

And I saw him as my protégé too. Imagine ...getting caught!

59

It couldn't last. The truce that existed between Derek and Jilly had been broken!

Being foolish enough to lift the pesky little terror, from a comfortable reclining position on a settee that her master wished to sit upon, meant the fracturing of good relations. He should have used gloves – he realised afterwards!

A painful index finger was the result.

To a certain extent, Derek accepted this as a sign that life in Toozlethwaite Manor was returning to normal, and being sleepless was part of normality these days, with little Edwin teething. It had to happen, just when Derek was beginning to think that sleeping through a night was a natural form of behaviour for adults. Young ET had decided to prove that idea to be wrong. Now, once more, Daddy accepted that to sleep soundly during the dark hours was never meant to be.

However, Derek told himself, *it won't be long before I and my son will be having intelligent conversations in the middle of the night – and all the troubles of the world will be righted.*

It felt strange for Derek to no longer be fighting fervently for a cause, strange, but nice, though they would have appreciated his presence over at Altchester. They were now facing the dilemma; the route of the High Speed Rail Line was about to spoil their lives…

Maybe I should have … But action, to be successful has to be generated from within the community; it has to come from the heart, he told himself. Someone would step forward to lead surely, someone local – secret information to use as a lever could also help!

And what a difference the new path made. It wasn't any wider than it was before, but the stream seemed less of a threat now. ET appreciated the lack of jolting as he was pushed along in the pram but, Derek decided, that would not be where he'd be taught to ride a bicycle. All thanks to Alexander. He had been generous, no ...more than generous – extravagant! Having lighting installed along the side of the road to ease the walk in the dark had made it almost a pleasure for Derek to take Jilly out on late night strolls.

At the Gazette Office, it was great that Derek was back, though some good came from his being absent: it gave the under-demanded skills of Spider and Christine a chance to be exposed. It was now a much stronger team with each contributing an extra tuppence-worth.

As for the Highly Confidential documents, Rob was very relieved that Derek had not forced him to publish any. That could have been disastrous for both the business and him. He sometimes wondered what Derek had done with the information; did he still have it?

Did he ever have it?

Wisely, Rob avoided asking. He saw little sense in stirring up a hornet's nest!

It had become a life of celebrity for Derek.

The inhabitants of Newingsworth, Slatterfoot and surrounding districts could not forget the part 'our hero' played in saving their community. As Hammy put it, Derek's face is 'weel kent', having been seen so regularly by the world. With appearances in person in a starring role at each of the rallies, was there anyone who didn't recognise him?

Everyone looked on him as their friend! His photo, regularly plastered somewhere in a newspaper, contributed too; even his television appearances had been difficult to avoid.

So, wherever Derek walked or cycled, someone was sure to shout a cheery "Hey, Sweaty – you'll be glad the WAARR's over," or some similar quip that the individual thought to be original. He always smiled back and waved acknowledgement.

However, 'our hero' recently had been having some doubts as to how it all came about, and questioned if the credit that came his way had been justified. His smartphone probably deserved just as much adulation. It had been involved in the fight as much as he had – and almost certainly had a better story to tell!

That phone was now back with him, thanks to DC Stuart Green. He promised himself that he would always remember where he laid it, and lending it to someone, even if a friend, was not on. He'd learned that lesson – even though it could occasionally appear churlish.

"Mr Toozlethwaite," asked Sally one day, "…if that phone was attached to your clothing, do you think you could avoid it being lost again? No, of course not; when you changed your clothes, it would still be attached and end up in the washing machine!"

Derek's epiphany was to be the challenge from Sam to play a new computer game.

"Everyone's on it at school," Sam told him.

"What chance," he moaned, "does a teacher have to teach when they are all playing LIBTORLAB in class?"

He, himself, was already addicted and wanting to rise to the next level. Solo against the computer, stage one of the game, had been successful. It had been a hard fought battle but he had beaten the machine.

He needed to earn more 'Mean Streaks'.

To do that meant entering the next level, in which a 'real live human' opponent had to be 'Ground Down'.

'Heartless' was the level he was aiming for, and to move forward, he needed someone to serve as a stepping stone! Angie, his wife refused to compete with him.

Sam tried persuading Sally, because he knew that Derek hated computer games, but Sally refused too.

So, it had to be Derek.

Derek disliked the obsessive use of electronic devices. Playing games constantly was definitely an obsession he wanted to avoid.

What would life be like when Edwin grows up – brain implants, incorporating today's game, plugged in and charged overnight, perhaps?

It worried him…

However, Sam's pathetic "Please… Derek... please…" was so repetitive that he gave in and said he'd consider the challenge …

So, Derek looked at the game, and it was only then that he realised!

"Sally. Got a minute? Frackaree! Powery-Wowery! Two-Speed-High!"

Sally's eyebrows furrowed.

"Are the names familiar?" he asked.

She gave a slow nod…

"Are you thinking what I am thinking?" he said.

"Yup..." she said, with a smile.

"About Highly Confidential documents?"

"Yup..." she said again.

"And that having inside knowledge must help if I play this game?" he said.

"Yup!" she said yet again.

So Derek took up the challenge.

From that day on, he was hooked, and won every single game he ever played with Sam!

www.ingramcontent.com/pod-product-compliance
Lightning Source LLC
Chambersburg PA
CBHW030637260626
47157CB00007B/2370